A DUET OF DARKNESS AND DREAMS

*To all the dreamers who were told
it would never work out.
Prove them all wrong.*

Playlist

The Rhythm is Gonna Get You - Gloria Estefan
Brown Eyed Girl - Van Morrison
She Works Hard for the Money - Donna Summer
Run to the Hills - Iron Maiden
I Will Survive - Gloria Gaynor
Hit the Lights - Metallica
Rock You Like a Hurricane - Scorpions
Call Me - Blondie
Rock the Night - Europe
Pour Some Sugar on Me - Def Leppard
Photograph - Def Leppard
Just What I Needed - The Cars
Drive - The Cars
White Wedding - Billy Idol
Hard Habit to Break - Chicago
In League with Satan - Venom
Don't Stop Me Now - Queen
Take My Breath Away - Berlin
Dancing in the Dark - Bruce Springsteen
Baby I'm-a Want You - Bread

What's Love Got to Do with It - Tina Turner
Voices Carry - 'Til Tuesday
Screaming for Vengeance - Judas Priest
You Shook Me All Night Long - AC/DC
Dress You Up - Madonna
Heartbreaker - Pat Benetar
Strike of the Beast - Exodus
Do You Wanna Touch Me - Joan Jett
Where Do Broken Hearts Go - Whitney Houston
Little Lies - Fleetwood Mac
Let Me Put My Love Into You - AC/DC
Take a Chance on Me - ABBA
Crazy For You - Madonna
Out Ta Get Me - Guns 'N Roses
Controversy - Prince
Don't Give Up - Peter Gabriel
Seek & Destroy - Metallica
These Dreams - Heart
Lucky Ones - Loverboy

CHAPTER 1

The Rhythm is Gonna Get You

ISABELLA

"I'm with the band," I shout over the blasting rock music to the massive bouncer. The stacked speakers practically vibrate the air, the cigarette smoke lingering above my head seeming to jump with every thundering bass note. This gigantic man looks down at me, and while I'm not super short, I feel like a munchkin in Oz compared to him. I think his biceps are bigger than my head.

"VIP pass?" he grunts.

I suck on my teeth. Shit, Becks hadn't mentioned needing to prove to anyone I knew her boyfriend's band. And, while the phrase *I'm with the band* isn't entirely a lie, it's also not quite the truth either since I don't really know the band yet. I've only met Becks's boyfriend, James, once. *Shit.*

"I . . ." I pat down the pockets of my jacket and fumble with my keys as if I might miraculously find a VIP pass hidden somewhere. "They didn't . . . I mean—"

He raises an eyebrow. "What's the band's name?"

He's on to me for sure. "Uhh . . . umm . . . Carnal . . . Carnal *something*—"

"Hey, Arnie, do you know where there's another cable? This one is fucked."

The bouncer—*Arnie*—steps back, unblocking my view into the darkened bar. Long, dirty-blond hair surrounds a chiseled jaw, pouty lips, and stormy blue eyes.

Major hottie alert.

He wraps a long black cable around his hand to his elbow, coiling it around his bare muscular arm, tendons and muscles flexing. Good god, I think I might start drooling. I swallow, then finally tear my eyes away from his biceps to glance up at his face.

"Extra equipment is behind the bar," Arnie says in a gruff voice. "There might be another one in the cupboard."

His mouth twists and he places his hands on his hips. "Okay, I'll check. Thanks, dude."

Stepping to turn toward the bar in the distance, his gaze finally catches mine and he stops. My belly swoops as his eyes travel down my body and back up to my face, a hungry smirk spreading across those pouty lips.

"Hey," he says.

Is he talking to me? I almost look around to check, but I can't tear my eyes away from him. I don't know how I manage it, but my right hand lifts into the tiniest little wave as I squeak out, "Hi."

"You know her?" Arnie asks the guy with the cable. "She says she's with the band."

His eyes flick up and give me another once-over. *Oh no. Don't tell him I said that. How embarrassing.*

"Oh?" He blinks a few times, then turns to Arnie. "Oh, yeah. She's with us. Let her through, will you?"

He's with the band? My eyes finally escape his gaze and land on his sleeveless shirt, where the name "Carnal Sins" is written across his wide chest. First James, and now this guy? Is this band just filled with absolute studs? How is that fair?

"Go on, then," Arnie grumbles out as he steps aside and gestures past him with his hand.

My feet are glued to the floor, the blond waiting for me with an amused expression. Finally, I shake my head and step forward. "Right. Thanks."

Looking back over my shoulder at Arnie one last time, I head inside, the humid smoky air filling my lungs and causing a trickle of sweat to drip down my spine. I expect the man to turn away, to go find the other cable he's been searching for, but he waits for me to approach as a wide smile grows across his face.

When I'm a few feet before him, he reaches out his free hand and wraps it around my shoulders, surprising me by pulling me against him. "Thanks again, Arnie," he says, glancing over my head at where I assume the bouncer is watching us. "We were wondering when this one would arrive."

He smells like ivory soap and something sweet like caramel, and his fingers are hot on my arm, goosebumps prickling up all over my skin as he steers me toward the bar.

"So," he says, leaning over to speak in my ear. "You're with the band, huh?"

Heat blooms across my face. *Shit.* "I just—I mean . . ."

He chuckles. "No harm, no foul. I'm Dave, by the way, and I *am* actually with the band."

I'm not sure it's possible for my cheeks to get any hotter. "Right, hi. I'm so sorry, the line was so long and, well, I was invited here tonight and . . . I didn't expect it to be this busy—"

"It's all good, sweetheart," he says, tossing the old frayed cable on the counter and crouching down in front of the cabinet behind the bar for another one. "Generally speaking, though, if you ever use the excuse that you're 'with the band' to bypass the line at a bar, know which band is playing."

Oh god, he heard that? "Right."

He continues looking through the cabinet, then with a groan, he mutters, "Fuck."

"Problem?" I ask, desperate to steer the conversation away from my embarrassing screw up.

Looking over his shoulder at me, he clicks his tongue. "No cable," he says simply. "Just my luck."

"Oh." Part of me wants to offer some kind of help, but what the hell can I do? "I'm sorry, that sucks."

He stands with a sigh. "Yeah, it really will. No cable, no show."

My eyes widen. "Shit, really? That's . . . that's—"

"Not for you to worry about," he cuts me off, leaning against the bar and lighting up a cigarette. He holds his pack out to me and I take one. A lighter appears in his hands and he holds it up to the cigarette between my lips. The nicotine smooths away a little of my embarrassment as I inhale the smoke. He watches my face intently as he lights his own cigarette, and I can't seem to break away from the intensity of his stare. "So, you got a name?"

"Isabella Rodriguez," I tell him, exhaling into the already smoky air.

He pulls the cigarette away from his mouth, blows the smoke out, then runs his tongue along his lower lip. Heat throbs through my body, pulsing in dangerous places. That lip would look so good with my teeth imprinted on it. His eyes travel over my body again.

"You here for a date?" he asks, those stormy blue eyes growing darker in the dim light.

"A date?"

He gives me a subtle nod, his top teeth biting down ever so slightly on that decadent lower lip as his eyes scan my face. Is he . . . is he asking me on a date?

Lifting the cigarette back to my lips, I try my best at a flirty smirk. "I mean I— Sure, yeah. Okay."

He tilts his head, a wide smile spreading across his face, then he rubs his hand along his jaw before taking another draw. "No, I meant . . . are you meeting someone here on a date?"

Oh my god. The inhale of the cigarette goes a little too deep, and I cough and cough and cough—eyes watering and my throat and lungs burning. My face must look like a tomato right about now. Could this be any more humiliating? I cover my face with my hands. "I'm sorry—" I try to compose myself. "I—I misunderstood. No, not—not meeting up for a date. I'm single."

He takes a step closer to me, a light in his eyes as he laughs. "Not for lack of trying, if you always look like that."

And just like that, my embarrassment is consumed by his flattery, and I release a breathy laugh. His smile widens further and my stomach clenches as he takes another step toward me, closing the gap between us.

"So, if you're not here because you actually know the band, and you're not here for a date—what *are* you doing here? You're not lost, are you?"

"No, I'm meeting a friend."

"Big fan?"

"Huh?"

He leans forward, finger wrapping around a strand of my hair, his breath in my ear making my brain go fuzzy. "The friend you're meeting. Are they a fan of the band?"

My eyes flutter as he pulls back to look into mine. Good lord, Dave is *gorgeous* with those deep-set eyes and full lips. He can twirl my hair all day if he wants. It would've been nice if Becks warned me. Wait, Becks . . . "I— Yes, I guess you could say she's a fan," I say. "She's dating the guitarist."

The smile drops from Dave's face in an instant, and he steps back, dropping my hair as he does so. "You're . . . Are you Becks's friend?"

The heat in my cheeks is suddenly replaced by a splotchy, uncomfortable prickling. Why did he pull away like that?

"Yeah, she told me to come to the show tonight. I told that guy I was with the band so I could get in. I didn't want her to think I ditched."

Dave's shoulders slump and he lets out a long breath, shoving his hands into his jean pockets. He mutters something, but over the music coming from the speakers, I can't hear what he says. "Oh. Well, I'll take you to her. She's backstage."

He turns and heads for a narrow hallway. Once again, my feet are stuck. *What the hell was that?* Did I say something wrong? He was flirting with me, right? Or did I imagine it all?

He looks over his shoulder to find I haven't moved, and waves to me. "Come on, Izzy. I'll show you the way."

Izzy. Some nostalgic feeling pulls at my heart. I haven't heard that name in so long. Moving to a completely new state to go to school meant leaving all my family and friends behind. And while at first I was excited to start this fresh chapter of my life, I soon realized making friends as an adult is a lot harder than it was in kindergarten. The familiar childhood nickname fills me up, as if confirming that coming here tonight was a good idea after all. Like maybe it was meant to be.

"You okay?"

Dave is in front of me again, a line creased into his brow as his eyes flick over my face. Taking a deep breath, I nod. "Yes, sorry. I'm fine."

I pull a smile onto my face, which seems to ease Dave's tension. He jerks his chin back down the hall and miraculously, my feet unstick, following him.

"So," Dave asks once I'm behind him, "how'd you and Becks meet?"

I shake my head. Come on, girl, don't blow this. Did he just ask me a question? My god, he has a great ass, and those jeans look like they've been painted on. *Jesus.*

"Still with me, sweetheart?"

I collide into Dave's chest, too zoned out to realize he stopped and turned around. His hands tighten on my upper arms to steady me before I topple backward. I need to seriously get a grip. What is happening to me?

"I'm so sorry. I swear I'm not normally this much of a klutz."

A soft smile pulls at his lips. The heat of his hands on my skin is electrifying, and that dark hunger in his eyes from a few minutes ago is back. Maybe I had just imagined the shift, maybe he's flirting with me after all.

His thumbs rub against my scorching skin and I take a deep breath, realizing for the first time that my hands are on his chest, the rhythm of his pounding heart just beneath my palms. His tongue wets his lips again and I can't help but mirror him—the desire to simply rise onto my toes and kiss this stranger is an overwhelming urge I've never felt so desperately before. His face tilts just a touch closer to mine, and I can feel his warm breath on my lips as his eyes drop to my mouth.

"Isabella?"

In a flash, Dave's touch is gone, and I wobble on weak knees trying to keep myself upright as he backs away. I'm disoriented and confused and so unbelievably horny I can't think straight. Then I see Becks's blonde hair and green eyes appear next to me, and I'm being wrapped up in a hug.

"I'm so glad you could make it!" she cries. "You didn't have any trouble getting in, did you?"

My mouth bobs open and closed for a few moments, eyes flicking back over to Dave, who is looking down at the floor and rubbing the back of his neck a bit awkwardly. I turn to Becks with a smile. "Yes, sorry. I was held up at the door, but thankfully . . . umm, Dave helped me out."

"Oh, gosh, I should've told the bouncer to keep an eye out for you. I'm so sorry."

I shrug. "It's okay, I'm here now."

"Well, if you ladies are all set, I've got to make sure we can all actually play tonight."

"What's wrong?" Becks asks.

But Dave is already disappearing down the long hallway toward the stage, leaving me completely flustered.

"Sorry about him," she says, waving her hand.

I can't help but stare after him. "Is that true?" I ask, turning back to my friend. "They might not be able to play?"

Becks grabs my arm and pulls me farther into the back. "I'm sure Dave will figure something out. Come on."

Maybe I should mention that he had tried to find another cable without success. Before I can though, she's pulling me toward a door covered in faded green paint.

Becks sighs. "I love these guys but sometimes it can get a little lonely all by myself. I'm glad to finally have someone to hang out with."

I try to push down the raw and exposed feeling that Dave left me simmering in and smile at my friend. "I get that," I say. I can understand loneliness more than she knows. "Dave seems," I pause, swallow hard, then finish with a lame "Nice."

She smiles. "Yeah, he's great. All the guys are. I'm so lucky to have them."

"And you live with all four of them?"

Something flickers across her face. "Mm-hmm. It gets a bit messy sometimes, but Dave, Joel, and Keith—Key, as he prefers —they're like my big brothers. And James . . ." She smiles. "Well, let's just say there's nowhere else I'd rather be than with him."

I don't know Becks very well. We only met a few weeks ago in our History of Fashion class at Stoneman College. I will admit

I was a bit shocked when she mentioned she lived with four men —four men in a heavy metal band, especially, since Becks is all soft pinks and quiet, feminine beauty. I'm sure there's a story there, but I won't push her to tell me until she wants to.

"The guys will be starting their set in an hour. You've already met James and now Dave, but I'll introduce you to the others and you can hang out," she says, pushing open the greenroom door.

Walking into the small space, I immediately spot James sitting on a chair and re-stringing a red electric guitar. He looks up and grins, his eyes focusing on the blonde beauty next to me until he looks over.

"Hey, you made it!" he says, setting the guitar down behind him and coming over. He kisses Becks on the temple and holds out his hand for me to shake. I grasp it, the tattoo of a raven staring back up at me. "Joel, Key," he calls. The other two men sitting on the couch turn and take me in, waving and smiling. But their eyes don't burn me from the inside out the way Dave's did. And while they're all ridiculously handsome—*seriously, how is this fair?*—they don't compare to the eyes that made all the breath halt in my body.

The door opens behind me and I know it's him. His smell makes the blood race in my veins.

"Crisis averted," he says, his voice whispering past my ear.

Glancing over my shoulder, my heart stutters when he grins and winks at me. He's standing so close behind me that I can feel his chest brush against my shoulder blades. Then he's moving across the room, tucking something into the front pocket of his jeans before grabbing a beer and sinking down onto the orange and brown sofa.

"You want a beer?" James asks me.

I nod, my pulse running a marathon. I need something to cool me down. Perhaps I should run out to the pier and jump into the bay. That might help.

"Are you a fashion major, too?" James asks, passing me an open beer and sitting down, then pulling a giggling Becks into his lap.

I take a long sip, grateful for the distraction. "No, I uh . . . I'm just taking the fashion course as an elective, and, well, because I love clothes. But, I'm actually in the writing and journalism program."

James's dark brows shoot up. "Journalism? That's cool."

"It's great," I lie. "Most of the time. I just—It's . . ." I shut my lips tightly together. These guys are metalheads and rockers, they won't care about my problems. Sure, James is sweet with Becks, but they're dating.

"What is it?" Becks asks as the silence stretches.

I lean back on the sofa. "It's nothing." Taking another long sip of beer, I look over at Dave, but he's engrossed in some conversation with Key, or is it Joel? I can't remember who is who.

I feel a soft hand on my arm where Becks has reached over to me. "Do you not like the program?"

Okay, I guess I can't avoid it after all. "No, the program is amazing, the best in the state. But, it's just . . . the majority of the program is writing for the college newspaper and well, I tend to get overlooked for the bigger stories. Which, now that I'm in my last year and looking for internships . . . isn't great."

Becks frowns. "Why would they overlook you?"

I wish I could say it's because I'm untalented. A shitty writer. That I have terrible grammar or can't spell without a dictionary open next to me. But none of that is true.

"It's because I'm a woman."

Blood pools in her cheeks. "They overlook you because you're *a woman*? It's 1986."

I take another long sip of beer. In for a penny, in for a pound, I guess. "It's very much a boys' club. I'm one of only a handful of women in the whole program, but I'm the only senior. And they're always giving me these shitty fluff pieces to write. Like, dating for college students, diet tips, celebrity gossip. Sure, that stuff can be fun to write, and yeah, I'll admit I might get a bit too excited when the paparazzi take a scandalous photo, but I also want to be taken seriously, and they won't give me the chance."

Becks chews on her bottom lip.

"And if I don't have anything decent in my portfolio soon, no publication is going to give me an internship."

"I'm sorry, that's awful. People can be so narrow minded," she says, then claps her hands. "Oh, I know! You should write something amazing, and turn it in under a different name. When they ask who it was because they all thought it was great, admit it was you. Then they'll *have* to give you a chance."

I fiddle absently with the paper label on my beer bottle then take another long sip. "Yeah . . . maybe. But what would I write about?"

She grins, her perfect white teeth gleaming back at me. "Write about them!" she says, gesturing to the men sitting around the room.

My eyes widen. "The band?"

Nodding enthusiastically, she leaves James's lap and scoots down next to me before lowering her voice. "Yeah. They're up-and-coming. And, between us?" She looks around, as though worried someone might overhear her. "They've had a stint of bad luck lately. A bunch of canceled gigs, and their manager, who was so confident, has been having trouble getting them studio time to record their first album."

Just my luck. Dave's words from earlier rush forward.

"Any publicity would help them build up their fanbase. Seriously, *anything* would help. And I can almost guarantee your journalism creeps wouldn't expect you to write an article about a metal band."

Mouth twisting, I consider it. It's true—the guys at the newspaper would never entrust me with an article covering a band, and being backstage and getting to know the band would definitely give me an advantage. And even though it gives me the heebie jeebies to even consider it, I *could* submit it under a man's name, then come forward when they ask who wrote it.

A sly smile spreads across my face. "Yeah, all right! That's a great idea. You don't think they'd mind?"

She turns to James. "You wouldn't mind if Isabella wrote an article about the band for the college newspaper, would you?"

He stops fiddling with the strings on his guitar and raises his brows. "No, that'd be wicked. Can you really do that?"

I lift my hands and shrug. "I can try, as long as you guys don't mind me hanging around, asking a few questions?"

James shakes his head. "Not at all. Hey, guys," he says to the others. "Isabella's going to write an article for the college newspaper about us. You'll be cool, yeah?"

Joel and Key nod their heads, and I smile as I reach for my bag.

"Do you need paper?" James asks.

"No, my notebook is in here somewhere," I say. "I never leave my apartment without it." Tissues, lipstick, chewing gum, a lighter, an unopened pack of cigarettes, my keys—oh . . . where'd my keychain go?

"We've got some paper over here, if that works," James suggests, but then I spot the little notebook and exhale triumphantly.

"I got it!" I look up, my eyes finding Dave's for the first time since I sat down, and nervous butterflies erupt in my stomach, the notebook toppling out of my grip and onto the floor. My face burns as I snatch it up, wildly flipping through the pages to avoid seeing any more of the amused smirk on Dave's face.

"So," I say, pulling the cap off a pen with my teeth. "How did you all meet?"

I TAKE AS many notes as I can, filling several pages on how Key and Joel met in military school and how they met Dave at a showing of *Evil Dead*. I'm surprised to learn that they kicked out their lead guitarist only to find James, who was working at a bar back in Iowa while finishing high school. From there, Dave received a letter from a Megaloud executive that he'd be in town and had listened to their demo tape. Next thing they knew, they were being asked to pack up and head out here to San Francisco.

While they tell me all of this like we're friends, there's definitely more to their story. It's in the way they look at each other for a long moment before answering some of my questions, even Becks looking nervous once in a while. Though I understand not wanting to spill your guts to a stranger, I'd never write anything they weren't comfortable with. I'm surprised that Dave is so quiet. In fact, he doesn't speak at all, and in the hour I sit here, he doesn't look over at me once. While I'm not so full of myself to think guys should be looking at me all the time, surely he'd look over and our eyes would meet purely by chance? But no. Not. Once.

I thought there was something between us. Some spark. I mean, I certainly felt it. But maybe he didn't. Maybe his finger twirling in my hair, or the way he whispered in my ear, or the way he stood so close to me even though he didn't have to was all just me reading too far into nothing. Maybe he does that to all women. Perhaps my loneliness is starting to make me lose my mind.

Or maybe he was just distracted by the broken cable.

"Why did you choose to be a musician?" I ask.

James fiddles with a silver rose ring on his hand. "I had a hard childhood. Music was the only thing that drowned it all out. I guess learning to play the guitar was one of the things that saved me."

Becks squeezes his thigh, and he gazes at her with such adoring sweetness that I have to look away. There's a knock at the door, and a short, stocky man pokes his head inside. "Carnal Sins, you're on in five."

I press my lips together and flip my notebook shut, stuffing it back into my bag as the guys collect their things. Becks sweetly kisses James before grabbing my arm to pull me along to a reserved table to the right of the stage. Pulling my camera out of my bag I set it down between us.

"Is it okay if I take some pictures for the article?" I ask.

Becks smiles wider. "Of course!"

I nod and pick it up to adjust the settings as the lights dim over the stage and the four boys take their places. Looking around, I can see what Becks means when she says the band has been having a bit of a hard time lately. While the bar isn't empty by any means, it also isn't full to the brim. Definitely not the kind of sold-out performance they probably wish for. My gaze turns back to Dave, and I watch as he settles behind the bass drums and spreads his legs—the words *Carnal Sins* written across the front in red letters. How can such a simple move be so sexy?

Key steps forward to the microphone and welcomes everyone to the show. I lift my camera and snap a few pictures, adjust the settings a little more, then look through the lens again. Dave's eyes are on me, searing me from the inside out even through the camera—looking at me like I'm the answer to all of his prayers.

The moment I drop the camera he looks away, and with a violent crash of his cymbals, my heart seems to shake, rattle, and boom right along.

CHAPTER 2

Brown Eyed Girl

DAVE

Why is it when you solve one problem, another pops up in its place?

Figures the hottest girl in here tonight is someone I can't have. My happiness at Becks finally making a friend is shattered by the fact that she happened to make friends with an absolute knockout. I mean, Isabella is smoking hot. She has that Phoebe Cates look from *Fast Times at Ridgemont High*. Fuck, she was hot in that movie. And that red bikini scene? I'm getting hard just thinking about it. I wonder what Isabella would look like in a red bikini. Any bikini. No bikini.

Okay. Now I have two problems.

I suppose this is my fault. I can feel her watching me. I never should've flirted with her. James warned me earlier to stay away from Becks's new friend. But when a girl looks like that and stares at me with those big brown doe eyes . . . well, how was I supposed to know she'd be the one woman here, other than Becks, who's off-limits?

Why is she off-limits? Because I don't do long-term. I don't do dating and I don't do relationships and James is well aware of that. He knows I'd leave her in the morning and doesn't want my dumb ass creating drama for his girl. And Isabella is no groupie—she's a writer. A journalist. A journalist who wants to write an article about *us*. I'd doom us all if I fucked her and ditched her. Besides, we need this. Things have been rocky since landing in San Fran four months ago. I suppose it was naive to think the band would take the world by storm overnight, but hey, a guy can dream, right?

So, even if the thought of stripping her down and fucking her brains out backstage is all I've been able to think about, *she is off-limits*.

Sweat drips down my nose as my arms start to burn, the droplets hitting the top of the snare drum, which promptly fly off when I hit the top with my drumsticks. Everyone is on fire again tonight, and I hate to admit that I might be showing off a little more than usual considering Izzy keeps pointing her camera my way. Damn, she would've been a sure thing too. The way her breathing sped up when I got close to her. Her gorgeous pink lips pouting when my eyes lingered on them. She'd look so pretty on her knees, looking up at me with my cock in her mouth.

Fuck, no.

I need to knock that shit off right now. My eyes scan the crowd and spot a few women farther back. They're attractive enough. Both blondes, or at least, trying to be. One with massive tits and . . . okay, I think I'm cured. There's plenty more women out there who are available, and if they look my way I might just . . . yeah, that flirty smile right there? They're interested. But even as I feel the excitement of burying my face in that chest later, I can't help but look back at the gorgeous brunette in the front row, her face hidden behind a camera.

Why is she taking so many pictures? Is she a photographer too? Shaking my head, I lick the sweat off my upper lip. Okay, time to focus. Last song is coming up, and it's complicated. James wails on his guitar, fingers flying so fast they blur. Key shouts into the microphone as he strums along with the chord progressions, and Joel plucks at those bass strings with surgical precision.

As the final notes crash, there's an eruption of noise from the modest crowd. Even though I search desperately for the dark-rooted blondes, my eyes manage only to find one face in the crowd, and it's still half-hidden behind a wide lens.

I'M the first to leave the stage, springing out of my seat and tucking my drumsticks into the back pocket of my jeans. The greenroom is at the back of the bar, which is where I grab a bottle of water from the cooler on the table and crack it open, draining the entire thing in one gulp. I'm overheated, and not just because I played for an hour and a half straight. I need a distraction. Something or someone to focus on. But then I hear the raucous laughter heading toward me from down the hall and before I know it, Key is bursting through the door, one arm triumphantly raised in the air and the other around a pretty waitress I noticed earlier.

"Dave," he says a little too loudly. "Where the fuck did you go? You shot out of there like you were going to hurl."

I slam the bottle onto the table and wipe the dregs that dribble down my chin.

"I was thirsty as a motherfucker. What's all this?" I ask as Joel stumbles in with a few more girls, followed by James and Becks and . . .

"You guys were incredible!" Isabella says, a stunning smile brightening her face.

Key and Joel look pleased as punch, the dickheads, but they're quickly distracted by the girls now hanging off their arms.

"Do you really think so?" Becks asks her friend.

Isabella grins. "Of course! I'll admit, I'm not super familiar with thrash metal, but I don't think there was a song played tonight I didn't like."

There's something too chipper about the way she says it. She's probably never listened to this kind of music before in her life.

"I guess you won't have to lie in your article then," James teases, pulling Becks back against his chest and wrapping his arms around her.

Her chin lifts indignantly, but there's a small smile pulling at the corner of her mouth. "I would never lie. I have journalistic integrity, thank you very much. My ethics are beyond reproach."

Both girls giggle, and fuck, a dimple appears in Izzy's left cheek that's so fucking adorable I want to gnaw on her face.

"You were really rockin' out there," a voice purrs in my ear.

I turn, and the big-breasted "blonde" from earlier settles into the seat next to me, her hand resting on my thigh. She sits a bit awkwardly, positioned to best show off her assets, even though I'd already appraised them as spectacular from afar.

"Thanks. Are you having a good night?" I ask, my voice a bit flatter than I intend.

Her hand slides a little higher up my leg and a sly smile pulls at her lips. "It's getting better by the minute."

I should say something back. This is normally so *easy*. She's clearly into me, and while we don't even know each other's names, she doesn't care what mine is. Blondie's just here to fuck a musician, and I wonder briefly if I could get through the whole night without ever learning hers.

"I'll be back. I'm just going to run outside for a smoke," Izzy says, then turns and starts toward the door.

Without meaning to, I find myself standing abruptly.

"Baby, where are you going?" asks the blonde, pulling on my belt.

I watch as Isabella's dark hair swings out of sight, the green door closing behind her. Blinking, I look down at the pouty face of this girl who's eye level with my dick. "Sorry," I mutter, "I'm going to grab a fresh bucket of beer." I pry her hand off my belt and head for the door, barely registering the whoops and cheers of the guys behind me at the prospect of more alcohol.

But before I'm even out the door, a large hand grasps my shoulder and I find myself staring into James's dark eyes.

"Where are you going?" he asks.

"Uh, for a smoke."

He frowns. "You remember what I said? Keep your paws off Becks's friend."

Goddammit. "Yes, yeah. I remember."

"Are you sure?" he probes. "Because you've been eye-fucking her the whole goddamn night."

I push his hand off my shoulder. "*Yes*, take a chill pill. I've got Blondie over there on the hook anyway."

He glances over at the girl I left by the couch and, seemingly satisfied, steps aside to let me leave. "Good."

"You have no faith, Walton," I say with a smile.

He rolls his eyes. "For good reason."

I shake my head and make my way down the narrow hall, searching for that white leather mini skirt and those silver wedge sandals. As I look over the heads in the crowd, wondering where the hell she disappeared to, I stop. What am I even doing? Why am I following her? What exactly is my goal here? I just promised James thirty seconds ago I wasn't going to go after her, yet here I am.

I just want to talk to her. That's all.

My eyes hone in on the patio door opening and closing, a head of dark brown hair and hoop earrings glinting in the neon lights. *There she is.* I squeeze my way through the crowd then push out into the cool autumn air. A few heads turn my way and another few guys congratulate me on our set, but I can't help searching for Isabella.

As if by sheer will, the crowd parts and I spot her leaning against the brick exterior wall, a cigarette pinched gracefully between her fingers. I swallow back a grin and head toward her. As I approach, I falter. *What's your plan here, Dave?* Closing my eyes, I scrub a hand down the length of my face. Before I can do the sensible thing and turn around though, she looks up, and I'm caught in her sights like a tractor beam.

"Oh, hey," she says, as she stands up straighter.

"Hey."

What the fuck? Her brows lift, waiting for me to say something. *Say something.*

"Can I bum one of those?" I point to the cigarette in her hand, still fixed between two long fingers tipped in red nail polish. "Forgot mine inside."

She blinks, then breathes out a laugh. "Yeah, of course." Opening her bag to pluck out her pack of cigarettes, she offers the box to me, and I take a smoke. "Now we're even."

"Huh?"

"From earlier. You gave me one, and now I'm giving you one. Even."

I chuckle. "Right."

"Need a light?" she asks, pulling a lighter out of the front pocket of her skirt. That damn mini skirt.

"Uh, yeah . . . I guess I forgot that too."

She clicks the lighter and takes a step toward me to hold it up. Leaning forward, I can't look away, and her eyes hold me to her as I light the cigarette and take a long drag. We're close, and I have to clench my hand to keep myself from reaching out and touching her hair. It was so soft before. Like a cloud. All of her looks soft.

The light extinguishes, and her eyes dart away. I step back, realizing I shouldn't be standing so close. Blowing out a plume of white smoke, I murmur quietly, "Thanks."

Isabella leans back against the brick. "No problem."

"So what did you think?"

She blinks. "About what?"

I can't help but smile. What about her face makes me want to smile so much? Is it that dimple in her cheek? I wish I could see it again.

"The music."

Her lips part. "Oh, I said . . . I thought you heard me—"

"I heard what you said, but I'm asking what you *really* thought. You know, away from the obligatory praise society expects you to dole out when you're hanging out with performers."

She shifts her weight between her heeled feet, color darkening her cheeks. She laughs, then takes a drag of her cigarette. "It was . . ." She blows out a cloud of smoke. "Interesting."

I can't help my grin. I knew it. "Interesting, huh?"

Covering her face with her free hand, she shakes her head. "God, I'm sorry. That was . . . and you asked—"

I laugh. "It's all right. I'm not offended."

She lowers her hand. "Really? You're not?"

"Not at all."

Tension leaves her shoulders, and they fall from where they were hiked up around her ears. "Good. It's not that I didn't like it, I did. It's just not usually what I listen to. I'm a little out of my element here."

I take another drag of my cigarette and inhale. "So, what do you normally listen to?"

She worries her bottom lip, her brows knitting together as

though she's not sure whether to divulge the truth. Like it's some big secret. Then she leans toward me and whispers, "Disco."

My face makes an involuntary spasm.

"Come on!" she says, stamping her foot adorably.

"I'm sorry," I say, chuckling. "Disco, yeah that's . . . *interesting.*"

She narrows her eyes, but there's a subtle smirk pulling at the corner of her mouth. "Yeah, yeah, all right. It happens to be very popular, you know."

I nod my head. "Unfortunately, yes. I'm aware. But don't worry, I won't hold it against you."

"Right." She looks at me for a long moment, then we both take another drag, her cigarette nearly gone. I find myself hoping she'll grab another so she'll stay outside. "Not a fan of interviews?" she asks.

My head tilts. "Interviews?"

She jerks her chin back toward the bar. "I don't think you spoke the entire time I was asking questions for the article." She looks down, tucking her hair behind her ear. "I assumed you weren't very comfortable with my inquisition."

My lips twist. *Shit.* So she did notice that. Normally I'm the chatty one. Happy to talk to anyone and answer any question, but I was so blindsided by trying not to stare at her like a creep that I wasn't able to contribute to the conversation at all. I shrug and smirk back at her. "Didn't want to overpower the other guys."

"Oh."

I take another drag and raise a brow at her. *What is she thinking?*

"Sorry," she says with a small laugh, stubbing her cigarette out on the bricks then flicking it into the ashtray. "I thought you . . ." Her face twists. "Never mind."

"No, what—? What were you going to say?"

She takes a long, deep breath, those brown eyes sparkling in the patio lights. "I thought maybe, I don't know, I said something to offend you. Before the show, in the hallway, you were—"

I already know what she's going to say. I was flirting—I was into her. So into her that I was five seconds away from pinning her against the wall and kissing her until she was breathless. But that all changed when . . .

"Then Becks came along and you went quiet, and I thought maybe I offended you."

I shake my head, flicking away the burnt-out cigarette between my fingers. "No, you didn't do anything. Sorry if I made you feel that way. I was just stressed over the busted cable."

"I'm glad you were able to fix the problem or I would've had a far less *interesting* night."

She smirks, and a laugh escapes me at her joke. In truth, it was the strangest thing. When I'd checked that cupboard Arnie pointed out earlier, there had been nothing. I looked and looked but it was empty and definitely wasn't housing amplifier cables. But when I checked again after Isabella went off with Becks, there it was. And on the floor was a small plastic keychain.

I'd picked it up, not thinking much of the little cloud-covered sun, but the words on the keychain had struck me.

Dreams are forged out of darkness.

That got me—a simple phrase that resonates so succinctly with me that I pocketed the keychain, not even bothering to look around for the owner. To be fair, there were no keys attached and the little metal clasp was broken. Lo and behold though, the moment that keychain was in my pocket, guess what I found? Another cable.

"Yeah, I was lucky."

She smiles, that glorious dimple indenting her cheek. My skin tingles with the desire to touch it. To touch her. To wrap that silky hair around my finger again and feel her breath on my face. But she's Becks's friend, and I made a promise. I can't fuck that up, so I take a step back to get some air.

"You seem like a cool chick," I say, my voice strained as I look away. "I'm glad Becks finally has a friend here."

"Thanks," she says, her smile disappearing. "I suppose I might see you again. You know, being her friend and all."

Fuck, I didn't think of that. I'll likely see her more often than is good for me. I'll see her, and every time I'll have to control myself. Not overstep. Not flirt too much, which is generally hard for me. Why couldn't Becks have made friends with a dull troll?

"Well, I'm usually pretty busy. I don't have much of a life outside of playing music right now."

"Right."

She frowns, looking down at her feet. Shit, that sounded like I don't want to see her at all. *Fuck, why is this going so bad?* I don't want her to hate me.

"Well, I should head back inside." She steps past me, heading for the door, and something inside me aches. I don't want this conversation to end. I know it also can't progress to where I want, but I don't want her to think I'm an asshole.

"It's how I understand people," I blurt out.

She stops in her tracks then spins around to face me, head cocked to the side. "What?"

I take a step toward her. "You asked earlier why we chose to do this, to be musicians."

Her eyes flick between mine, waiting for me to continue. I take a deep breath and sigh.

"I—I've never been good at understanding people. I can be too trusting, too optimistic, too oblivious for my own good. Being able to recognize people's patterns, it gives me insight into who they really are. How they're feeling. Like my own personal litmus test."

"Oh," she exhales in a breathless whisper.

I bite down on my lip and shrug. "Drumming is rhythm and pattern. Everything has a rhythm—a way it should sound. When someone isn't being honest, their rhythm falters. It . . . helps me, I guess."

I look away, unable to handle the intensity of those brown eyes, so I brush my hair away from my face.

"Wow," she finally says. "That was— Thank you, that answer was . . . great."

"You're welcome."

"What does it tell you about me?" she asks.

I pause to think. "I'm not sure yet."

"Baby! What are you doing out here? You're missing all the fun." Arms wrap around my neck, the smell of some candy-like perfume permeating the air until my head is swimming in it. Bleach blonde hair obscures my vision as the girl from earlier presses her body into mine. She hangs off of me, and I can't help but grab her around the waist to keep her standing.

"Just having a smoke, and talking to—" I break off. Isabella is gone, and her long dark hair is already disappearing through the door.

Fingers grasp my face, and my gaze is pulled away from the door to find large blue eyes covered in blue eyeshadow. "Talking to who?"

I shake my head and smile down at the nameless woman. "Never mind."

She smiles slyly then leans forward, her lips kissing the underside of my jaw as her hips grind against mine. "Buy me another drink, then you can take me home and we can do whatever you want," she whispers, sharp teeth tugging on my earlobe. My cock throbs, and part of me wonders how fast I can get this girl her drink so we can get out of here. But the other part wishes I had one more minute with Isabella as I rub my thumb over my new good luck charm in my pocket.

When we get back to the greenroom, she's gone, and it's both an ache and a relief. And when I stumble home an hour later with tonight's conquest, I'm ashamed to admit that it's someone else I imagine as she strips down in the light of the moon shining through my bedroom window.

CHAPTER 3

She Works Hard for the Money

ISABELLA

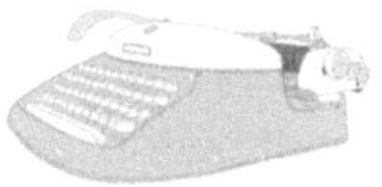

"Isa, *cuando vas a venir a casa?*" my mom asks through the phone.

I sigh, twirling the phone cord around and around my finger. "Maybe for Thanksgiving, okay, *Amá?*"

"But that's so far away!" she nearly sobs. "Isa, please, this must be hard on you too. Your family misses you. It's like you're running away from us."

"I'm not running away," I counter, rolling my eyes. "Don't be so dramatic. We only get certain holidays off from school."

There's a whispered prayer coming through the line, and I close my eyes and rest against the cool window. "*Amá*, it's fine." Lie. "I'll make sure I arrange to come and visit over Thanksgiving." Another lie.

There's a frustrated *Hmph* from her end. "I just want us all to be together. Remember when we went home to Santa Ana to visit your *Abuela?*"

I roll my eyes. "Yes."

"And remember when we saw Timbiriche perform while we were there? It was so fun."

She's trying to make me feel bad, and it's working wonders. Finally she sighs. "We miss you, Isa, that's all."

My face heats, my nose begins to run, and I look down at my shoes to try to stem the flood of tears that angrily pushes itself forward, desperate to be free. "I miss you too. I have to go."

Before she can protest, I drop the phone onto the receiver and press my palm to my heated forehead. I take several long breaths until my heart is calm again and the tears have miraculously receded back from whence they came. The last thing I need right now is to walk into the school newspaper office looking like I was just crying. They're all sharks, and tears are blood in the water. Pulling out my compact mirror, I check that my mascara is still in place, reapply some lipstick, then pull my article out of my bag.

When I got home from the Carnal Sins show, I stayed up all night writing. I know it's just a college newspaper, but I want to be taken seriously—as a real journalist—and I can't do that unless I approach every article and every opportunity as if I'm writing for the *New York Times*. Besides, how the hell am I going to have any chance of getting an internship if my portfolio is nothing but crosswords and makeup trends?

Metal Music Sensation Hits Stoneman College Scene

Not to toot my own horn or anything, but this article is definitely the best I've ever written. I don't know what came over me, but I was like a woman possessed. It was nearly three a.m. when I finished writing. I swore I wouldn't do what Becks suggested and put a man's name on it, but as I stand here, part of me is terrified that if I don't, no one will ever take it seriously. Just like everything else. I tilt my face up, my head resting back on my shoulders.

I'm running out of time.

"Screw it!" I finally mutter, scribbling the name Santiago

Morales across the top of the typed pages. God, what if they kick me out for this? Is this against the law? No, it can't be. It's not much different than using a pseudonym, right?

Sure, that sounds reasonable enough . . . for now.

I tuck my camera back into my bag and leave my apartment to head over toward the north building. The college newspaper office is on the main floor, and as usual the air reeks of smoke and the place is obscenely bright, the fluorescent lights giving me an instant headache. I sneak toward the editor-in-chief's door, glancing around as subtly as I can. I look down at my article one last time and stare at the picture I took paperclipped to the front.

It's a group shot, one of several I took last night, but this one is the clear winner. Probably because each member of the band is smiling in one way or another, whether it's at each other or the audience. And I'll be honest with myself when I admit that the real reason why this picture won over every other one I took, is because of the way Dave is looking right at me through the lens. His blue eyes are clear even from afar, and his teeth are biting down on that gorgeously full lower lip.

My stomach does a little tumble. He's so handsome. Also, incredibly confusing. The best line of the article came from him. The rest of the guys had given me fairly shallow answers. I assume "safe" is what they should be called. But Dave? He opened up, told me something personal about himself, and it made me so weak in the knees I nearly collapsed onto that patio floor.

Then that beautiful woman came along and reminded me of exactly where I stand when it comes to Dave Noblar. Not good enough. My pathetic attempt at flirting was just that—pathetic. And while he indulged my sad efforts, it dawns on me now that he maybe he flirts with every girl who walks his way. As soon as he found out I was there to see his friend's girlfriend, he backed off. He has to play nice, especially since I'm writing an article about his band for publicity.

I take a long look at the picture again, some fluttery sensation springing to life in my chest. Pulling it from the paperclip, I tuck it into my purse while pulling another great photo out of my bag. It's not *the* photo but it's a close second. I think I'll keep the other one just for me, and that will be the end of it. We have a working relationship now, and I have to keep things professional. Swapping the picture, I turn, then beeline for the editor's door and slide my article through the drop-off slot, burning with determination to finally be seen.

As the morning turns into early afternoon, the office fills up with more and more students, and more and more smoke. It's too much for me. While I do smoke cigarettes myself, I'm by no means a chain-smoker and usually just do it when I'm drinking . . . or after sex. God, there's nothing better than a smoke after sex. To think I imagined for one moment I could've had that last night.

No. Stop it.

"Eh, Bella baby, how about you head on down to the diner and grab everyone their lunch orders?"

If vomit took on a human form, it would have to be Simon Cranmer. I don't even need to look up from my desk to know he's leaning cross-armed over my cubicle wall and trying not-so-subtly to stare down my button-down shirt. "If I remember correctly, waitressing isn't my job here."

"Come on, now," he says, and I can hear the smug smile in his tone. "Everyone takes their turn."

Slamming my pen down on my desk, I swallow against my gag reflex and look up. Yup, there's that smile. *Ugh.* There's a piece of gum smacking between long chews like it's some kind of flirtatious mastication, but it makes the bile in my stomach rise dangerously fast up my throat.

"And when was the last time you fetched everyone's lunch orders, Simon?"

The idiot guffaws and steps around to the side of the cubicle to slide his flat ass onto the corner of my desk, knocking over a pile of papers in the process.

"Cool it, Bella, I'm only teasing. You know that's what I'm like."

Unfortunately. "If you don't mind, I'm busy."

"Heard back from any internships yet?" he asks in a surprisingly serious tone.

I bite the inside of my cheek. "That's none of your business."

He smirks. "So . . . no."

Choosing to stay quiet, I turn back to my work—but he still hasn't budged.

"Starting to run out of time, little Bella."

I pull some stale air through my nose. "Are you deaf? I said I'm busy."

"Doing what? Writing about which mascara is the best bang for your buck?"

I try to unclench my fists, but my knuckles pop anyway. "No."

"Is it which lipstick won't rub off when you're"—his eyes scan me up and down—"on a date?"

Barf. "Actually, I was thinking of writing an article on the best way to kick a man in the balls. Care to be my test subject?"

He shakes his head and rolls his eyes, then he finally stands and walks away. "Jeez, smile a little. Can't ever take a joke, can you?"

When he's gone and out of sight, I sink back into my chair and it takes me a full minute to steady my heart rate, but at least he should leave me alone for the rest of the day . . . perhaps two days. That would be a real treat. With the weekend coming up the day after tomorrow, I might have a whole *four days* without him pestering me like the gnat he is.

The saddest part is that while his teasing is horribly sexist and slimy, he wasn't entirely off base. Randall, our editor-in-chief, insisted I write an article about the best beauty products and trends happening at the moment with the reason of *We need to bring in more female readers*. I tried explaining that women also enjoy articles about college sports and academics as long as they're written in a way that doesn't talk down to them, or better yet, when they feature actual women, but he couldn't be swayed. It's why so much is riding on that Carnal Sins article. I can't write about eyeshadow anymore. It might kill me.

And his jab about internships—it's quite possibly the biggest stress in my life. The last semester of the program here at Stoneman requires journalism majors to complete a four-month internship at a publication company. If I don't get at least something, I won't have the necessary requirements to qualify for my degree. Four years of studying down the drain. The only thing keeping my head above water right now is the fact that it doesn't seem like Simon has managed to land an internship yet, either. If he had, everyone would know about it, I'm sure. The bragging would be unbearable. Plus, the fact that he was asking me about mine makes me think he's sleuthing for information.

One thing's for sure, though—if Simon gets an internship before me, I'm kicking him in the balls.

"DID YOU HAVE FUN LAST NIGHT?" asks Becks as we break away from our History of Fashion class and head into the building atrium.

I nod. "Yeah, it was great."

"I know metal music isn't everyone's cup of tea. It never used to be mine, but I can appreciate its complexities and beauty now," she continues.

"Yeah, it's not bad. Just not really what I'm used to. But I suppose it helps when you're dating one of the band members, huh?"

Her cheeks flush, and there's a shy smile that crawls across her lips. "James opened my eyes to it. To a lot of new things actually. I wouldn't be who I am today without him."

My brow furrows. The way Becks talks about her boyfriend, it's like he saved her life or something. "How did you two meet, anyway?"

"He moved in next door and we finished senior year at the same school," she says quickly. "It's kind of a long story."

She looks away, and I get the sense that she doesn't want to elaborate, so I drop it.

"What about you?" she says, finally turning her smile back on. "Meet any cute guys last night?"

I nearly trip over my own two feet and have to skip on one foot to right myself. Did I meet a cute guy last night? I met a guy so cute I wanted to climb him like a tree. "Uhh . . . not really. No one seemed interested."

She pulls her face back and scoffs. "You're crazy! There's no way guys weren't interested in you last night. I saw at least three sizing you up during the show alone."

Not the one I wanted though. "Well, point them out next time, will you?" I say, laughing.

We walk through the glass doors and sit on the steps facing the street.

"How did the article go?" Becks asks. "You said you submitted it, right?"

I twirl a strand of hair around my finger. "Yeah, I think it's my best work, if I'm honest. I hope they see that."

"Did you submit it under another name?"

I sigh. "I did. I didn't want to, but I can't stand the thought of no one reading it."

"They're going to love it," she says, her eyes sparkling. "Then they'll all be eating their hats when they realize they never should've underestimated you."

Becks is sweet—naive, but sweet—and I wish I had the optimism she does. "I guess we'll see."

"It'll all work out. I know it. Oh! There's James."

A black van pulls up along the curb and the tall, attractive guitarist hops down out of the driver's seat. He smiles widely at her and we both stand.

"We should hang out sometime. You know, outside of school, and maybe without all the loud music," she says, pulling her bag over her shoulder. "Being new to the area and working so much, I haven't had a chance to get out much."

Dave's comment from last night pings in my mind, and I'm surprised all over again. Becks is beautiful, and bright, and genuine. She reminds me of the popular cheerleaders from my old high school, so to hear she's been struggling to make friends is hard to believe. Me, on the other hand, I've closed myself off from everyone. Becks being the exception, because she wouldn't take no for an answer. And truthfully, I'm flattered she wants to be friends. It's why I pushed myself out of my comfort zone by going out last night. "Sure. I'd like that."

She pulls a piece of paper and a pen from the inner pocket of her bag and writes something down. "Here's my number at the house. Call me whenever, okay?"

"Sure. Thanks."

"See you!"

She practically skips down the steps and jumps into the wide, waiting arms of James, who wraps her up and spins her around like they haven't seen each other in days. I'm envious. I can't help it. They look so *happy*. And I just feel . . . so alone. I look down at the paper with the phone number on it and tuck it into my purse.

My fingers slide over the photo I hid away, and I pull it out. Eyes zeroing in on the sexy smile on Dave's face. The way his teeth gnaw into his lip, and that piercing look that makes my insides turn to liquid. Even through the photograph, he has me nearly in a sweat by the time I tuck it away. I can't help but remember the heat of his body close to mine and the way he'd twirled my hair.

But I also can't forget how he pulled away. How he flirted with that woman. Did they go home together? What a stupid question, *of course* they did. I'm not an idiot. Dave is hot, and she seemed eager for whatever he was willing to give her. Again, that ugly green monster rears its head. When I saw how he held her, I couldn't stay. I didn't want to be a spectator to that show. So, I wave goodbye to Becks and James, watching them drive away into the sunset, and I ask myself another question: what would it be like to be in bed with Dave?

Would he be rough and punishing or would he be slow and gentle? Or would it be all of that somehow at the same time. Would his touch burn me from the inside out, and his kiss— It would be a crime against humanity if he wasn't a good kisser.

I turn back inside to head for the newspaper office, and I'm so caught up in my own ridiculous fantasy that I don't register someone calling my name until they tap me on the shoulder.

"Henry?" I ask, my heart jumping in my chest at his sudden appearance.

"Good, you're still here. Come on," he says, gesturing to the building I just left.

"What—?" I start, but Henry runs back inside the doors, and

while I wish I could simply walk home after my long day, I've always been too nosey and curious for my own good. Hiking my bag up on my shoulder, I head back inside, where I notice the gathering of people outside the editor's office. I sidle up behind Henry, who's obnoxiously chewing on his thumbnail like a toddler.

"What's going on?" I whisper.

He leans over but doesn't tear his eyes away from the front of the room. "Randall called an emergency meeting."

My heart begins to race. "About what?"

"No idea."

From a quick look around the room and the way the other men quietly chat amongst themselves, it appears like no one else has any idea what this is about either.

After several painful minutes of waiting, Randall finally materializes out of his office. It's not unusual for him to go on a long tirade about sloppy editing or bad story assembly, but those freak-outs usually happen on Fridays at four thirty. Not on a Thursday.

"Thank you everyone for taking a moment before we close up for the day to come to this meeting. I'll try to keep this short."

A cold sweat sweeps over me as I see Randall hold up several pieces of paper with a photograph paperclipped to the top. My article. "Oh, shit."

"It appears we have a serious issue," Randall continues, holding my submission between his hands. "You see," he says, thumbing through the typed pages, "this article was submitted today and, I'll be honest . . ." He trails off, rubs at his chin thoughtfully. Oh god, he's going to say it's the worst thing he's ever read in his life. He's going to humiliate me in front of the entire program. Simon will be intolerable. I'll never be able to show my face again. *Wait, they don't know I wrote it.* I can just pretend I— "This is the best written article we've received all year. And the kicker? The writer isn't even enrolled in the journalism program."

Wait, what? He liked it?

Something like a squeak fights its way through my lips, and Henry gives me a look. I try with all my strength to keep my smile at bay as the men all turn, murmuring to each other.

"What do you mean?" Simon speaks up. "Someone submitted an article, but they're not in the program?"

Randall looks up. "Apparently they don't even attend Stoneman."

"That's ridiculous!" a redheaded man with freckles and glasses cuts in. "You can't write for the college newspaper unless you're enrolled."

Randall narrows his eyes. "Well, considering this is work above and beyond what you manage to turn in, Peter, there's no way I'm going to toss it in the trash."

"Well, who wrote it?" Simon calls out from the crowd.

My heart is beating so hard I worry I might have a heart attack and die before I'm able to explain it's mine. "Someone by the name of"—Randall looks at the article again—"Santiago Morales."

Oh god, oh god, *oh god.*

The whispered discussions continue around me, and I'm suddenly losing my nerve. I was so sure I would be able to say that it was me who wrote it, but in none of those scenarios had I imagined an audience—or at least, not one of this size. This may have been a terrible idea.

"Does anyone know a Santiago Morales?" Randall asks.

Everyone looks around, perhaps waiting for someone to miraculously appear with a nametag.

Randall sighs. "Listen, I want to run the article, but I can't unless I can confirm they're a student. Did anyone see a man they didn't recognize loitering around the submissions box?"

Again, everyone looks confused, and I'm so nervous my legs are quaking. Finally, Randall shakes his head. "It's a shame. Whoever wrote this is talented. This is by far the best—"

"It was me."

As if in slow motion, every head turns my way. Every mullet and pair of large framed glasses looks toward me, slack-jawed and eyes bulging. The crowd parts, and it's as if someone has turned on a spotlight over my head.

"You?" Randall asks, dumbfounded.

I swallow, hard. "Yes, sir."

He narrows his eyes, his astonished face folding into a menacing frown. "My office, now."

Oh no.

He turns and disappears through the door, and I walk with heavy steps through the crowd, hearing the murmured whispers of *There's no way. She couldn't have written that* and *Makeup girl? I thought she just wrote the crossword* and, most unoriginal: *Bullshit, she's stealing credit for someone else's work.*

Thankfully, when I shut the door behind me, the whispers are drowned out, but a far more terrifying beast stands across from me behind a desk. Slamming the article down between us, he slumps down in his chair.

"It appears you have some explaining to do. Sit."

Face boiling, I shuffle forward to sit in the green leather chair across from Randall, who looks like he's one embarrassing typo away from exploding. He sits and picks up the article again.

"Who wrote this, Miss Rodriguez?"

I blink, not sure if I heard him correctly. "I'm sorry?"

"Who wrote this?"

"I did."

"Bullshit."

Pulling my face back, I frown. "It's not bullshit! That's my article."

"Are you trying to tell me that you wrote an article *this good* about an up-and-coming heavy metal band? Do you even listen to metal music?"

"I'll admit, it's not my preferred type of music, but I hung out with the band, and they're really cool, and I thought—"

He shakes his head. "Okay, now I know you're lying. You 'hung out' with the band? Did they pick you out of a crowd and serenade you too? What kind of childish fantasy are you trying to spin?"

My shock and disbelief start to give way to anger. "What is your problem?" I shout.

"My problem is that I have this great article, I don't know who wrote it, and a fucking senior journalism student thinks she can take credit for someone else's work."

"Why is it so unbelievable that I could write this?"

"Because I've never read anything from you that would indicate this level of talent."

I cross my arms over my chest. "Maybe you would if you ever bothered to read what I write, Randall."

He leans forward, menace scrawled across his face. "What did you just say?"

"All you ever do is have me write stupid fluff pieces. You never give me anything worthwhile. I put a man's name on this article because I knew it would be the only way you'd actually bother to read it. Thank you for proving me right."

Grabbing the article again, he flips through it several times before looking back up at me. "How can you prove this is you? It could be anyone."

I open my purse and grab the photo I swapped earlier. My favorite one. The one with Dave's beautiful smile directed at me. "Here's another version of the cover photo. I took several."

For several long minutes he does nothing but flick his eyes back and forth between the article, me, and the door, as though contemplating whether or not to kick me out of his office. Maybe even out of the program. *Shit.* I can't get kicked out. No, I won't let that happen. I just proved, in albeit an underhanded way, that I'm the best journalist he has, and that he hasn't taken me seriously for years simply because I'm a woman.

He seems to come to the same conclusion as me, and he sighs.

"Listen, Isabella," he starts, placing the papers down and flattening them out gently. "I apologize. Perhaps I haven't been giving you the right attention. This article is . . ." He pauses, then looks me dead in the eye. "It's excellent."

My heart is leaping around my chest, relief starting to feel like a possibility. "Really?"

"Yes."

"Thank you."

He pulls at the collar of his stiff shirt and clasps his hands together in front of him. "I want to put it on the front page. Under your *actual* name. Are you okay with that?"

My face is begging to split into a grin, but I'm still negotiating here. "Yes, if you agree to stop giving me shit assignments. No more crosswords and no. More. Makeup."

He pauses for a long moment, and while I'm flirting with the boundaries of my limited power here, I have to try.

"Deal."

CHAPTER 4

Run to the Hills

Something warm and soft brushes against my chest as I roll over in bed. A low groan escapes my lips, and I attempt to pry my eyes open against the late morning sun filtering in through the blinds. The warm, soft thing on my chest moves, and my eyes shoot open to find a nest of blonde hair that's attached to the hand currently resting on my torso.

Oh yeah, I forgot about her . . . And her name. Shit, was it Tiffany? Stephanie? It definitely ended with an "e" . . . I think. Forgot she was blonde too. Why did I dream about a brunette?

So, you got a name?

Isabella Rodriguez.

Oh, right.

I gently grab the tanned wrist from my chest and try to move out from under my guest. As much as I don't have any intention of seeing this girl again, I'm also not a complete dick and am not willing to wake her up only to tell her to get her shit and go. Whoever she is, she's obviously a sound sleeper, because she doesn't wake as I sit up on the side of my bed and pull on a pair of boxers and my jeans.

There are clothes strewn across the floor. She obviously didn't care that my room was a mess when she got here last night, but that might change with the light of day and a hangover. So I pick up her discarded bra and underwear, leaving them on the bed along with her dress, and grab the remaining clothes from the floor. I quietly open and close my bedroom door, heading for the laundry room. There's already a load going, so someone else must be up by now. Thankfully, there's a load of freshly washed clothes in the dryer, which happen to include one of my favorite Metallica shirts, so I pull that on and head out into the kitchen.

"Morning."

I look up and find James sitting at the breakfast bar, drinking a cup of coffee. "Oh, hey."

He's looking through the newspaper with a pen in his hand but puts it down when I pass. "Have a good night?" he asks with a smirk.

I roll my eyes but can't help returning the smile. "Not too shabby."

"She still here?"

Nodding, I pull down a mug from the top shelf and fill it with coffee. "Yup."

"Key and Joel's dates just left," he says, picking up his newspaper again. "So it seems like everyone went home happy."

"It would seem that way."

"Thank you."

My brows furrow. "For what?"

"For not going after Isabella. I could tell you were into her."

I shrug my shoulders and scoff. "It never would've worked out between us."

"Why not?"

"She likes *disco* music."

James laughs. "Yeah, okay. Fair enough."

I take a deep breath. *Okay, crisis averted.*

"Pretty cool that she's going to write an article, huh?"

I turn to the fridge to get the creamer out, and also to hide the way my skin heats at the thought of Isabella in her mini skirt. "Oh yeah, that's right. Forgot about that."

"It probably won't be huge, but the college scene is kind of our core audience right now. So the more people who come out the better, right?"

My head bobs as I turn back to James, who's circling something in the paper. "What are you doing?"

He shrugs but doesn't look up. "Looking for another job."

I pause with my mug at my lips, coffee sloshing over the rim. "Why? Surely you're making enough from the gigs that you're not strapped for cash."

"No, but, if we were playing more often, or to bigger audiences, the money would be better. Becks's tuition is expensive and I want to be able to help her with that. She's already working her ass off and she doesn't say anything but I know worrying about paying for her education stresses her out."

While I haven't had the desire to be in a relationship in years, I have to admit that I have huge respect for James with the way he takes care of his girl.

"Dude, we can all help pitch in on that, if need be. You know we all love her like a sister," I say, placing my hands flat on the counter. I mean it too. I didn't know what to think when I first met Rebecca, but after everything she and James have been through—we've *all* been through—I've grown to adore her. "Besides, maybe things will pick up soon. Al could call any minute with some studio time."

James offers a small smile and looks up at me. "Thanks, man. And I know that, but a few hours working in the afternoons won't kill me."

Taking another sip of my coffee, I close my eyes and swallow, relishing in the bitter taste and the burn on my tongue. My hand lands on my hip when I feel something hard. And not *that* kind of hard. Digging my fingers into my pocket, I pull out the little sun and cloud keychain from the bar last night.

"What's that?" James asks.

I stare at the words etched in the plastic again. *Dreams are forged out of darkness.* "Found it last night."

"The way you're staring at it makes me wonder if it's made of gold," James says with a chuckle.

"Huh?"

He raises his eyebrows, glancing between me and the keychain.

"Oh, right." I tuck it back into my pocket. "Thought I would turn it into lost and found last night, but forgot."

Then everything goes dark, hands pressing over my face and a warmth closing in on my back.

"Guess who?" a feminine voice coos.

Fuck. Forgot about her. And I still can't remember her name. "Uhh . . . sexy?" Better than getting it wrong, I guess. Apparently that's good enough, because she giggles and lets go of my face to spin me around. She's managed to tame her hair a bit and pull her clothes back on, but there's still some remnants of blue eyeshadow and mascara smudged under each eye.

"I was so sad when I woke up and you weren't there, pumpkin," she says, then pouts while batting her eyelashes. I woke up feeling fine, but this display makes me suddenly nauseous.

"Oh, yeah, I thought, coffee . . ." I mumble.

"Coffee? That sounds great," she says, cutting me off and stealing my mug from my hand to take a long drink. I hear a quiet laugh and glare at James out of the corner of my eye, watching as he hides behind his newspaper.

"Right, well, I guess I'll give you a ride home, then?" I say, wanting to get this over with.

"You know," she says, turning and plopping onto the chair

next to James, "I'm starving. You wouldn't happen to have anything to eat, would you?"

"Uhh." *How the hell do I get rid of this girl?* James meets my gaze over his paper and I throw him a pleading look. Mercifully, he rolls his eyes and lowers his paper.

"Sorry, we're in a hurry. Have a meeting with our manager in fifteen minutes," my friend says, hopping down and closing his paper.

"Shit, yeah," I say, feigning disappointment. "Sorry, darlin'. Raincheck?"

She gives me a dramatic pout. "Fine. I'll leave you my number and you can drop me off at Broadview and fifth."

"Perfect," I say, backing away and offering her a thumbs-up.

I brush my teeth, and five minutes later James, Blondie, and I are climbing into his black van and heading out to the main road.

"You know," she says leaning over to James. "You're seriously hot and exactly my friend's type. You interested in a date?" she asks slyly.

James clears his throat but smiles politely. "No thanks, I'm taken."

"Taken?" she says surprised. "That skinny blonde girl from last night?"

He nods. "That'd be her."

"Hmph," she huffs, folding her arms and sinking down into her seat. "Well, that's no fun. How are we all supposed to go on a double date if you have a girlfriend?"

James's cheek twitches as he turns the knob on the volume, and I rub at my temple. This woman is ridiculous. A few awkward minutes later, we pull up at her street, and before the van even fully stops, I'm opening the door for her to get out.

As she climbs down, she turns and wraps her arms around me and kisses me full on the lips. "I had a great time, pumpkin. You'll call me?"

"Sure, yeah . . . I have your number."

"Don't keep me waiting," she whispers, her teeth nibbling on my chin.

I pull back, prying her arms out from around my neck. "Right. Thanks again. Bye."

Before she can even respond, I'm slamming the van door and telling James to floor it.

"You sure you don't want me to wait while you profess your love for each other on the street corner, pumpkin?" James asks through a wicked grin.

I shove his shoulder and slump in my seat. "Just shut up and drive."

"I'M TRYING to get you guys into the studio the moment there's a cancellation. We need to get those drum sets on tape, so you'll be up to bat first, Noblar," Al says through the phone. "Are you guys good with something last minute?"

"Yeah, man. We're ready," I say, nodding.

"Good to hear."

Al shouts something at someone on the other end of the line, his hand obviously covering the speaker to muffle the noise. "Sorry about that. I wasn't able to get that Wednesday gig locked down unfortunately, but I still have a few more lines in the water. I'll let you know what I can come up with. Hang in there."

"Okay," I say, trying to cover the disappointment in my voice.

"I'll be in touch."

The line goes dead and when I hang up, the receiver feels heavier than ever before.

"Well?" Key asks from his place on the couch.

"Nothing until the weekend, and no studio time yet. Al's

hoping for a cancellation." I sigh. "He'll let us know, so we need to be ready to drop everything and go."

Key curses under his breath and takes a long sip of beer. "Yeah, all right. Well, I'm sure it'll pick up soon."

"Only if our luck changes," I mutter. Key holds my gaze. It's hard to stay positive when things keep going wrong.

We both look over at the sound of a grunt to find Joel passed out on the couch with his mouth hanging open and his beer precariously perched on his knee. I walk over and grab it before it makes a mess on the shag carpet.

"I think that redhead tired him out last night," Key observes. "How was your night?"

I glance back at the kitchen, where I found the daintily scrawled number earlier and promptly tossed in the trash. Apparently her name is Ashley. "It was good."

"James came to your rescue, I heard," he says smiling.

I shrug. "Asshole can't keep anything to himself, can he?"

Key slaps me on the shoulder as I sink into the cushions next to him to watch *Days of Our Lives*. "She just wants to go on a double date with her pumpkin," he simpers, screwing his face up and giving me the most grotesque puppy dog eyes.

"Fuck off."

He laughs and Joel looses a startled snore from a few feet away.

"I'm just busting your balls, man. I've been there. Chicks can be nuts."

A smile starts to pull at the corners of my lips, but a pressure I haven't felt in a while creeps over my chest, and my breath halts. "Yeah. Yeah, they can."

Five Years Ago

DAVE

"I called that place in Cleveland and left a message. Should hear back soon," I say, bursting through the door to Sam's garage and easing onto the stool behind my drum kit. Reaching forward, I adjust the cymbal and tap my foot on the right bass.

"Sorry?"

My eyes widen as I look up and realize Sam isn't here. Instead, there's a brunette with bright eyes and long legs. *Fuck, she's pretty.*

"Oh," I say, jumping to my feet and nearly toppling over the bass pedal. "Hi, sorry, I thought you were Sam."

She grins. "He'll be back in a few minutes. He just went to grab some sodas."

"Right."

"I'm Emily," she says, walking forward and holding out her hand for me to shake. I take it gently, noticing the way her bare arms are covered in beauty marks, like a constellation.

I manage to swallow. "Dave."

She smiles again then takes a step back, clasping her hands

behind her. "You must be the drummer I've heard so much about."

Heat rushes into my cheeks. "I . . . uh, really? I mean," I say, fidgeting with my drumsticks to expel the nervous energy that's suddenly coursing through me. "I am the drummer." As if to prove it, I hold up the drumsticks, but in my enthusiasm they fly out of my hand and shoot toward the back wall, nearly hitting the window.

Thankfully, Emily doesn't laugh at me, and I can't help but notice her smile. "So, what's in Cleveland?"

"Huh?"

"You said you left a message for someone in Cleveland?"

My brain finally catches up and I part my lips. "Just this little recording studio."

She angles her head, brown eyes probing. "Really?"

Nodding, I continue, the words spitting from my mouth uncontrollably. "We're trying to record a demo track to send to some record labels out west."

"That's amazing! Sam told me he was in a band, but he didn't make it out to sound like it was anything serious. I thought you guys just got together to jam and drink beer."

I rub the back of my neck. "It can be that way sometimes, but the dream has always been to make it big."

"You and Sam go to school together?"

I hastily pick up my drumsticks and tuck them into the back pocket of my jeans. "Yeah. We've, uh . . . gone to school together since kindergarten. Weird to think we'll be graduating high school in five months."

She nods, and for a long moment, we just stare at each other.

"Uh, so . . . how do you know Sam?" *Please don't say girlfriend, please don't say girlfriend.*

"He's my cousin."

Yes! "Oh, cool. He's never mentioned a cousin."

She shrugs and walks over to the counter where Sam's dad stores all of his tools, then hops up on top of it like she's made of air. "We never got to see each other much growing up, as my dad was usually deployed, but since he's been back, home has been rough. My mom took off, and my dad apparently can't be bothered to do anything except drink himself into an early grave, so I'm staying with my aunt and uncle for a while."

"Oh. I'm sorry, that sounds awful." So she'll be around for a while. Perfect. "My mom took off too."

"Really?"

"Yeah, when I was five," I say, walking toward her.

"Shit, that's—I'm sorry."

I shrug. "It was a long time ago. And while my dad doesn't drink, he's not exactly a peach either."

She smiles sadly. "Guess we have quite a bit in common already."

I can't help but grin at that. "Will you be going to school with us?"

"That's the plan."

"Maybe I could drive you to school?" I blurt awkwardly. But I can't help myself, I want to be near her.

She smiles a wide, toothy grin and my insides turn to liquid. "Pretty sure Sam can do that. You know, since I'll be living with him."

"Right." *Fuck, I'm an idiot.*

"But, maybe you can show me around? Other than Sam, I don't know anyone. And who better to make introductions than a rad drummer?"

I think my face might literally be on fire. "I don't know about that . . . I'm not exactly Mister Popular."

She gives me a long look—one that does nothing to ease my flaming cheeks. "I find that surprising."

I clear my throat just as Sam bursts through the door with an armful of Dr. Pepper bottles. "Okay, Em, so all we have is this—oh, Dave, I didn't know you were here. I take it you met Emily, then?"

"Yeah."

She takes a bottle from Sam, and as he turns away, she winks at me with her bright eyes and long lashes and I know right there, I'm in a whole new world of trouble.

CHAPTER 6

I Will Survive

ISABELLA

My palms are sweaty and my heart gallops as I hold the note in my hand with Becks's handwriting. Why is making a simple phone call so nerve-racking? *Come on, don't be ridiculous.* We're friends, and she gave me her number expecting I'd call at some point.

But that little sabotaging voice in the back of my mind might as well be saying, *Maybe she was just trying to be nice but doesn't really like you.*

No. Becks doesn't seem like the type of person who would be phony like that. Also, she admitted it's been hard for her to make friends.

"Okay, just call. No big deal," I say, finally picking up the phone and punching the buttons with shaking fingers. The phone begins to ring, and I nervously chew on my cuticle. Wait, what if one of the guys answers? What if *he* answers? But before I can hang up and panic, the line connects.

"Hello?"

Goddammit . . .

"Hello?" Dave says again, drawing out the O like he's searching for the caller.

Come on, Izzy, say something. "Uh, hi."

There's a pause. "Who is this?"

"It's uh—sorry, it's Isabella?" Why am I asking him? "I'm looking for Becks."

"Oh hi, it's Dave."

The deep timber of his voice already clued me into that. "Hey."

"Becks isn't here," he says. "But I could pass along a message."

My heart needs to get a grip, how can a voice make its rhythm so completely erratic? "Sure, I—thanks, that would be great."

There's a long pause as I wait for him to say . . . something, but nothing comes.

"Uh . . . what should I tell her?" he asks.

Did I not tell him? Oh my god, what is wrong with me? "Yes, I—" But the phone slips through my sweaty palms and hits the floor. I bend down to chase after it but the spiral cord catches the fallen receiver and it bounces back up—hitting me square in the nose. "Fuck!"

"Isabella?" I hear from a distance. My eyes are watering and my nose is throbbing. "Isabella, hey, are you okay?"

I stand, shaking out my hands and letting go of a long breath before lifting the phone back to my ear. "Yes, sorry. I uh —"

"Dropped the phone?" he asks. Somehow I can sense it. The sound of a smile in his voice. Can practically picture it in my head.

Sighing, I nod my head and tenderly touch the bridge of my nose. "Yeah . . ." I mutter.

Even though there's no noise, I can almost hear him vibrating with laughter.

"Anyway," I say, continuing on even though my cheeks burn, "I just wanted to let her know that my article about the band—

well, I guess, your band, actually—it's going to be on the front page of next week's paper."

There's a moment of silence, then Dave's excited voice sounds. "The front page? Izzy, that's amazing!"

That name again. It cracks open my chest. The tiniest fracture in the walls I've built up around myself beginning to form.

"Isabella?"

I close my eyes, realizing I haven't breathed in almost a minute, and I sharply inhale.

"Hey, are you still there?"

"Yes, I—" Another few deep breaths. "Sorry, yes. I'm still here."

"Thought I lost you for a minute there," Dave says. I glance down at the picture in my hand, the one I kept, the one I used to prove I actually *can* write, the one Randall convinced me to let them have a copy of for the paper. I wish I didn't have to share it.

"I hope it helps you guys," I say into the speaker. "Surely it'll bring people out to your next show."

"Yeah."

There's a long moment and my brain is spinning, not sure what to say. Should I hang up? Is he still there? I realize I only just called to leave Becks a message, and now I'm wasting his time. But what do I expect? If last night is any indication, he's not into me the way I wish he were, so why am I grasping the phone like it's a lifeline? Why am I secretly hoping and praying he'll confess that he was sad I left, that he wished I had gone home with him last night, that he wants to see me again?

"You know," he says, breaking the silence, "if we ever manage to score some studio time, you should come and check it out."

My chest suddenly lightens. "Oh?"

"For a follow-up piece, maybe? You could write an article

about the process of making an album. People would eat that shit up."

"Oh." Not quite the invitation I was hoping for. But it's an invitation nonetheless. "I'll have to run it by my editor, but you're right. It's a great idea."

"Bitchin'."

Another pause. It's like neither of us wants to hang up . . . or maybe I'm just reading too much into this again, but either way, I find myself saying, "It's actually thanks to you that the article made the front page."

"Me?"

I nod even though he can't see me. "What you told me about why you chose to play music. How it helps you understand people . . ."

He's quiet, but I can hear him breathing.

"I think it really helped make the article relatable and compelling in a way you don't normally get. Most people with incredible talent tend to be full of themselves and lose sight of why they're in the business they're in," I ramble on quickly. I don't even know what I'm saying. "So thank you, is all."

"You're welcome," he says. His voice is soft and breathy and it both turns my legs to jelly and my stomach to lead. This isn't healthy. How can I have developed a crush so fast? How am I going to stay professional if I have to write about him again? "Anyway, I better go," I mumble.

"Right."

"Bye."

He doesn't say bye back, and after a few long, quiet moments, I hang the phone back on the receiver, my hand lingering on the plastic like it might somehow keep us connected through space and time.

BY MONDAY AFTERNOON, the college newspaper has sold out every printed copy, and while I never could have predicted this in my wildest dreams, it appears it's all because of my article. Something *I* wrote. It's surreal. Of course, Randall has gone on a rampage, blaming me for the demand like I could have possibly predicted this. I know he's just projecting because of the stress, but it's caused me to be jumpy and on high alert all day.

"We're all sold out! Go away!" Randall yells at the line of people banging on the glass door. "Simon! Can you please deal with those idiots?"

Simon swivels in his chair and glares at me. God, you'd think these guys hate success. Or, I suppose they just hate *my* success. He pulls himself up, then stomps his way past my desk like a petulant child. "I still don't believe you wrote this," he says, pointing his finger at me. "And I'm going to prove it."

Dropping my pen to my desk, I cradle my head in my hands and sigh. I need to get out of here or Randall might get so annoyed that he fires me.

"Rodriguez!" Randall shouts from his open office door. "Get in here now."

Too late.

"Enjoying your success?" Henry asks with a grin.

Getting up from my desk, I stick my tongue out at him and head toward the office door. When I poke my head inside, I find that Randall has sweat through his shirt and his normally slicked-back hair is falling over his forehead.

"You wanted to see me?" I ask.

He looks up, loosening his tie. "Yes, we need to talk about what's next for you." He gestures to the seat across from him and I sink into it cautiously.

"What's next—?"

"Yes, yes, what's next. What you're going to *write* next. My phone has been ringing off the hook from students demanding to know where they can find out more information about this . . . this . . . Carnal Sins band. So what have you got for me?"

My jaw drops open. "I . . . I don't really know—"

"Don't come in here telling me you have no ideas, Rodriguez. You said you met the band right? Do you think they'd let you tag along backstage again? Get you another peek behind the curtain, so to speak?"

"Well, I—" My mind spins, trying to think of something. "Actually, they said I could come along when they manage to get some studio recording time."

Randall's eyes light up like he's five years old on Christmas morning. "They asked—in a studio? I thought these were just some local losers."

I frown. "They're not losers. In fact, they're signed to Megaloud Records. But I don't know when the studio thing is supposed to happen. They didn't have a date yet."

Randall closes his eyes and rubs at his temples. "Okay, okay, I get it. Rodriguez, this could be huge. If these guys make it big, and we're the first ones covering their rise to fame? I've already had to order three times as many papers to fill the demand, but if you can keep churning out stories like this one, people might actually care about our paper. In the four years I've been here, we've never sold as many as we did this weekend."

My frown eases, but my stomach begins to twist. On one hand, this is great for my career—my portfolio. Maybe this is my ticket to an internship. And not just any internship, but a really, *really* good one. Like something notable that my parents could be proud of. I can use these articles as a jumping off point for my career in journalism. Surely magazines and papers are all about making money, so if I have a history of high-selling papers under my belt, no one will say no.

On the other hand, it seems Randall only wants me to write about the band.

"Are you sure we need another article about Carnal Sins? I've been working on this piece regarding the Chernobyl disaster in Pripyat, and I—"

"No one wants to read about that!" Randall says, exasperated. "One thing I know for sure, is that when there's interest, you keep feeding it. You keep writing about it until the interest tapers off. Maybe that'll be after next week's paper. Maybe it'll be in two months. But right now? I want your sole focus to be on the band. Besides, you somehow have this connection with them, and that's invaluable."

I uncross my legs with a huff. "Okay, fine."

"Submission deadline is Thursday at noon, as usual."

Standing, I nod my head and make for the door.

"Isabella?"

I turn around and find Randall staring off into space, squeezing a stress ball like his life depends on it, before he looks back at me.

"Don't fuck this up."

CHAPTER 7

Hit the Lights

DAVE

"The place is packed, can you believe this?" James says, coming back into the greenroom at the back of Legendary, the bar Al got us into for the night.

While we haven't been playing *empty* gigs, a crowd chanting our name like they bought tickets to Madison Square Garden is definitely something new. And I'll be the first to admit that lately I've been questioning whether things were ever going to pick up. That maybe Al is wrong and we'll simply be like hundreds of other hopeful bands who fade away into nothingness. But tonight, things are different.

I tuck my hand in my pocket and grasp my new keychain. It's stupid, I know, but I can't help feeling a connection to the little plastic token. Like the sudden change is because of its presence.

"What do you think happened?" asks Joel, tuning his bass guitar.

"It's obvious, isn't it?" James says, still with a smear of pink lip gloss on his cheek from where Becks gave him a kiss earlier. "Obviously Isabella's article is pulling people in. Most of the crowd are students. In fact, I saw two people with Stoneman College sweaters on, so they must be here because of the article."

I haven't seen or spoken to Isabella since she called and let me know about her article. And while exposure is what we wanted, I didn't think it would work this quickly or be so effective. I guess these students are hard up for decent music. And Izzy, well, other than being friendly, there isn't much I can do about her. She's off-limits but fuck, that doesn't mean I stopped imagining her in that white leather miniskirt, those thick tanned thighs bare and that skirt riding up just a little higher than is decent as she walks.

"Dave?"

Looking around, I find the guys staring at me. "Huh?"

Joel raises an eyebrow. "You okay, man?"

I shake my head. "Yeah, sorry, just kind of zoned out for a minute."

"Well, are we ready to give these people the most metal night of their lives?" Key asks, his smirk roguish.

"Fuck yes."

It's wild how much a crowd can influence a performance. I don't think any of us have ever had more fun, except maybe that first gig back in Iowa. The first time we played together on a stage for an audience—the night we met Al—and changed all of our lives. But tonight is a different kind of atmosphere. It almost makes me feel like we're actual rockstars. Sure, it's not the Garden or some big fancy sold-out arena, but the energy is sizzling and all of that pent-up aggression pours out of us onto the stage.

The only thing that would make it better is if Isabella were here.

Who am I kidding? She doesn't even like metal music, she told me so herself. And it's not like I invited her. I don't even know her number. I briefly wonder if she's at some disco club. If she's dancing in a pair of go-go boots, shorts, and a halter top. Fuck, she'd look downright edible in a getup like that. She's got that old-Hollywood pinup body too—curvy like a country road. Guys would be all over her; they'd have to be crazy not to be. Jealousy creeps up my spine like ice. It's awful and I hate it.

I attempt to look through the crowd for a new distraction but the lights from the stage are too bright. So I'm doomed to spend the rest of our set fantasizing about a girl I can't have. When the final chord is struck and the last cymbal crashes, the crowd erupts into an enormous roar, and by now I've sweat through my shirt and pants, my long hair sticking to my neck and shoulders.

I should be happy, and I am, but there's also something I haven't thought about in a long time. Guilt. And it's festering, rotten . . . Curdling in my stomach. And while I can normally contain it, right now it gurgles up quickly—like I couldn't stop it even if I knew how. Maybe I don't want to. That guilt reminds me of what's come before. That James telling me to stay away from Isabella was for the best because I'll be damned if I let history repeat itself. There's too much to lose now.

After we change, the four of us head out into the bar. The crowd is still buzzing, and soon enough I'm pulled into a seemingly endless circle of praise and admiration that makes me feel on top of the world—my guilt temporarily forgotten. Then I see a mop of pretty dark brown hair and a curvy figure and I stop in my tracks. Maybe she came after all. Did Becks invite her? The woman turns though, and while she's beautiful, she's not who I thought. She smiles at me anyway and waves, and I lift my beer to her, smirking as if I'm on autopilot.

She accepts my quiet invitation and heads toward me through the crowd until she stands a foot away, the smell of her perfume making my head dizzy.

"Hi," she shouts over the bumping music. "You were great up there." She hikes her thumb over her shoulder.

"Thanks."

She smiles. "I'm so glad I came tonight."

"Yeah?"

"I was sure that photo in the paper was fake, that there was no way you were that hot in real life. Imagine my surprise to find out that picture doesn't even do you justice." She bites her lip and that familiar aching, throbbing sensation pools in my groin, waiting to be satiated. She reaches forward and grasps my forearm. "I'm Libby, by the way," she says, stepping closer.

The heat of her is pleasant, and I can't stop myself from enjoying the way her body leans into mine, the soft touch of her skin and how those eyes gaze up at me, like she doesn't know exactly what she's doing.

Libby rises onto her tiptoes. "Maybe you could show me around backstage," she whispers in my ear, then leans back with a wink.

The straining in my jeans urges me on, to take this girl into the back and do unspeakable things to her. So why, then, are my feet stuck to the floor, like a mouse caught in a glue trap?

The keychain burns a hole in my pocket. I've always fantasized about hooking up with a hot chick backstage. I mean, what musician hasn't? And here is this gorgeous woman, practically begging for me to fuck her in the wings. I grab her by the hips and she giggles while I inhale the feminine scent of her, hoping it'll erase all memory of Isabella from my mind, and whisper against her ear, "I'll give you the full tour."

Taking her by the hand, we head through the black door, past the bar. As it shuts behind us, the noise is muffled, and I can hear the clattering of the employees scurrying around.

"Oh! I've never been backstage anywhere before," Libby admits, and I find myself wondering how long this tour has to be before I can push her up against a wall.

"Afraid it's kind of boring," I say. "Not really much to see except curtains and pulleys, sometimes some speakers and a long hallway."

The *click-clack* of her heels on the floor are muted in the dense space. Muffled by the velvet curtains and narrow walls. "Well, maybe you could make things a little more interesting then," she says coyly.

I stop and turn, eyes on the flirty smile gracing her face. "I could think of a few ways to spice things up." Stepping toward her, I cage her in between my arms against the nearest wall. While she makes a tiny squeak of surprise, it's impossible to ignore the way her chest starts to rise and fall, the way her eyes darken. She wets her lips as I begin to lean toward her and inhale the scent of her flowery perfume.

But it's wrong, somehow. I search her face, my gaze latching on to her sparkling blue eyes and, however beautiful they are, they're wrong too. Everything is wrong. This woman isn't *her*. She isn't Izzy, with her fluffy hair and chocolate brown eyes. Her soft, delicate smell and adorable clumsiness.

"Something wrong?" Libby asks.

I realize then that I'm frozen, standing over her with a glazed look. "I . . . uh, sorry. I—" I clear my throat and step back. "You know, I actually forgot, I was supposed to meet with my manager immediately after the show."

She frowns. "Oh."

"Yeah." *What is wrong with me?* "I wish I could give you a more thorough tour, but duty calls, you know?"

"I—"

"You can find your way back out to the bar, right?"

Her mouth drops open, but I don't linger. I turn to the right and head down a corridor toward the back exit. Air . . . that's what I need. Fresh air so I can kick myself in the ass. What am I doing? Never have I shot down a willing woman before. Well, except Izzy, I guess.

I burst out through the back where mine and James's vehicles are parked. It's deserted back here. Everyone is partying inside, and it's quiet though my brain is spinning. I don't know what this feeling is . . . this lack of desire I have for that woman inside. The disinterest to go back in and pick up any other girl. It's all gone. Shit, what if this is what death is like? But then I think of Izzy's hips, and her freckled shoulders, and how she moves as she talks.

Okay, so the rush of blood to my groin indicates I'm *not* dead. Just . . . infatuated? Is that what this is? Perhaps denying myself of her company makes me compelled not to want anyone else. Well, fuck, that might not be a treat. I lean back against the brick exterior and sigh. This is stupid. Izzy's just one woman . . . she's not all that different from every other woman.

That's not true though. She listened when I shared myself with her, like she understood me.

I might not want to admit it, but Izzy *is* different. She's rare. And wanting her is complete pandemonium.

THERE ARE one thousand three hundred and forty-eight plaster daisies on the ceiling of our living room. I know because I just finished counting them from my spot on the shag carpeting. James and Joel are sitting on the couch, working on some new song, while Key is playing Trivial Pursuit against himself. He asked us to join him an hour ago but I didn't think I could push my brain today. Besides, no one can beat Key at Trivial Pursuit. Apparently he can't even beat himself. Instead, my half-empty brain decided to lie on the floor and as I stared up at the ceiling, I noticed for the first time the plaster pattern of flowers.

I imagine the person who was tasked with it. I think about it for so long, because it's very easily a job I could've ended up doing. I didn't have the brains like Key or James. I didn't even graduate high school. But one thing's for sure, if

I hadn't ended up here, my dad would've made sure I worked my ass off at some manual labor job everyday of my life.

Probably still wouldn't have been proud of me then either.

Ring ring.

I lift my head off the floor toward where the phone is hanging on the wall in the kitchen. The others look up as well, but no one seems remotely motivated to move. Spirits have been low this week even after a great show, and I think it's finally starting to get to us.

"I'll get it," I say with a groan as I roll over onto my knees. My back cracks as I stand, causing a slight wobble to my walk before I pick up the phone. "Hello?"

"Who is this?"

It's Al's voice, and he sounds crazed. "Al, it's Dave. What is it?"

"You're not going to believe the news I have for you boys."

My pulse beats in my neck as I clench my fist around the phone cord. "What?"

He stalls, perhaps for dramatic effect, but I'm about to have a heart attack. "I just booked you for twelve new gigs over the next three weeks!"

I spin and face the others on the couch, who have stopped what they're doing and are now looking over with interest. "You what?" I ask. I need to hear it again.

"Twelve more shows, Noblar. That's four days a week. Not only that, but the venues are bigger!"

My jaw has dropped somewhere between my shoulders and the floor. "How—how is that possible?" I ask.

He scoffs. "Honestly? I don't really know. But we got a call from the manager at Legendary saying his place had never been busier and asking when could you come back. Next thing I know, I've got phone calls coming in from all over Oakland!"

"That's incredible, Al! I can't— Wow, that's amazing fucking news." I say, my mouth finally settling into a permanent grin.

"There's more!" he continues.

"More?"

"I may have managed to book you guys four solid days of studio time."

"Holy shit, really?"

Before Al can even give me the details, James, Joel, and Key have jumped over the couch and are trying to tear the phone out of my hand to listen in.

"Next week on Monday and Tuesday, and the week after, too! Who knows, maybe there'll be more. But this is what we needed —a foot in the door. I don't know how you guys managed to do it. You're either magic or the luckiest sons of bitches I ever met."

Lucky.

I've never been lucky before the past few months. My whole life seemed to be one unlucky and unfortunate event after the other. Key grabs the phone out of my hand and I back away as the others yell for Al to tell them what he just told me. From my pocket, I once again draw out the plastic keychain. It's warm because it's been in my pocket all day. Can this silly thing really be lucky? Everyone will call me crazy if I ever admit to it, but there's something about *this*. Something in my gut that tells me this is special. That finding this little lost artifact in my hand was the turning point. Or maybe I'm just desperate not to feel so cursed.

As the guys scream and yell with excitement over the news, the idea solidifies in my mind that after so much failure, so many bad things and broken dreams, maybe this is finally my time. Our time. But luck doesn't tend to give with both hands. It gently offers fractions at a time, as if to a starving dog. There always has to be balance. So now I'll wait . . . for the other shoe to drop.

CHAPTER 8

Five Years Ago

DAVE

"**D**ave, what the hell is this?" Emily asks, holding up the report card I'd purposefully tossed in the trash. I briefly look at her as the piece of paper I'd been writing on falls to the floor at my feet.

"It's not a big deal."

She disappears behind the report with the school emblem at the top, then lowers it, her eyes narrowing on me. "Seriously? You only passed PE and wood shop?"

I scuff my foot along the carpet on the floor of the garage, trying to hide the fallen note. "It's fine. It doesn't matter."

She crumples my report card and squeezes the bridge of her nose with her fingers. "Baby, what do you expect to do for a job if you can't even fucking graduate high school?"

Shrugging, I cross my arms over my chest. "Like I said, it doesn't matter. I won't need a regular job, I—"

"I swear to Christ, if you say you're going to 'make it big' in music one more time, I'm going to throw myself off the roof."

I scoff. "Don't be so dramatic."

She shifts her weight and places her hands on her hips. "I'm being dramatic? What the hell are you going to do come June, Dave? Sell your kidney?"

Tilting my head, I feign an interested expression. "How much do you think I could get for one?"

"And what is your dad going to say?"

I shrug. "Probably about as much as he'd say if I got all As. Which is nothing. I'm just a huge loser to him, no matter what I do."

She sighs and turns to storm away, but the paper I dropped gets caught under her feet and her eyes lock on it. Before I can grab it, she scoops it up, her eyes narrowing as she reads.

"What is this?" Emily says, looking up at me.

She turns the handwritten note toward me, and I want to sink into a hole in shame, so I avert my eyes to the floor.

"It's nothing . . . it's stupid . . ."

She scoffs. "Stupid?" She holds it up with a shaking hand and starts to read in a too-loud voice. "*Be asked for an autograph, See the band's name on a marquee, Play at Madison Square Garden.* I don't know if stupid sums this up. This is idiotic, Dave. How can you think this is ever going to happen?"

"You don't know it won't."

She crumples the paper further and presses her bone-white knuckles to her lips. "So is this what you're doing when you're supposed to be getting your high school credits? Daydreaming and making lists of what you want to do when you're a rockstar?"

Leaning forward, I reach a hand out. "Em, come on," I say, pulling her toward me. She hesitates at first, but after a few tugs, she relinquishes and comes to stand between my knees. I wrap my arms around her thighs and rest my forehead against her stomach. "I'm sorry," I whisper, defeated. "I tried."

She's stiff at first, not touching me. Then her hand strokes the top of my head. "I just don't understand how this happened. Why didn't you tell me you were struggling? I could've helped."

I shake my head. How can I explain to her that school hasn't mattered to me in months? That I know what I want to do with my life, and it's *not* being an accountant like my dad. That what grades I had in high school won't matter. All I want is to play music, and I have no problem flipping hamburgers for minimum wage until that happens. To be honest, it scares me. Like if I find myself in a job that pays well and has a future, I'll lose sight of the dream—the prize. I won't push myself to do what it takes to make it as a drummer. But to Emily? That sounds crazy.

"I know," I say finally, looking up at her beautiful face. "I fucked up."

She sighs. "I just— I love you so much, and I know this isn't what you want to hear, but . . ."

My muscles tighten, waiting for the words I know she's going to say.

"I know you think that music is all you're meant to do. But . . . that's not real life. The chances of you succeeding the way you want are lower than getting hit by lightning. You need to grow up."

I let go of her and push myself off the couch, snapping up the handwritten list crumpled at her feet. "At least I have a dream. A goal. What do you have?"

She spins and blinks at me, her face turning a deep crimson. "Don't try to turn this around on me. You're the one with this stupid dream that's ruining your life. Just how much money have you spent on cassettes and audio recording equipment, huh?"

"You're one to talk! At least I'm spending my money on something that will help me achieve what I want. What do you do?" I spit back, knowing I'm out of line, but too angry to care. "Partying every weekend? How many times have I had to come pick you up when you're passed out on someone's lawn?"

Tears well in her eyes, and I'm immediately filled with regret. That was uncalled for. I take a deep breath. "Emily, I—"

But she turns on her heel and stomps into the house, bumping her shoulder into Sam on the way.

"Em?" he asks.

She doesn't stop, and a few moments later, we both hear the sound of a door slamming shut.

Sam turns to me, his lips pursed with annoyance. "What the fuck did you say?"

I run my hand down my face and sigh. "It's nothing."

"It's not nothing. I warned you, Noblar. I warned you not to hurt her."

"I know." I shake my head. "I'll go apologize."

I head into the house and toward Emily's bedroom on the second floor. Her door is shut, so I tap my knuckles against the hollow wood.

"Go away."

I smile. "You know, I think it's obvious from my report card that I'm terrible at following instructions."

Turning the handle, I open the door and step inside. Emily is sitting on the floor, her back against the bed with a cigarette burning in one hand. I approach her tentatively, but as I do, I see a half empty bottle of vodka sloppily hidden behind the corner of her dresser. My chest aches.

I slide down to sit next to her on the floor and point to the bottle. "You should give that to me," I say gently, holding out my hand. She doesn't move for a while, just sits like a statue with her cigarette.

Finally she lets out a long breath, then reaches over and hands me the bottle. "Fine. Take it," she says simply.

"It's not good for you, Em," I say, placing my hand on her knee and giving it a gentle squeeze. "I wish you wouldn't drink this shit."

She scoffs. "Like you're in any position to make demands.

Who are you anyway?" she mutters, her eyes blurry and fixed on something in the distance. "You and your pathetic dream. Just some high school dropout, wannabe-rockstar going nowhere."

CHAPTER 9

Rock You Like a Hurricane

The bus jostles me back and forth as it trundles its way down the street, heading for downtown. After the success of the article about the band and more pressure from Randall, I immediately set out to find Becks to see if she could get me any information about checking out the band at their recording studio. I've since wrestled for three days whether Dave just invited me because . . . well, because it was just the polite thing to do. But, also, why invite me if he didn't actually want me to come? Then there's the whole crushing realization that he probably only wants me to come to write another article and, lucky for him, that's exactly why I'm going.

I'm overthinking everything again. I should remember that I'm going for *me*. Because this is good. I'm finally being taken seriously, and I need to cling to that for as long as I can. If I "fuck this up" like Randall warned me not to, I'll be back to writing about the newest nail polish trends, and even if I happen to love the idea of two-toned nails and may have done my own last night in green and pink, it doesn't mean that's the extent of what I can write. I need people to pay attention to my internship applications, and nail polish won't cut it.

I check the slip of paper that Becks gave me. She wasn't able to make it to the recording studio this week because of classes and her job at the boutique, but she guaranteed me the guys would be there all day. So here I am, with my camera and notebook, a few pens, and a buzzing, nervous energy under my skin. I didn't have the courage to call and let them know I was going to show up. What if Dave answered the phone? No, I'm just going to show up and pray that, just like at the show, they recognize me enough to let me in.

"Next stop is Gordon Avenue," the driver calls out.

I reach above me and pull the bell. The bus slows and I step out onto the street, looking up at the numbers as I figure out which way I need to go. After about three wrong turns and some help from a homeless man who I gave the last of my spare change to, I find myself outside of a dark-brick building with the words "Lancaster Recording Arts" above the door.

I shake out my limbs, my bangle bracelets clinking rhythmically from the action. Taking one last look at myself in the reflection on the glass door, I turn the knob and head inside. The moment the door opens, the sound of metal music greets me. It's not like anything I've heard before and doesn't sound like anything I remember them playing at the show last week. For a moment, I wonder if maybe I have the wrong place and the wrong band, but I force myself forward anyway. The long narrow hallway is deserted, but there are pictures in black frames lining every square inch of the walls.

As someone without a huge knowledge of metal music, I don't recognize most of the faces, but there are a few who seem familiar. Like I might have seen them on TV or a poster somewhere.

"Can I help you?"

Startled, I spin at the sound of a gruff voice and find myself face-to-face with an attractive young man. One that I recognize from the other night—one of the band members. What's his name again? Key, I think.

"Hi . . . Key?"

He crosses his arms, looks me up and down, then his eyes brighten. "Oh, hey! The girl with the notebook. Isabella, right?"

I dig into my purse and pull out the very same notebook. "Yeah, that's me."

Finally he smiles, and the crushing weight in my chest eases. "What are you doing here?"

"The article I wrote about you guys did well. Like, really well. My editor wants me to write another. And Becks told me you were all going to be in the recording studio . . . she gave me the address and—"

"You're here to write another article?" he asks, surprised.

I nod. "I mean, if that's okay with you guys. There's a huge demand on campus for more information about Carnal Sins."

He grins wide. "Hell yeah." At my tentative smile he claps his hands then rushes up to usher me onward. "Come on, Dave's recording a track right now. You can watch."

My stomach flips. Oh god. Dave's on the drums right now? I look up at the speakers still broadcasting the music and realize that's him playing. Live. Heat rushes up the back of my neck but thankfully the lighting in this place is dim, and if Key notices, he doesn't say.

"You'll have to be quiet, but when he's done with this take, I'll tell everyone you're here."

"Okay."

There's a red light above a door ahead of us, and he opens it. The music gets a bit louder as we sneak inside. The low light continues in here and there's a huge control board with dials and knobs and sliders. Immediately I spot James, and next to him is the third member of Carnal Sins, Joel. Which means . . .

I turn and see two men, one with a low ponytail and one with a tight afro. They're sitting at the control panel and looking through a pane of dark glass. My eyes follow theirs and my breath catches in my throat. Dave sits at a massive drum arrangement. His arms are slick with sweat and his long dirty blond hair is damp and clinging to the straining muscles in his neck and traps. His scrap of a shirt sticks to his chest and abdomen.

This man . . . *This man* is quite possibly the sexiest man I've ever seen. I swallow hard against the lump that forms in my throat. *Cool it.* I'm a professional. No one here needs to know that it's a water park in my panties right now. The track comes to a final, crashing stop and my chest heaves almost as much as Dave's does through the glass.

"That's great, Noblar," the guy with the ponytail says through a microphone. "Why don't you take five?"

Dave gives a thumbs-up while taking a long swig of water. He stands from behind the drums and moves toward a door—the door I happen to be standing right in front of. Before my brain can tell my feet to move, it swings open and there he is. He stops short of walking into me, and his eyes widen as they land on my face.

"Izzy?"

"Hi."

He pushes his damp hair off his face and I can't help but notice the way his skin glistens like gold in the dim orange light. Something heats in my belly and I find myself wanting to lick his skin. *What is wrong with me?*

"You're here," he says finally. "I—uh, didn't think you'd take me up on my offer."

The heat vanishes. My biggest fear has been realized. Did he really invite me here just to be polite? He never actually thought I'd come. That's the only reason he—

"She's here to write another article," Key pipes up, appearing at my shoulder.

Dave's eyebrows lift. "Oh?"

I shrug. "The first one was wildly successful. My editor is a bit crazed and wants to keep up the momentum because we're actually selling papers."

He grins. "That's awesome." He steps forward, passing me and heading for the burly man with the afro. "Hey, Al. You should meet Isabella Rodriguez."

Al comes over and shakes my hand. "You're writing about the band?" he asks, scratching at his bristly beard.

"Yes, I came to the show a few weeks ago and asked the guys some questions. It made the front page of our college paper."

"No shit?" he says in a low rumbling voice. "And people are wanting more?"

I nod. "Students have been calling the office all week asking about upcoming shows."

"And you're here to write another?"

"If that's okay with you," I state, not wanting to step on any toes.

"Are you kidding me?" Al boisterously chuckles. "That article is probably what spawned the sudden upswing in gigs. Hell, it's probably what got us this studio time. You can write about these guys all you want. As long as it's good."

I smile. "That's the plan."

He pats my shoulder and moves past me to head out into the hallway beyond, leaving us behind. Dave leans in until his breath is skirting the shell of my ear, and goosebumps prickle all over me.

"I'm going to head out for a smoke, want to join me?" he asks with a small grin.

"Sure."

He places his hand on the small of my back, urging me forward, and thank goodness it's still dark in here because my cheeks are burning.

We walk past the pictures and finally, out into the low sunlight of early evening. He leans against the brick exterior and pulls a pack of cigarettes from his back pocket. He looks over at me and offers the pack. I shake my head. "No, thanks."

His eyes narrow as he pulls out a cigarette with his teeth. "I thought you smoked."

"I try not to."

"Oh," he says, lighting his cigarette. "I thought—last week you did. Sorry. I wouldn't have asked you to come out here if I knew you were trying to quit."

"No, no, it's fine. I'm not quitting and . . . I do smoke, sometimes. Mostly when I'm drinking."

"That's fair."

I shrug. "It's stupid, I know. I feel like a huge hypocrite."

He grins. "I get it. It's nice to be bad every once in a while. You have to break your own rules now and again."

A shiver races up my spine to the crown of my head and his blue eyes shine in the light of the sun. "So, how do you break the rules? Be bad?"

I ask because the journalist in me would find the answer interesting. But I also ask because the woman inside of me is dying to know what Dave Noblar does when no one is watching.

"On the record?" he asks.

Right. He's only viewing this as an interview. "Yes."

He takes a long drag of his cigarette. "Well, like with the other guys, there's a lot of anger inside of me."

This makes me pause. "Anger?" Somehow the image of Dave being angry is a foreign concept. Unimaginable. He's so bright.

He nods. "I think that's what ultimately connects all of us to metal music. Being angry and needing a way of dealing with it. We work that darkness out through our drums and guitars. By screaming into a microphone rather than getting ourselves into trouble."

I lean against the brick wall next to him and inch my body closer. "And what does Dave Noblar get angry about?"

Something dark flashes across his face for an instant but then it's gone. It's not scary, per se, but it's disarming, and I fight against the chill that has suddenly crept into the air. But then he smirks at me, and I feel a touch warmer. "Afraid I don't feel comfortable sharing that with a journalist. Even off the record."

Nodding, I cross my arms. Okay, he's not willing to open up about that, but maybe one day he might. "That's okay. You don't have to tell me. I'm just surprised. It's hard to imagine you being angry at anyone."

He holds my gaze as he inhales his cigarette. "There's a lot about my life that I'm not particularly proud of. Things I'm still trying to let go of—things that haunt me."

"Oh."

He leans forward with a coy smile, the smell of him overwhelming me. "What about you? Why did you turn into a Disco queen? Anything haunting you?"

At first, it sounds like an insult. That because of my stupid taste in music I can't possibly understand what he means. But the way he doesn't laugh. Doesn't flinch. Doesn't pull away, makes me think otherwise.

"Disco music is happy. It makes me happy. And . . . I need that. It brings people together and after I left home, I was lonely. It helped." I shrug.

He takes a final drag of his cigarette and flicks away the butt before blowing the smoke up into the air. "Why'd you leave home?" he asks.

I try to keep my gaze locked on his. "Afraid I don't feel comfortable sharing that with a drummer. Even off the record."

He grins. Maybe he's amused or maybe he's intrigued because I'm not as open a book as I can seem at first glance. But damn, that smile is magic and makes me want to spill my secrets and fears and desires all over the sidewalk for him to sift through as he pleases.

"Come on," he says, jutting his chin toward the door. "I'll give you a private tour of how an album gets recorded. That should please your editor, right?"

I grin back, and as he opens the door for me, I laugh. "Definitely."

CHAPTER 10

Call Me

ISABELLA

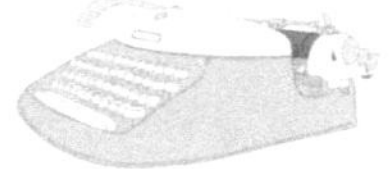

I frown and grip the phone. My chest tightens as I disappoint my mother by telling her I won't be home for Thanksgiving. Just how many times can I let someone down before they give up on me?

"What do you mean, Isa?" she says, her voice choked with emotion.

I sigh. "I had to finish my internship applications so now I'm way behind on work for all my other classes. This last semester before work placements is so important. Plus, Randall has me answering the phones because almost everyone who calls wants to ask about the band I'm writing about every week. I've just been so busy that I can't risk leaving to come home now."

"*Pero—*"

"You know that if I come home, I won't have any privacy or quiet time to do my work."

Silence. She knows I'm right. One thing my family is not, is quiet.

"Besides, if I'm there, I won't want to do work. I'll just want to hang out with you."

"Promise me this isn't because of Miguel."

I twirl my finger into the payphone cord until it's so tight the skin begins to turn purple. "No, it's not."

"Because he wouldn't be here, you know."

"I know, *amá*."

A sigh. "Do you still have that cassette player?" she asks.

I glance behind me at the top of my dresser. "Yes."

"Good, I have that new Dana Raina album to send you."

A chuckle bursts out of me. She knows music is always the way to my heart. "*Gracias*."

"*Te quiero, Isa*."

Hanging up, I slump against the wall. It drains me to tell my mother bad news. But I've sacrificed so much to get to my senior year. I can't lose focus now.

A knock on my door makes me practically jump out of my skin. Who the hell is here?

"Isabella?"

I blink. "Becks?" Crossing the room to the door, I open it to find Becks grinning from ear to ear. "Hey, what—?"

"Theyfinishedthealbumanditscomingoutnextmonth!"   she squeals in the doorway. Grasping at my hands, she shimmies and shakes with excitement, and I can't help but grin even though I have no idea what she just said.

"Hold on, what?" I ask.

She steps into my apartment and I shut the door behind her. "The band, they finished their debut album in the studio. They're releasing the EP in November!"

Something viciously happy explodes in my chest. "Oh my god! No way, that's incredible!"

"I know, right? It's happening," she says, beginning to pace.

"James and the guys must be so thrilled."

"They are over the moon," she says. "They needed this. They needed *you*."

Huh? "What do you mean?"

"Oh come on, don't be so modest. Everyone knows your articles helped put them on the map in San Francisco."

"They do?"

"They must."

"Oh, well I—"

"Isabella," Becks scolds. "You're a talented writer and, yeah, you needed something good to write about and they needed the boost. Everyone benefited."

"Right."

She finally perches herself on the arm of my couch like a dainty little bird. "What's wrong?" she asks.

"Nothing's wrong. It's great. The best news I've heard in weeks," I say, and really, it's true.

She tilts her head. "Have you heard anything about an internship yet?"

I bite my lip. "I sent in my applications two days ago, so it'll be a while before I hear back."

"You're going to get one. I just know it. How could they pass you over?"

Smiling, I nod encouragingly, but I still don't know how much of that I believe. I got lucky with the opportunity to write about the band, but maybe that's where it stops.

"Oh!" Becks says, clapping her hands together. "So, I need a favor."

"A favor?"

"I need help shopping for an outfit," she says. "Want to come with me?"

I laugh, the tension that has somehow built in my chest easing. "Shopping for clothes? I'm in. What's the occasion?"

"Well, the band thought it would be fun" —her face turns bright pink—"to put me on the cover of the album."

My jaw drops. "Really? I thought metal bands usually put, like, demons and monsters on the covers."

Her nose scrunches with distaste and she shakes her head. "Yeah, usually, but James had a different idea." She smiles a little wickedly, her lips quirking. "Do you know what 'carnal sins' are?" she asks.

"Yeah, of course. I grew up Catholic."

She opens her mouth for a moment, her eyes scanning my face but before I can ask her what's wrong she continues. "Well, they thought I could be on the cover, you know . . . indulging in such things." She raises her hands. "I mean, obviously nothing graphic. I wouldn't want to do that anyway. But, something sexy. With maybe a bit of Christian imagery thrown in, you know, like a middle finger to the church."

"Oh. I didn't realize you were an atheist."

"I'm not!" she says, a little panicked. "I just—" Her shoulders turn in, as though she's protecting herself from something painful. "I'm a Christian, I just don't exactly have the best relationship with some institutions."

"Sure. I get that. I'm Catholic, but it's not really something I practice on the daily, you know? Usually just on Christmas and Easter."

She smiles brightly and I smile back.

"So something sexy that says a big F-U to organized religion. Got it."

I DON'T THINK I've ever been so busy in my entire life. What I told my mom was mostly true. Life the past month has been . . . in a word, chaotic. The phone rings on my desk and I snatch up the receiver.

"Stoneman Press," I mutter.

"Hi, yes, I saw this article in your paper about that band. Uh, what was the name . . . ?"

I roll my eyes. "Carnal Sins."

"Right! Yes, do you know when their album is coming out?"

I clear my throat. "It's coming out November 18th, and they're also performing this weekend down at Pier 22 if you're interested."

"Thank you so much! It's my boyfriend's birthday coming up and I need a present to give him."

A smile breaks across my face. "That's nice. You should take him to the show."

"Great idea. Thanks again."

She hangs up and I replace the phone on the receiver. A low whistle hits my eardrums, and as I look up, Simon is headed my way.

"Bella, Bella, Bella," he says, tsking at me like I'm some impudent toddler. "I'm amazed you can get anything done with that phone ringing all day."

I feed a new piece of paper through my typewriter and shuffle around the papers of my finished draft, ready to be typed. "You could always help, you know."

"I'm afraid my voice doesn't sound nearly as appealing on the other end of a call. Besides, most people would expect a woman to answer. It makes us sound legit that we have a secretary."

My molars grind together. "I'm not a secretary, Simon. I'm a journalist, and apparently the only one in the building who can actually sell papers. So why don't you run along?"

Anger flashes across his face for a brief moment, then that condescending smile is back as he leans forward on the edge of my cubicle. "You know, I was just chatting with Randall. It seems unusual that you're able to manage all that you are. Writing the articles, answering all the calls, going to classes . . ."

My eyes narrow. "What are you trying to say?"

He shrugs. "Lots of people hire ghost writers, but I think you'll find that colleges would frown upon that. Considering you get credits for providing your own original work."

I shoot out of my seat, heat blistering my face at such an accusation. "Are you suggesting someone else is writing my articles?" I ask through gritted teeth.

"All I'm saying," Simon says standing back, "is it would make sense. I mean, it's unbelievable enough that you hang out with metal musicians." He picks up the stuffed googly eyed pepper from my desk, shaking it so that the eyes rattle. What does he think? That just because I have a stuffed pepper on my desk, I can't also hang out with guys who thrash around on stage to aggressive music?

"What's unbelievable, Cranmer, is that you think you know enough about me to make judgments about who my friends are," I spit back.

"At least it'll give you something for your internship applications. I suppose it was slim pickings for a while there," he jabs, ignoring my ire completely.

How can someone be so intentionally cruel? "One of my articles is better than fifty of yours," I say.

He smiles in that self satisfied way. "I think a few publications would disagree. Already have a few bites coming in for a place in January."

My heart falls out of my chest and onto the floor. "You—you have?"

"They aren't my top choices—I'm still waiting to hear about those—but at least I know I'll have something next semester."

I bite the inside of my cheek so hard I taste blood.

"I guess you had to do something to get a decent story. Can't exactly expect to get in with the *East Bay Chronicle* with crossword puzzles and makeup. I wouldn't blame you for doing what needed to be done."

I narrow my eyes. "What needed to be done?"

"You can be honest with me, Isabella," he whispers. "I'm a feminist. There's no shame in being a groupie in order to get your stories."

Tearing around my desk, I storm up to him and his awful, smug smile. "Say that again and I'll slap you across the face."

He steps back with his hands held up in mock surrender. "Whoa whoa, easy. I always knew you were a hot tamale." He chuckles to himself and turns to walk away. My fists are clenched at my sides, my chest heaving with righteous indignation, and there's a ringing in my ears.

"*Pinche pendejo*," I mutter.

It's a full five minutes before I can bring myself to move, and when I do it's only because that stupid phone won't stop ringing.

"What?" I growl into the phone.

"Uh . . . Isabella?"

Something twinges in my chest. Like a balm to a burn—soothing. How can the voice of someone I barely know have such a visceral effect on me? My knees buckle as I sink back into my chair.

"Hey, are you all right?" Dave says through the phone.

I swallow down my anger and sniff. "Yes, yeah, I'm fine. How are you?"

There's a pause. "I'm good. I—Are you sure you're okay?"

"Yeah, sorry . . . I just ate something really spicy and my nose is running, that's all." Great. What a lovely visual for sexy Dave to have of me.

"Oh, well, I hope it was good."

I clear my throat and rearrange myself on my chair. "H-How can I help you?"

"Al wanted me to call you and give you an updated list of show dates and venues."

Of course.

"With the huge turn out of the last few weeks and the album coming out, he's added a shit ton more shows."

"That's great."

"It's because of you," he says, his voice gentle.

I scoff. "Hardly. You guys are the talented ones."

"Yeah, but what you've done . . . You gave us great exposure. Got people to give us a chance and build up momentum. I just want you to know how grateful I am—we—are," he finishes quickly. "Besides, from what I've read, you're pretty damn talented yourself."

My cheeks and the tips of my ears heat but it's not the uncomfortable feeling from earlier with Simon. This time it's like the heat of a warm hug. God, I wish someone would hug me. "Thanks. That, uh, that means a lot to me."

I can almost hear him smiling through the phone. "It's the truth."

"I should go. I have a lot of work to do. Can you give me that list?"

"Sure."

He rattles off five additional show dates and venues with their times, and I write them all down on the notebook on my desk.

"You should come to the release party. Becks would be thrilled if you came."

Right, Becks. "I wish I could, but I have a mountain of schoolwork to catch up on before finals."

"Come on, you can't take one night off?"

I could. I want to. I want to stare at his face and body and fantasize about that first meeting and how he twirled my hair. How that all stopped in an instant.

"I shouldn't. But maybe some other time."

"Promise?"

There it is again. That soothing, familiar feeling spreads throughout every cell in my body. Almost like the altercation with

Simon never happened. My heart slows and my knee that's been bouncing uncontrollably is finally still.

"Yes," I whisper. "I promise."

A long silence stretches, and it's strangely intimate. How it feels like he's right beside me. How dare he.

"I have to go."

"Okay."

"Bye, Dave."

"Bye, Izzy."

There's a charged pause until finally I place the phone back on the receiver. Before I can fall down a self-obsessive spiral, the phone rings again, and again, and again. And soon enough the office is closing and I have to haul the typewriter all the way back to my campus apartment in order to have my article typed up before the deadline tomorrow.

Five Years Ago

DAVE

It's dark by the time I open the back door into the kitchen. There's dirty dishes covering the counters and spilled milk that seems to have dripped onto the floor—hours ago, it seems, from the way it's congealed on the tile. My nose scrunches at the smell as I decide I'll try to tackle the mess in the morning. Opening the fridge, I grab a soda then head for the stairs.

"Where the fuck have you been?"

His voice stops me in my tracks. A light turns on in the corner of our dusty living room to reveal my father, his shirt unbuttoned and tie gone, sitting in his recliner. I swallow hard against the sudden lump in my throat.

"At Sam's."

"Playing that goddamn music again?" he asks. It's not really a question. He knows the answer, so I keep quiet and wait for the real purpose behind this conversation. "Got an interesting call from the guidance counselor at your school today," he says, and it's as if I can feel the blood drain from my face. "She told me that my son—my only child—won't be graduating."

"Dad, I—"

He holds up one finger, and I know by now to shut up and wait.

"I always knew you were stupid, Dave," he says, gazing out the dark window into the night. "A dumb kid—even as a baby— late to learn how to talk and walk . . . couldn't even recognize the letters of the alphabet for years. Always mixing them up."

The blood rushes back, my face burning with shame and anger.

"But even though I knew that, I never thought you were stupid enough to fail high school." He laughs. "But I guess I've been wrong about a lot of things, haven't I?"

He pushes himself out of the recliner, and every muscle in my body tenses as he stalks toward me. In the dark shadows of our living room, it's as if I'm an injured gazelle being stalked by a lion. I can't help my lip from trembling as he stops in front of me and takes a long inhale.

"Thought your mother was a decent woman," he whispers. "But she abandoned me with you. Did she see what I do now? Was it because she knew what a deadbeat her son would become?"

My body is shaking, my fist clenched around the soda can.

"Wish she had told me that's why she was leaving. I would've left with her and dumped you off to become someone else's problem."

"Stop it," I spit through clenched teeth.

But there's a maniacal gleam in his eye now as he continues on. "I had your mother and she was perfect. We were so happy before you. Then you came along and it all just . . . ran out. It was like you ate it all up and left none for anyone else."

My heart is beating so hard it might just give out. I can't take it anymore.

"Now you've got that nice girl. God knows what she sees in

you. But I know how that'll end. You'll ruin her life too. Just like your mother's. Just like mine."

"*Shut up!*" I scream.

In one swift motion, he grabs me by the collar of my shirt and slams me up against the wall. "*Don't you raise your voice at me,*" he yells in my face, spit flying everywhere. "Or you'll find your sorry ass sleeping in that piece of shit car."

I want to tell him I'd rather sleep in my car than under his roof. That living with him for eighteen years has been nothing short of torture. That I already blamed myself every day for Mom leaving and that he didn't need to tell me he blamed me too.

"All right, Dad," I whisper through sharp, frightened breaths.

His grip finally relinquishes on my collar, my skin aching, but I'll continue this little game. I can't afford to try to live on my own yet, because every dollar I've ever earned has gone into equipment, drumsticks, and saving for studio time. I'm so close now to the band being legit that if I blow this free ride with my dad, I'll never make my dreams come true.

He scoffs. "You're lucky I even let you stay."

Before I can say anything else, he turns and passes me up the stairs, the bedroom door slamming shut behind him. There's an immediate release of tension. Not all of it, but the most painful kind when your body is still deciding what to do—fight, flee, or freeze. I take a long, deep breath and turn toward the stairs. But there's a letter for me on the entryway table. From the recording studio in Cleveland?

I tear at the paper envelope, my eyes nearly glazing over as a smile creeps its way back onto my face.

DEAR MR. NOBLAR,

YOUR REQUEST FOR STUDIO RECORDING TIME HAS BEEN APPROVED. PLEASE CHOOSE A DATE FROM THE LIST BELOW.

"Holy shit," I whisper, and my knees give out from under me as I sink down to the floor.

Maybe my dad's right about one thing. Maybe I am lucky . . . just not for the things he and Emily think are important.

CHAPTER 12

Rock the Night

ISABELLA

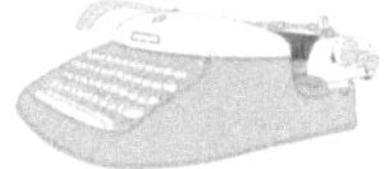

It only took until the end of November, but for once, I'm early to my History of Fashion class, and as I take my seat, I wonder where Becks is and— Oh, wait. It's release day. How did I forget? I've only been telling everyone who calls into the newspaper office for weeks. Maybe she's out celebrating with the guys. At the thought of the five of them out together without me, my chest aches.

"Isabella!"

I look up, and there Becks is, skipping toward me with an absolutely stunning smile.

"You're in a good mood," I say as she falls into her seat next to me.

"It's release day!" she sings. "I haven't been able to sleep for a week. James either. Actually, none of the guys have been sleeping. I swear our neighbors must think a group of vampires live at our house. Everyone is both excited and scared out of their minds."

I think of Dave. Has he been mindlessly wandering around San Francisco in the middle of the night? Has he passed by the phone and thought of calling me? I think of all the times I've dialed their house, punching the numbers in—all but the last one. I wish I were brave enough to make those calls. Certainly it would take my mind off the endless obsession of checking the mailbox, hoping for any news pertaining to an internship.

With every day that passes, my hope slips away a little more. At this point, I would take anything. I wish I could tell him how nervous I am about my future. How I'm so excited for his. Other than the newspaper office, it's not like much goes on in my life, but his is full of adventure. I wish I could be more like that, but I've never been overly outgoing. I wish he would call me, but I doubt he ever will—he's not lonely like I am. He no doubt has loads of beautiful women he could call to keep him company.

"I'm sure it'll be amazing. You'll see."

"Actually," she says, rolling her lips. "I have a gift for you." She opens the flap of her bag and pulls out a large flat cardboard square.

"Is that—?"

"It's a copy of the EP!" she says, grinning widely. "The guys wanted you to be the first to have one after everything you've done."

She hands me the vinyl album, and I can't help but let the grin overtake my face. "Thank you so much. Hey . . . oh my god, is this *you* on the cover?"

Becks's cheeks turn bright pink. "I mean, yeah." She tucks her blonde hair behind her ears. "What do you think?"

I take in the sultry, scandalous image of Becks in basically her underwear, a cross, and her boyfriend's guitar. "This is so hot. Guys are going to want to buy this even if they aren't into metal."

"That's what James thought too. Good thing for him, I'm a loyal girl."

I turn the vinyl cover over in my hands, admiring her photo and reading the names of their songs, when a small card falls out onto my desk.

"What's that?" Becks asks.

I set the record down and pick up the card. "No idea. You didn't put this here?"

She shakes her head, so I open the card to find a handwritten note.

Izzy,

Thanks for everything. I know metal isn't your thing but you might find track 5 interesting.
Dave

The breath whooshes out of me on a laugh.

"What does it say?" she asks, leaning closer to read over my shoulder. "Oh, that was sweet of him," she says. "What does he mean by interesting?"

I shrug, not sure how much I want to go into detail of that first night I met Dave. That maybe I want to keep that just for me. But I can't keep the smile off my face that we have a joke. A joke between just us. "I don't know. Guess I'll have to listen to it and figure it out."

"You're coming tonight, right?"

"Hmm?"

"To the release party," Becks adds, raising her eyebrows expectantly.

"Oh." I shake my head, tucking the album and the card into my messenger bag. "I don't know. I'm really busy and have been trying to catch up on everything. Finals start in just a couple of weeks."

She grabs on to my arm. "No! No, you have to be there. Please? You don't have to stay all night. Just come for an hour or two."

I bite the inside of my cheek and look away, knowing my resolve is already failing.

"There'll be lots of hot guys there," she probes.

Sighing, I nod, unable to resist Becks's charm. "Well . . . where is it again?"

Clapping her hands together, she bounces on the stool. "It's at The Drop. Do you know it?"

The Drop is a huge open-air theater down by the wharf, named for the massive drop ledge and view of the bay. "Yeah, I do."

She nudges my shoulder. "Perfect. Nine o'clock and look hot. Not that you don't already, but they'll probably be taking pictures and stuff."

"I don't think anyone will compare next to that album cover photo of you," I say, tipping it toward her. "Yowza."

She giggles behind her hand as our professor clears her throat for class to begin.

"Just make sure my name is on the guest list this time, okay?" I say.

CLIMBING OUT OF THE TAXI, I readjust my dress—a red strapless number with some gorgeous ruching over my butt and a hem that hits mid thigh. I piled my hair on top of my head in an elaborate twist to show off as much skin as possible, keeping my neck bare but donning a large pair of silver hoop earrings. The moment I step toward The Drop, it's abundantly clear that I'm overdressed. Most people here are in denim and leather jackets, long hair and mullets with big mustaches and patchy beards. Band T-shirts with demons and pentagrams as far as the eye can see. Me in my red dress? I stick out like a sore thumb. Why didn't I at least wear black?

Several men's eyes from the line turn to look at me, but I

won't shrink away. I roll my shoulders back and smile as I approach the bouncer at the door. Another massive man, he gives me an appraising look up and down as I come to stand in front of him.

"Hi, I should be on the list," I say, thankful my voice sounds confident and steady this time. "Isabella Rodriguez." I swear, if Becks forgot to put me on the list again, I might just die right here and now.

The bouncer consults his list, and when he sees my name, checks me off, then steps back to move the red velvet rope. "Go right on in, Miss Rodriguez."

Tension melts off my shoulders as I enter the darkened club. There's a large space with tall tables and stools, each one lit by a small candle, flanked by a bar that must be thirty feet long and accessible from all sides like an island made of booze. Bartenders hurry to and fro inside the enclosure as people shout out their drink orders. Just beyond that, the roof opens up to the night sky and in the distance, I can see a raised platform stage. Then there's the drop.

"Right, first things first," I say, heading for the bar. A little liquid courage will get me through this night. After a few minutes waiting for a whiskey sour amongst the crowd, I begin to look for Becks. It doesn't take me long to find her, nuzzled up to James at a booth just under the canopy of the roof.

"Isabella!" she cries, spotting me and waving me over toward her seat. She's wearing a silver halter dress under a cropped leather jacket that looks like it might have at one point belonged to a man.

"Oh my god, you look incredible!" I say, reaching the table and giving her a hug.

"Doesn't she, though?" James smiles. "So glad you could make it."

I smile. "Becks promised it wasn't something to be missed."

Taking a place opposite them, I sip on my drink, my lips pursing at the sour taste.

"Becks tells me you've been super busy at the paper," he says, leaning forward so his dark curly hair brushes the top of the table.

Nodding, I steal a glance at Becks. When I told her I was busy, I hadn't mentioned the unfair treatment of becoming the unofficial secretary, nor the additional editing work I'd been "entrusted" with, which forced me to set back the work for all my other classes.

"Everyone wants more information about Carnal Sins," I say brightly. "And I'll continue to give the people what they want."

James grins wide. "Well, whatever you need. Don't hesitate to ask. We really appreciate everything you've done."

"Walton," a voice calls. Turning, I see the bassist, Joel, running up to our table. "Come on, the place is filling up and Al wants us to do that grand entrance. Oh. Hey, Isabella."

I wave, and he wraps his arms around my shoulders for a quick squeeze. James slides out of the booth, before turning back to me. "Take care of my girl, okay?" he asks.

"Of course."

Once he's out of sight, Becks's grin fades. "Holy moly, I'm so nervous," she confesses, grasping at her chest.

"Don't be," I reassure her, reaching across the table to take her hand. "They've done dozens of performances by now."

She nods a bit frantically. "I know but . . . now everything is happening and the EP is out. And it's so fast. I feel like they only took my picture for the album cover yesterday."

"But just think what all this could mean," I say. "With the way they've been gaining more and more traction lately? This time next year they could be one of the biggest metal bands out there."

Becks takes a sip of her drink and nods again. "Yes, you're right. Just . . . one day at a time, right? For now, I should just be enjoying tonight."

She takes a deep breath, and I seize the opportunity to distract her as the bar continues to fill up. "So, have you decided what fashion decade you're going to do for your term paper?"

AFTER CHATTING to Becks for a solid half hour about our classes, we head toward the open-air and the stage. Lights of all colors dance, glinting off the metal of the double bass drum kit. *Dave's* drums. I swallow. Seeing him play again is not good for my sanity. Maybe I should go. I made my appearance. But something glues me to my spot, and I remember I have a job to do. A purpose for being here outside of my strange little friendship with this metal band. I'm a journalist.

I reach into my bag and pull on my camera, dislodging pens and my notebook to free it. As the music from the speakers starts to fade, the lights that dazzle across the stage go steady on what I now realize is a large rectangular hole in the floor. Slowly, lit with red lights and smoke curling into the air, a platform lifts and the band appears. It's as if they're rising from the depths of hell itself. The noise from the crowd is deafening. I look through the camera lens as the four men materialize, their long hair, denim, and chains on display for all to see. Dave is in a cut-off shirt that shows off his arms in a way that has me clenching my thighs.

Keep it together.

My camera clicks as they take their positions, pulling guitars over their shoulders. Key steps up to the microphone and holds a copy of the album over his head to a raging crowd.

"Today marks a day that none of us on this stage ever thought would really happen. Our self-titled EP album is officially released!"

The audience explodes. The sound shakes the walls, and dust particles fall in the stage lights like fairy dust.

"This album is for all the freaks out there. The weirdos and the misunderstood people that don't feel like they fit in. Know that here, you fit in with us."

Like a woman possessed, I grab the notebook out of my bag and furiously write down the beautiful words that Key said as the crowd throbs around me. The next article I'm going to write starts to take shape in my head, and watching the four of them start their set, I can't help but feel like I'm included in that group. How all of them have been so kind to me, and even though there's this weird tension between Dave and me, I'm really glad I'm here to help document this moment for them.

THE SHOW IS INCREDIBLE, and while it's true that metal isn't exactly my favorite genre, no one can deny their presence on stage. Besides, it's kind of growing on me. Their passion and aggression is palpable. I think I finally understand what Dave meant when he told me underneath everything, they're all angry. That they all wrangle with a darkness. I see it now. How that anger comes out through their music, their performance. How what Key said must ring so true to them. Maybe they always felt like outsiders, and finally having each other helped them cope.

It's amazing.

Becks, of course, is over the moon, dancing in her own little hypnotic way, and James seems to play just for her. God, to be that in love. After the show, the guys disappear back below the stage, and Becks and I head for the bar.

"Whiskey sour, please," I shout, putting my almost full notebook on the bar next to me. To my right there's a massive lineup of people waiting to buy a copy of the album. I wonder vaguely if the guys plan to come out and sign them. Surely people would also line up for their autographs based on the reaction of the crowd tonight. I smile to myself, thrilled at their success. It almost feels like my success as well, which sounds crazy, but the energy in the air is electric just like their music.

I scan the crowd across the island bar, and as if I've jumped off the wharf into the freezing bay water below us, my blood runs cold. There, waiting for a drink at the bar across from me, is Simon. Quickly, I turn away, hiding my face.

"What's wrong?" Becks asks.

I raise my hand, using my other arm to shield my body. "What the hell is *he* doing here?"

"Who?"

"See the guy across the bar with the blond crew cut and the bad mustache?"

She glances over my shoulder. "The guy in the sports jacket? Does he even know where he is?"

I groan. "He works with me at the school paper and he's an absolute buffoon."

"What *is* he doing here?"

"I don't know, but he's probably up to no good. He's been insinuating for weeks that I haven't been writing the articles myself or worse, that I'm some"—the word gets caught in my mouth—"groupie."

Becks whips her head my way. "What? How awful!"

Simon turns his face toward me, and I duck on instinct below the bar.

"Isabella?" she calls, peering down at me.

I put my finger to my lips. "I'm just going to go, okay? Is he walking toward or away from the front door?"

She looks up, her green eyes scanning the crowd, then frowns.

"He's right between here and the door. But maybe if you keep to the edge, he won't see you."

I nod. "Right. Thanks, Becks. Tell the guys they were amazing for me."

Before waiting for an answer, I walk, hunched over underneath the bar until I'm at the very edge, then I bolt for the perimeter of the room. The bar is packed, and even if I wanted to run at this point, that would be impossible because of the crowd. I glance over my shoulder toward where I last saw Simon, but he's gone. Stopping, I push up onto my tip toes trying to see over top of the crowd. Then, just like the sea parted for Moses, the crowd shifts and Simon is only a few people ahead of me.

In my panic, I stumble toward the wall with a loud thump, then notice a sliver of light next to me. A closet? I weigh my options. Hide in what I assume to be the coat check closet, or potentially face Simon as I try to leave.

Closet it is.

I slide along the black painted paneling and grasp the door handle, throw it open, and hurl myself inside. Turning toward the door, I close it behind me and step backward, expecting to feel coats behind me. But I meet a wall instead—a contoured wall that smells like Ivory soap.

"Izzy?"

CHAPTER 13

Pour Some Sugar on Me

DAVE

A small yelp escapes her red lips as Isabella spins around, her dark eyes growing comically large as she takes me in.

"Dave?" she asks, bewildered. She scans the space. "Oh, I'm so sorry. I thought this was a closet."

I tilt my head as I take her in now that she's so close. I feel like the biggest creep ever, watching her throughout the night without her knowledge from the moment she walked through the door in her little red dress. I'm ashamed to say I leered at her as she leaned over the bar to give her drink order, the backs of her thighs straining in a way that had me nearly pitching a tent in my jeans.

Eyes finding her face again, I gesture with my head toward the stairs disappearing down into the dark unknown. "No, it's the way to the stage from down below. Wait, why were you looking for a closet?"

Even in the dim light, her cheeks flush. "I—Well, I . . ."

My chest swells at the adorable way she gets so easily flustered. I wonder if she gets flustered with everyone or just me.

"I was just getting a bit overwhelmed by the crowd," she

finally spits out. "I'm not used to the noise and . . . well, everything else."

She looks away, and a loose strand of hair sweeps over her collarbone. My hand flexes as I use all of my strength not to reach out and brush it back.

"Yeah, I can understand that."

"Wait," she says, eyeing me up and down, "why are *you* in here?"

"Considering this is technically backstage, I'm allowed to be here," I say with a smirk.

She rolls her eyes. "I mean, why aren't you out there." She juts her thumb over her shoulder toward the door. "Why aren't you meeting your fans and signing autographs and partying?"

The smile falls from my face and I look down at the floor, stuffing my hands into my pockets to keep myself from touching her. "I'm just—I don't know, I'm a bit overwhelmed too, you know?"

Her expression softens from something accusatory to sympathetic.

"What Key said . . . the four of us were never popular kids. So I know it looks like we're eating up all this attention, but the truth is, it's—it's . . ."

"A lot?" she finishes.

I release a breathy laugh. "Yeah."

She smiles. "I get it. And for the record? Totally normal."

Sighing, I turn and sit down on the top step. "I just need a few more minutes, I think." I lean against the cool plaster wall and hear the sound of Izzy's heels clicking against the groaning floorboards. For a moment, I think she's going to leave, that she'll assume I want space and head back out, so I'm surprised when she sits down, her hip touching mine on the narrow staircase.

She wraps her slender arms around her knees and for a few minutes, we just sit together in the muffled quiet.

"Thank you for the album, by the way," she says.

"You're welcome."

"And the note."

I turn to look at her. "You got it?"

She nods. "And you're right. Track five was very *interesting.*"

I resist the urge to let my grin take over. "You thought so?"

"Oh yeah. Metal with a disco influence? That song's going to be a hit."

She smiles and it seems to lighten the whole room, as if her face is a bright sun finally appearing after days of dark storm clouds.

"I think I get it now," she says. "What you meant by being angry."

I blink. "Really?"

She nods. "When you're on stage, you're aggressive, passionate . . . loud. You're able to just let all of that energy out. You don't have to contain it, or pretend." Playing with the hem of her dress, she looks down. "It must feel cathartic."

"Well, it's a lot less problematic than getting into fights all the time."

Turning her head toward me, she rests her cheek in one hand. "Was that something you struggled with?"

I shrug. "They happened, but not as much as you might think. I wasn't like Joel, getting into fights at any and every opportunity. My dad would say I was too soft for that."

"Is your dad proud of what you've accomplished?"

Scoffing, I shake my head. "My old man was never proud of anything I did, ever. Probably because I never did anything *he* wanted me to."

"So he had different plans for your life, then?" she asks, smiling sadly.

"Everyone did."

She holds my gaze for a long moment, then looks away. "But you did it. You made it. That must feel great."

"It's fucking incredible. It feels like a dream."

"Just promise you won't let your ego grow out of control." She smirks.

I place my hand to my chest in mock outrage. "Me? Never."

"You say that, but after a few more months of people constantly asking you for your autograph? That head is bound to inflate."

Pushing back my hair, the back of my neck tingles, the list I made as a teenager practically burning a hole in my pocket. "No one's asked for my autograph yet, so I think I'm safe for now."

Her smile falls and her joking tone desists. "What do you mean? No one—"

"Nope. No one."

"What about that blonde girl? The one . . . ." She swallows, and her eyes dart between mine. "Surely she asked—"

I rub the back of my neck. "She wasn't exactly looking for a souvenir."

"Oh."

She turns away, and I inwardly curse at myself. I'm such an idiot. What kind of moron admits to that kind of thing? Telling this girl that the previous one she met was just there for a hookup. *Idiot.*

Isabella pulls her bag into her lap and digs around in the bottom before extracting what looks like a marker. "Here."

I blink at her. "Here, what?"

She holds out the marker to me. "I'd like your autograph, please."

The knots in my chest seem to liquify. A gooey, fluttering feeling filling up my insides like warm honey. "Really?"

She nods and smiles sweetly.

"I . . . okay, well—" I stammer. "What do you want me to sign?"

Her eyes widen. "Oh, shit. I left the copy of the album you guys gave me at home. Ummm . . . hold on." She digs through her purse for a moment, and I can't help but smile at the frantic little way she wants to do this for me. "Shit, where's my notebook?" she mutters, throwing her bag down on the stair below us.

"It's okay. Don't worry about it."

"No," she says forcefully. "This is happening." There's a fire burning in her dark eyes when she looks at me, and it's as if the noise outside of the room fades away. She twists her upper body. "Here."

"Huh?"

She reaches around and taps her bare shoulder with her finger. "Autograph me here."

My jaw nearly hits the floor. "Wh—what?"

"Come on, Noblar."

Pulling the wispy hairs away from the nape of her neck, she looks back at me. Her skin is gorgeous, smooth and tanned, and it feels like a crime to mark her up. The only saving grace is that she wants *me* to mark her up. To brand her with my name and, fuck, if that doesn't make me want to also sink my teeth into her, I don't know what will.

"Okay."

I pull the cap off the marker with a pop. Reaching up with my left hand, I brace myself along the skin of her shoulder blade, the feel of her under my fingertips sending a jolt right through me. Lifting my other hand, I pause as I let my thumb brush ever so gently across the landscape of bare skin.

I hear and feel her sharp intake of breath, and my cock strains in my jeans. What would it be like to have every square inch of her under my hands? I swallow hard, then swipe the marker across her skin, leaving a glistening black trail in its wake. A few more careful strokes as I unabashedly take too long writing out my autograph.

"There," I choke out, looking away only for a moment to recap the marker and hand it back to her.

"How—How does it look?" she asks, her voice deeper than normal.

"It's still a bit wet, here—"

I lean forward and blow, watching with fascination as goosebumps scatter all over—up and down. Her eyes fall closed and her lips part, fuck, she's the sexiest thing I've ever seen. My thumb grazes over her skin again and again, back and forth like I'm stuck in a trance.

"Dave."

Barely above a whisper, the sound of my name forces my gaze up to where she watches me. Her brown eyes sparkle in the dim light but also ignite something deep and yearning in my belly. The world seems to disappear, and there's no more anger or guilt. There's just her and this staircase when I lean forward, dropping my eyes to her lips.

Cacophonous noise pours in as the door snaps open behind us. Like a bubble bursting, I pull back, hands retracting as I realize what I'm doing.

"Dave, there you are. Come on, Al's waiting for us," Key says, then retreats again, pulling the door closed. The quiet this time is different, uncomfortable, and the two of us shift on the stairs. *This shouldn't be happening.*

"I better go," I murmur, unable to meet her gaze. I know what I'll find there if I look, and I can't stand to see her hurt.

"Right," she whispers, my chest squeezing at the choked way it sounds.

We both stand, and in the confined space, we bump together, me trying to angle my hips outward so she doesn't feel exactly how much my body longs for more of hers. But I can't. I just can't. Not with the promise to James and the guilt of my past weighing heavy on my shoulders. Not tonight, when everything is finally becoming real.

"Thanks," I murmur, gesturing wildly in the area of her shoulder as I look everywhere but her.

A deep breath, then: "No problem. I'm honored to be your first."

I can't avoid it anymore. Looking up, my gaze latches on to pools of warm chocolate. The fire in them is gone, and I hate myself for it.

"Listen—"

The door opens again, and Key reappears. "Noblar, what the fuck?"

I bite my lip then jut my chin forward, indicating for her to lead the way out the open door.

"Come on, Al needs us over by the stage."

"I'll be right there," I say.

When Key gives me a look of annoyance, I hold up my hands. "Promise, I'll be right over. I want to grab a beer."

Key turns away to walk toward the drop, and I turn back to Isabella. Only she's not there. She's gone. Looking around, I search for her brunette hair and that red dress, finally spotting her heading for the door.

"Izzy!" I call. I can't let her leave like this. Maybe I could explain or at least try and make it right.

Almost to the door, I catch her by the arm to stop her and she spins to look up into my face, but now that I'm here and she's looking at me, I realize I have nothing to say. How can I possibly tell her everything? How can I explain the promise to James? Or the fact that I'm terrified falling for her will ruin everything, just like it did before? I stand staring at her, my jaw flapping like a fish gasping for air.

"What?" she asks, a note of annoyance creeping into her voice.

I swallow, and my mouth is as dry as the desert. Really wish I had that beer right about now. "I just—I'm . . . I—"

"Bella! There's my little tamale."

From out of nowhere this blond-haired dweeb with a terrible mustache slides right up to Isabella, throwing his arm around her shoulder. Who the fuck is this? And what the fuck is he wearing? The guy looks like he wandered in from shooting an ad for JC Penney. Does Isabella know this douchebag?

"Oh, hey man," the guy says, and holds out his free hand to me. "Simon Cranmer."

My eyes flick between his outstretched hand, the way Isabella is frozen, and up at the smug smile on his face. "Hey, man, you lost?" I ask, pointing to his attire and disregarding his open hand.

Discreetly, he tucks it away and opens his chest up a little further. "No, man. Just never been to a metal concert before. You guys were great though. I mean, I assume. Metal's not really my thing."

Isabella tries to shift away from Simon, but I see the way his fingers tighten on her arm.

"Then I'm not sure why you're here," I say, trying to bite back the venom in my voice.

He laughs. A stupid, high-pitched laugh. "Just came for an inside scoop. Bella and I both work for the *Stoneman Press.*"

So he knows her from school. They're classmates, colleagues. Okay, maybe punching this guy in the face isn't such a good idea. But why does she look so uncomfortable?

"No one asked you to be here, Simon," Isabella says, her cheeks turning a splotchy kind of red. Not the pretty way they color when she blushes. No, there's something up here.

Mercifully, he lifts his arm off of her and holds both hands up.

"Calm down. Randall just wanted to make sure the release was properly covered in case you got . . . distracted."

His index finger trails down her exposed shoulder—the one I autographed, and she jerks away with a horrified look.

"Simon—" she gasps.

But before I can hear what she says, I step between them. "Don't fucking touch her."

He merely chuckles, the smug grin on his face widening. "No harm meant," he says backing up. "Was just here to fact check some things anyway. You're Dave Noblar, correct?"

I don't say anything, my jaw is clenched too hard.

"Yeah, I thought so. Anyway, other than hot tamale here and a blonde with legs for days, there's no decent women around, so what's the point in staying, am I right?"

"For someone in journalism, you should know it's pronounced tamal. No need for the *e*."

Izzy's head whips toward me but I don't take my eyes off him. He laughs again, and it makes me physically sick to my stomach to think that this guy shares a work space with Isabella. Does he harass her at her job like this, too? Did he follow her here?

"Right, well, I'm out of here," he says.

"I think you leaving is the best news I've heard all night," I say dryly.

His smile falters, just for an instant, before it blazes brightly again. "Good luck with the album," he states finally before turning and disappearing into the crowd.

My blood is pulsing, and the muscles in my tired arms twitch. I highly doubt Al would appreciate it if I assaulted a member of the press on the night of our release. But that guy is a creep and it physically pains me that he felt he could touch Isabella when she clearly didn't want him to. Speaking of . . .

I turn around, but she's gone. Again. I swear this woman is like a ghost, disappearing into the crowd like vapor. This time I can't find her though, and when I feel Key's hand clamp with deadly force around my bicep, I allow him to carry me away from the exit and back toward my duties.

SUNLIGHT STRETCHES across my face and I groan. My head is throbbing as I step into the shower. But not from a hangover. I wasn't drunk last night. In fact, most of last night is a blur with random moments in focus. I remember lots of people and playing an amazing set. Handing out copy after copy of our album to a wild crowd. I remember signing my autograph over and over and over again until my hand ached. Then I remember a dark closet— wait, no a staircase—and writing my name on beautiful tanned skin.

Isabella.

I almost kissed her last night. That would've been a huge mistake.

But she looked so fucking delicious. Like a red velvet cupcake in that red dress with her dark hair and her bare unblemished skin. Or at least unblemished until she let me write on it. My cock hardens immediately as I imagine what it would've been like to kiss that shoulder. To pull that slinky dress down and away, exposing her breasts. The thought of tweaking her nipples while her lips punish mine has me grasping and stroking myself under the stream of water. I would've reached down under that dress to find her panties soaking wet. A moan bursts past my lips and my head tips back as I think about fucking her right on those stairs in the dark with just a wall separating us from hundreds of people. How she could have screamed my name as loud as she wanted because the music was blaring.

My stomach contracts and I come hard with panting gasps,

immediately cursing at myself for getting so worked up about her when I know that scenario can never happen. I turn off the water and towel off, grabbing a clean pair of boxers, jeans, and T-shirt from the laundry basket by the door, which I haven't bothered to fold or put away.

Sitting down on the edge of the bed, I grab my jeans from last night. First, I pull out my wallet and remove the worn and wrinkled paper. The one that Emily sneered at so many years ago. I wonder what she would say if she could see me now. Would she be sorry? No, I don't think she would be. She would've found a way to make it all about her. I sigh and fall back onto the bed.

How can I think such a thing? I'm a horrible person. Maybe because I'm still wounded— haunted by what happened. I wonder what Izzy would think of my stupid little list. Would she behave the same way as Emily?

Be asked for an autograph.

Izzy asked me. The very first person, without even knowing I desperately craved it. I didn't think it would hit me so hard, but as I painted my name across her skin, something fundamental changed in the way my heart beats. Like it was changing its rhythm. Even though I was asked for my autograph dozens more times last night, something about Isabella being the first makes me smile, and a curious, deeper something in my bruised heart begins to heal.

CHAPTER 14

Photograph

ISABELLA

Simon Cranmer. That *leech*. Just what the hell had he been doing at the bar at all? And what had he meant by fact checking? None of my articles have been reported for inaccuracies. Maybe there's a more sinister reason—with Simon there always is. If he's trying to discredit my journalistic integrity or my abilities as a writer, then he might have all the ammunition he needs from just looking at my shoulder, where Dave's name is still prominently displayed across my skin.

Goosebumps scatter up my spine at the memory of sitting with Dave on that dark staircase. The way his eyes lit up when I asked for his autograph, and the subsequent way they darkened when I offered myself up as his canvas. I can still feel the brush of his thumb on my skin like a ghost, haunting me even as I strip out of my dress and heels. He was going to kiss me. I know it. I could feel it.

So why didn't he? Aside from being interrupted, I mean.

Then he just stared at me like I was an alien from another planet. Like he forgot who he was when the intimacy of that moment broke. Walking into my bedroom, I stare at myself in the floor-length mirror in the corner. I step closer to it and try to imagine what he sees when he looks at me. I turn, looking over my shoulder at my reflection, standing in nothing but my thong. At this moment, I don't know how he couldn't find me at least a little attractive.

I feel incredibly sexy. I've never hated my body. Aside from a few minor insecurities about the strange dimple in my cheek and the dips in my hips, I've always been pretty confident. But maybe there's something I don't see. Grabbing my camera from my purse, I walk back to the mirror. Angling myself so Dave's autograph is on full display, I cover my chest and snap a picture. It's a silly thing to do and I wouldn't dare ever show him . . . or anyone, but I feel compelled to capture this moment. Who knows, maybe it'll help me understand what he doesn't like about me. Maybe he just only likes blondes.

As I slip into something more comfortable and settle in at my desk to write my article, I wonder who Dave took home tonight. And who he decided was worthy of a kiss over me.

STANDING OUTSIDE of the newspaper office, I shift my weight back and forth on my feet. I'm exhausted after last night. I had to write my entire article from memory after misplacing my notebook, and I wonder if it's covered in beer under a table at the Drop. There are bags under my eyes and my hair is flat in a way no amount of AquaNet could fix. I really don't want to face Simon. But I have an article to submit and film to develop. I'll admit that taking that photo of myself last night was stupid. Especially when I took it on a roll of film with pictures I need to submit with my article. Well, maybe I'll get lucky and the darkroom will be deserted. I would probably throw myself off a balcony if anyone ever saw it—oh god, if Simon ever saw it. Is it illegal to pour bleach in someone's eyes?

You've done nothing wrong. You're a journalist and Simon is a gremlin. You don't need to be intimidated by him.

I manage to push myself through the newspaper office doors. I have a deadline after all, and even though the piece I wrote for this week isn't as edited as I wish it was, I can't miss out. Not when this opportunity to be taken seriously may not last forever.

After dropping my article in the basket on Randall's door, I head for my desk. Maybe I can use the time between classes to catch up on the last few assignments I need to turn in before finals begin. Amazingly enough, it's quiet here. So quiet, I take the opportunity to slip away and quickly develop my film before anyone can find it. A few people are typing away at other desks, and miraculously it appears as though Simon has retracted into whatever hole he lives in. Even the phone has stopped ringing off the hook.

If life has taught me anything though, it's that it's always calmest right before the storm. So, as I wait for the inevitable chaos, my heel bounces against the floor, keeping time with my racing heart.

I'M WAITING for my pictures to dry when I hear some chatter near the front of the office. A few of the guys are standing around Simon, who looks like a cat that just swallowed a canary. Something twists in my stomach as his eyes catch mine and he offers me a saccharine grin. Oh god, I'm definitely the canary.

"Rodriguez."

I nearly drop my pen as I jump at Randall's voice. There's an expression I've never seen before on his face. Normally he looks like his veins are about to explode at the temple or he's so red he's turning purple. But, right now? He looks . . . tired.

He waves me over then retreats into his office, leaving the door open. My heart sinks. If Randall looks like that, it can't mean good news for me. And the fact that Simon looks like he just won the lottery doesn't bode well either. I make my way across the room, the group of men quieting as I approach, but all with the look that they were just talking about me. I try to keep my head up high, but every step I take feels like I'm about to crumple into a heap on the floor. No, I can't do that. Not in front of these assholes.

I enter the office and close the door. Randall is sitting at his desk with his head on one hand.

"Sir, you wanted to see me?"

He looks up and gestures to the seat across from him. "Yes. Have a seat, please."

I sit down, but nothing about me relaxes. For a long tense moment, he says nothing, just rotates back and forth on his chair. "Randall?"

Finally, he looks up at me and leans forward. "Listen, I'm really sorry to have to tell you this, but we're not going to be running the article you submitted."

"What? Why not?"

He sighs and picks something up off of his desk. "Because of this."

I gingerly take the newspaper from his hands and find myself peering down at the front page of the entertainment section of the *East Bay Chronicle*. My eyes focus on the handsome face blurred behind a drum kit, surrounded by his bandmates and friends.

"Seems like we won't be the exclusive source of Carnal Sins news anymore," Randall says with a resigned sigh.

I let out a breath. To be honest, I was sure it would be worse news than this. I knew I wouldn't be the exclusive journalist for

Carnal Sins forever. In fact, this is great news. The band will get more widespread coverage and now that I've shown I can be taken seriously as a writer, maybe Randall will be more inclined to let me write stories that mean something. Not to mention I can distance myself from a guy who isn't interested in me like I am him.

"Well, it's not the end of the world," I say breezily, trying to make Randall see that this isn't the worst news I've ever gotten. "We both knew it wouldn't last forever."

Randall looks up at me and stares for a long moment. "Did you not see the name on the article?"

I narrow my eyes and look down under the title of the article *Thrash Metal's Newest Stars* to the author's name.

"Simon Cranmer . . . Simon—" I look up and Randall nods his head.

This is what the storm feels like. My hands begin to shake and the blood rushes into my face so fast it's as though my skin is on fire. It suddenly makes sense why he was at the release party. He was swooping in from under me to steal my story. But . . .

"How—" I splutter, gripping the edge of the paper so hard it begins to tear. "How did he manage to—"

"Apparently Simon has been trying to get accepted for an internship position with the *Chronicle* for weeks. He is in his final year of the program after all, same as you. This article he submitted solidified their decision to bring him on."

I scoff loudly. "He could've literally written about anything!" I say, my voice rising. "Why was this the winner?"

Randall's eyes flick down at the article, and taking his cue, I read. But as I do, nausea begins to surface, hot tears boiling up behind my eyelashes as the paper shakes in my hands with poorly restrained rage. The next moment I'm up, throwing open the door and marching across the room to Simon and his gang of wannabes.

"You!" I say, throwing the paper at Simon's chest. "You stole my work, you pathetic, slimy snake!"

The other posers disperse but Simon grapples with the paper and holds up his hands. "Whoa there, little Bella, what's the problem?"

"This," I say, pointing my finger so hard at the paper in his hands it punches right through. "This is my work! You took all of the articles I wrote and mashed them together. The details in here are things the band told only to me! This is plagiarism!"

Simon's smirk vanishes. "It's your word against mine."

My mouth drops open. "How could you do this?" I ask, my voice growing hoarse.

He shrugs. "It was easy, really. Or rather, you made it easy." He takes a step closer to me then removes a notebook from his pocket. *My* notebook. The one I lost at the bar last night. The one with a dozen pages filled with notes from the release party.

"You *stole* my notes?" I shout.

"More like . . . recovered. You really should be more careful about leaving your stuff around."

"You—You can't! I won't let you do this!"

"It's done," he says. "No one in here really believed you wrote those articles anyway. I dare you to try and prove it to anyone other than Randall." His eyes are like ice—completely devoid of emotion. He returns the notebook to his pocket and leans toward me, speaking loud enough for everyone watching to hear. "But first tell me, because I'm dying to know, was the band only interested in you hanging around so you could write about them, or"—he reaches out and swipes his finger down my shoulder, Dave's autograph zinging under my shirt—"did they have other uses for you too?"

I stumble back, desperate to escape his touch, fully aware that all eyes are on me.

He sighs. "Whatever the reason, I wouldn't worry. I'm sure

everything will work out for you. Even a rockstar wouldn't give up that bangin' body of yours too fast."

I want to scream. I want to slap him across his smug face. I want to beat my fists so hard into his chest it caves in. But I can't. All I can do is stand here and cry like a little girl whose favorite toy was just taken away by a bully. With a guttural sound squeaking past my lips, I whip toward the dark room. Furiously, I rip the hanging photos off the line then storm toward my desk. When I reach it, I start shoving whatever I can find inside of my bag. Notebooks, pens, my stuffed googly eyed pepper.

A concerned Henry peers over the wall of my cubicle. "Isabella, what's wrong?"

"I'm leaving."

"For the day? Or—you weren't fired, were you?" he asks, glancing over toward where Simon is still chatting with some of the other guys.

"No, I— I just can't stay here any more," I say, my voice breaking again. "I won't continue to work for people who will sit back and let my work be stolen."

Henry blinks. "Who stole your work?" His eyes flick over to Simon. "Wait, did Simon—"

With the last of my few personal things stuffed haphazardly into my bag, I head for the door. "It doesn't matter. Nothing matters."

"Wait! Isabella!" Henry says, jogging around to step in front of me. "What the hell happened?"

I'm seething. All I see is red. Red and a deep, dark despair. "Move, Henry."

"You're just leaving? What about your classes?"

I press my lips together and wipe my eyes. "Next week is finals. I'll finish the term then decide what to do."

"But the paper—"

"I'm only required to be on the school paper for two terms. At this point I've been on it for three. The prerequisites have been filled, I just stayed because . . ."

Because I thought it would help me be a better writer. Because I thought the experience could actually help me get an internship. Because I love it.

"I don't need to stay anymore. Hopefully Randall will write me a good letter of recommendation."

I try to walk around, but Henry stops me in my path again. "Wait, just . . ."

"Just what, Henry? Sit back while someone else decides to steal my work to help their own career? Wait for Randall to ask me to start getting everyone's lunches and coffee again? No one respects me here, and I'm not going to wait around for the next time someone decides to fuck me over."

He opens his mouth, but I don't care what he has to say. Nothing will make this right, and while I know—I know deep down running away isn't the right choice, I also know I can't stay here. So I turn, the weight of the overstuffed bag on my shoulder cutting into my skin, and head for the exit.

The fall air chills the tears on my face as I head back toward my apartment. It's not until I pass the dining hall for the second time, though, that I realize I've been wandering around campus for the last hour and a half. This is where I'll always end up, isn't it? Alone and lost.

Maybe one day I'll finally disappear. Maybe one day someone will notice.

It's quite possible I've turned into a vampire.

I hiss at the sight of sunlight when it peeks its way into my room. I've avoided my shower like it's holy water. And rather than blood, I've lived off a diet of cold pizza and cereal.

Not really a vampire then, I guess—just your everyday depressed girl.

I thought I felt better today, until I decided to unpack my bag from the office and found a copy of the *East Bay Chronicle* article that Simon had kindly decided to leave on my desk with a note that read, "Thanks for the tips, hot tamale."

At least cereal isn't too unpleasant on its way back up.

As my body shrinks away from the morning light creeping across the bed, I push myself up to sitting. I need to get out of here. I can't hide away forever, and besides, I'm starting to really smell.

After a long, hot shower, I start to feel a bit better. Taking the time to pick out a nice outfit and do my hair and makeup makes me at least *look* like I have my shit together. The *Chronicle* article has been out for two days now, so there's officially nothing I can do anymore, not that there was before either. But now everyone will read it.

The band will be thrilled. They tolerated me, sure, but I'm still just a journalism student for a college paper. This, even if it was stolen, is a real news source. It's not the *New York Times* or *Rolling Stone* magazine but it'll still be read by thousands of people. With their EP album out now, the more exposure the better. I just—part of me really wishes it had been me. That I had been the one to finally break them out, that I would be known as the girl who helped a band get discovered. And the kicker? I haven't even gotten an internship out of all of this.

If they get really famous now, I'll be annoyed. And I know that makes me a terrible person.

I wonder if they've seen it yet. Would they even know to check the *Chronicle*? Should I call and tell them? Oh god, I don't even know what to say. And what if Dave answers the phone?

Picking up the article, I tear it out and stuff it into my notebook for History of Fashion while I finish getting dressed. I'll give it to Becks. I may feel dead inside about it, but I can fake being happy for a few hours, right? If I can fake an orgasm without anyone being the wiser, then I can fake this too.

CHAPTER 15

Just What I Needed

DAVE

Part of me is still in shock as I stare at the article, my eyes glazing over as I read it again for what must be the fiftieth time. This is incredible.

"I'm running out to the store, you want anything?" Joel asks before grabbing my keys and heading for the door.

I look up, then glance at the fridge. "Uh, yeah, hold on, there's a list." Once I pass him the short list of groceries, he grins at me.

"Careful, you look at that too long and it'll burst into flames," Joel teases from the other side of the counter, nodding to the paper still clutched between my fingers.

Flipping him off, I head back toward my bedroom to tuck it into the shoebox with the others from the *Stoneman Press* that Izzy wrote. On the way, James rushes out of his room and our shoulders collide.

"Hey, hey, whoa, you okay, man?" I ask, steadying him as he nearly topples over.

He rights himself before pulling on his denim jacket. "Yeah, sorry. I uh . . . I'm going out for a bit."

I cock a brow. "For food? Joel already left."

James laughs a little nervously, his weight bouncing between his two feet. "No . . . no, actually. For something else."

Something's up. Why is he so jumpy? "Dude, what the fuck is up with you?"

He settles and sighs, leaning back against the wall behind him. "I'm going to ask Becks to marry me."

My eyes nearly bug out of their sockets. "You what?"

"Don't try to talk me out of it. It won't work."

He sets his dark eyes on me with a determined stare, and after a moment, I smile. "I wouldn't dream of it, congrats, man."

His face melts into the most repulsively happy grin. "Well, she still has to say yes."

"Pigs will fly before that girl says no."

"Do you want to come with me?" he asks.

I narrow my eyes. "You trying to brainwash me into monogamy?"

He shrugs. "Can't help but notice you've come home alone the past few weeks, and not for a lack of girls falling all over you. What was it that girl with the black hair said last night?" He pouts and bats his eyelashes, placing his hands under his chin in a show of dramatics. "Oh! Mr. Noblar, how do you drum so fast? Do you want to practice on my ass?"

I laugh and shove his shoulder. "Fuck off. That is not what she said."

"One hundred percent that's what she said."

Sighing, I hook my thumbs in my belt loops. "So what? You're concerned about my ability to get laid and your solution is to show me how perfect your life is with just one woman?"

"Just wondering if maybe there was something going on."

At my blank expression, he continues.

"I mean, if you met someone that's cool. You don't need to hide it."

"I haven't," I state, now serious. "Just been tired."

"Never stopped you before."

I frown. "Okay, what are you, the pussy police? First you forbid me from going after Isabella, and now I'm not bringing home enough girls?"

He shakes his head and turns to walk away. "Fine. Forget I said anything."

After he disappears down the hall, I head back to my room. Sitting on the edge of my bed I fall backward to stare up at the ceiling. Okay, fine. So for the past few weeks I haven't taken advantage of the girls who've thrown themselves at me. Not because I wasn't attracted to them but because . . . because . . .

"Fuck," I whisper, the truth hitting me square in the face after dodging it for nearly a week.

Because they're not Isabella.

What the hell is wrong with me? Before she came into my life, I wouldn't have batted an eye if a woman asked me to use her ass like a bongo drum, but now? All I can think of are the things I would do to her if I had her underneath me, on top of me, pinned up against my shower wall. And the worst part of it all? I think I could if I wanted to. I could so easily call her at the newspaper office, invite her over, and let things happen the way they've been raring to for weeks.

But I won't. I can't let feelings for a girl I hardly know get in the way of everything I've worked so hard to achieve.

"I can't believe he proposed!"

I freeze, last night's water glass hanging suspended in the air, and my heart thuds as I recognize a familiar voice. A voice I may have, only a few minutes ago, dreamt moaning my name in my sleep.

Isabella is here. In my house.

"Can you believe it?" Becks says, her voice almost an octave higher than usual. "Just look at the ring."

"It's— Wow. It's just gorgeous, Becks," Isabella says. "But . . . you're only eighteen. Isn't that a bit young to get married?"

There's a pause. "I don't think so. James and I—We've been through a lot together, and I know there'll never be anyone else I could love as much as I love him. So we just figured, why wait?"

I can't help the smile that tugs on the corners of my lips. Maybe monogamy *is* contagious, because listening to the way Becks talks about James is inspiring. It's something I wished for, once upon a time in my life.

"So you'll what? Get married in a year? In the summer? What's the plan?" asks Isabella.

"Actually," Becks says, her tone mischievous. "We're going to drive to Vegas as soon as possible." The words burst out of her in a giddy rush.

"What?"

At Isabella's shrill exclamation I jump, the glass tumbling from my fingers and shattering to pieces on the floor. "Fuck," I whisper, and I only now remember that I'm barefoot and in nothing but a pair of boxers.

Isabella and Becks run into the hallway and stop at the sight of the glass on the floor, their eyes trailing from my feet to my face.

"Dave?" Becks asks.

I stare open-mouthed at them, totally incapable of forming words.

"Hold on," Becks says hurriedly. "I'll go grab the broom. Don't move. I don't want you to cut your feet."

Fuck. Now I'm alone with Isabella wearing hardly anything. Now would be an incredibly unfortunate time to get a boner.

"Hey," she says, crossing her arms over her chest.

"Hi," I respond awkwardly. I realize this is the first time we've spoken since the release party. Since that jerk of a colleague made her feel uncomfortable. Since I autographed my name on her shoulder. I wonder if it's still there . . .

"Are you okay?" she asks, gesturing to the ground, where the shattered glass keeps me locked like a prisoner under her gaze.

Sighing, I scratch the back of my neck. "Yeah, just . . . you know, wish I'd put on pants before deciding to go to the kitchen."

She chuckles, then her eyes dip down, traveling over my chest, my abs, my hips, and I have to force images of dead animals to the forefront of my mind as her gaze lingers just a little too long on the spot I'm desperately trying to keep the blood from rushing to. Even still, I can't quell the goosebumps that prickle up all over me at the sight of her drinking me in.

After what feels like the longest moment of my life, she looks up and smirks. "Were you eavesdropping on us?"

I scoff, knowing immediately that the jig is up by the obnoxious sound I just made. "No! I mean . . . not intentionally."

She smiles a little wider.

"I didn't realize you were here. Why are you here? I mean . . . How—how are you?"

Her face darkens for a moment before she shakes her head, her smile brighter than ever. "I'm great. Becks invited me over to make scarves for that AIDS charity she volunteers with. Plus she wanted my help proofreading a pamphlet for this new safe sex campaign."

"Oh." Why did she have to say *sex*?

"I saw the article in the *Chronicle*," she says, but I can't help noticing the way her eyes shine and how her voice breaks on the last word. "It was glowing. I'm sure it'll do wonders for you, publicity-wise."

My mouth twists. She's happy, but there's an edge to her voice that catches me off guard. From what I know about Isabella, which admittedly is far less than I'd like to, she would never be unhappy at anyone else's success. Especially when she helped to create it in the first place. She worked tirelessly to promote us the best way she could. Something she never had to do.

"It *was* great," I say, softly. "But I prefer yours."

Her cheek twitches and her face softens, the phony smile changing to something more sincere, sweet. More like her.

"How's it going anyway?" I continue. "At school, I mean. I didn't see anything written by you in the paper on Monday."

"You were looking?"

I move to step forward, then remember I'm surrounded by glass. I'm stuck. Where the hell did Becks go to get a broom? Outer space? "Yeah, I always do. Becks brings them home. You're a great writer."

Her face turns the most brilliant shade of red, and her arms drop to wrap around her waist. Her posture becomes more protective, like she's shielding herself. "Thanks. I uh . . . I had an article written for this week but my editor got wind of the piece in the *Chronicle* and—well, he decided not to run it."

My heart sinks. "Oh. That sucks."

She shrugs.

"Does that mean you won't be writing about us anymore?"

The thought of Isabella never coming to a gig again, or never showing up at a recording session, of never reading her words on a page about us and feeling like she knows me—understands me . . . My heart aches at the thought.

Her eyes drop to the floor, where she's shifting her weight between her feet. The sight makes me want to reach out and touch her. To be fair, most things make me want to touch her. But when she looks back up, her eyes are shining in the late morning light.

"Actually, I won't be writing anything for the paper anymore."

I blink, confused. "What?"

"I quit."

My eyes widen at her confession. "You—"

"Sorry, that took forever. Apparently, Key had the broom outside his window after trying to chase away a noisy pigeon."

Becks comes back into view and starts sweeping up the shattered glass fragments, the sound of them tinkling against the floor. When I look up, Isabella has turned and is walking back toward where she and Becks were sitting earlier. But even from where I stand, still half naked, I see her wiping her cheeks furiously with the back of her hand.

Almost like the conversation with Isabella never happened, I watch as she smiles and laughs over the Chinese takeout the six of us got for dinner. What is she talking about? She quit the paper? Doesn't she need that for school? And what would make her quit? Writing is something she clearly has a gift for. Did something happen?

Maybe the story with her editor dismissing her wasn't true. She didn't seem genuinely happy about the article, not at all. I take another bite of my Chow Mein and swallow, watching the way she happily chats to James and Becks about their upcoming nuptials.

A reel of film races through my mind. Images of words and pieces of information flipping through like stop-motion as they try to form a coherent thought. Something is off. And that article, it was like . . . like, I don't know, familiar? Like I've read it before. Am I crazy?

The phone rings in the background, and James jumps up from the table to go and answer it. I bite into a spring roll as I watch Isabella drown the rest of her beer.

"You want another one?" I ask.

Startled, she brings a napkin up to her mouth, wiping away the moisture that escaped. "Oh, I—no, I shouldn't. I need to get home eventually."

I have to bite my tongue. The words to tell her she can stay here begging to burst out of my mouth. That she can sleep in my bed and I'll take the couch. Or . . . we can share. But even I'm not that delusional. I know exactly how that will go and why it can't.

James bounds back into the room with a shit-eating grin on his face as he stands at the head of the table.

"Who wants to drive to Vegas on Monday?"

The room goes quiet for a moment until finally Joel speaks up. "Wait, Monday?"

James rounds the table and sits next to Becks, kissing the top of her head. "I just cleared it with Al. He doesn't have anything booked for us until Thursday, so after the show on Sunday we're all free for a few days."

I find it hard to keep my jaw from falling to the floor. They just got engaged, and now they're planning on running off to Vegas to get married? Officially? Legally?

"What do you guys think?" James asks hopefully. "You all up for a road trip?"

There's a beat of silence but then Key jumps up out of his seat. "Fuck yeah!"

At that, there's a chorus of excited chatter, myself included, as plans for the following Monday are drawn up and discussed. It might seem like a crazy plan to me, but who am I to dictate how they live their lives. Besides, I don't think I've ever seen two people more in love than James and Becks.

"You'll come too, right?" I hear Becks ask Isabella from across the table.

She looks like she's lost for words. "I mean, of course I'd love to, but I don't have a car."

"That's okay," Becks says. "One of the guys can drive you." I see her green eyes flick to me for a moment before she asks the table at large. "Hey, there's room for Isabella in one of the cars, right?"

"Hell yeah," James says. "We can take my van and one of the other cars. There's plenty of room in both."

Noticing the way Isabella's ears flush a shade darker makes my stomach flip. Shit, I could be stuck with her in a car for hours. I bet she'd look gorgeous with the wind blowing through her hair. *Damn.* Well, at least we won't be alone. That'll offer some reminder to stay platonic.

"Dave?" James asks.

I look up to find everyone watching me. "Huh?"

"Is it cool if we take your car?"

Nodding my head, I sit forward on my chair. "Yeah man, that's cool."

"Thanks."

Isabella tucks her hair behind her ears and stands from the table. "I should head home," she says, turning and pushing her chair in. "I still have a few assignments I need to finish before exams."

"Did you take a cab or the bus?" Becks asks.

"Bus."

She makes a face. "Oh, you shouldn't take the bus alone this late. Dave can drive you."

I think my heart actually skips a beat. "What?"

Becks tips her head toward a very embarrassed-looking Isabella, then lowers her voice so only I can hear. "You're the only one who hasn't been drinking. You don't mind, do you? It's not far."

I clear my throat and stand. "Yeah, sure. Of course." Her lips twitch, and I still have no idea what she's thinking. "You ready now?"

She nods and gives Becks a hug, offering her congratulations again and telling her how excited she is for Vegas. Then she casts her eyes down as I grab my keys and head for the door, holding it open for her as we head out into the chilly November night air.

We head for my Buick wagon in the driveway and I fumble with the keys when I stop to unlock the passenger-side door for her. She smiles shyly at me, and my heart flutters. "Thanks," she says.

"No problem." She gets in while I walk around to the driver's side. Sitting quietly, she watches as I turn the car on and adjust the radio. "Cold?" I ask.

"A little."

I turn the heat on low then pull out onto the street.

"My apartment is on the outskirts of the campus. Just off Brandy Street," she says, watching the lights go by.

"Okay."

We drive in silence for a while, and the whole time I'm thinking of something to say. How to bring up the conversation from earlier. How her skin looks so gorgeous in the street lights. How to apologize for the release party.

"I appreciate you not saying anything to Becks," she says suddenly. "About me quitting the paper, I mean."

I take a quick look at her, her shoulders tight up against her ears and her arms hugging her body.

"Will you not tell her?" I ask.

She shakes her head. "Not yet. It's such a happy time for her. I don't want to be the thunder cloud to her sunny day."

"But you told me."

She turns to look out the window again. "Yes."

"Why *did* you tell me?"

She doesn't answer and she doesn't look back. Okay, new tactic, I guess.

"This isn't because of that guy, is it?"

Her head whips around to look at me so fast I'm surprised she doesn't break her neck. "What?"

"That guy—" The guy I wanted to punch until his face was mush. "What was his name? At the release party."

"Simon."

"Yeah." I take a left turn toward the college. "What the hell was he even doing there? What a fucking douchebag."

She utters a dark laugh and fiddles with the tassel on her purse. "You don't know the half of it."

"You could tell me."

Her face seems to crumple, her eyes shining again. "I—" Her chest rises and falls sharply, as if she's working up the courage to say the words out loud. "He kind of stole my work."

My knuckles tighten on the steering wheel. "What?" I say a little too loudly. "What do you mean he kind of stole your work?"

"All of my articles, he— He mashed them together."

Hot anger bubbles up my throat, heating my skin and turning my stomach.

"Remember how I couldn't find my notebook? He found it and took everything I'd written about the release party and got it published in the *Chronicle*."

I slam on the brakes, but luckily it's late out so the roads are empty. Isabella's hands shoot out to brace herself against the dash as I pull over on the shoulder, unbuckle my seat belt, and wrench open the door.

"Dave!"

There's a commotion coming from the inside of the car, but all I can focus on is the pounding of blood in my ears and the roaring in my chest, like a caged animal desperate to be set free. I try to focus on the white lines on the side of the road, pacing back and forth as my hands shake. A car door slams, and I hear the sound of footsteps on asphalt approaching.

"Dave, please."

I stop pacing and look up at her. "I fucking knew it!" I shout. She flinches, and a wave of shame washes over me. Taking a moment to try to calm myself, I hold up my hands. "I knew there was something up with that article. It sounded so familiar, like I'd read it before in a dream. But I have read it before. From *you*."

"It's fine."

"How did I not notice earlier? Who other than you would've picked up on the disco influence of track five?"

"Seriously, Dave, it's—"

"No! Don't say it's fine." I step forward. "That fucking asshole stole your work and pawned it off as his own? I should break his fucking knee caps."

She shakes her head. "It's done. It doesn't matter."

"And you quit?" I ask incredulously. "Because of some jerkwad?"

"Dave—"

"I know what we'll do," I say, walking back to the car. "We'll call the paper in the morning. We'll show them all the original articles. I have them all on top of my dresser—"

"*Dave!*"

I stop and turn, the sight of her so defeated stealing my breath. That sparkle in her eyes is gone.

"Just stop, please."

"What? No! I can fi—"

"Just stop!" she screams. "It's over."

For a long moment we just stare at each other, our chests heaving in the light of a single streetlamp. Isabella's eyes close, and she turns to lean her back against the car, her bracelets jingling as she raises both forearms to cover her face. My hands tremble, and I shake them out. I can already feel the anger giving way to concern. Slowly I walk toward her until we're standing toe-to-toe.

"I'm sorry," I whisper. "I didn't mean to get so carried away."

When she lowers her arms, her face is blotchy but she's still agonizingly beautiful. She lets out a sad sort of laugh. "I wish I had the energy to want to fight like you do."

"You know what's awesome about having friends, Disco Girl?" I ask, leaning down to peer into her eyes.

A crease appears at the bridge of her nose. "What?"

"They can help you fight the battles you can't win on your own."

Pushing herself off the car to stand, her chocolate brown eyes flit over my face. "Is that what we are? Friends?"

We're close. So close the air seems to crackle around us like it does before a thunderstorm. I want to spend every thunderstorm wrapped around her, tangled up in her limbs, my face buried in her slender neck. Her dark hair picks up and blows across her chest, and my fingers tingle with the desire to brush it back, but that would contradict what I say next.

"Yeah, friends. Of course we are."

She searches my face as if trying to find the lie—the crack in my shield. Then, for one painfully long moment, her eyes drop to my mouth.

"I've never been friends with celebrities before," she says, looking away and sniffing. "I suppose this Vegas trip will be high luxury and first-class accommodations the whole way."

I laugh, and I'm glad to see her smiling back. "Afraid we're not quite at that level yet. Motel 6 is our kind of luxury. However, I'll tell Joel to keep the farting to a minimum for the most luxurious driving experience I can muster."

This time she really laughs. I wish I could record the sound so I can play it for her whenever she's down, but for now I try to memorize every lilt and cadence to it so I can replay it in my head.

"So, you really aren't going to do anything about the article?" I ask.

She shakes her head and clears her throat. "No. I mean, there isn't anything to be done anyway. He's a conniving son of a bitch. Besides, the *Chronicle* will realize soon enough that he can't write worth a damn when he starts his internship."

I frown. "Internship?"

She shrugs. "They offered him one, you know—based on the caliber of the article."

"Bastard," I mutter. "He stole that from you too?"

"I applied, but . . . who am I kidding? If publications are anything like how it is at Stoneman, I won't get a single internship. They never took me seriously and treated me like a goddamn secretary . . . I only stayed as long as I did because I love to write. It's been my dream since I was a kid to be a journalist—a writer. I thought if I stuck it out things might change, and it did . . . for a while. But it's not worth it anymore."

"But it's your dream," I say softly.

"It still is. I just have to find another way to get there. That's all."

My eyes close, and I take a calming breath in through my nose and out my mouth. "Izzy—"

As I open my eyes, I catch her flinch.

"I—sorry," I say, "do you not like that name?"

She shakes her head. "No, no . . . it's not that. I love it. I just —I don't hear it often enough anymore."

"Oh."

"Just promise you won't call me Bella, okay?" she says with a smirk.

I grin widely. "Deal."

After dropping Isabella off at her place, I drive for hours, just letting the road take me where it wants.

Is that what we are? Friends?

Fuck how I wanted to say no. To grab her face in my hands and kiss her, press her body up against the car and ravage her. But no, that definitely crosses the friendship boundary, although I suppose between Izzy and I, it's been a bit blurred from the start.

The logical part of my brain knows what I'm doing is right. That what comes along with my dreams will crush her. Run her over like roadkill left behind for vultures like Simon to pick and feed off of. And I don't want that for her. She has dreams too. Dreams that she deserves to have come true.

What does it say about me that I'm not willing to sacrifice my dreams for her? I've worked too hard and too long to get where I am. I can't risk losing it now. What woman wants to come second to a man's ambitions? No, I've seen what that does to someone— what it did to Emily, my mom—and I won't make that mistake again. Besides, Isabella deserves a man who will drop anything and everyone to be there to support her, and I can admit I wouldn't be able to do that. So I'll support her as best as I can. As a friend, from the sidelines.

THE NEXT DAY I'm on my fourth cup of coffee by the time I walk into the dimly lit bar to set up my drum kit. I'm always the first to arrive. My equipment takes the longest to set up, and I'm a bit obsessive with making sure everything is in place because the guys wind their amps and cords across the small stage.

As I stifle a yawn, I spot Al talking to the bartender and wave him over. Sitting at my kit, I stomp on the bass drum pedal, taking note of how it's a bit sticky and could use some grease.

"Noblar, how's it going?" Al asks, leaning his protruding belly against the stage.

I cross my arms. "It's been an interesting few days."

He chuckles and shakes his head. "I'll say. Walton is nuts to be getting married. He's only nineteen."

"You'll never convince him he's not doing the right thing."

"I guess not," he says. "You going with them to Vegas?"

I nod. "Yeah, we're all heading out Monday morning."

"I'll get you guys some motel vouchers as a wedding gift," he says thoughtfully. "I know you're not raking in the big bucks yet, but it's coming. We just have to be patient."

"That's decent of you, Al, we'd all appreciate that."

"Sure thing. You'll have to get used to sleeping in motels when you guys head out on tour."

Going on tour. I grin like an idiot, my cheeks straining. "Holy shit, really? A tour. For real?"

"Guess your days are going to get even more interesting."

"God, I can't—you have no idea what this means to me . . . to us."

He waves me off. "I knew when I saw you guys in Iowa you were something special. It just took us a little longer than I thought to get things going. But you deserve it Dave. All of you do."

I can't believe this is happening, that any of this is. Somehow I still need to remind myself this isn't a dream. That I'm not eighteen years old in Sam's garage anymore. That I made it. Then the image of Isabella's defeated face swims before me. She had dreams too, and that scumbag took them away from her and made her feel like she's not worth fighting for.

Al turns to walk away, but an idea springs to mind so fast I can't keep my mouth closed.

"Hey, Al?" I say, stopping him. "Can I ask you for a favor?"

CHAPTER 16

"Estelle called me the other day," my mother says into the speaker.

My eyes close, a headache throbbing to life at the base of my skull. "Oh?"

"She said that Miguel broke up with Ana. That he's been very unhappy."

I sigh. "*Mamá*, why are you telling me this?"

"I just thought—"

"What? You just thought that now that Miguel is single again and probably regrets ditching me for some backstabbing weasel that I'd race home to take him back?"

"No! No, Isa—of course not. I just thought that if you wanted to, you could give him a call."

"*He* dumped *me*," I say. "He couldn't deal with me chasing after what I wanted. He wanted me to follow him around like a lost puppy. He *never* supported my dreams, *amá*. Why would you ever suggest that relationship could be rekindled?"

"Now, Isa, I only suggested it because you loved each other so much," she says, her tone accusatory. Like I don't remember it myself.

I sigh exasperatedly. "Well, things change."

She groans into the speaker. "Why do you always have to be so stubborn?"

"And why does everyone seem to think they can just do whatever they want and I'll rearrange my life to suit them? Why do I always have to be the flexible one, huh?"

"*Mija* . . ."

"No," I say, my voice rising quickly. "I've had enough of everyone telling me I'm not doing enough for *them*. Who's doing stuff for me? Huh? No one."

There's silence on the other end as I pant into the speaker from my outburst.

"I have to go. I'm going away for a few days, but I'll call you next weekend."

"Wait, where are you—"

But I don't let her finish, instead hanging up the phone on the receiver with a loud crack. A painful prickling races over my skin, but I shake my head, willing the anger and frustration to recede. I've spent too much time being everything but happy lately, and I won't let it consume me. Besides, I need to figure out what the fuck I'm going to do after exams. Without the paper, and with no news from any of the internships I applied to, I need to start actively looking into other ways I can finish my degree. The thought of taking on a full course load of stuffy English classes for one more semester is exhausting. But honestly, what other choice do I have?

I also have no idea what to wear at the wedding.

Shit, what does someone even wear to a Vegas wedding? I don't imagine the guys will dress up. No matter how hard I try, I can't picture them in suits and ties. I wonder if they even own them. I think I have a halter dress that might be suitable. My ass looks great in it, plus my back and shoulders will be exposed. By now, Dave's autograph has faded completely. Sometimes it's like

I can still see it there—the memory of it burned into my retinas. If I show up wearing this dress, will he be looking for evidence of it?

I can't explain my behavior from last week. Telling Dave about everything—I don't know why I did. But there's something about him—something just made me feel . . . safe, I guess. It's not like I expected him to come to my rescue or anything like that. No, it was more that he seemed to genuinely care. He seemed to know, just by looking at me.

Packing my halter dress into my bag with an oversized ABBA T-shirt and a pair of flannel shorts I use as pajamas, some overnight toiletries, and a change of clothes for the next day, I grab my camera and purse. But when I walk toward the door, there's a stack of letters on the floor in front of the mail slot.

I don't usually get mail unless it's a package from my mom, and even though I shut down our conversation pretty quickly earlier, she didn't say to expect anything. Oh god—what if this is about my applications. I put my bag down and stoop to pick up the letters.

Turning over the envelope in my hand, I see the *East Bay Chronicle* emblem front and center. I frown at it, but tear it open nonetheless.

MISS RODRIGUEZ,
AFTER CAREFUL CONSIDERATION, IT IS WITH REGRET THAT WE MUST DECLINE YOUR APPLICATION FOR THE WINTER INTERNSHIP PROGRAM.

My eyes burn. I figured this would come, considering Simon got the internship at *East Bay*, but it still stings. Rejection never feels good on any level. As I look at the stack of other letters, an ominous feeling washes over me. Like a dark cloud rolling in when you're frolicking in the sun. Surely there must be at least one here that says yes, right? But as I tear open the letters, that dark, sinking feeling presses in on me until I can hardly breathe.

WE'RE SORRY, BUT WE ARE LOOKING FOR SOMEONE WITH MORE EXPERIENCE WITH SERIOUS GLOBAL ISSUES AT THIS TIME.

UNFORTUNATELY, WE ARE UNABLE TO OFFER YOU A PLACE ON OUR TEAM.

YOUR WRITING HAS FLAIR AND WE WELCOME YOU TO REAPPLY WHEN YOU'VE HAD AN OPPORTUNITY TO EXPAND YOUR PORTFOLIO.

Rejected.
Rejected.
Rejected.
Pain tears through me like a white-hot knife, stabbing and slicing through the layers of my very soul as I drop to my knees. The tears I've been fighting fall in rivulets down my face, sobs wracking my body like it's forgotten how to perform its basic functions.

Every application is a rejection. A sea of nos, and it's like I'm drowning.

After a while, my breathing starts to even out and I wipe at my face, numb. The overarching emotion that lingers is anger, and when I stand, I tear at the letters. Tear and tear and tear. Then I walk to the bathroom and let the pieces flutter into the toilet before flushing them away down the drain.

The sudden laughter of someone walking past my door makes me jump. *Shit.* For a moment I forgot the real world exists. Funny how that happens. When everything around you is falling apart— but for everyone else? The world just keeps on spinning.

I quickly gather my makeup from the counter and pile it into my travel bag. I'll have to do it in the car on the way to Vegas. I promised Becks I'd do hers too. It'll be fun. I can pull it together for one night. She deserves it, so fun it will be, even if it kills me.

ALMOST FIVE HOURS into the drive, I have fixed my makeup, done Becks's hair in a beautiful twist at the back of her head, and learned more about her past than I ever would've dared to guess. Thinking back to the first night I met the band, the first night I'd gone out in months, I now realize why Becks and James were so cagey when I asked my silly journalism questions. I can only imagine the trauma that goes along with escaping what is, as far as I see it, a cult. No wonder they're so obsessed. They saved each other.

Halfway through the drive, we pull up to a diner off the I-15 to stretch our legs and grab something to eat. Carefree smiles plaster the faces of our eclectic group as the waitress delivers baskets of fries, onion rings, and cheeseburgers. Everyone is happy. And they think I'm happy too—thankfully. And while I do my best to avoid eye contact with Dave, I know he's looking at me more carefully than anyone else.

I don't know what to think about him, or us, if there even is an us. Somehow these situations keep piling up on top of one another. The phone conversations, the staircase at the release party, the car ride home the other night where he looked like a rabid wolf who would tear Simon to shreds if I asked him to. Again, I thought he might kiss me.

Or maybe it's just that I *want* him to kiss me.

Dave is a passionate person. Maybe I mistook his exuberance for life and flirtatious flair as affection beyond that of what he defined our relationship as. Friends.

"Are we shuffling around the driving arrangements for the

second half of the drive?" Joel asks. "I'd like to take a nap so I'm fresh as a daisy when we get there."

"I don't think you could ever be fresh as a daisy, Joel," Key says. "More like fresh boiled cabbage leaves."

Joel shoves his shoulder. "Fuck off. You're one to talk. You snore so fucking loud the walls shake."

"I have a medical condition, thank you very much," Key says defensively.

"A deviated septum is hardly a medical condition," James counters. "Your halitosis on the other hand—"

Key leans across the table and points a finger at James. "You watch yourself, Walton, or I'll mess up that pretty face of yours."

"Not on my wedding day you won't!" Becks says sternly, and I'm surprised by how quickly the boys switch from playful aggression to repentant children. She really has them all under her thumb.

"Anyway, what was I saying before being so rudely interrupted?" Joel ignores the way Key flips him off from across the table. "Dave can drive while I sleep, and I think Key wanted to have a nap in the back of your van, right, James?" he says finally as the waitress leaves the bill. A flurry of cash starts to appear, and I drop five dollars down to cover my food and drink and a small tip.

James nods, and I can practically hear the smirk spread across Dave's face before he says, "That means you're riding shotgun with me, Disco Girl."

He smiles, and my heart flutters at the sight. No, Isabella. No. Stop it. It's just a drive.

As we head out to the parking lot, Joel jumps in the back seat of the station wagon, taking no time to ball up a few pieces of clothing to put under his head before lying down across the seat. Dave shakes his head, his dark blond hair swaying. He walks me to the passenger-side door, and I'm surprised by the chivalry when he opens it for me.

"Thanks," I say, sure my cheeks are flaming. If only my heart would calm down.

Dave slides casually into the driver's seat and follows James's black van back out onto the interstate, and after only five miles, the sounds of soft snores reach us from the back. Dave and I look over our shoulders to find Joel fast asleep, and even though I had the absolute worst morning in months, I actually smile.

"I thought Key was the one who snores," I say.

Dave grins. "Both of them do. They used to share a single room bachelor apartment back in Iowa. Pretty sure they used to wake each other up."

My eyes widen. "Sharing one bedroom? Sounds like it would interfere with their . . . social activities."

Dave rolls his lips, his smile settling into a smirk. "It didn't."

My face must look shocked, because Dave looks away from the road for a moment and laughs. I'm still trying to sort through that information in my head. "So they would just wait outside while the other . . . ?" I trail off, deep in thought.

Dave glances at me, that look of amusement still dancing on his face. "Not always."

"Not always, meaning sometimes they—? Oh."

"Yeah, they're really good at sharing."

"Wow, okay."

"If you get any redder, I'll have to start calling you Rudolph," Dave teases.

I clear my throat, glance out the window, and try to erase the mental image of Joel and Key with the same woman. Like some gigantic fleshy pile of throbbing bodies.

"You're picturing it, aren't you?"

I bury my face in my hands and try not to laugh. "I'm trying not to."

"Uh oh," he says, pointing at my face. "You've reached disco ball status. That face is so red you could light up the dance floor."

I quickly pull my sweater over my head to block myself from his stare. "Stop, oh my god!" Then it bursts out of me. Laughter. Pure, unfiltered laughter that makes my eyes water and my breath come out in sharp pants. Finally, I regain some control, my laughs fizzling out into chuckles then finally a wistful hum as I wipe my cheeks.

"It's nice to hear you laugh," Dave says quietly.

Peeking out of my sweater, I find him stealing sideways glances at me. "I feel like I haven't in a while."

"You needed it."

There's my heart fluttering again. "Yeah, well, life's been shitty lately."

He frowns, then reaches into his back pocket for his wallet. "Here," he says, holding out a folded five-dollar bill.

"Are you trying to buy a smile?" I ask teasingly.

The corner of his mouth quirks up. "Okay, first of all, smiles shouldn't be bought, they should be earned. And second," he continues, pushing the bill into my hand, "I paid for your food, so you can have this back."

I stare at the money in my hand. It's still folded the same way as it was when I put it down in the diner. "No, Dave, you— you didn't have to do that," I stammer, holding the money back out to him. "I'm more than capable of paying for my own things."

He pushes my hand holding the money back at me, and that small contact zings through me like an electric current. "I know. I wanted to. Consider it a small consolation prize for having such a shitty time lately."

My lips part as I try to formulate an argument, but he turns away, looking out his window. *I assume the conversation is over?* Sighing, I tuck the bill into my bra, and when I look up, I notice how Dave's eyes flick back to the road and the way a muscle in his jaw flexes.

"Thank you," I say quietly. "I appreciate it. The meal and the laughs."

"No problem. Like I said, you needed it. Your rhythm," he says simply. "It's been off all day—for a while actually."

I turn back, my head leaning on my fist to stare at him. "Explain it to me."

"What?"

"This rhythm thing. I want to understand it better."

He's silent for a long time, then: "If I do, will you explain to me why you were in such a terrible mood up until a few minutes ago?"

My lips twist and I turn away. It's quiet for a few minutes other than the sound of the road and Joel's quiet snores.

"It's your cycle of behavior." Dave's face is serious as he stares out over the dash, the setting sun behind him casting an orange halo around his face. "Your rhythm, I mean. It's not like I assign a tap dance melody to each person."

My eyebrows lift.

"It's just—I can usually tell if people aren't feeling themselves. Like right now? James is nervous, and he's almost never nervous. If he wasn't getting married, I'd be worried about him."

I smile at that.

"Becks gets real stiff . . . like a mannequin, or a doll, when she's upset. It used to happen all the time after we came out here, but it's been less frequent the past few months. I think you've helped with that."

Gazing down at my lap, I fiddle with the hem of my shirt. "Yeah, she uh . . . she told me about all that."

Dave nods and continues. "Joel, back there? He gets loud when he feels like no one's listening to him. And Key? Nothing really ever bothers him much, but he gets irritable after conversations with his family."

"Oh."

"And you, there's something on your mind. Am I right?"

Offering him a small nod, he smiles gently. Maybe his theory about people's rhythms wasn't so far-fetched after all.

"You don't have to talk about it if you don't want to, but you can."

Talking to Dave . . . it feels so easy. Like a lifelong friend who would never judge you. Who accepts you even when you make mistakes. Even the most horrible of them. How this same sweet man gets up on stage and beats a drum kit to music that sounds like it comes from the devil himself is beyond me. I thought I had that kind of friend in Miguel.

We dated all through high school. My mom doesn't know, but Miguel actually proposed. That night at prom, as the two of us lay sweaty and naked in the back of his car. But his idea of a future for us was me working for him when he took over his father's construction business. That's not what I wanted, and even though he promised to love me through anything, my dreams weren't a part of his plan.

"Not today," I finally whisper, then roll down the window a little to let the cool November breeze skip over my skin and blow through my hair.

"Here," Dave says, reaching across and pulling something out of the glove compartment. "I've got ABBA or Gloria Estefan. What'll it be?"

Surprised, I stare at the two cassette tapes between his long fingers. "How on earth do you have these?"

He shrugs, looking out his window to change lanes. "I might have stocked up knowing you'd be in the car."

"Really?"

He grins and shakes the cassettes at me. "Come on, Disco Girl, give me an education."

I'M NOT sure when it happened or for how long, but when I open my eyes again it's dark. The sun has set and the Gloria Estefan tape I made Dave listen to is over, a rock station on the radio now playing gently in the background. Blinking the sleep from my eyes, I register a subtle pressure on my calf muscle.

I must have fallen asleep. Trying not to move, I take in my surroundings. The upholstered bench seat beneath me, and a ball of fabric under my head. I turn my face inward and inhale the clean soap smell of Dave, all with a faint touch of smoke. It's his jacket. It comes back to me then. How I mentioned I was tired and how he offered me his leather jacket as a pillow. It was softer than I expected but smelled far more delicious than I could've imagined. I realize then that I'm laid out across the front bench seat, my bare feet in Dave's lap while his right hand rests on my calf.

He hasn't noticed I'm awake yet, so I resolve to watch him for a minute. His blue eyes are focused on the road ahead and his sharp jaw has the barest hint of a five o'clock shadow forming. My eyes follow down his neck to the top of his chest, hard and tanned and just barely visible at the top of his shirt. Then his arms —good lord. Without the jacket on I can see every line of muscle, the product of his drumming. The way they stretch and flex like a marble statue that's come alive.

Then I feel his thumb brush against my skin, and my breath catches. It's callused, just below the knuckle. When I look back up to his face, he seems to do this absently rather than giving it any real thought, but it catapults my heart into a thrumming nervous wreck. I can't deny all of this—I never want it to end.

"Are we there yet?" A voice from behind me breaks the silence, and I nearly jump in my seat. Joel yawns. "We have to be getting close."

Dave's hand moves from my leg to the steering wheel as if he's been electrocuted. My heart is a traitor of the worst kind. How dare she grow attached to his touch so quickly, and how dare she ache like this when it disappears.

Dave looks over his shoulder. "Almost. About twenty minutes away. Your impeccable nap timing is truly a wonder." His clear eyes find mine before he turns back toward the road.

Pushing myself up, I pull my feet away from his lap. "Sorry," I croak, my voice still sticky from disuse. "I didn't mean to use you like a foot stool."

"It's fine."

Something's wrong. There's a hardness to his tone that makes me feel like my feet ending up in his lap isn't fine at all. Where is the sweet and flirty Dave from hours ago who made me laugh? The one who went out of his way to have music in his car that I would enjoy? The one who was just touching my leg with the same tenderness you might pet a kitten?

Sitting up properly in my seat, I pull his jacket out from under my head, sure there are grooves on my face from the seams. Maybe I'm thinking about this too much. He couldn't be mad at me, could he? I hand him his jacket.

"Thanks for the pillow," I say sheepishly.

Without sparing me a glance, he takes the jacket and drapes it across his hips. "You're welcome."

I stare at him for a long moment, but he doesn't look at me. *Purposefully* doesn't look at me, his focus trained on the road ahead while his grip tightens on the steering wheel. What the hell is up with this guy? All of this back and forth, hot and cold is giving me whiplash. A scoff crawls out of my throat, and I turn my body toward the passenger-side window, crossing my arms and legs away from him.

I don't need this in my life. I don't have the energy to constantly interpret how someone feels about me, and with Dave I feel like I'm doing mental gymnastics every time we interact. It's not normal. It's not healthy. But it's like a drug. Like feeling high only to crash and crave your next fix. Addictive.

"Hey, I see the lights, look," Joel says, popping his head over the bench and pointing out the front window.

True enough, the bright lights of Las Vegas can be seen in the distance, surrounded on all sides by a dark desert. As we follow along behind James's van, the lights grow and grow until they sparkle and shine off the cars we pass on the streets. I take a deep breath. Okay, I need to be happy. I'm happy my friends are getting married. Tonight will be fun. I can do this. I can forget about last week with Simon and this morning with all of those rejection letters. My dreams may be in the toilet, but I can pull it together for a few hours. I can even forget about Dave in order to be happy for James and Becks, even though he's right next to me.

I can do this.

"We're here," Dave says. He pulls into a parking lot with a neon chapel sign, turns off the engine and gets out without ever looking back.

Another deep breath. I can't do this. I need help, and I know exactly where to find it.

CHAPTER 17

White Wedding

DAVE

Watching James and Becks get married feels like a goddamn fairytale. And while I know it's not something that will ever be in the cards for me, I allow myself to fantasize about it—for a few moments at least. I imagine myself dressed up in a pair of black jeans and a tailed tuxedo jacket over a T-shirt, vowing to love one woman forever. It wouldn't need to be a big wedding, or as small as this one, maybe it could even be on a stage somewhere. I almost laugh at the thought of getting married in a little white church. If I didn't burst into flames, it would be ironic to say the least.

I'd wait at the top of the aisle for my bride to walk toward me, her face shrouded in a gauzy white veil. We'd swear to love each other always, under the watchful eyes of our friends and families. Then I'd lift the veil for that first newlywed kiss to find the most beautiful brown doe eyes staring back at me.

I shake my head, as though I might be able to shake away the fantasy. To remove the image of Isabella looking back at me from beneath long lashes. Turning my head, I can see her now, standing closest to the aisle next to James's aunt Noreen, snapping away with her camera in a dress that should be illegal. Her ass looks like a ripe peach that I want to take a bite out of. But she's mad at me.

I know why, and honestly, she has every right to be. I behaved terribly earlier. I lost my self-control in that car as she curled up around my jacket, her breaths evening out to a steady rhythm until she fell asleep with the last rays of sunlight shining on her face. She looked so beautiful. Then when her legs curled up and her feet landed in my lap, it felt . . . right. I hadn't even realized I was touching her until Joel snapped me back to my senses.

Fuck. I'm giving this girl all of the wrong cues. We're supposed to be friends. Just friends.

"I now pronounce you husband and wife. James, you may kiss the bride."

I turn my attention back to the front, where James kisses Becks like he's the luckiest man on the planet, and if I'm being honest with myself, he is. There's a shuffle of bodies as we follow the happy couple out into the lobby, and while I've been more than happy to witness all the lovey-dovey stuff until now, we're in Vegas, which means that there are literally a hundred places more fun than this overly bright wedding chapel.

"Okay, okay, can we hit up a bar now?" Key asks. "First round's on me."

Thank god someone said it. I wonder how many bars are between here and a motel? Oh, that reminds me . . .

"Key, Joel . . . Al gave me some vouchers for motel rooms. Here," I say, passing them each a slip of paper.

"Awesome," Joel says, taking the paper and tucking it into his wallet. "Should come in handy."

Looking past them, I spot Isabella standing on her own and fiddling with her camera. Taking a deep breath, I walk toward her. "Hey, Izzy," I say. Her head shoots up, and I cringe at the way she rolls her eyes when she realizes it's me. "Our manager gave us some motel vouchers for the night. I've got one for you."

Her forehead scrunches under her fringe. "For me?"

Not technically. Al only gave me four, one for each of the bandmates, but with James, Key, and Joel taking the other three, she doesn't need to know I'll pay for my own to give her the last one. "Yeah. Free is good, right?"

"Right." She takes the voucher and stares down at it before tucking it away in her bag. "Thanks."

She doesn't look at me, and my chest tightens when I realize all I want is for those brown eyes to flit over my face. "Izzy," I sigh. "Can we talk about earlier? I feel like I need to explain—"

"Actually," she says, her face rounding on mine with the sharpness of a knife blade. Her eyes crackle like they're simmering with stored up electricity. "I think I'm done with the talking. Talking is exhausting. I'm here to have fun." She pushes past me to speak to Key. "Where are we heading first? I desperately need a drink."

"That's the spirit," Key says. "There's a club just down the street there, we can walk to it."

"Perfect," she says. Her eyes find mine for just a flash of a moment before she turns a sparkling, disingenuous grin at me.

My mouth drops open, but whatever I might have said dies on my tongue. What the hell *can* I say? Maybe it's best that she's mad and stays mad.

Shrieking and yelling from just inside the chapel doors make all of us jump. With a quick look at one another, we all bolt for the double doors, wrenching them open to find James with Becks in his arms as coins fall in a waterfall of metal out of a slot machine in the lobby.

"You fucking won, angel!" James shouts, pressing kisses to Becks's stunned face.

"You know, I take back what I said earlier," Key says from next to me as we watch the coins form a small mountain. "Seems like the first round is on you two."

I HATE THIS.

I thought I could come in here and distract myself, but all I've been able to do for the past hour is watch Isabella in the middle of the dance floor. Joel is chatting up a couple of girls at the end of the bar and James is leaning against the rail, happily watching his new wife enjoy herself.

"What's going on with you two?" Key asks, appearing at my side from out of nowhere.

"Huh?"

Key points to the two girls. "You and Isabella."

I take a sip from my beer bottle and shake my head. "There's nothing going on."

"Bullshit."

I look up at him and he narrows his eyes at me. "What bullshit?"

"Bullshit there's nothing going on," Key says.

Rolling my eyes, I press against the bar to order another beer. "You don't know what you're talking about."

He watches me for a moment, then his eyes widen. "Hold on, you *like* her."

I turn away. "No."

The lie is hollow though, and Key pushes his way in front of me along the bar. "You do! You like her."

"Fuck off, Prentiss."

He smirks, knowing he's caught me now. "Come on, man, could you make it any more obvious? You've been staring at her since we got here."

I say nothing. What *can* I say? I *have* been staring at her, and apparently enough for others to notice too.

"Wait," he says, holding up a finger with a metal skull ring on it. "Is this why you've been coming home alone after gigs?"

"Shut up, Key."

He grins. "Holy shit, it is! How long has this been going on?"

I hang my head back, knowing he won't back off. "I don't know . . . a while."

"Are you hooking up?" he asks.

"No."

"What the fuck are you waiting for? Go dance with her."

"Look," I say, turning to face him. "I don't *like* her, I just want to fuck her brains out. But I can't do that because she happens to be Becks's only friend, and Walton forbade me from sleeping with her. And now with the articles she wrote, she's too involved with the band. If we hook up, it'll just get messy for everyone."

Key rolls his eyes then shrugs. "Since when do you listen to James? And for the record, I think you're crazy. Isabella is awesome. But . . . looks like you might have missed your opportunity."

"What do you mean?"

He looks past me over my shoulder and points. Spinning around, my eyes lock on Isabella, her arms wrapped around some douchebag in a baby blue silk shirt with one too many buttons undone. Her gorgeous body is pressed up against him as she tosses back another drink. That's her third in only an hour, and while I don't pretend to know the science behind it, I know damn well for her size she'll be feeling pretty tipsy right about now.

My jaw and fists clench as I watch this guy's hands slide over her bare shoulders, the shoulder I marked—he's touching what's mine. He leans forward to whisper something in her ear, and she smiles . . . fucking *smiles*, before his hands start to slide down her body. All of her delicious curves are at his fingertips while her eyes close and her head tips back as he grinds himself into her. That anger—that terrible, debilitating darkness—comes to life under my skin, my arms vibrating with it. Then her eyes open and those chocolate brown pools lock on me and before I can stop myself, I'm moving toward her through the crowd.

Becks finds me first, a gentle smile growing across her face. "Dave, you coming to dance with us?"

I shake my head, my fists still clenched as I try not to reach out and strangle this guy. "No, we're leaving. Izzy, Becks, let's go."

"What?" Becks asks, her brows furrowing. "Why?"

Fuck, this is her night. "I just mean, we're going to head out onto the strip for a bit. Check things out."

"Oh!" she says with a smile. "Yeah, okay!"

But Isabella hasn't taken her narrowed gaze off me, like she knows exactly why I chose this moment to interrupt them.

"You're not leaving too, are you, dollface?" the guy says as he presses his face to hers.

"Yeah," I say, grabbing her arm and pulling her away from the dance floor, "she is."

I can hear Isabella protesting but I don't slow down. I toss her jacket at her as we head for the exit. For all his being nosy, Key seems to have caught on to the fact that I want to leave, because he's rallied everyone together. It's not until the six of us are out in the parking lot that I let go of Isabella's hand.

"Asshole," I hear her mutter under her breath, but as everyone starts to walk toward the strip, she follows along whether she wants to or not, pulling her jacket back on. Peeking over my shoulder, I find her glaring at me, but I'm not sorry. I'm still seething, even though I have absolutely no right to. Isabella's not mine, never has been, never will be, but that doesn't mean I need a front row seat to some idiot grinding all over her.

"Is that a tiger?" Becks cries, pointing toward the front entrance of a casino.

Sure enough, there's a huge white tiger lying on a platform

outside. Isabella pushes past me, her shoulder knocking against mine in what I sense is an intentional way to tell me she's still pissed. Even though it's well past midnight now, the streets are alive with people. Lights and sounds come from every direction as we take in everything around us. I don't know how, but Isabella and a few others end up with a drink in their hands. Are we even allowed to drink outside?

But as I glance around, it seems to be the norm. Showgirls in bright feathered headdresses are passing out oversized shots, and my stomach churns at the way Isabella throws back two in a row. *Shit.* It's not long before she's stumbling a little, losing her balance every few steps along the chaotic street. I suggest that we all stop somewhere for food, thinking it'll help soak up some of the alcohol. She hasn't eaten since Bakersfield, but when we find a food truck, she ignores my attempts at trying to get her to eat some french fries.

It's not until later, when we end up near a lavish hotel across from what appears to be a strip club, that I'm able to speak to her without drawing too much attention from the others.

"Izzy," I say, tugging on the sleeve of her cropped jacket. "Are you okay?"

She rolls her eyes lethargically and starts to walk away.

"Izzy!"

Spinning around to face me, she almost topples over. Apparently those two shots on an empty stomach were enough to take her from tipsy to drunk. "Don't *Izzy* me," she says, her nose scrunched up. "And don't call me that."

"Look, I'm sorry about earlier, I was—"

She holds her hands up. "It's fine. I'm fine. I don't care. Whatever you were earlier . . . whatever you are now . . . *I don't care.*"

"Hey, guys," James says, walking toward us. "Becks and I, we're going to get a room at the Flamingo for the night. You know, honeymoon and all." He grins. "How about we meet up at that diner by the chapel in the morning for breakfast?"

Key wraps his arm around his shoulders. "Aww, Jamesey's got to go take care of his wifey," he says, making an obscene kissing gesture as James pushes him away.

"That's cool," Joel says. "We were thinking about hitting up the strip club anyway."

"Yeah, well, don't blow all your money," James warns.

"There's no greater purpose for hard earned cash than spending it on tits and ass," Key says, pulling Joel away.

James turns back to Becks, and I watch as Isabella hugs her friend and wishes her a good night before they disappear into the lobby and the two of us are alone together.

"Isabella," I say softly. But when I turn to find her, she's gone. "Isabella?"

Where the hell did she go? After three full circles, I spot her dark fluffy hair bouncing away in the distance. "Isabella!" I call after her, already pushing through the crowd. "Hey!" I say, running up and grabbing her by the wrist just as she wobbles on the uneven sidewalk.

She falls against my chest and looks up at me blearily. "Dave?"

"Where are you going?"

For a long moment she just looks at me, trying to focus her gaze, her head rolling to the side. Then she blinks rapidly and pushes against my chest. "Let go of me."

The harshness in her tone catches me off guard, and a tightness in my chest uncovers a painful memory from long ago, like the shore when the tide goes out.

She starts to walk away again, so I follow after her. "Isabella, what are you doing?"

"I want to go dancing," she says. "I'm going back to that place with the fish in the dance floor. That was fun."

"No way. You're wasted, you can hardly walk, let alone dance," I say, following behind her like a shadow.

She bares her teeth at me. "I am not. I'm having fun. Tonight's supposed to be fun, Dave, and you're ruining it."

Jogging to get in front, I stop her before she can step out onto the road. "I'm ruining it?"

Her eyes close for a moment, and when she opens them back up, her gaze is unfocused and she talks to a point past my shoulder. "I'm sorry I put my feet on you, okay?"

"Your feet?"

"In the car." She pushes away from me and begins stumbling down the sidewalk back the way we came, laughing darkly to herself. "I didn't realize my feet were so offensive."

"They aren't."

She spins around, nearly hitting me with her bag. "Then what the hell, Dave?"

Her eyes are clear suddenly, focused. Like the only thing she can see is me, and I don't know what to say. I don't know how to tell her why this can't happen between us.

"Nothing?" she asks, her voice shaky. "Nothing to say?"

"Izzy," I say, stepping toward her.

"I said don't call me that!" she shouts. Stepping backward, she stumbles, loses her balance, and I move before thinking. My arm wraps around her waist, catching her before she can topple onto the cement.

"Whoa," I breathe, pulling her against me as her legs give out from under her and she wraps her arms around my neck. "You okay?"

Her face is pressed against my chest but she says nothing. Instead all I can hear is the sound of her quiet sobs. I take a deep breath and scoop her legs up under my arms. "Come on, Disco Girl, you need to get some rest."

She continues to quietly cry, her arms tightening around my

neck as I carry her down the sidewalk and back toward the chapel. There's a motel around the corner with a Vacancy sign, and I head toward it.

The door of the motel office jingles as I back my way in, Isabella still snugly wrapped up in my arms. I set her down on the bench by the window, careful to keep her propped up against the wall. Her hair is falling out of its arrangement, and there's some mascara smudges under each eye, but she's still undeniably beautiful.

"Can I help you?"

I startle at the man behind the counter's scratchy voice. He looks like a gremlin, with beady eyes that are exponentially magnified by coke bottle lenses. His comb-over is greasy and there are sweat stains under the pits of his gray shirt. I fight the urge not to contort my face but . . . hasn't this guy ever showered?

"Uh, yeah," I say, pulling out my wallet. "We need two single rooms."

"Not one?" he asks, looking past me to where Isabella is sitting lopsided on the bench.

"No, two."

Reaching into my pocket, I pull out the paper voucher. Shit, I forgot to ask James for his back. It's not like the honeymoon suite at the Flamingo takes motel vouchers. It's fine, I'll just pay for my own.

"She okay?" The man eyes me shrewdly, then he turns toward the wall to grab a ring of keys.

"Yeah, she just drank too much," I say, pulling out a few twenties to pay for the second room.

"Hmm," the man hums. "You can have these two. They're right next door to the office."

The man makes no attempt to hide the way he looks at Isabella. He licks his lips and cracks a devious smile, and I find myself suddenly nauseous.

"Actually," I say, taking back the cash from the counter and grabbing only one of the keys dangling from his yellow fingers. "We'll just take the one room. We're on a budget."

The man's gaze snaps back to me with a disappointed glare, but I don't stay long enough to say more. With the room key in hand, I pick Isabella back up and push my way out the door. There's no fucking way I'm leaving her alone in a shady motel room with that lecherous creep probably waiting for his chance to attack her.

"Dave?" Isabella whispers, her head burrowing into my neck. "Where are we?"

"At a motel. You need to sleep."

"It still hurts when I sleep," she whispers.

My brows furrow as I look down at her. "What still hurts?"

She sighs, her face pinching. "My heart."

I hoist her up a little higher. Biting the inside of my cheek, I can't help the sharp stab of guilt that plunges its way through my chest at her words. Is she hurting because of the school paper? Or is it because of me?

I insert the key into the lock and after a few tries, it pushes open. It's a bit of a struggle to find the light switch, but when I do, the dim light reflects off the wood paneling on the wall and the burnt orange and brown bedspread. The room smells like smoke and reminds me that I'm desperate for one myself, but Isabella is the priority right now. Setting her down on the bed, I turn the bedside lamp on and begin to take off her heels.

"You don't need to touch my feet again," she slurs. I look up at her, eyes half open as she watches me from her pillow.

I chuckle. "I have no problem with your feet. In fact, they're beautiful feet."

"So it's just the rest of me that's ugly, then," she says, her face buried in the pillow.

Sighing, I remove her shoes and place them at the foot of the bed. I sit down next to her and brush back the hair covering her face. "Trust me, there's nothing about you I don't find beautiful."

She sits up on the bed and cradles her head in her hands. "I think—I might have drunk too much."

A smile tugs at the corner of my mouth. "Yeah, I think so."

"I just wanted a distraction, but I should've known it wouldn't compare."

"Wouldn't compare to what?"

Her eyes close and she sways where she sits. "You."

"Me?"

She scrunches her face and nods.

"What do you mean?"

Her hand reaches out to touch my chest. "You're the best distraction."

I don't know what she means, but her eyes close and her hand begins to trail down my chest and over my stomach, causing a rush of blood to throb in my groin.

"Isabella—"

She shakes her head and leans toward me, her fingers fumbling with my belt buckle. "Call me Izzy again."

I grasp her wrist, pressing my thumb against her racing pulse. "No," I say, realizing what she's attempting to do. "This—no, this can't happen. You're wasted. You don't know what you're doing."

Her eyes open, and even though they're a little unfocused, they make my breath catch. With surprising steadiness, she pushes herself up onto her knees. "Please, Dave, I just want to feel something good."

My resolve cracks enough for her hand to free itself from my hold, and a shudder ripples through me as her fingertips slide under the hem of my shirt. My body betrays me, every cell desperate to devour her right here in this scummy motel room. I want to tear her dress to pieces, the one that's been teasing me all night. I want to finally see and feel every inch of her gorgeous skin while she moans my name. And she would. She would moan and scream my name with how good I would make her feel. I'd make her forget all of the shit she tried to vanish by drinking tonight. I would be the distraction she so desperately craves.

But it would be wrong. And as amazing as it would feel to finally kiss her, touch her, consume her—in the morning, it would be a mess. A mess I might regret for the rest of my life.

I push her away and stand up from the bed, painfully aware of the bulge in my jeans. "Izzy, stop, you need to go to sleep."

Her face drops, the color draining away.

"Actually," she blurts, "I think I'm going to be sick."

She rolls off the bed and runs for the bathroom, then promptly retches into the toilet. Well, that's one way to deflate my hard-on. I take a few steps toward the bathroom. "Do you want some help?" I ask, forehead resting against the cool door.

"No!" she says in a strained voice. "Just—don't come in here, please."

At the sound of her throwing up again, I back away. "I'm just going to go get you some water, okay? I think I saw a vending machine outside."

Grabbing the key, I head outside, spark up a cigarette, and lock the door behind me. Don't want that office creep to find his way inside while I look for something to help with what I'm sure will be a nasty hangover in the morning. Luckily, there's a vending machine at the end of the row of motel rooms, so I grab two water bottles and take my time walking back, reveling in the comforting smoke of my cigarette before I go back in.

Staring at the door, I hesitate. It's all too familiar and suddenly, my heart begins to pound in my chest and my muscles lock up. I back away from the door, leaning against a support beam for the second level. No, this can't be happening again. It's not the same—she's not the same—but someone should tell that to my body, which seems programmed to protect itself. Protect my heart.

It seems like no matter where I go, and whatever I do, this follows me. Am I being punished? Forced to live out the same horrible scenario over and over again? Is it just a coincidence? Or is it maybe an opportunity to change? To fix the mistakes I've made and do the right thing for once?

As I stand outside of this motel door, I think I can finally admit to myself that I'm scared. I'm scared to lose what I've found. Scared of losing the success I've worked my whole life to achieve. Scared of being lied to. Scared of opening my heart because it's too vulnerable, too damaged, and too accustomed with being thrown away like garbage. If I keep it closed off to everyone, I'll never get hurt again. I'm scared of my luck running out.

Isabella is in bed when I walk back through the door. After making sure everything is secure, including the chain lock, I set one of the bottles of water down on the table next to her head and shift to the edge of the bed. Her face is pale, but it looks like she's washed her makeup off—the mascara that had been under her eyes is gone and her lips, while still dark, no longer have the reddish tint.

She's still wearing her little dress but she's taken off the cropped jacket, and I can't help my heart from trying to find where my signature was on her shoulder.

"Isabella?" I say softly, wondering if she's truly asleep.

Her forehead pinches and she groans. "Hmm?"

"Are you feeling better?"

"I'm so sorry. I'm so, *so* sorry."

"It's okay, we all get carried away sometimes." I take a deep breath. "You're safe. Just go to sleep."

"Dave?" she whispers, and her eyes flutter open to find me.

"Yeah?"

"Will you stay with me?"

Seeing as how there's only one bed in here, no chairs to sleep on, and I suppose the alternative is the floor . . .

"Please?" she whispers.

I nod. "Yeah, all right."

Kicking off my shoes and removing my belt and wallet chain, I turn off the lights and get into bed, making sure to keep a respectable distance between us, even if the memory of her touching my stomach earlier is making it very difficult to focus. Especially with how the light of the moon through the window makes her skin glow.

"I'm sorry I ruined your night," she says, her voice still soft.

"You didn't."

She sighs contentedly. "I'm having a nice dream now."

"Are you?"

"Mm-hmm. You kissed me."

A breathy laugh escapes me. "Did I?"

Her smile turns into a frown. "But then you stopped."

I reach out and tuck her hair behind her ear, listening as her breaths even out and she falls asleep.

"Trust me," I say, my thumb caressing her cheek. "If I kissed you, I wouldn't be able to stop."

CHAPTER 18

Five Years Ago

DAVE

"Sam, you promised you'd give me forty bucks for the studio rental. Now what the fuck are we supposed to do?" John and Charlie both turn toward us as Sam hangs his head. "I'm sorry, man. I had it, I swear."

My eyes narrow. "You fucking lost it?"

"I don't know!" he says, fumbling through his wallet and checking his pockets again. "Maybe it's upstairs . . ."

He disappears out of the garage and into the house.

"Pretty sure I know where it's gone . . ." Charlie mutters under his breath.

I spin around. "What do you mean?"

He shifts uncomfortably on his feet, avoiding my eyes as he fiddles with the E string of his bass guitar.

John sighs. "He means that if there's money missing, you might want to ask Emily."

I pull back, affronted. "What the fuck is that supposed to mean?"

He pulls on the chain at his throat. "Look, man, I know she's your girl and all, but you must see it. Emily is a fucking mess."

Stalking toward him, I clench my fists at my sides. "Watch your mouth."

"Where do you think she's getting the money for booze?" Charlie speaks up finally, possibly with the hope he can distract me from pummeling John's face.

"She works!"

"She got fired two weeks ago for missing shifts at the diner, Dave," John says with a frown.

I feel like I'm being blindsided. "What?" *Fired?* No, that's impossible, she's at work right now. She told me that's where she was going. I asked if she wanted a ride but she said she was fine to walk.

John holds up his hands. "You know the line cook who sells weed? Danny? He told me yesterday."

"But—" I don't have a response. What the fuck is happening right now? Is this true? Has all of this really been happening right under my nose and I've been too caught up in my own dreams to notice?

Sam reenters the garage looking frazzled. "I can't find that cash anywhere. What the hell could've happened to it?"

John and Charlie look at me as if to say, *You know where it went. You have to be the one to tell him.* But how can I, when I don't even want to believe it myself?

"Do you think the studio will let us postpone so we don't lose the deposit?" Sam asks hopefully.

I shrug, still desperate to believe that John and Charlie are wrong. "I can call them and ask, I guess."

Another delay. Another setback. Another thing to deal with. Why does this keep happening? It's like every step I take forward, I end up three steps back. And Emily . . . I fucking love this girl with all of my heart. Could she really lie right to my face? Could she really steal money from her cousin?

"Dave, you okay?" Sam asks.

I shake my head. "Yeah, sorry. Let's get back to practice and we can sort the money issue out later."

But all through practice I'm distracted. Off time and off beat. Thankfully, John and Charlie don't mention it—they know why. Maybe if I'm lucky, I can pick up some extra shifts at the lumber yard in the evenings to make up for the missing money.

By the time the sun has set and all of us are sweating and exhausted, my stomach gets more and more twisted as I think about what's going on with Emily. When she finally walks up the driveway, I can't help but want to throw up when I notice the way she stumbles and walks on an angle. Is she drunk?

"Hey, guys," she says with a cheerful voice.

"Hey, Em," John and Charlie reply, giving me a loaded look.

She walks up to me, wraps her arms around my neck, and kisses me on the lips. She tastes like mouthwash, but there's a familiar scent that lies buried underneath.

"How—how was work?" I ask, pulling away. I wonder if she can see it on my face. That I know something's going on.

She rolls her eyes and sighs dramatically. "Ugh, same old, same old. The fryer broke down, so that was a nightmare. I'm going to go have a shower and change."

I look away. "Yeah. Okay."

"I missed you," she whispers, brushing another kiss to my lips.

Grasping her face with my hands, I stare into her eyes. Eyes that used to sparkle but now are glazed over and dull. "Em?"

"Yeah, baby?"

Ask her. Just *ask* her. Did you get fired? Did you steal Sam's money? Are you so drunk right now that you can't even walk a straight line? "I love you."

She smiles and giggles, kissing me again only to disappear into the house. Shame crawls over my skin. I couldn't do it. I can't believe it. I love her, but if everything else is true it might mean she doesn't really love me back. Maybe she's just been using me. Maybe everything has been a lie.

That's the funny thing about a lie, I guess. All it takes is *one* to question all of someone's truths.

CHAPTER 19

Hard Habit to Break

ISABELLA

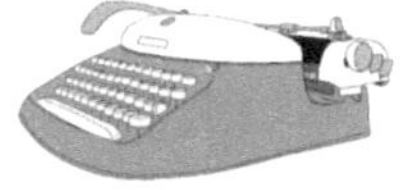

There's a pounding on my bedroom door. An incessant *bang, bang, bang* that wakes me from a colorful dream of music and flashing lights, palm trees and stormy blue eyes.

Bang, bang, bang.

"Mmhfm," I groan, attempting to open my eyes, but everything feels so heavy. Finally, I manage to, and an unfamiliar room is revealed. Wood paneling and a buzzing light in the bathroom and a scratchy bedspread under my cheek. Then I realize that the pounding isn't on the door, it's in my head. Stretching out my limbs, my hand lands on something soft and hard at the same time. Sitting upright in bed, I look down to find Dave sleeping peacefully at my side.

Oh no.

My head feels like it's being crushed by an elephant, but after a quick check, I realize I'm still dressed and so is Dave. What the hell happened last night? Where are we? We didn't—

No, we both still have our clothes on. Besides, Dave . . . He doesn't seem like the type to take advantage. Actually, I think I remember him carrying me. Him putting me on the bed . . . Oh god, did I— I remember my hands touching his skin. A muscled stomach that felt as smooth as velvet. Did I come on to him? And he pushed me away. Embarrassment makes me squirm, my gaze landing on the bottled water next to me on the nightstand.

My mouth feels stuffed with cotton and I chug the water, some semblance of life coming back to me. What would really help is a shower. Looking back down at Dave, I take in his dark blond hair framing his face, his strong jaw and slightly parted lips. I definitely dreamt of him last night, and I wonder achingly if he dreamt of me too.

I try to sneak off the bed, the weight of his hand resting on my hip sending a shiver down my spine. He groans and shifts but seems to fall back asleep as I dash for the bathroom. Looking at my reflection in the mirror, I'm a little pale, but I've seen myself look worse as steam begins to settle on the glass from the shower. Slipping out of my dress and underwear, I pull the last few remaining pins from my hair and let the tangled strands fall down my back.

The heat from the water helps me feel a little like myself again as I try to piece together the memories from last night. The incident in the car and how Dave proceeded to ignore me. Ignored me until he saw me dancing with another man. Then he behaved like a caveman, dragging me out of there like I was a dog on a leash. How the drinks helped me forget about Simon and the pile of rejections I flushed down the toilet. Then there's the fuzzy memories of Dave laying me down in the bed. I think I might have thrown up. I definitely threw up. Ugh, hopefully I had the decency to do that in privacy. I don't know if I'd ever be able to look him in the eye if I threw up in front of him.

I dreamed that you kissed me.

Did I say that out loud? I drag a wet hand down my face. What he must think of me.

When I've scrubbed my body clean and untangled my hair, I

dry off and pull my clothes back on and wrap my hair up in the towel. I wonder if Dave is still sleeping. Was he drinking too? How did we end up in the same motel room? But when I walk out of the bathroom, the bed is empty. The room is empty. He's gone.

"Dave?" I call, opening the closet door. "Dave?"

Did he . . . leave me here?

Before I can start to spiral, I notice a note on the bed.

ISABELLA,

I WENT TO GET MY CAR FROM THE CHAPEL. THERE'S A DINER NEXT DOOR, MEET ME THERE AFTER YOUR SHOWER FOR SOME BREAKFAST.

DAVE

At least he didn't take off on me. Right, well, this won't be awkward at all. I wish I could remember exactly what I said last night, then I could at least find a way to make a U-turn out of this mess. Or . . . maybe this is a good thing. Dave and I have been dancing around this weird flirtatious will-they-or-won't-they for months now. Maybe after last night, I can finally get some straight answers out of him.

I towel dry my hair and I put my heels and jacket back, then head out the door, dropping the key back in the slot on the office door. I peer left and right of the motel, my eyes landing on the diner right across the parking lot. Feeling a little ridiculous in my halter dress and heels on a Tuesday morning, I open the door, immediately feeling my queasy stomach settle at the smell of fresh coffee and bacon and eggs. I'm starving and so desperate for coffee I would accept an IV hooked straight to my veins.

Looking around, I spot Dave sitting at a large booth, sipping a glass of water. How does he look so handsome after a night out like we had? As I approach, I notice he's reading a tattered piece of paper. There's an expression on his face that reeks of concentration, and his brows pinch together as his eyes travel over the small crinkled note. I'm not sure why I stand and stare at him. I suppose it's because interrupting him like this feels indecent. Like I would be intruding on a very personal and private moment.

As though sensing my thoughts, he looks up, those stormy eyes finding mine across the row of tables. My cheeks burn as though I've been caught doing something I shouldn't be, but he smiles gently and waves me over, folding the piece of paper and tucking it into his wallet on the table. I sit down across from him as he picks up his cigarette from the ashtray and takes a drag.

"Good morning," I say shyly.

"Morning," he says as he watches me fiddle with my bag. Once I'm settled, he steeples his hands under his chin. "How are you feeling?"

I slump in the squeaky vinyl seat. "Like my head is about to explode."

He laughs. "Yeah, you really tied one on last night."

I snort. "We all did. Even Becks, and I've never seen her drink."

The grin fades from Dave's face, but the waitress comes by asking if I would like some coffee and I nearly burst into tears as she fills the ceramic mug in front of me. I add one cream and sugar and take a long sip, relishing the way the bitter coffee burns and rids that stale morning taste from my mouth.

"Heaven," I sigh, and I notice Dave is looking at me with a strange expression. "So, can I ask?"

"Ask what?"

I bite my lip. "Last night, we didn't—"

He pulls back, shaking his head. "Oh, no. No, definitely not."

Relief scatters across my skin. I didn't think it had happened since we both woke up in clothes, but you never know.

"And was us ending up in the same room just . . ." I'm not

sure how to end that sentence, so I wave my hand to encourage him to finish it for me.

"Yeah, sorry about that. You were . . . well, you were wasted and could barely walk. I was going to get two rooms, but the guy who worked in the office looked like he might try something fishy and I didn't want to leave you alone in that state."

My heart swells. He was trying to take care of me? "Thank you for that. I'm sorry you had to babysit my drunk ass. I'm just glad you were coherent enough, otherwise we might both have ended up in some back-alley dumpster."

He takes a drink of his water and looks away. "I wasn't drunk."

I narrow my eyes and laugh. "Oh, come on. I watched you drink at least seven beers within the first two hours that we were out. How can you not be drunk after that?"

He fidgets with the salt and pepper shakers on the table. "I uh —I only drink nonalcoholic beer."

The smile falls off my face. "You—wait, what?"

He shrugs. "I don't drink. But people expect me to, so . . ."

"Dave, that's—but why?"

He looks up at me, and that's when I register the tiredness in his eyes. "I've seen what alcohol does to people. And I—I don't trust myself enough not to turn into someone who abuses it."

My stomach flips. "Oh." Is that what he thinks of me? Does he think I abuse alcohol to escape my problems? I mean, last night I kind of did . . . but it's not like I do that all the time.

Almost as if on cue, the waitress returns to take our order. After we've both said what we want and she's left, he continues to stay quiet while simultaneously organizing the sugar packets in the container.

"Dave, it's fine if you don't drink. There's nothing wrong with that. Why do you feel like you have to hide it?"

He shrugs.

"Oh god," I say, the realization that I acted like a total buffoon in front of someone completely sober creeping up my neck and into my face. "You must have thought I was a total idiot last night. I'm so embarrassed."

"No, no," he says, and his hands abandon the now color-coded sugar packets to pull mine away from my face. I should just tell the cook to fry my eggs right on my forehead. "You weren't an idiot. You were adorable, feisty, and . . . rightfully mad at me."

Is he actually admitting that he acted like a jerk? "I wasn't mad," I say, giving a half-hearted shrug of my shoulder.

He grins. "Yeah, you were. And you were right to be. I—" He rubs the back of his neck again. "I wasn't exactly . . . I was a jerk to you yesterday, in more ways than one, and I'm sorry. You didn't deserve that."

I wasn't expecting a flat-out apology. "Wow, well . . . thank you. And for the record, I'm sorry too. For . . . you know, getting wasted. That's not—I'm not normally like that."

He nods. "I know. It's okay."

"And thank you for taking care of me last night. I can only imagine what a mess I was."

"You weren't so bad. At least you threw up in the toilet."

I can practically feel my soul leave my body. "Oh god."

He laughs while I want to crawl into a hole and never come out. "It's fine!" He laughs again. "Isabella, it's fine."

Isabella . . . not Izzy. Why isn't he calling me Izzy anymore? We're quiet for a few moments, and Dave finishes his cigarette as the waitress brings our food. I reach for the ketchup bottle, my fingers brushing his as we go for it at the same time, and there's an awkward chuckle from us both.

"Dave?"

"Hmm?"

I need to know. "Can I ask—why *were* you such a jerk yesterday?"

He takes a bite of his scrambled egg–covered toast and looks at me before swallowing. "Can I be honest with you?"

I blink. Honesty is good, right? So why is my stomach in knots? "Yeah, of course."

Dave sighs and puts his cutlery down on the table. "Look, I think it's obvious by now that I'm very attracted to you."

Wow, okay, I guess we really are doing honesty. My heart begins to tap dance in my chest, but stops dead at the resigned look on his face. "But?"

"But I can't do a relationship right now. I honestly don't know if I ever can. And while I'd like nothing more than to throw you over my shoulder, take you back to that motel, and worship that gorgeous body like you deserve," he says, and I think every cell in my body is burning up under his gaze. "I also know that's all I can offer you. I can't be your boyfriend. I can't be someone who falls in love with you."

If anyone ever looked shocked before, it's me. I'm taken aback by his candor, and while I know it shouldn't hurt me, I can't help but feel my chest aching with the barrier he's so clearly defining.

"Oh."

"I'm sorry," he says looking down at his plate. "If you were any other girl, I would've had my way with you that first night we met, then promptly ditched you. I'm not proud of it," he rushes to add when he sees my mouth drop open. "But Becks is like my sister and you're her only friend at Stoneman. I couldn't risk you hating me and never speaking to her again. Or never speaking to *me* again because . . . I like talking to you."

I blink.

"And last night when I saw you dancing with that guy—well, something snapped. It was wrong of me. I don't own you."

"I . . . don't know what to say."

"Say we can be friends. Real friends."

Realizing my mouth is still hanging open, I take another sip of my coffee. "Friends. Yeah . . . I mean, of course. But that also means you can't behave like that again when a guy wants to dance with me."

His spine straightens and he swallows hard. "I know."

"And, if I can ask a favor?"

"Sure."

I take a deep breath. "If I'm around, could you . . . not flaunt the girls you plan to hook up with and ditch?"

"Shit, it sounds so terrible when you say it like that," he says with an embarrassed smile.

"Well," I say, taking a bite of my bacon, "it is the behavior of a total skeev."

He narrows his eyes at me, but I can't help the smile that pulls across my face. Soon enough he's smiling too, then we're laughing, and while it's not the outcome I was hoping for, I can't help but feel a *little* happy. After all, if I can't have him romantically, we can still be in each other's lives. Only now, there's a set boundary. A clear line in the sand. No more flirtation or lingering looks. No more darkened staircases where I'm unsure of what might happen. And I won't kid myself into thinking I can change his mind.

Besides, we really won't be seeing much more of each other. I'm not writing articles about his band anymore, and other than this impromptu trip to Vegas, it's not like we hang out. I can keep my distance and move on from this schoolgirl crush.

"Thank you," I say finally. "For being honest."

He scoops more egg onto his toast. "No prob—"

"Good morning, gorgeous." A voice vibrates in my ear and Joel flops down next to me. "And Dave."

Dave flips him off and, turning my attention to the others, I try to smile and focus on the new arrivals.

"You boys seem like you had a good night," I force myself to say, focusing on their tired yet smiling faces and ignoring the way Dave's rejection burns.

"Made off like bandits at the strip club," Joel says. "Did you know you can gamble in there? So, I'm two songs deep with this gorgeous redhead, her huge—"

"Joel," Dave interrupts, "is this really a conversation for Isabella, or is it one you can tell me about in the car on the ride home?"

Joel holds up his hands. "Right, yeah, sorry."

"Not exactly a story to tell over breakfast," Key adds with an odd look on his face.

Dave makes a gagging noise and I smile. "Anyone know when the happy couple will appear out of their fancy honeymoon suite?" Joel asks.

"Probably not for a while," Key says. "They need to get their fill of each other before we head out on tour."

I turn to look at Key. "What?"

He turns to Dave. "You didn't tell her?"

Dave takes another sip from his water, and there's an unusual look that passes between them. Finally he shrugs. "I guess I figured Becks would've mentioned it."

They're going on *tour*?

"No, she didn't mention it," I say.

"We're heading out after Christmas," Joel says, leaning toward me like it's a big secret. "Becks can't come because of her classes."

"Will you look after her for us while we're away?" Key asks me. "Keep her company?"

The way they love her like a sister makes my heart ache with longing. "Of course I will." I plaster an easy grin onto my face, refusing to let my emotions get the best of me. "How long will you be gone for?"

"Three months," Dave says. "Twenty-six cities."

I lift my mug up to my mouth and take a sip. They'll be gone for three months. *Dave* will be gone for three months. It sounds like such a long time, but maybe this will be good. Having Dave gone from my life for a quarter of a year will help me get a grip on my feelings. I can focus on figuring out what the hell I'm going to do without an internship, I can look after Becks, and I can get over this silly crush.

Dave watches me from across the table. Maybe he's thinking the same thing as me. That time away from each other is exactly what we need to move on from this attraction to each other. He'll hook up with and ditch a new girl in every city to forget about me, and I'll—well, I don't know yet, but I'll think of something.

Becks, James, and his aunt Noreen, who I recognize from the chapel, join us not long after and I'm awed by how much this little group makes me smile. Becks tells me about their elaborate honeymoon suite and flushes bright pink when I point out the love bite on her collarbone.

"What about you?" Becks asks. "Did you have a good night?"

"I'm pretty hungover, but"—I catch a quick glimpse of Dave laughing at something James said, then quickly look away—"yeah, I had a lot of fun. It was a much-needed distraction."

Dave's gaze whips to me and I'm thrown off-kilter by the intensity of that look. It's like he's stripping me down to my soul, and I'm vulnerable and exposed. I definitely think three months away from each other will help this problem we're having, because the way he's watching me now . . . that is not the way friends look at each other.

"Come on, let's get out of here. We've still got a few hours to sightsee before we have to head home," James says.

Everyone stands and throws down a few bucks for their food. I open my mouth to tell Dave I'll pay for his meal today, but he shakes his head, picks up my money, and pushes it into my hand as he pulls out his wallet. Yes, three months apart will be good.

"Isabella, you'll ride with us?" Becks asks.

"Yeah, I'm just going to use the bathroom first."

Running to the back of the restaurant, I relieve myself, realizing with horror that I just started my period.

"Fuck," I mutter. But my purse isn't here. "*Fuck,*" I shout when I remember I left it in the booth. The door opens, and I spy through a crease in the door a young woman with more glitter around her eyes than I thought possible. "Umm . . . excuse me?" I say, embarrassed. "I'm sorry to bother you, but do you happen to have an extra tampon?"

"Oh! Sure honey," the young woman responds in an accent that sounds Texan. "Here you are." A glittered hand appears under the stall door proffering a tampon, and I sigh with relief.

"Thanks, you're a lifesaver."

"Don't think anything of it. Us girls got to stick together, don't we?"

I smile and once I'm situated, I exit the stall to find a beautiful bedazzled redhead. She's wearing a silver mini skirt, a yellow crochet halter top, and denim platform heels that put her easily at six feet tall. Washing my hands, I get carried away watching the hypnotizing way she reapplies her lipstick in the mirror.

I try to think of something to say, and settle on, "I love your shoes," hoping it didn't come out as lame as it sounded in my head.

She grins at me from the mirror. "Like 'em? I just got 'em this mornin'."

My eyebrows disappear under my frizzy hair. "You've already been shopping this morning?"

She giggles. "Of course. This good-lookin' fella came into the club last night and treated me real well." She proceeds to hold up a stack of cash with a Cheshire cat–like grin. "Took me out to get these shoes. Wish all our patrons were so sweet."

It suddenly clicks into place that this girl is a stripper. I mean, who else would have a stack of ones the size of my fist. It also explains the glitter. "Well, you have excellent taste. Thanks again for the tampon, I really appreciate it."

"You're welcome, darlin'," she calls as I head back to the table.

Thankfully, my purse is still here, but it slipped down under the table, and I have to slide along the bench seat to reach it. Pulling it up, I eye the five-dollar bill that Dave put down for me and swap it with the one I intended to pay with myself. Maybe I can find a way to sneak it into his pocket or something. But amongst the bills on the table, there's a folded piece of paper.

Pulling it toward me, I open it up. It's covered in faded blue and black ink.

SEE BAND NAME ON A MARQUEE.

COMPLETE FIRST NATIONAL TOUR.

What is this? It's like some kind of list.

GET ASKED FOR AN AUTOGRAPH.

This one is struck through with a line, and my heart flutters in my chest like a wild bird at the sight of my name next to it.

"Holy shit," I whisper. Is this . . . ? This is Dave's list. Is this what he was looking at so intently when I came in this morning? My eyes flit over the things he's written. Most are music related, like 'Sell out tickets to a show.' I can't stop the smile that pulls the sides of my lips up. 'Be featured in a newspaper article.' Something *I* helped him complete. Actually, two of these items I've helped him complete.

But some others look like things he simply wants to do, like 'Try each city's signature dish' and 'Go skinny dipping.' I laugh at that one. Has this man never been skinny dipping before? My eyes catch on the last one: 'Hook up backstage.' Heat creeps up my neck all the way to the tips of my ears. Does this mean he hasn't hooked up with someone backstage? I remember the night we met. How he had twirled my hair around his finger. How he had so confidently flirted with me and made me feel like I was the only woman in the room.

If you were any other girl, I would've had my way with you that first night we met, then promptly ditched you.

At least I have the answer to one question: it hasn't all been in my head.

"Isabella!"

I look up to find Becks's head floating through the doors to the diner.

"I'm coming!" I quickly stash the list in my purse then walk toward the door. "Sorry," I say when I catch up. "I had a tampon emergency."

"Oh." She frowns. "Are you okay?"

"Fine, just tired and now . . . bloated."

"You and me both. You don't mind sharing a mattress with me in the van, do you? I need a nap."

I grip her around the waist and squeeze. "Only if I can be the big spoon."

Later that afternoon as we head back to San Francisco, I watch Dave's station wagon following along behind us on the highway in the side mirror for a while. I haven't found a time to return his list to him, or his money, and I'm ashamed to say that I've discretely opened it and read it through five times since we left Vegas—one entry sticking out in my mind the most. The one at the very bottom of the list.

PROVE THEM ALL WRONG.

I don't know who "them" is, but it does tell me more about who *Dave* is. That he has something to prove and people who didn't believe in him. I hope he knows I'm not one of those people. When he goes out on tour, he'll be able to do so many of these things and prove to himself *and* everyone else that he made it. And even though I know it's not meant to be between us, I hope while he's out there being a wicked cool rockstar, that he thinks of me. That I cross his mind once in a while. If he does, then maybe I won't feel so stupid for thinking of him.

CHAPTER 20

In League with Satan

ISABELLA

"So, how does it feel to be a married woman?" I ask Becks while we sit and eat our lunch in the cafeteria. It's the first time I've seen or spoken to her since they dropped me off last week.

"Honestly? It doesn't feel much different," she confesses. "I was brought up to believe that marriage would solve all of my worries and make me feel fulfilled, but . . . I already felt that way."

I smile. "I'm jealous," I confess. "You and James—You both seem so happy."

"Well, what about you?" she asks and leans in closer to me, like we're sharing a secret. "Did anything happen between you and Dave? I thought maybe . . ."

Part of me wants to confess everything. The way we confided in each other on the ride there, how he freaked out when I got too comfortable. How he acted like a total jealous asshole but most of all, I want to gush about how he took care of me, then told me it'll never work out between us. But I don't. Something tells me Becks would understand, and I would be mortified if she went home to chastise Dave about the choices he made for his life because of me. The list he wrote burns a hole through my pocket and I'm ashamed to admit that even though a few opportunities presented themselves to return it to him . . . I kept it anyway. I guess I just had a harder time letting go of the small, secret part of him I discovered than I thought I would. It doesn't change the fact that Dave Noblar is a man who knows what he wants, and the best thing I can do now is move on.

"No," I say. "I mean, nothing romantic," I continue. "I got pretty drunk and he took care of me, made sure I was safe, but . . ." The memory of his hand on my waist makes my stomach clench. "No. Nothing happened."

Becks huffs. "Did you tell him you like him? Or, I don't know, make a move?"

Shaking my head, I take a sip of my coffee. "No, but I'm pretty sure it wouldn't work out anyway."

"Why not?"

I shrug. "I think he wants to live that rockstar player life. Dating me would really cramp his style." She laughs, and I blink at her strange reaction. "What?"

"Dave is hardly living his best rockstar life," she says.

My brow furrows. "What do you mean?"

"I mean, sure he was sleeping around a lot when we first got here, but the last couple months? It's been less and less . . . in fact, I don't think I can remember the last time he brought a girl home. Certainly not since the EP was released."

My heart picks up to a steady gallop.

"James even thought maybe he secretly met someone, but apparently not."

Dave hasn't brought a girl home since . . . No, don't read into this. Becks is naive, maybe she just hasn't noticed or maybe he's been hooking up backstage like he wants.

"Dave—He's a fairly secretive guy," Becks continues. "He doesn't drink. He thinks no one knows but . . . I noticed he only ever drinks Clausthaler beer. I haven't brought it up—" She suddenly turns to me like she just spilled a huge secret. "Oh! I shouldn't have—please don't mention it, okay?"

I shake my head. "No, of course I won't."

She takes a deep breath and sighs. "Thanks. I don't know *why* he doesn't but . . . he obviously doesn't want people to know."

"I'm sure he has his reasons. Oh," I say, remembering, "by the way, I took some pictures of the wedding. I'll make you copies once I can find a place to get them developed."

She frowns. "I thought you used the darkroom at the newspaper office."

Shit.

"Uhh . . . well, Randall said he doesn't want us using it for our own personal stuff anymore."

"Bummer, but that's fine. Can't wait to see them, though. You take the best photos."

MY APARTMENT DOOR is a welcome sight after I finish my last exam. My hand is cramped from so much writing but it's over, and I very much plan to get into my coziest pajamas, pour myself a cup of tea, and crawl into bed with one of the many books I've been neglecting stacked in the corner of my room. But when I get inside, the red light on my answering machine is blinking.

Randall's voice crackles to life when I press play on the tape. "Rodriguez. I need you to come by the office as soon as humanly possible. It's important. Don't make me walk all the way across campus to bang on your door."

What the hell could Randall possibly want from me? Maybe he's pissed at my abrupt exit. Maybe he was expecting a new crossword for this week's paper then suddenly, when there wasn't one to be had, he realized I was gone. I shake my head and check the time. It's only four thirty and it's a Thursday. Randall will definitely still be at the office. Maybe if he's in a good mood I could even persuade him to let me develop Becks's wedding pictures. Grabbing my bag, I walk across campus, the sunlight disappearing behind the buildings as I wrap my jacket around myself to keep the chill away.

When I finally reach the double glass doors, it seems empty, but just like I knew it would be, there's a light on in Randall's office. The doors are locked, but I knock loudly, hoping he'll hear me. After a few minutes, he appears. First he looks annoyed at having been disturbed, but his expression softens when he sees me, and he jogs over to let me in.

"Miss Rodriguez," he says unlocking the door. "You got my message?"

"Yes."

"Please, come in." He steps back and lets me into the office, relocking the door behind me. He gestures toward his office and I follow along behind him. "I wasn't sure I'd hear from you," he admits, sitting back down at his desk, which as usual is covered in piles of spreads. "After you left, I—" He looks up at me sheepishly. Like he knows that what happened to me was shitty and he did nothing to stop it. "Well, I just have to say that I hope what happened doesn't deter you from pursuing a career in journalism. Out of everyone in the program, you show the most promise, and I'm sorry it took me so long to recognize that."

This is surprising. "I . . . well, thank you." When I received his message, the matter sounded urgent, not him needing to clear his guilty conscience. "To be honest though, with no internship prospects for after the holidays, I don't think I'll get very far."

His lips part. "None?"

I shrug and sit down across from him. "Well, then maybe your luck is changing because someone called our office trying to locate you."

I freeze.

Randall holds up a piece of paper. "A mister Lewis. He said he wanted to know how to get in touch with the woman who wrote the Carnal Sins articles in the school paper. I didn't exactly feel comfortable giving out your number or address, so I told him I would find a way to pass along the message and that you would call him."

This keeps getting more and more surprising. "Lewis, you said?"

He hands me the slip of paper where the name Harold Lewis is written in Randall's messy scrawl, along with a phone number. "Did he say why? You don't think it has to do with the *Chronicle*, do you?"

Randall shrugs. "I honestly don't know. He just said it was important you call as soon as possible."

"Right. Well, thank you for this. And, for the record, I'm sorry for just up and quitting. That wasn't really very professional of me."

He shakes his head and smiles. "Honestly? I would've had the same reaction. Actually . . ." He stops himself. "That's not true. I would've punched the fucker in the face a few times first."

I smile at that. "That's something I'd like to see."

"Isabella," he says, leaning forward. "If there's anything you need. References, letters of recommendation, you name it—"

"Thank you, I really—actually . . ." I turn to my bag and the rolls of undeveloped film. "Do you think I could use the darkroom to develop some pictures? My friend got married and, well . . ."

He smiles. "Sure. I'll be here for another hour at least. But"— he reaches into his desk drawer and pulls out a key—"if you need to stay later, just lock up behind you and drop the key off before the holidays."

"Thanks."

Tucking the note with Mister Lewis's phone number into the outer pocket of my purse, I head down the hallway toward the back of the office. As I pass my old desk, I'm pleasantly surprised to see it hasn't been filled by someone else. Although it's more likely that they haven't had need of it yet, part of me wishes it's because they couldn't bear to replace me so quickly.

Turning on the red lamps, I shut the door, then the blackout curtain. I grab the film from my purse and place it in the enlarger, methodically working my way through the roll of pictures I took in Las Vegas. Becks and James look so happy and she looks so beautiful in her feathered coat and silver heels. Considering the amount of pictures I took, there's hardly any of Dave except for the group photo that James's aunt took of the six of us.

I watch as the picture develops in the solution, the photo paper coming to life as it gently floats in the tray. Once it's finished, I hold it up and hang it to dry on the line but stop. I'm surprised at how genuinely I'm smiling in this photo. I think Noreen had told us all to yell sex instead of cheese as she took it, which promptly caused me to burst out laughing. Everyone looks happy, like they're having the time of their lives. Except Dave.

He's at the opposite end of the group and while he's smiling, it's different than the rest of ours. At this point in the night I had been too annoyed with Dave to look at him, but it appears he was looking at me. Smiling at me. Like the only thing he can see is *me*.

I don't think I can remember the last time he brought a girl home. Certainly not since the EP was released.

Was Becks telling the truth? Has Dave not been hooking up with anyone recently? If that's so, what's the reason? Surely it can't be because of me. He told me two weeks ago that the life he wants doesn't include getting into a relationship with me. Because he wants to fuck around with no strings attached. But he's . . . not.

I blow a long breath out of my mouth, the breeze ruffling my fringe. No, Becks must be wrong. Maybe he's just been more discreet about it.

"I'm surprised you came back."

I jump and spin around, the developer solution tray nearly toppling over as my eyes focus on Simon standing across from me.

"What are you doing here?" I bite out.

Simons smirks and takes a step toward me. When I step back, he stops and puts his hands behind his back. "Little Bella, I work here. You, on the other hand, do not."

I narrow my eyes and clear my throat. "That may be, but I have permission from Randall to be in here."

"Is that so?"

"Yes."

"Is he aware that you use the school newspaper darkroom as your own personal print service?" he asks.

Taking a deep breath, I turn toward the photos hanging from the line and begin to pull them down, placing them in a pile to take home with me. "I don't need to explain myself to you, besides it's not like you're unfamiliar with breaking the rules."

Before I can turn, he steps right up behind me so his sour breath is in my ear.

"I'll break any rule to get what I want, Bella," he whispers, his fingertips grasping onto my hip tightly.

I shove off his hand and spin around, pushing into his chest with the limited strength I have. "Don't touch me again or I'll make sure you lose that arm." There's heat waves coming off my forehead and I'm sure I look like a raccoon with how furious I am that this prick thinks he can touch me. But all he does is smirk.

"Ah, now *there's* my little hot tamale," he goads.

"Stay away from me, Simon," I spit. "Or maybe I'll give the *Chronicle* a call about what inspired their new intern to write about an unknown metal band."

The smirk falls from his face.

"You may think you've won, but all I have to do is make one phone call. I doubt the *East Bay Chronicle* wants someone on their staff who is a liar and a thief."

He stares at me, his lips turned down into an unappealing frown, so I take my opportunity to move around him for the exit.

"Did you take the film out of the enlarger?" he asks.

I stop and turn around, my eyes locking past his shoulder where I did in fact forget to remove the film. Dropping my bag to the floor, I move past him to take it out and put the film back in the roll while he silently watches me.

"Seems like you have a bad habit of that," he says quietly.

I work as quickly as I can so I can get the fuck out of here. "My only bad habit, Simon, is allowing you to walk away from me repeatedly with that pathetic dick still intact between your legs."

Again, I turn and walk for the door.

"Then how is it that I managed to make a copy of a certain photo of you?"

I freeze, the blood in my veins turning to ice, and as I look over my shoulder at him, I can sense the smugness radiating out of him like an x-ray.

"You're quite forgetful, but that works out for me as a nice insurance policy," he says, that self-assured smirk pulled tighter across his face.

"Wh—what photo?"

Dread like a boulder settles in my stomach as I watch Simon pull a photograph out of his pocket and turn it toward me. All the breath in my lungs evaporates as my own eyes stare back at me. The autograph on my shoulder, my bare skin, my thong . . .

"You," I whisper. There's no air to get the words out.

"I always knew you had a great ass, Bella. Never dreamed it would be this delectable though—"

I grab for the photo but he raises it over his head and out of my reach.

"Give it to me now," I grit out, my chest pulsing erratically.

"Ooh, I like it when you beg," he whispers, leaning his face closer to mine.

The anger is too much and it has nowhere to go but down my arm and through my fingers as I slap Simon sharply across the face. I want to do more. I want to scratch out his eyes and tear his tongue from his throat. I want to hurt him, but all I can do is seethe like a snarling bull stuck behind an iron gate as my hand throbs.

Surprisingly, he doesn't react much other than flexing his jaw before he hands me the photo. I eye it apprehensively for a moment, then snatch it from his grasp with my sore hand.

"A thank-you would be nice," Simon says.

"Go to hell."

"Now, now, Bella, play nice. Remember I still have the film. I can make a hundred copies if I want."

Shit, I forgot about that. It's as if the fight whooshes out of me and tears sting the backs of my eyes. "What do you want, Simon?"

"For now? Nothing. You just keep your pretty mouth shut about our misunderstanding," he says. "And I promise that film will never see the light of day."

"You're blackmailing me?"

He shrugs.

"How can I possibly trust you?"

"You can't. You never could. But, trust *me* when I say, I enjoy having this image of you all to myself. It wouldn't be as special if everyone had access to it."

I sneer at him. "You're disgusting."

He steps toward me, invading my space once again with my bright red handprint glowing on his cheek. "I have to know though," he says, pushing the hair back over my shoulder. My muscles tense but I can't bring myself to move. "Are you fucking the whole band or just the drummer?"

I suck in a breath and raise my hand to slap him again, but he grabs my wrist.

"Uh uh. You don't want me to change my mind about sharing this, do you?"

My feet unstick from the floor and I run from the darkroom. Again, I'm running. I don't know anything else. The cold night air burns in my lungs until I collapse on a bench by the buses.

I'm so stupid. How could I have been so careless? I took that picture so recklessly, then like an idiot left the film in the enlarger? Of course, out of everyone, Simon was the one who found it. Of course he was. When he stole my work, it was a simple he said/she said situation, and he's right. Other than Randall, I could likely never convince the others it was really mine and not his work all along. But now? He finally has the ammunition to pull the trigger.

To silence me for good.

Don't Stop Me Now

ISABELLA

Knock, knock, knock.

I look over at my door, my heavy eyes narrowed as I wonder who on earth it could possibly be. With my luck, it'll be Simon somehow, coming to make me feel even worse than I already do. Setting down my tub of cookie dough ice cream, I peel myself off my couch and pull my robe on over my pajamas that I've spent the last several days wallowing in.

Knock, knock, knock.

"I'm coming," I call out, my voice hoarse after not speaking to anyone for so long and eating nothing but ice cream and taquitos for three days. Unlocking the door, I pull it open to find Becks standing in the doorway. Her eyes widen as they focus on me, and I'm sure she's wondering where her friend went only to be replaced by this troll.

"Hey . . . ?" She says it like she's unsure.

"Hi," I reply, my head resting on the edge of the door.

For a moment we stare at each other until Becks smiles and asks, "Can I come in?"

I nod and step back for her. If I had the energy to care, I'd be embarrassed about the state of my room. How the dishes haven't

been done in a week, how it probably smells like sweat in here . .
. The size of my massive pile of laundry. Instead I go back and sit
back down on my couch to continue watching *The Golden Girls*.

Watching Becks out of the corner of my eye, I see her take in
her surroundings, then she sits down beside me, moving a dirty
plate out of her way onto the coffee table.

"Isabella," she says. "Are you okay?"

I laugh abruptly. "Me? Of course I'm okay. Just peachy."

"I—"

"Why are you here?" I ask.

She tilts her head and reaches for my hand. "I came by to
invite you over for Christmas dinner. But . . . I wish I'd come
sooner."

"How did you even find out where I live?"

"I stopped by the newspaper office a few times hoping I'd run
into you. But after not seeing you for a few days, I thought it was
strange since you're always there. So I asked someone if they
knew where you might be and they said you'd quit."

I sigh.

"Is that true? You quit the paper?"

"Becks," I say, pulling my legs underneath me. "I don't want
to talk about that."

"Well . . . we are," she says, taking on a tone of stubbornness,
albeit a weak one. "What is going on with you? You love the
paper and you quit? Weeks ago, without telling anyone? I thought
we were friends. Then I find you like this with . . . Is that nacho
cheese in your hair?"

I grasp at my head, feeling some kind of sticky substance over
my ear. Then, as if it's been trying to burst out of me for days, I
confess everything to her. Or at least what happened leading up to
me quitting the paper. How I was finally being taken seriously.
How Simon had shown up at the EP release party, stolen my
work, and then weaseled his way into an amazing internship. She

listens intently as I spill my guts, squeezing my hand when I need it the most.

"Isabella, that's— You should've told me. You've been living with this all on your own with no one to talk to about it?"

Dave knew. I could talk to Dave. He always tried to make me feel better. "I'm sorry," I whisper.

She shakes her head. "No . . . don't be sorry. Just remember that I'm here, okay? You can talk to me."

"Okay."

"Now," she says sternly, "I want you to go have a nice long shower. Then we'll tidy this place up."

BECKS MUST BE SENT STRAIGHT from heaven, because after an excessively long and much-needed shower, I come out to an almost entirely clean apartment.

"You didn't have to do all this," I say, wrapping my arms around her.

She shrugs. "Oh, I don't mind. And don't think it's an inconvenience. Sometimes we have to rely on our friends."

"Thank you."

Becks helps me change my bedsheets, put on a load of laundry down the hall, then the two of us fall back onto my newly clutter-free sofa.

"So," Becks says. "I found this phone number on the floor for a . . . Harold Lewis?"

Crap. I completely forgot about that.

"Who's Mister Lewis?" Becks asks teasingly. "Some hot guy? Please don't tell me he's a professor."

"No, no, he's— He called the newspaper office looking for me. Randall gave me his number and told me to call him."

"What about?"

"Randall said he was looking for the girl who wrote the Carnal Sins articles," I say, taking the slip of paper.

"Really? Why?"

"I have no idea."

She jumps up out of her seat. "Well, come on! Let's call and see what Harold wants."

Before I can stop her, she's picking up my phone and holding it out for me. With half a smile, I dial the phone number. It rings and rings and I'm about to hang up when finally, someone answers.

"Harold Lewis speaking."

But my throat is suddenly constricted, and I can't force the words past my tongue.

"Hello?"

Oh no. I can't speak.

"Hello? I swear to god, if this is Theresa again, I told you to send the papers to my lawyer—"

"Mister Lewis?" I finally blurt out.

There's a pause. "Yes . . . ?"

Becks waves at me frantically. "Hi, sorry, my name is Isabella Rodriguez. I got your number from my editor at the Stoneman Press. He said you were looking to get in touch with me."

"Ah, Miss Rodriguez, thank you for finally getting back to me. I'll be honest, I'd given up hope that I'd hear from you."

"I apologize for not getting back to you sooner."

"I'm glad I've got you now. I'm Harold Lewis with *Earworm Magazine*."

"*Earworm Magazine*?" I ask.

He chuckles. "Don't worry, I won't be offended if you've never heard of it."

"I'm sorry. I haven't."

"Listen, I'll be perfectly honest with you, Miss Rodriguez,

you've probably never heard of our magazine before because, well, it's struggling to survive."

"Oh?"

"Our publication is old and unfortunately stuck in the past. I can't get any new subscribers, and the promising young journalists that come on all ditch me at the last minute."

"That's . . . I'm sorry. That sounds hard."

He sighs. "I know we're no one's first pick, but I loved your articles in the *Stoneman Press*."

"Really? I didn't think anyone but college students were reading them."

"I'm trying to build up a younger audience for *Earworm*, and where better to find talent than a college paper. Both musician-wise and journalist."

"Makes sense."

"Is that what you want? To be a journalist?" he asks.

My heart is pounding so hard in my chest I wonder if he can hear it through the phone. "Yes, I do. More than anything."

"Well, I'll cut to the chase then, Miss Rodriguez. I've read the articles you wrote about Carnal Sins and I have to say, you have a real knack for talent coverage."

Shivers break out across my arms and there's a pinching in my cheeks. Am I *smiling*? "Really? Thank you, sir."

"I wanted to discuss an internship opportunity with you."

"Are you serious?"

"Yes, very serious. What do you say?"

"I would be thrilled for any opportunity to work with *Earworm Magazine*."

Like he's been holding his breath waiting for my answer, I hear him sigh. "That's wonderful. Well, I happen to know that Carnal Sins are going out on their first tour in the new year and I'm looking for a journalist who can tour with them and chronicle their experience as new and up-and-coming stars."

My knees buckle beneath me. An internship. A real one. Albeit for a small magazine, but this could be huge. He's asking me to write about Carnal Sins. He's asking me to *tour* with Carnal Sins. Becks mouths something to me, but she's out of focus.

"I—You . . . I'm not sure I understand," I whisper.

"It's obvious you have a connection to the band. They've opened up to you, connected with you. As a journalist I'm sure you know how important that is. We'd put together a feature in the magazine based on what you submit. I think it would really help to pull in young readers. Build up our audience again. I heard you take your own photos as well."

"Ye—yes, I do."

"I'm afraid we can't provide much for expenses but perhaps if you only join them for the last few weeks of the tour, we could at least cover some accommodation costs," he continues.

I don't even know what to say. If Becks wasn't pinching my arm, I would think I'm having the most wonderful dream but . . . how did this even happen? There's no way a magazine editor, even a failing one, reads a school newspaper.

"I'm sorry, Mister Lewis, but . . . I have to ask. Why me? I mean, surely you don't expect me to believe that you read my college paper for fun and stumbled on my articles."

He laughs. "See, I knew you'd be sharp. You're right. Your articles were pointed out to me by the band's manager. We go way back."

Al sent my articles to *Earworm Magazine*?

"And I'm sure you must have dozens of other more experienced staff far more qualified to write this feature than me —"

"I don't," he interrupts. "My journalists are dropping like flies. I don't know why. Perhaps because, unlike me, they see the writing on the wall. That the magazine is one bad print away from tanking. So, this is my last-ditch effort to save it. Will you help me? I realize it's probably not as appealing as some of your other offers—"

I bite my lip. Why am I arguing with a man trying to give me potentially the biggest break of my career? Deep down, I know why. Because it means I'll be following Dave for a few weeks. Following him and his band while they finish out their first real tour. Watch as he flirts with women while he lives his bachelor lifestyle. And I'll never get the distance I need to get over my crush.

But I also need an internship, and even if the magazine folds, it's something when I have nothing. That dream I've had for so many years hasn't quite extinguished yet.

"Okay, Mister Lewis, I'm in."

CHAPTER 22

Take My Breath Away

"**H**ow the fuck do you check if this thing is cooked all the way through?"

Joel and James look at me from across the counter, all with expressions of utter confusion as I hover over a steaming turkey.

"How the hell do I know?" Joel shrugs, reaching forward to poke it.

I slap the top of his hand. "No, don't touch it! Who knows where your hand has been."

"Yeah, that's fair," Joel says, tucking his hand back in his pocket.

"Do we just cut into it?" I ask.

James shakes his head. "No way, Becks will kill me if we make a hack job of this turkey."

"Where the hell is she anyway?" I ask.

"She said she had to get some last-minute things for tomorrow," James says.

"Just take its temperature."

We all turn to stare as Key walks up to us from the hallway.

"What the hell are you talking about?" I ask.

He rolls his eyes and walks away.

"Key!" I call after him.

"Now what?" Joel asks.

"Well, maybe we just turn the oven down and keep it in there until Becks gets back," James suggests.

"I got it!" Key says, running back into the kitchen with a thermometer, sticking it under the tap, and washing it with soap and water.

"You've got to be kidding me," Joel mutters. "You were serious?"

"Yeah, you've got to make sure the internal temperature is right."

He sticks the end of the thermometer into the turkey, all of us standing wide-eyed and concerned for his sanity.

"There," he says, removing the thermometer. "One hundred and sixty-six degrees. Perfect. Leave it on the counter to rest." He looks up at the three of us not trying to hide our shocked expressions. "What?"

"Where the hell did you learn that?" James asks, crossing his arms.

"The army." Key shrugs, taking the thermometer and cleaning it off.

Joel scoffs. "I was in the army too, fuck nut, and I never learned that shit."

"Maybe you would've if you ever followed orders long enough to get kitchen duty."

"Meh, I'm a loose cannon. Always have been, always will be."

With the turkey taken care of, and the list of other tasks Becks left for us to do completed, I sit down at one of the stools and sigh. I haven't had a proper Christmas in years, and it warms something deep in my heart to be having a real celebration with my new family. I even went out of my way to buy a small Christmas tree for the living room. We don't have any ornaments on it, but I did manage to find some lights so it glows prettily in the corner.

The front door opens, and a cold breeze blows through as Becks walks in with several bags and . . .

"Isabella!" Key says, weaving around the kitchen counter and wrapping his arms around the shivering brunette.

My insides squirm at the sight of her nuzzling into his neck and I have to actively stop the frown that threatens to grow across my face. I promised her I could do this. Promised I wouldn't act like some jealous caveman. That's not fair. I told her I don't want a relationship, but it's been a few weeks and how could I have forgotten how pretty those eyes are—that mouth . . .

I stand and make my way over, sure that it would seem weirder to ignore her than to hug her in what is a normal holiday greeting.

"Hey," I say, her body folding into mine. The smell of her hair hits me as her head tucks in under my chin. The scent of vanilla and just . . . her.

"Hi," she says, and her arms take a beat too long to let go, but so do mine.

"I didn't know you were coming," I admit, feeling uncomfortable I didn't get her a Christmas present.

She tucks her hair behind her ears. "Becks invited me at the last minute. Is that okay?"

Her expression is nervous. Perhaps she's thinking that because of our last conversation, I might not want her here. But I do. I've thought about her every day since Vegas. I've thought about the way she danced like she had no cares in the world on that dance floor. I've thought about the way her brown eyes flared when she talked back to me. I've thought about the way her hands touched me before I stopped her.

I'm the fucking idiot who told her I want to be just friends. *Friends*. I need to remember that's what we agreed to. And she accepted it so easily. Because of course she would, she's cool. She's chill. And I'm just a distraction for her. Does she have a lot of other guys she uses as a distraction?

I nod. "Yeah, of course. I'm happy you're here."

"Me too," she says with a small smile. "Actually, I was . . . Can we talk for a minute? In private?"

A lump forms in my throat, but I nod and follow her out the back door and onto the patio. My brows furrow as I notice the way she paces, her feet shuffling their weight around. "Want a smoke?" I ask, knowing it's something that always helps me calm down.

I'm surprised when she nods. "Please."

Passing her my open pack, she pulls one out and I hold up my lighter for her. Her eyes look like two pieces of burning coal in the cherry of the cigarette and I follow along, lighting my own and inhaling deeply. She visibly relaxes in her shoulders, but she still continues to shift back and forth.

"So, what's on your mind?" I ask.

"I need to run something by you," she blurts out.

My eyes widen. What the hell could she possibly need to run by *me*?

"I had a call today with the editor of *Earworm Magazine*, Harold Lewis," she says, and takes a long drag of her cigarette.

Wait. *Earworm Magazine*? Isn't that . . . it's a music magazine, I think. "Really? What did he want?"

Her face twitches like she can hardly believe what she's about to say. "He wants . . ." She pauses and looks up at me nervously. "He wants me to write a feature for the magazine about Carnal Sins."

My mouth drops open. "Holy shit, really? That's—"

"He wants me to go on tour with you guys . . . follow and document your experience for the final three weeks of it."

"Well that's . . . that's . . . great." *Shit.* She'll be there, every city, every show, every moment for three weeks. My Disco Girl with a backstage pass. After what I told her in Vegas, she'll be expecting me to be partying, chasing after girls, doing whatever stupid thing I feel like, but how can I keep this up if all I feel like doing is talking to her?

Her face crumples. "I would've said no, but . . . it's the only internship I've been offered."

"What do you mean the only one?" I ask.

She stubs the toe of her shoe into the concrete and takes another drag of her cigarette. "All of my applications were rejected," she admits, her voice cracking on the last word.

My heart drops. "Shit. Isabella—"

"I hate feeling like a charity case, but . . . I really need this," she whispers. "And it came up out of the blue. I didn't even apply. In fact, I don't even think they have an internship program but—"

"It's fine." I say, interrupting her rambling.

She sighs. "It's not a problem?"

"I . . . no, it's not a problem. Why would it be a problem? This is great. And you'll be amazing."

She arches a brow, clearly not convinced. "Really? You'll be okay with my lame ass tagging along while you and the guys become superstars?"

I shrug and take a drag. "Yeah, of course. And this will be amazing for you too. You'll leave that fucking toe rag Samuel in the dust."

She grins. "You mean, Simon?"

"Yeah, that idiot. He'll choke when he finds out you're doing an internship covering a band on tour."

"Well, this could be big. But I wanted to check with you first.

After . . . well, after Vegas and what we talked about." Even in the darkness, I can see her cheeks flame. "I needed to make sure you would be okay with it."

"You thought I wouldn't want you to do it?" I ask.

She shrugs and takes the last drag of her cigarette before flicking it off into the darkness, her dark lips blowing out the smoke into the air between us. "I just want to make sure we'll be able to maintain being friends. We'll be around each other almost every day for a few weeks. I want to make sure you meant what you said. That it wasn't just some roundabout way to reject me. That you really want to be friends."

I finish my cigarette, flicking it off to join hers in the dark, and take a step toward her. "Of course. Isabella, you have to do this. And for the record," I say, my voice quieting. "I can't think of a better person for the job."

"Thank you, Dave," she whispers, then smiles. "I'll have to thank Al the next time I see him."

"Al?"

She nods. "Yeah, he was the one who sent Harold Lewis my articles. I owe all of this to him."

She slides open the door and heads back inside where the others are at the kitchen counter mixing up Christmas cocktails. Meanwhile, my stomach is in knots. I asked Al if he knew of anyone looking for an intern weeks ago after I found out what happened to Isabella. I didn't think he'd find her a job at *Earworm Magazine*. That the job would be to follow me on tour. Should I tell her? What kind of message would that send? That's crossing the friendship line, isn't it? Even if it wasn't, she might interpret it as meaning more than it does.

The truth is I do want her to know. I'm just terrified of what that might mean. That she'll realize how much I do care for her. That I'm scared of how it seems to consume me more and more, every day.

Shaking my head, I turn against the cold wind and head back inside to find Isabella taking a mug of hot chocolate.

"So, guys," she says, wrapping her hands around the cup. "I have some news."

CHAPTER 23

Five Years Ago

DAVE

Loading the last few things into the van, excitement is coursing through me so much I'm almost vibrating. It's finally here. The day I worked all those extra hours to make back the money that went missing from Sam is finally here. It's demo recording day, and the first step toward actually making it.

I still haven't confronted Emily about it. I think part of me isn't ready to accept that it might be true. Also, I don't know what it means for us if she did do it. I love her and I want to help her, but if she stole money and lied about her job, I don't know if I can look past that.

"I think that's the last of it," Sam says as he closes the van doors. "Ready to go make a demo?" he asks with a wide grin.

"Fuck yes." Charlie claps his hands together.

"Dave, you ready?" Sam asks.

I grin. "Yeah, man. Oh, wait, let me just grab my spare drumsticks. They're inside."

I head inside the house and look through the living room. Locating my spare sticks, I tuck them into my back pocket and head back toward the garage. Just before I reach the door, the phone on the kitchen wall rings. I stop and stare at it for a long moment. Normally I wouldn't answer someone else's phone, and I certainly wouldn't answer the phone when I'm headed out the door. But something about this phone call—this one time—makes me double back and pick up the receiver.

"Hello?"

"Hey, Sam?"

"Oh, no, sorry, it's Dave."

"Dave, good. This would be harder if it was Sam."

My forehead creases. "Wait . . . Tyler?"

"You need to come to the diner."

"What? Why?"

"It's Emily."

My stomach drops like a lead balloon. "What—what about Emily?"

"Dave, she's wasted. She stumbled in here and started shouting at everyone. She said she was here for her shift, like, dude, she doesn't even remember she was fired."

I fall back against the kitchen wall and close my eyes. "Fuck, man . . ."

"The girls got her sitting in a booth with some coffee, but she's starting to get agitated again."

"Yeah, I'll . . . I'll be right there."

I hang up the phone and head back out to the garage, grabbing my keys off the counter before heading for my station wagon.

"Hey, Dave, where the fuck are you going man?" Sam calls from the van.

Shit.

"Uh . . . my dad just needs me to pick up a prescription for him. I'll just swing by the house and I'll meet you guys there, okay?"

"You can't do that later?" Sam asks.

I drum my fingers on the top of the car door. I should tell

Sam. She's his cousin. But what if I do and he cancels out on making the demo to take care of her?

Fuck.

I'll tell him later. I'll bring her back here, go do the recording, then tell him everything when we get back. "No, the pharmacy will be closed by then. I promise, I'll be right behind you."

"Yeah, okay," Sam says, a hint of distrust in his tone.

Throwing myself into the car, I peel off down the street. Fuck, fuck, *fuck*. Of all the fucking days.

Thankfully, the diner isn't far, and when I pull into the parking lot, I can already hear the chaos from inside, glass shattering and voices shouting. I race up the steps and run inside to find Emily sitting on the floor in the corner of the diner, the shattered remnants and puddle of dark brown liquid surrounding her like a debris field.

"Em?"

She turns to face me, but her eyes are unfocused and swollen. "Davey! Baby, you have to help me," she says, attempting to stand, but she slips on the spilled coffee. I rush over, my arms scooping under her to try to help her up, aware that every eye in the diner is on the two of us.

"Come on. I'm going to take you home."

"I'm not going home!" she yells, pushing me away. I lose my grip on her and she stumbles back against the counter. "These assholes are trying to keep me from doing my job."

"Baby," I say, approaching her like one would a frightened deer. "No one's trying to keep you from doing your job . . . You don't work here anymore."

She scoffs. "What are you talking about?"

"You got fired. Remember?"

Her eyes seem to focus on me for a moment. Then I see the moment she understands the mess she's made. The way everyone is watching her and waiting for her to attack. "I . . . no. No, that's not true, I—"

"Em, it *is* true. Just let me take you home, okay?"

Tears fill her eyes as she looks around and takes in the terrified faces of what used to be her friends—her coworkers.

"Come on," I say, edging toward her slowly. "Let's go. I'll put on *The Blue Lagoon* and you can rest on the couch."

She nods, tears running down her face. "I love that movie," she whispers.

"I know." She looks right at me as I reach for her hand, and for a moment I recognize the girl I met that first day in Sam's garage. How did we get here? How did things get so bad so quickly? "Come on, Em, you're scaring everyone."

My hand touches hers, and it's as if a light goes out. Her eyes squint and her face contorts in anger, her arms thrashing out at me and her nails scratching my arms and face. "No! Let go of me! Help!" she screams. "Someone help me!"

I try to subdue her, to protect myself while also trying to get her outside. I'm vaguely aware of Tyler shouting that the cops are pulling up. Emily's hand slaps me across the face, her nails scraping my cheek.

"Help, he's hurting me!"

In a flash, I'm being pinned to the ground. I grunt as a knee lands on my back, metal cuffs clicking into place against my skin. Emily cowers in the corner watching an officer haul me to my feet, and utter betrayal rips apart my heart.

"He has to control everything I do," I hear her, but the sound is hollow, like I'm hearing it from somewhere under water. "He hits me. I'm scared to go home with him."

"Wait! Officer, that's not—" Tyler shouts over the commotion.

But the officer elbows me hard in the ribs so I double over. "Don't worry, m'am. We'll take care of him for you."

"No, officer. You don't understand—"

"Shut up!" he yells. "Whatever you say can and will be used against you in a court of law."

A few of the other waitresses try to speak up, but this asshole isn't listening.

"You kids with your violent music," he spits as I'm dragged outside and shoved into the back of a police cruiser. "Think you're so tough with your leather and chains." He pushes me into the back of the car and stares at my face, where Emily's scratch marks burn against my cheek.

"You fucking coward. Is that how you get your kicks? Beating the shit out of your girlfriend?"

I say nothing, knowing better than to talk without a lawyer, but it does nothing to stitch together the remnants of my heart. Like that shattered coffee cup, it's scattered in jagged pieces across the floor.

CHAPTER 24

Dancing in the Dark

ISABELLA

All the worries I had about Christmas with Becks and the guys vanished hours ago. My heart swells at the way they all so effortlessly include me. Even Dave, making good on his promise that we can be just friends. Twenty-four hours ago, I was sure I'd be spending the holidays alone in my sad little apartment with a giant bowl of peppermint bark and telenovelas on in the background.

But we've laughed, played games, and talked for hours in the glow of the twinkling lights strung around the Christmas tree. All we need is some glittering snow to fall, but that's wishful thinking for California. When Becks starts to yawn sometime after midnight, she and James quietly slip away, but not before she brings me a pillow and some blankets for the couch.

"Are you sure you don't want one of our beds?" Joel asks. "I don't mind sleeping out here. Maybe I'll see Santa." He chuckles.

"No, I'm happy to sleep on the couch. I can't kick you out of your own beds on Christmas."

"I'm okay with sharing," Joel says, wiggling his eyebrows suggestively.

I grin, but a loud scrape of a chair leg moving across the floor makes it disappear. Dave stands and heads for his bedroom without looking back.

"You're not even going to say good night?" Key asks after him.

Dave waves over his head then disappears, his door clicking shut behind him.

Joel scoffs. "He's such a moody bastard lately." He stands and stretches. "Last chance to steal my bed."

My eyes flick to where Dave disappeared. "I promise, I'm okay out here. Besides, I have this to keep me warm," I say, gesturing to the gas fire warming the large open space.

"Right, well, good night then," says Joel, picking up his glass and patting Key on the back.

Then it's just Key and me left. "I'm going to sleep too," he says. "I just wanted to say that we're all glad you're here."

"Really?"

"Yeah. And not just today. You've done so much for us . . . for Becks . . . and with you agreeing to come on tour, it's going to be great. I just wanted you to know how much all of that means to us."

"Thanks, Key. It means a lot to me too."

He smiles softly, then stands and disappears down the hallway. Then it's just me with the lights of the tree, the sound of the wind blowing outside, and the whooshing noise of the gas fire. Taking a deep breath, I stand and get the couch ready for sleeping on before grabbing my bag and heading for the bathroom.

Teeth brushed, I slide under the covers of my makeshift bed and reach for the wrapped package in my bag. My fingers brush along the snowman-covered paper. It's not much, but it's something. I place the little box under the Christmas tree with the handful of other gifts already there, then climb into bed.

Two hours later, I'm still awake. What had at first been soothing white noise from the wind outside has turned into a full-blown howl. And the fireplace, when left on for too long, makes me sweat, but then it's too cold out here when it's off, forcing me to continually switch between the covers on or off of me. Another sleepless half hour, and I get off the couch and head to the kitchen for a glass of water. After filling a glass, I hop up and sit on the cool counters.

The kitchen light flickers on, and my eyes clamp shut against the brightness.

"Oh, shit, sorry. I didn't know anyone was in here." The lights go off again and when I open my eyes, white spots dance in my vision as the silhouette of Dave walks toward me.

"I was just getting a drink."

"Me too," he says, opening the cupboard across from me and getting his own glass. "Didn't mean to blind you."

As my eyes adjust back to the darkness, I begin to see Dave a little more clearly. Thankfully, he's not just in his boxers like last time. He's wearing a pair of sweatpants and a T-shirt with the sleeves cut off, and he looks *good*. Outrageously good.

"Can't sleep?"

"Hmm?" I ask, blinking a few times.

He smiles and takes a sip of his water. "Is that why you're up at three in the morning? You can't sleep?"

"No, I can't."

"Me neither."

"Christmas excitement?" I ask.

He laughs through his nose. "Hardly." He walks over to lean against the counter next to me. "Not much for me under that tree, not that I really need anything. Christmas was never really a big deal at my house growing up. I wasn't like Joel and Key, who waited up all night for Santa. My dad told me flat out when I was five that Santa was bullshit and since that moment, I guess, he figured since I knew Santa wouldn't come, he didn't have to bother doing anything."

My chest aches. "Dave, that's so sad."

"Anyway, it's been a while since I've actually had fun at Christmas, but I'm not sleepless because of it."

"Why can't you sleep then?" I ask.

He shrugs and takes another sip of water. "Probably because I feel guilty that, out of all people, Joel offered you a bed before I did."

I look away, grateful for the shadows that hide my hot cheeks. "You don't need to feel guilty about that. I'm perfectly happy with the couch—"

"I can't sleep with you out here on the couch and not in my bed."

I set my glass down, watch the ring of liquid pool on the countertop. "Dave . . ." I sigh. "You can't say things like that."

He chugs the rest of his water and groans. "I know." He leans back against the counter, hand next to mine, and my skin tingles at the heat of him so close. It burns like reaching toward an open flame, then his pinky makes contact with mine and I inhale a deep breath as goosebumps sprout over every inch of my body.

He turns to me in the dark. I can feel him watching me as his fingers crawl over mine to take my hand. My body is electric, an intense energy flooding through my veins at his touch, his gaze, his everything. I keep my eyes forward. I know if I look at him right now, I won't be able to control myself. I'll simply throw caution to the wind and climb him like a tree. I squeeze my thighs together and I know he sees it—I can hear him swallow next to me as his hand twitches and tightens over mine.

I can't be your boyfriend, I can't be someone who falls in love with you.

The words he spoke in Las Vegas rush back to the forefront of my memory. Slowly, I slide my hand out from under his and hide it in my lap. Next to me, he lets out a long breath.

"So . . . are you excited about going on tour?" I ask, grateful my voice is moderately steady.

I chance a look at him, and he grins. "Yeah, it's still a little hard to wrap my head around. All of it is, I mean. But, it's literally a dream come true. I feel incredibly lucky. I can't wait to get on the road and meet other bands and the fans. Play music almost every day . . ."

"It's going to be great."

"And you'll be there too," he adds. "Documenting everything." Even in the dim light I can see him grin widely. "I mean, that's a hell of an opportunity for you too."

"It is. Sometimes I feel like . . . Like I don't deserve it," I admit.

"What?"

"I just mean I'm . . . me. Surely there are other people far more qualified. I just got lucky." I pull my lip between my teeth, feeling a little lighter having voiced how I really feel.

"You didn't just get lucky," Dave says, bumping my shoulder with his. "You deserve every good thing coming your way. Wait here," he says, bolting from the kitchen.

I open my mouth to call after him, but then remember it's three in the morning. I down the rest of my water and hop down off the counter to put my glass in the sink. A moment later, I hear footsteps and watch as Dave rounds the corner with a shoebox in his hands.

"What's that?" I ask as he takes off the lid.

"This is why you deserve this," Dave says, pulling pieces of paper out of the box. "This was the first article you published about us," he says, showing me a clipping from the *Stoneman Press*. "And these," he says, showing me a handful of ticket stubs, "are all the extra gigs we picked up because people read your article and wanted to see us perform."

My stomach flips.

"This," he continues, holding up a piece of yellow paper, "was our schedule from the studio that day you came to visit after we kept getting denied recording time. And this is the first royalty check I received because expected sales tripled with what you wrote."

"You kept all of this?" I whisper. "Why?"

"Because I don't want to forget anything. I don't want to wake up in twenty years and think I might have missed out on doing something I wanted. I guess it's a way of keeping track . . . like —"

"A list?"

His gaze finds mine, those blue eyes searing into me in the dark. I shouldn't have said that. Does he know I found his list? That I haven't had the courage to give it back to him? Has he made a new one since he realized he lost it?

"Yeah," he whispers. "Exactly. So, don't go thinking you don't deserve this, because you're just as integral to all of this as any of us."

His face is so sincere in that belief that I can't help but smile. He smiles back briefly, then looks away.

"Actually, I uh . . . got you something for Christmas," he says.

"You did?"

"Yeah. It's not much since it was last minute, but I— Maybe you can make better use of it than me while we're on tour."

He moves the shoebox and reveals a brown leather-bound journal. He holds it toward me and my fingers skim across the smooth cover, my heart beating frantically in my chest at his gesture. "Dave, I . . . don't know what to say."

His gaze on me is too intense, so I look down at the journal and open it to the first page.

"I thought you could make a list of the things you want to achieve. That way you'll always know you deserve your success."

This man . . . if it weren't for my bones keeping me upright, I'd be a puddle on the floor right now. "Thank you," I say breathlessly. "I umm . . . I actually have something for you too."

Now *he* looks surprised as I turn and head back toward the living room. I bend over and pick up the wrapped package from under the tree. When I turn around, he's standing behind me by my makeshift sofa bed. I take a few steps toward him to close the distance

"Here," I blurt out.

He takes my modestly wrapped box and unwraps it. Pulling the lid off, he looks up at me. "A tape?"

My skin flushes with heat. "It's a mixtape," I explain, stepping beside him to look at the cassette in the box. "Contrary to popular belief, I don't just listen to Disco music, so I made a mix of my favorite songs across all genres."

"You did?"

I shrug. "I thought, you know, a well-rounded music education is always beneficial, and you never know when inspiration will strike."

He grins. "That's true."

"Who knows? Maybe something on there will influence a song on your next album."

Picking up the cassette tape out of the box, he walks over to the stereo by the fireplace.

"What are you—"

Popping the cassette in, he adjusts the volume so it's quiet and the sound of "Baby I'm-A Want You" by Bread fills the room with its groovy, quiet melody. Dave looks over at me and I think I probably really am as red as Rudolph right now.

"I like it," Dave says, walking back to me.

"It's a classic." I smile.

"Why is it one of your favorites?"

I let go of a breathy laugh and wrap my arms around myself. "It was the first song I ever mustered up the courage to ask a boy to dance to."

"Hmm."

"It's silly, I know—"

"What did he say?"

"Oh . . . he—well, he said no . . ."

"Dance with me."

I blink. "What?"

He extends his hand. "Come on, it's Christmas."

This is a bad idea. It was hard enough to pull myself away in the kitchen when it was just his hand on mine. But in the light of the tree, his blue eyes are bright and sparkling as I step toward him and take his hand.

He closes the distance between us, his one hand grasping mine and the other gently weaving its way around my waist, pulling my hips against his. My face is close to his chest as I place my hand on his shoulder and he starts to move, the two of us swaying to the beat. He's warm, and I sink into him a little more as he adjusts his grip on my hand. His smell is overwhelming and my stomach lurches when his hand on my waist tightens. This feels so right, so easy that I can't help but sigh as I rest my forehead on his shoulder.

"What are you thinking?" he whispers in my ear as he lets go of my hand to wrap both of his arms around my waist.

I loop mine around his neck and look up at him. "I'm thinking about how glad I am that I took the advice of a girl I didn't know, and came out to see her boyfriend's band perform."

He chuckles. "I heard they were 'interesting.'"

This time, I laugh. "I stand by that statement."

"You were the most beautiful woman there that night."

My body tenses. Here he is again, crossing the line. Okay, maybe this entire night has crossed the line we drew, but this is so far over I can't even see it anymore. "Dave—"

"You're the most beautiful woman anywhere, any night," he blurts out.

We've stopped swaying now. My heart is running a marathon, and his words turn that twisting sensation in my belly to butterflies that flutter lower and lower. I bury my face in his neck. "See, this is exactly why I shouldn't be anywhere near your bed."

"You're right," he says, his teeth snagging on his bottom lip. "But honestly? There isn't a surface in this house I haven't imagined fucking you on."

My eyes widen on a gasp, and before I know what's happening, his mouth captures mine. The music fades into the background as his lips learn the shape of mine and, like a dam that finally breaks, I am flooded with every lustful and arousing thought I've kept contained since I met him. He tastes like peppermint as my tongue massages his, and my grip on his neck tightens when he pulls me against him. Skin tingling and heart hammering, a moan escapes from somewhere in my throat.

The kiss breaks and Dave pulls back, his blue eyes almost black as they dart over my face. "Izzy, I—"

My heart has whiplash. He just called me Izzy and he kissed me and he still hasn't let me go. This wasn't supposed to happen. "Dave, you— Friends aren't supposed to kiss like that."

He breathes out, eyes closing, and rests his forehead on mine. "I know . . . I'm sorry. I just—I had to know what it's like to kiss you."

"And . . ." I say slowly, "has your curiosity been satisfied?"

His hands grasp my face. "Fuck no."

He kisses me fiercely, one hand lingering to cup my cheek while his other moves to caress my nape. My hands trail down his hard, muscled chest as he wraps my hair around his wrist and tips my head back. His lips attack my jaw, then my neck, and I gasp again, grinding my hips against his as the ache that's been lingering between my thighs for months grows to near unbearable levels. I can feel him, feel how turned on he is too, and it makes me want to do something reckless.

He sucks on the pulse point below my ear and my knees turn to jelly. A long guttural groan vibrates in my ear as my palm brushes over the length of him.

"We should stop," he murmurs as his teeth tug on my earlobe.

I subtly shake my head. "I don't want to stop."

It's possible he stops breathing, and maybe so have I, because everything freezes. Like someone pressing pause on the VCR, the world halts in place as we silently make the decision. Maybe it's my loneliness that is making me wild for any intimacy I can get, or maybe it's that I hate myself just enough to want to live in the knowledge that this will never go further than physical between us. But I also can't go on not knowing what his body feels like against mine.

With more gentleness than I would've expected, he brushes my hair back from my forehead and looks right into my eyes. "Tell me what you want."

"I want you."

"Then fucking have me."

CHAPTER 25

Baby I'm-a Want You

DAVE

I lift her up, crushing her body against mine as she wraps her legs around my waist. Kissing her again, I revel in the taste of her. She tastes so goddamn sweet that I curse myself for not kissing her sooner. This is dangerous. I can't fall for her, and I try to remind myself it's purely physical, an itch that is in desperate need of scratching, and I need to make sure she's on the same page before this goes any further.

Her thighs squeeze my hips as I bury my hand in her hair, holding her to me as I walk us down the hallway toward my bedroom. Her lips never leave mine, and I'm grateful that I know my way well enough to do this without needing to see where I'm walking. The lamp on my dresser is still on when we enter, casting the whole room in a subtle reddish glow.

A gentle moan escapes Izzy's lips, and it makes my cock throb. She sucks on my bottom lip and I grip her tighter, my fingers pinching into her soft thighs. Whoever gave her the idea to wear shorts like that to bed should be given a medal. I never stood a chance. I close the door behind us then walk toward the mattress. I lay her on the sheets, my weight sinking down on top of her. A gasp leaps from my lips as my swollen cock nudges against the heat coming from between her legs.

Fuck.

"Izzy," I say, pulling away from her luscious mouth. I catch a glimpse of her, dark hair splayed out on the bed, chest heaving and her lips swollen and red. She's the most beautiful creature I've ever seen. "Are you sure this is what you want?"

She nods frantically. "Yes, just this time—I need you just this once."

Just this once. "One time," I agree. "To get it out of our systems."

"Then we'll go back to being friends," she whispers, gripping the neck of my shirt and pulling my face back to hers.

I nod. "Friends. Right. But not tonight. Tonight, you're mine, understood?"

She pushes up to touch her lips to mine. "Tonight, I'm yours."

A shiver of anticipation runs down my spine. The amount of times I've fantasized about exactly this moment—all the things I've dreamed of doing to her. But I only have one night. How can I fit an infinite number of touches and kisses and moans into one sleepless night?

Her lips latch on to my jaw and I groan before her hands slide down my stomach to grasp the bottom of my shirt. She lifts it up, and I help her take it off, tossing it aside somewhere on the floor. She places one hand on my chest, the other holding her up on the bed, and I watch as her eyes travel over my torso. I cover her hand with mine and lean down to kiss her again. Fuck, her kisses make every nerve come alive.

My mouth moves down to her neck, her throat, and her hot breath pants in my ear. My hands find their way to her hips and slide up, touching the soft skin of her stomach that sharply contracts at my touch. And the way she gasps . . . I wish I could record it. I'd make an album of just the sounds she makes when I touch her.

I push her T-shirt up and move my way down, kissing just over her belly button.

"Dave," she whimpers.

"Goddamn, that's music to my ears, Disco Girl," I say with a smirk.

A soft smile graces her face, and I watch in fascination as her head drops backward while my kisses continue their trail up her body. Her shirt lifts higher and higher, and she sighs as my thumbs brush the underside of her breasts. I grip the fabric with my teeth, pulling it up, exposing her. They're so perfect, each fits in my hand like she was made for me. Gently massaging them, she squirms under my touch.

"Take it off," she says.

I don't hesitate, the shirt disappearing into the dark mess of my floor. Her nipples are peaked and dark, like two chocolate kisses, and I'd bet my life they taste just as good. My tongue flicks out to tease one. There's a startled gasp, then a deep moan as my mouth encircles her nipple. Her fingers glide up the sides of my head, her nails scraping my scalp euphorically. My cock throbs desperately as her hips grind against mine. I need to be inside her—but first . . .

Kissing back down her gorgeous body, my fingers hook into the top of her shorts.

"Please," she groans, her face flushed.

I run my tongue along her hip, then blow on it—the act causing goosebumps to sprout up all the way to her chest. I reach up and pinch her nipples, knowing they'll be extra sensitive right now.

She cries out and I smile as my hands come back to her little shorts meant to torture me. "If I only have one night with you, Izzy," I say, "I'm going to take my time."

Her head shakes. "I might lose my mind if you don't hurry up."

As slowly as I can manage, I pull the shorts down her thighs, over her knees, her calves, then they're gone. She clamps her legs together but I can smell her arousal, see the hint of her glistening wetness dampening her thighs.

"If you move any slower, I'm going to go blind," she mutters.

I chuckle. "Who knew you were so impatient?"

"I'm not impatient. You're deliberately torturing me."

I slide my hand up her silky thigh, but her legs stay firmly clamped together.

"You know, generally speaking, you have to open your legs for this to work," I tease.

I feel her muscles relax a bit. "Sorry, it's just . . . it's been a while. I'm nervous."

Climbing over top of her, I stare into her dark brown eyes. "Do you want to stop?"

"No," she breathes.

"Then spread those legs for me, Izzy. I want to feast on your pussy until you're begging me to stop."

Her eyes widen, and I take the moment to sear her lips in a devastating kiss. She wraps her arms around me, holding me to her as our mouths wrestle for dominance. Her thighs relax and slowly spread apart, my hand climbing up the inside of her thigh one inch at a time.

"That's my good girl," I murmur against her mouth.

Her knees fall open, and my hand reaches the apex of her thighs, my fingers finding the skin there drenched.

My stomach contracts with my own harsh gasp as my cock throbs painfully. "Fuck, you're so wet for me. Let's see how you taste."

In a moment, I'm back between her legs to lick her dripping pussy.

"Oh god!" she gasps, her hips bucking up toward my face. I plunge my tongue inside of her, my left arm wrapping around to press her hips into the mattress. Her fingers plunge into my hair, gripping the strands sharply with each swirl of my tongue on her clit. I watch as her chest rises and falls, faster and faster until her legs begin to twitch. With one hand guiding my head, she loses herself, grinding her pussy against my mouth. I let out a low groan as I watch her free hand tease at her stiff nipples. Her legs shake, and with a teasing flick of my tongue and a sharp suck on her clit, she falls apart. Back arching off the bed, she holds me to her as she gasps and pants and moans.

"Oh, fuck! Yes!" she cries.

I don't relent. Her body twitches beneath me but still I lick her, my tongue tasting her pleasure as she writhes and moans so beautifully. She twists and turns and I grin against her as I pull her into place beneath my mouth.

"Dave," she pants. "Stop."

"I told you," I say. "Not until you beg." I suck her swollen clit into my mouth and she gasps louder than ever, her thighs squeezing my head, but that doesn't deter me. I press down against her thighs, opening her back up to me, and continue the assault. Her whole body trembles and shakes like an earthquake until she comes again. Harder and so forcefully, it bows her back into a sitting position.

Dark, glazed eyes stare down at me from above.

"Please," she begs. "Please, fuck me."

I grasp the nape of her neck and rise to my knees between her still shaking legs. "You sound so pretty when you beg." I kiss her hard and she whimpers against my mouth. I want her to taste herself, taste how delicious she is, and know that I'll never forget what it's like for her to come on my tongue for as long as I live.

CHAPTER 26

What's Love Got to Do With It?

ISABELLA

"Your wish is my command," Dave says as he pushes himself up. He stands at the foot of the bed before me—this gorgeous man—then drops his pants to the floor in one fluid motion to reveal . . .

My pussy clenches hard but my eyes widen as I take him in. A sudden swoop of nervousness twisting my belly as I gaze at his perfect, *massive* cock.

"You—" I stammer. "You're never going to fit."

He glances down at himself, his hand gripping the base before working himself slowly, spreading the glistening precum over his sizable length. Those stormy blue eyes flick back up to mine and he grins. "Trust me. It'll fit. Now, get on your knees."

I blink a few times as he waits for me to decide what I'm going to do. No man has ever bossed me around before in the bedroom. But then again, there's only been one other and we were both kids—barely adults, sneaking off in secret to do whatever we could manage.

This though—I didn't know it could be like this. Perhaps it's the euphoria clouding my mind from those earth-shattering orgasms or simply that I want to do whatever he asks of me, but I find myself getting on my knees before him at the end of the bed. He takes a step toward me, his cock jutting out, hard and straight.

"Do you know how many times I've thought about this mouth?" he whispers, his fingers gripping my chin as his thumb runs along my lower lip. "Dreamt of your mouth full of me?"

"That might be physically impossible," I say, crawling closer to him and wrapping my hand around his thick cock. He gasps and his eyes close as my fingers fight to encompass more of him, but they don't even reach all the way around. His eyes open and both of his hands grasp my hair, piling it up on my head and out of my way. "But I'll try my best."

Just like he did to me, I lick him, tease him, swirl my tongue around him until I can see the muscles flex in his jaw. I want to torture him just as much as he did me. To watch as he attempts to restrain himself. It's so hot, and I feel unbelievably sexy to be the one who makes him lose his mind. Something rumbles in his throat, signifying he's had enough of my teasing, so I open my mouth and do my best to take as much of him as possible, which . . . arguably is not much.

"Fuck," he moans. "I knew that mouth was going to ruin me."

I bob my head, my hand gliding up and down his length to make up for what my mouth can't hold. It's barely been a minute and my jaw aches, but it's a delicious sort of burn. I try to take him deeper, feeling him hit the back of my throat, and I breathe through my nose as his hand slides down my spine and his fingers dip into my pussy. I'm overwhelmed, his weight against my back and my mouth full as his fingers plunge into me from behind. This can't be real life. It's too good. I moan around his cock before his fingers retreat and one slowly breaches its way into that forbidden hole.

My eyes roll back and I moan around his cock. Oh my god, he's so filthy, I fucking love it. He tugs my hair to pull me off of him and grasps my chin again, lifting my body up to kneeling so we're almost at eye level. "You're dangerous, Izzy," he groans, kissing me hard. "Now, turn around and kiss the mattress."

I swallow and grip the back of his neck. "You'll be gentle with me?" I ask, my eyes searching his face. "Remember . . . I—"

"Don't worry, Izzy," he whispers against my lips. "It was made for you."

All of the breath rushes out of my lungs, and I'm left lightheaded and aching to feel him inside me. Gently, he turns my face and places his hand between my shoulder blades, pressing down so my chest makes contact with the sheets. They smell like him and it warms my heart. I watch as he grabs a condom from the top drawer of his dresser. I swallow the nervous lump in my throat as I once again consider his size, but he adds what looks like lubricant over himself before finding his place behind me.

"You tell me if it's too much," he says, his cock gliding through my drenched skin and brushing against my sensitive clit.

He grasps one of my hips and breaches my entrance, stretching me open in a way I— actually, I don't think I've ever felt it like this. I bury my face in the mattress, my fingers gripping the sheet for something to hold on to as he fills me. Fuck, it feels so good. He pulls back, then forward a little more, then again and again, each time burying himself deeper inside me.

I can't help the moans that escape me now. I've lost all sense of myself. There's just him and me and us together.

"You're taking me so well," he praises, his hand running up and down the arch of my spine. "That's it. Arch your back for me —just like that."

"Oh god," I cry, my voice muffled by the sheets. I'm so full. So overwhelmed, but still he sinks into me deeper. I feel his hair tickle my back, kisses peppered along my shoulders, as he waits for me to adjust to him. But I need more—my body is desperate for friction, so I push my hips back. My eyes roll as the pressure glides over that perfect spot inside me, and my legs tremble again.

"That's right, fuck yourself on my cock," he says.

Something wild seems to take over me as I rock my hips back, impaling myself on him over and over. Nothing has ever felt so good, so purely animalistic and uninhibited.

"Do you have any idea how fucking gorgeous you look right now?"

Closer, closer, and then it's as if all of me shatters at once. Like hurling a bowling ball at a mirror, I splinter and shake and scream out with the sheer force of my orgasm. My thoughts are incoherent, time ceases to exist, and all I can feel is Dave thrusting in and out of me, coaxing out the ripples of my pleasure.

"You're so goddamn perfect," he groans, grabbing my arms and pinning them behind my back as he drills into me. All I can do is hold on for dear life as he fills me over and over, before finally his rhythm falters.

"Fu—ck," he cries.

He lets go of my arms and they drop to my sides like dead weight, then rests his chest on my back. He's breathing hard and so am I. I can barely move. There's no strength left in me, so I just stay where I am. After a minute, he pulls out of me, and while I had originally been sure I wouldn't be able to accommodate his size, now with him gone, I feel empty.

With a kiss to my spine, he gets up off the bed. "I'll be right back." He walks away and out the door and I fall to my side as I try to regain some control over my limbs.

It was just one night. One time to get it out of our systems so we could go back to being friends—or whatever we were before this—but now . . .

Maybe this was a huge mistake.

He returns a moment later and sits next to me, wiping my damp hair away from my face. He grasps my cheeks in the palms of his hands and darts his eyes between mine. "You okay? I wasn't too rough, was I?"

"I'm fine . . . just—I'm just a bit overwhelmed."

"Are you sure? I brought you some water, and here, let me clean you up."

There's a damp cloth in his hand, and a smile pulls at the corners of my lips as I let him wash me with it. Then he hands me the glass of water. When I'm done, he climbs over me and pulls me into him. He nuzzles his face into my hair, closes his eyes, and sighs.

"Uh, Dave?"

"Hmm?"

"I should go back," I whisper.

"Why?" he asks.

I blink. What does he mean *why*? "Because that's where I'm supposed to be sleeping."

He opens his eyes and looks down at me. "Oh, right." His fingers twirl in my hair and it's so euphoric I almost forget why I said I need to leave. I've been waiting for him to do that to me for months.

"Will you lie with me for a few minutes?" he asks.

"Just a few minutes," I agree warily.

He smiles and closes his eyes again, and I'm surprised by how he pulls me into him. How he wraps his arms around me, his legs, like I'm the most precious thing in the world to him.

"I should really get back—"

"Just a few more minutes, then I'll walk you back out there and tuck you in," he says.

"Okay."

I rest my hand over his heart and feel the steady beat tapping my palm. His index finger traces up and down my arm, and I close my eyes at the feeling of calm that washes over me.

"See? That's better," he yawns out.

"What's better?" I ask.

"Your rhythm."

I crack my eyes open to find a subtle smile on his face and his eyes closed peacefully, like he's having the most wonderful dream. Maybe he is. Or maybe I am, because the truth is I don't want to wake up from this. I simply want to drift off in his arms forever.

CHAPTER 27

Voices Carry

DAVE

Something tickles my nose as I wake up from the best dream I've ever had. Slowly, my eyes open against the daylight that peeks through the sliver of my open curtains. There's a mop of brown hair in front of me, and my eyes widen as I remember it wasn't a dream. Izzy is cuddled up next to me in my bed, her beautiful face so peaceful as she sleeps.

Shit . . . what time is it? I hadn't meant to fall asleep but really, what did I expect when I insisted she lie in bed with me after . . . The memory of her soft skin, her breathy moans, the way she screamed and the way she clenched around me as she came threatening to rush my blood right back to my cock. Maybe it's early enough that no one is up yet. I should go out and pretend to have slept on the couch. That'll work, right? If anything, we can just say that neither of us could sleep, which is true, so I offered to switch. *Perfect.*

As gently as I can, I pull my arm out from under her, taking the time to memorize every inch of her skin. Silently, I pull on a pair of sweatpants and a T-shirt, then exit the room, pulling the door closed behind me with a *snick.* The house is quiet so it must still be early, and while I slept better in just a few hours than I have in weeks, I could definitely use some coffee. Walking to the kitchen, I try to tamp down the smile I know is front and center on my face.

"Hmm—hmm."

I freeze, my stomach dropping as I look to my left to find four pairs of eyes watching me from the living room. *Shit.*

"Morning," I say, trying to be casual.

James throws out his hands. "Dude, it's twelve thirty."

My shoulders slump and my eyes close as I realize the jig is up. "Right."

Becks is sitting ramrod straight, her big green eyes wide as they flick between me and the hallway.

"Merry Christmas . . . to you?" Key asks.

I scratch the back of my head. "I—yeah . . . Listen, I really need some coffee and a smoke before . . . before—right."

I slink into the kitchen, pouring myself a coffee from the pot then grabbing my smokes and running out to the patio. I can barely get my cigarette lit before James, Key, and Joel stumble out behind me. I should've known I wouldn't get away so easily.

The three of them stare at me for a long moment before I ask, "What?"

"You know what" says Key incredulously.

"You're fucking Isabella?" Joel asks.

"Look," I start. "It's not—"

"No," Key interrupts. "None of this it's-not-what-it-looks-like bullshit. Do you think we're idiots? All things aside when neither of you could be found on the couch this morning, did you really think none of us would hear the two of you going at it like gorillas last night?"

"Ugh," I groan, dipping my face into my hands.

"How long has this been going on?" Joel asks.

I take a deep breath. "Nothing is going on."

"Cut the bullshit," Key says.

"It's not bullshit, last night was—" Amazing. Life-changing. The best sex I've ever had in my life. God, why does James have to look at me like that? I feel like the biggest shithead. "It was just a one-time thing, okay?"

They all gape at me. "A *one-time thing*?" asks Key.

"Yeah, it was. It is," I insist at James's glare. "Here's the thing. She's hot. She thinks I'm hot. And we've been on the verge of it for a while, but that's it. It was just to clear our heads so we can go on tour and not be constantly thinking about the other person naked."

"And you expect her to be fine with that?" Joel asks.

"She is!" I say. "It was just. One. Night. We didn't mean for anyone to find out. Nothing's going to change."

"James," Key says, dismissing me with a limp hand. "You're awfully quiet about all this."

He frowns and shrugs. "Dave already knows my thoughts on this."

"You knew?" Joel counters. "You knew they were dying to rip each other's clothes off and said nothing?"

"I knew before they even met," James says. "I told you to stay away from her, Noblar."

Joel turns to James. "Why would you tell him that?"

"Because Dave isn't interested in relationships and she's Becks's only friend!" James shouts. "I wasn't about to have him screw that up by ditching Isabella after a quick fuck. And . . . oh my god, have you been fucking her this whole time?"

"What?"

"You haven't brought a girl home in weeks—months. Have you been secretly hooking up with her behind my back?" James asks.

Key and Joel stare at me.

"No! Of course not. Last night was the first time—"

"Holy shit, James, you're right," Key says. "How did I not notice? Is this why you acted like a jerk to her in Vegas?"

James looks between us. "What happened in Vegas?"

"You said it was just because you thought she was hot," Key says. "But you *do* like her. Why else would you not be hooking up with other girls?"

"You *like* her?" James asks.

I close my eyes. "Can I fucking speak, please?"

Joel's not ready to drop it though. "Wait, is *that* why you took off in such a mood last night after I jokingly offered to share my bed with her?"

"*What*?" James asks, rounding on Joel.

"I offered her my bed instead of the couch," Joel says, rolling his eyes. "I joked we could share, which I *wouldn't* have done if I knew Davey boy had heart eyes for her."

I groan. "I don't have 'heart eyes' for her."

"Oh please." Key laughs. "It suddenly makes so much sense."

"What makes sense?" I ask, forgetting about the cigarette as it burns down to my fingers.

"The two of you at the release party—" adds Key.

"What happened at the release party?" James interjects.

"Nothing happened—"

"The way you trailed after her in Vegas—" Joel throws in.

"I wasn't—"

"You can't deny, you did go practically feral when she started dancing with that guy," Key chimes in.

"Will you all just fuck off?" I shout, head pounding.

They go quiet for a few minutes before James finally says, "Dave, I told you to stay away from her thinking you'd break her heart. But if you have real feelings for her, then go for it."

"I don't have feelings for her," I lie. "It was one night to work it out of our systems and I'm sorry I broke that promise to you,

James, but she and I both agreed to it. Now, everything can go back to normal."

"It's okay to like a woman for more than one night."

Not for me it isn't. "I appreciate the concern, but we're not the same, James. And I don't need to stand here and convince any of you."

James shakes his head and holds up his hands, then he turns toward the house and disappears back inside.

"Dave," Joel starts, but I glare daggers at them both.

"No offense, guys, but I don't want or need your advice on this," I say sternly.

"Fine," Key says, crossing his arms over his chest. "But you better be nice to her today. This may have been some onetime thing you two decided on, but she's still coming on tour with us—to write about us—don't fuck it up by being an asshole."

I tilt my head back and sigh. "I know . . . I *know*. I won't. She's not like the others anyway." I catch the way that Joel and Key look at each other. "I just mean, she's my *friend* and other than what happened between us last night, I won't do anything to jeopardize that."

"Whatever you say, man," Joel says, and they both turn to head back inside.

They leave me on the patio, and a sudden strong gust of wind lifts my hair and makes me shiver. I pull out another cigarette and light it, inhaling the calming smoke. It's fine. This is fine. Izzy and I—*Isabella* and I, we're adults. Adults who both made a consensual decision last night to rid ourselves of some pent-up sexual tension. Now that it's over, we can move on, focus on what we're supposed to be doing over the next couple of months, not obsess about what the other person is doing when they're around —or not around.

It's fine.

Even though I can't stop the memory of her lips as she moans, the way her legs shake right before she comes, the way she fits me so perfectly. Like the satisfying way a puzzle piece slots into place after searching for it for hours, days, years. I flick the cigarette away and take a deep breath before walking back inside.

They're all still there, avoiding my eyes, carrying on with exchanging modest presents and talking about the upcoming tour, when I spy Isabella peek her head out from the hallway.

Don't fuck it up by being an asshole.

Key's words twist my stomach, but the way she looks right now—how could I ever be intentionally mean to someone so perfect? Her dark hair is a tousled mess. Her lips still a little swollen because of *me*. It makes me want to scoop her up and take her back to bed. But that wasn't the deal. The deal was one night, so . . . why do I suddenly want more? I've never wanted more. Not since—

"Merry Christmas everyone," Isabella says joyfully as she waltzes in.

Everyone looks up, unsure of exactly what to say as she sits down on the arm of the couch.

"Merry Christmas," Becks says with a smile. "Do you want something to eat? Or maybe you need some coffee?"

"Definitely coffee, but I can get it," she says with a smile, before turning and heading into the kitchen.

Four pairs of eyes turn pointedly back to me, the sound of cupboards opening and closing a soundtrack to my discomfort. James crosses his arms and Becks gives a very deliberate tilt of her head. I get the hint and push myself up off the couch, ready to have a conversation that I'm sure my friends will be straining to overhear.

Turning the corner, I watch as Isabella pours herself a cup of coffee from the carafe and adds her cream and sugar. She turns her head when I enter, a smile on her face.

"Hey," she says.

"Hey."

She stirs her coffee, the spoon clinking around in her cup before she takes a long sip and sighs.

"So, I'm guessing everyone knows?" she says, not looking up from her mug.

"Yeah." I nod, the awkwardness now palpable. "I tried to deny it but . . . apparently they heard us."

The blush starts all the way from her chest, rushing up her throat to her cheeks and her ears. "Oh."

"I'm sorry," I whisper. "I didn't mean to fall asleep."

She nods a few times. "It's fine. I mean . . . they probably would've found out eventually, right? I mean, isn't that what guys do?"

"Huh?"

She shrugs. "Don't you all like . . . I don't know . . . share details?"

"What? No. *No*, Isabella, I wouldn't—" But the way she looks up at me when I say her name—her full name—stops me in my tracks. I swallow hard. "I wouldn't do that."

"Okay, well, thanks."

"Are you okay?" I ask, leaning toward her.

She smiles widely. "Yeah, I'm great. Last night was . . . interesting. But now we can move on. I feel better already."

I manage to keep my jaw from dropping, narrowly. Last night was *interesting*? She's already moved on? She grabs the leather journal from the counter where we left it and tucks it to her chest.

"Thanks for my gift. I'm sure it'll come in handy on tour. I lost my last one." She reaches out her hand and tucks a piece of hair behind my ear before pressing her palm against my cheek. "I'm fine, Dave," she whispers. "We agreed—one night." She sighs. "This wasn't supposed to change anything. You don't need to check on me. I was fine before you and I'll be fine after you. We're still friends, so promise me you won't be weird about it."

"I won't—I'm not going to be weird about it," I say, cringing at the way my voice stammers.

"Good." She grabs her coffee mug and turns back for the living room, acting like her usual bubbly self.

I watch from the doorway as she smiles and sits between Key and Joel, both of whom look back over at me like they're worried I might storm off because they're near her. She's acting completely normal. But that was what I wanted, right? I didn't want her to be mad or regret what we did. We just wanted some relief, and it appears as though she got it. She's relaxed. Happy. Perfect.

So why do I feel so out of sorts that it's over?

CHAPTER 28

Screaming for Vengeance

ISABELLA

"**M**amitá?"

There's a beat of silence on the other end of the phone line before a tearful sob cuts through. "Isa? Oh, thank goodness. I've been calling and calling and leaving messages. I've been so worried about you."

Tears spring to my eyes knowing that I've hurt her. How I keep hurting my mother, who's never done anything but love me. "*Lo siento, amá.*"

"Oh, my dear." She pauses. "Everyone has been asking where you are. *Tu papá* made your favorite, *sopaipillas*. He was so upset when you didn't come home for Christmas."

"I know, but something came up and . . . I couldn't make it." It's only half a lie.

"Were you all alone?"

The warmth of sitting around a fire with my friends while they made metal covers of Christmas Carols and the turkey that Becks cooked all make me smile. "No, I wasn't alone. I was with some new friends."

"Oh." She sounds surprised. "And these new friends are what is keeping you from coming home to visit your *amá y apá*?"

I roll my eyes. "Yes and no."

"Isa—"

"I was offered an internship—with *Earworm Magazine*," I say, cutting her off.

"An internship?"

"Yes. They want me to travel around with a band and write a feature for the magazine about their first tour."

"With a band? What kind of band?"

I pause. "A rock band."

She laughs. "Isa, what do you know about rock music?"

"I've had a bit of an education recently," I say indignantly.

"This is a rock band of women?"

"No . . ."

She sighs. "So a magazine wants to send an unknown, inexperienced journalist to follow around a group of male rock musicians? Unchaperoned?"

"*Ay mamá, que es esto los 50s?*"

She's quiet, and I can practically visualize the scowl from the other end of the line.

"I met them through a girlfriend and they're really nice. They won't let anything bad happen to me. They're my friends."

"Uh-uh, boys cannot be friends with girls. Especially pretty girls like my Isa."

Part of me wants to argue, but then the night that Dave and I spent together two days ago reminds me that maybe she's right. We couldn't be just friends because there was always that attraction between us standing in the way. It was really just a matter of time before it happened and, my god, did it ever happen. The way he made me feel is like out of the most scandalous romance novels—or a porno. But that's it. It's over and done. He's moved on and so have I. I definitely haven't spent the last forty-eight hours thinking about his touch, his kisses, his moans.

"*Isa*, are you listening to me?"

"Sorry, yes. I'll be fine. It's just for a few weeks and I promise I'll call every few days, okay?"

"Just . . . promise me you'll be safe," she pleads.

I nod absently into the phone. "I will."

Hanging up, I look around my apartment. It's surprisingly clean and empty, thanks to Becks and her heart of gold followed by the fact that I've been away for two days. The only thing out of place is the leatherbound journal on my bed that Dave gave me for Christmas.

I snatch the journal back up and flip it open. It's really beautiful, and I wonder briefly if he bought it for himself after losing his list—his list that still lives secretly in my purse. At this point he must know it's gone, meaning it's too late now to somehow sneak it back to him. I can't tell him I found it or he'll ask why I didn't return it sooner, and what could I possibly say? That part of me wanted to hold some secret, intimate part of *him* in my hands?

Then after what happened between us on Christmas . . .

My stomach jolts and there's a tingling rush between my legs as I remember that night once more. That unbelievable, mind-altering, wonderful night. And while we promised it wouldn't change anything—something has shifted. Of course, everyone finding out about it wasn't exactly in the plans, and it took all of my energy to avoid being alone in a room with Becks so I could dodge what I'm sure would've been a thorough interrogation. But Dave acted so strangely. Nervous and not his usual, confident self.

I knew it would hurt. I knew in my heart that after that one devastating kiss that led to so much more, it would never be enough. So I put on my best performance to date and convinced everyone in that room I was fine—it appears even Dave, with all his talk of understanding people's rhythms, didn't pick up on it.

I just hope he can keep up his part of the deal. That this won't change anything between us, because my attraction to him aside, he's actually a really great guy and I'm lucky to have him in my life—even if that means keeping things strictly platonic.

"I've arranged for you to go on the bus with the band for the last three weeks of the tour," Harold Lewis says.

My mouth drops open for the millionth time as I sit across from him in his Bay area office. "Really?"

"It's really the most practical and cost-efficient way to do this. It's just for traveling purposes. When you get to each city, there will be a motel room available for you to have some privacy."

"Right."

He grins. "I realize having to sleep on a tour bus with four grown men may not be the most decent thing . . ."

I nod my head. "My mother would agree."

Lewis chuckles.

"But it's fine. It won't be all the time and it'll give me lots of down time with the guys to chat with them about their experiences while they're touring."

He claps his hands together. "Yes, exactly what I thought."

"It'll be great."

"You have everything you need?" he asks.

I nod, the enormity of this opportunity settling over me. A handful of motel vouchers, deadlines, contact information . . . it's a lot of responsibility.

"Mister Lewis?" his secretary interrupts. "Your two o'clock is here."

"Thank you, Eliza. Now, Miss Rodriguez. Any more questions?"

I can't help but grin. "No, I think I have everything I need. Thank you, sir."

He nods and I'm ushered out into the outer office, where a man with black curly hair longer than James's and a pair of sunglasses walks past me, shutting the door behind him.

"You think you're ready for this, do you?" Eliza says once we're out in the hallway by her desk. Her tone is tight though she smiles widely.

"Oh," I say, turning toward her as she retakes her place behind her desk. "Yes, I think so."

Her nose twitches. "Well, you should *know* so. We here at *Earworm* have something of a reputation for excellence to uphold. If you don't think you can rise to the occasion, then you should reconsider."

My mouth drops open. Is this secretary really saying all of this with her wide, plastic-looking smile?

"Close your mouth, dear," she says through gritted teeth. "It's not a good look for a young lady."

Pressing my lips together, I breathe through my nose. Does Mister Lewis know she speaks to people this way? Or is there just something about me in particular she feels the need to be a total bitch about? "I'm definitely ready for the challenge."

She scans me from foot to face. "We'll see about that."

What the hell is this woman's problem? If her boss thinks I'm capable then that's all that matters. Besides, I hardly think she's in a position to be picky, if their magazine can barely stay afloat.

"Here are your accommodation vouchers," she says, handing me a large brown envelope with a scowl. "Make sure you keep receipts for everything."

"Of course."

"Did Mister Lewis explain our professionalism policy to you?" she asks, typing furiously on her typewriter.

"Uh . . ."

She looks up and places her hands under her chin with a tsk. "He's a very busy man so I'll give you the short version. As an employee of this publication, you are expected to conduct yourself in a professional and dignified manner at all times. If at any point you are seen or reported for behavior that violates our guidelines, your employment shall be terminated."

My mouth opens and closes a few times before I can finally speak. "Who dictates what is professional and dignified?"

She sighs and rolls her eyes. "If you have to ask such a thing, you'll probably be out of here before you can even make your submission deadline. Especially if you're covering one of those devil bands." She says the last part under her breath.

"Devil bands?"

Not looking up, she mutters something again and I roll my eyes. Perfect. "They're actually wonderful people, if you bothered to get to know them."

Her eyes flick up and narrow on my face. A chill sweeps down my spine at the icy cold nothingness in their depths. Again, she gives me an appraising look. "Let me give you a piece of advice," she says sweetly. "Girls like you shouldn't be covering stories like this, but seeing as how we're here, I highly recommend you make sure you're only going to be working."

I take a step closer to her desk. "As opposed to what?"

She twists her mouth. "Our reputation is very important to us," she says, dodging my question.

"I get it," I say.

"I wonder," she continues. "Just how did you get involved with a band like Carnal Sins?"

I meet her judgmental gaze with fierce pride. "None of your business."

Her nose pinches as though she's smelled something foul.

"Have a great day," I say with an overly chipper smile. She blinks, and after scooping up my documents, I turn on my heel and storm out of the office. I've walked almost five miles by the time I've calmed down, realizing I just as easily could've taken the bus.

What the hell was all that about? Like I wouldn't behave professionally . . . What does she think? Does she think the same as that foul bastard, Simon? That I'm sleeping my way to the top? I mean, yes, Dave and I have slept together now, but—oh god, if Eliza ever found out about that . . . Would Mister Lewis really fire me for that? He seems desperate to keep staff but maybe this is why the magazine is failing. Someone who holds no modern views would surely tank any business. I'll have to be careful, but it's not like I'm going to be sleeping with Dave again.

No, it was just once.

I stop in the middle of the sidewalk and press the heels of my hands to my eyes. What if they try to bring groupies back to the tour bus with me inside? What if Dave does? No, he promised me he'd keep it discreet if he was hooking up with someone else. But that anger and irritation bubbles up again at even the thought of him hooking up with anyone.

I take a steadying breath, put one foot in front of the other. Three weeks. That's all I need to survive. Maybe establishing some rules with the guys right away will benefit everyone. No hooking up on the tour bus. Outside of that . . . it's free game. But I need the tour bus to be a safe place.

MY FISTS clench as I stare at the glass doors of the *Stoneman Press*. I suppose I do have *some* fond memories here. It wasn't all horrible . . . just most of it. I hold my head high and pull on the door. The place is fairly quiet, which makes sense considering it's the holidays, but this couldn't wait and I have no idea where else I might be able to borrow one.

"Excuse me, Randall?" I say, knocking on the editor's door.

Randall looks up, and though there's no paper to run at this time of year, he looks as disheveled as ever. "Miss Rodriguez," he says. "What are you doing here?"

I step inside the chaotic office and sit in the chair I'm all too familiar with. "First of all, I wanted to thank you."

"Thank me?"

I nod. "Yes. For making sure I got that message from Harold Lewis."

"Oh, right, right. What was all that about anyway?"

I bite my lip. "He uh . . . he offered me an internship at *Earworm Magazine*."

"Oh," he says, sitting up. "That's great news. I'm glad you found something."

"He wants me to write a feature on Carnal Sins actually. Follow the band while they're on tour. But I need a typewriter. Do you think I could borrow one?"

"I—uh—yes, of course. There's still one on the empty desk in the back corner you can borrow."

I stand. "Thank you."

"Uh, Isabella," he says, reaching out his hand. At my puzzled look, he continues. "That's wonderful news. Congratulations." He smiles. Warmly, genuinely.

"Thanks."

Offering a subtle nod, I return it then step out of his office and head toward the back.

"There's no way that's true."

I stop in my tracks. Not this. Not again. When is murder a viable option? I won't let him bully me. I'm the one with the upper hand now.

Turning, I pull a smile on my face. "Simon. How unfortunate to see you."

His face is menacing. "There's no fucking way you're working with *Earworm*."

I place my hand on my hip. "Why would that be so unbelievable to you? I'm surprised you even know who they are —"

He moves quickly, his hands shooting out on either side of me, pinning me against the wall. "Tell me you're lying," he says with a snarl.

"Believe what you want. I don't need to prove anything to you." But as I watch his face, something pulls at his features in a way I've never seen before. His eyes are manic and searching and his lip twitches. Why is he so desperate to believe I'm lying? He swallows hard and it hits me. "Wait," I whisper. "They rejected *you*."

A muscle jumps in his jaw and while he says nothing, it's evident all over his face.

"You applied to *Earworm* and they said no," I say again.

"Shut up, Rodriguez," he says. He never calls me that.

"What's wrong?" I ask. "Can't stomach the fact that someone accepted me over you?"

He says nothing but seethes, his arms strained tight on either side of me and his horrible coffee breath on my face. "Is that why you stole my work?" I whisper. "Because you couldn't get an internship with your own?"

"Don't fuck with me, Rodriguez."

"Get away from me—"

"You weren't supposed to get anything," he shouts.

My lips part and my heart beats in my throat. "Wh—what?"

His frightened, watery eyes flick over my face and he finally takes a step backward.

"You . . . Did you blackball me?"

He clears his throat and looks away. "Look. I did what I had to do."

"You prevented me from getting an internship?" I whisper.

He says nothing.

"How could you? You already took so much from me!" I scream.

"I couldn't have anyone tracing the articles back to you, could I?"

"But my name is on them!"

He shifts uncomfortably, the first time I see him squirm, and there's a small part of me that ignores the anger to revel in him feeling uneasy. "I removed the original articles from the school archives."

A horrified laugh bubbles out of me. "Then what? You wrote to every publication I applied to and told them I was plagiarizing *you*?"

His eyes stay trained on mine.

"You—" But words elude me. The absolute betrayal. Not only has this asshole stolen my work and sabotaged my chances at an internship, but he went so far as to remove any evidence I could use to help me clear my name.

"How did you even know where I applied?" I ask, trying to make all of the pieces make sense. "Wait, my notebook . . ." I kept a list of all of the outlets I was waiting to hear back from in my notebook. The one he stole from me. No wonder everyone rejected me. And the only reason I was still able to get any internship at all was because *Earworm* reached out to *me*.

This time, I do rage. Like an animal that's been captive for years and is finally let out, I hit and scratch and thrash and cry with all the strength I have, and while I get a good few swipes in, I can't compete with his size and strength and he easily subdues me, pinning my wrists against the wall.

"Calm down," he shouts. "I still have that picture. Remember what I can do to you."

"What the hell is going on here?" Randall yells as he pulls Simon away from me.

I collapse in a heap on the floor, unable to speak as Randall sends Simon out the door.

"Isabella," Randall says. "Did he attack you? Are you okay? What the hell happened?"

But I can't breathe. No air will enter my lungs, and the small ray of light at the end of my long, lonely tunnel extinguishes into total darkness.

CHAPTER 29

Five Years Ago

DAVE

T he cuffs tighten for a moment before they release, the skin pinched and sore from the metal digging in for the last eight hours. I rub at the raw skin and push my hair back.

"We're sorry about the mix up," Officer Daniels says, remorse ringing out in his tone. "From our perspective, it looked . . . well, I'm sure you're aware that we need to take domestic abuse allegations seriously."

I nod, his voice and words barely registering. "Right."

He lets out a long breath. "But the statements from the diner employees made it very clear that you didn't do anything wrong. You're free to go. Here are your personal items back—wallet, keys—and your car is parked out back."

I take the brown envelope from him. "Thanks."

"Any questions?"

"Where—" I clear my throat. It aches from the pressure of grinding my teeth for hours on end. "Where is she?"

The officer sighs. "She was taken to the hospital by one of our officers, but we got a call from triage saying she left."

I sniff and nod.

"You should get that girl some help," he says.

I don't say anything. All I feel is defeat. I back toward the door, trying to hold it all together before I fall apart. Stepping out into the warm midsummer night from the stagnant air of the police station, I head around the back for my car. My station wagon is at the far end of the lot, and it's as if I'm a marionette. Some other divine being puppeteering my body through the motions.

Unlocking my door on autopilot, I get into the front seat and slam it shut. In the privacy of my own car, I finally let everything out. I break down. A horrible sob wrenches its way through me, and I can't stop. I cry like I'm five years old and fell off my bike only for my dad to tell me my mom couldn't kiss my scrapes all better because she was never coming back. Now, in the back of the police station parking lot, all of that pain comes rushing out as tears stream freely down my face.

I'm hurt, betrayed, heartbroken—but most of all I'm angry. Angry at everything. At how, no matter what I try to do, the good things in my life always get fucked up. My luck always runs out. The anger tears through me, manifesting in my fists until I'm punching the steering wheel and the dash until my knuckles are bloody and my hands are shaking.

I just wish I could fall asleep. Everything would quiet down if I could just sleep. Because if I leave this parking lot, I'll have to face the real world and everything that's broken, and I don't know if I'm strong enough for that yet.

Wiping my face with an old bandana from the back seat, I finally pull out and head toward Sam's house. I won't go home. My dad didn't even answer the phone when I called from the police station. I suppose I finally lived up to everything he always thought I'd achieve. At least I won't have a record, but he won't ever believe I didn't do anything wrong. So I head to Sam's.

I wonder if Emily will be there. Will they know what

happened? Will she have told her cousin the same story she told the police? Is she still so drunk she can barely stand? Will they ever forgive me for not showing up at the studio?

WHEN I PULL UP, the garage door is still open, my headlights illuminating Sam as he sits on a folding chair with a cigarette between his lips. As I kill the engine, his eyes find mine through the windshield. For a long moment we stare at each other until finally, he takes a deep breath and looks down.

The door opens and my whole body is tense as I walk toward him. I stop short when I'm a few feet away.

"Where were you, man?" Sam asks quietly.

"Jail."

His eyebrows shoot up, some of the anger he's hiding in his features disappearing with my answer. Obviously, he hadn't expected that.

"What the hell for?"

What do I even tell him? That Emily, his cousin, is an alcoholic? That she was so drunk she accused me of hitting her? That she's the one who's been stealing money from him? How is it fair that I have to be the one to tell him everything?

"Is Em here?" I ask, looking toward the door into the house.

"No, we're not doing that. You're going to fucking tell me what the hell is going on before you race off to her."

I shake my head. "No, it's not like that. I—I just want to make sure she's somewhere safe."

"She's in her room."

Letting out a breath, I rub my chin where some stubble is already growing. "Good."

"Dave?" I look up, and Sam's eyes are angrier than I've ever seen them. "Tell me what's going on. Right now."

I cross my arms over my chest, my heart anxiously pumping as I try to decide how to tell my friend. "Em . . . she's . . . She has a drinking problem."

Sam's eyes widen. "A drinking problem?"

I let out a breath. "Yeah."

There's a moment where I think the truth will hit him like it did me. Some lightbulb will go off and he'll finally be able to piece everything together. But then he laughs.

"What could possibly be funny?" I ask.

"Emily doesn't have a drinking problem," Sam says, screwing up his face.

Now it's my turn to look surprised. "Yes, she does."

He rolls his eyes. "She's a party girl, Dave. You know that. Sometimes she parties a bit too hard, but which one of us hasn't? Do you know how many times I've had to babysit your drunk ass after you got wasted? Remember that Fourth of July weekend two years ago?" He chuckles, remembering. "You were a mess."

"This isn't like that, Sam," I say sternly. "She hides it well but today she— Today, she . . ."

"What?" Sam asks. "She what?"

I look over my shoulder, worried someone might hear. "She was wasted and causing a scene at the diner. That's where I went."

"Causing a scene?"

I bury my face in my hands. "She was out of her mind. Breaking shit, and I thought if I could just get her home, get her to sober up or fall asleep—" Taking a few deep breaths, I force my heart to slow down its frantic pace. "She fucking accused me of beating her, Sam."

His brows furrow so low over his eyes they nearly disappear, a look of utter disbelief on his face.

"And right in front of two cops. They tackled me and threw me in the back of their cruiser. You know me, Sam. You know there is nothing that could have kept me from making that recording session. You know it had to be something bad to keep me from being there. I've tried to help her, Sam, but she won't listen, and I don't know if I can do this with her anymore."

"Dave, stop," Sam cuts through my rambling.

"What do you mean—?"

"I mean stop this bullshit, man," Sam says, standing up.

Ice floods my veins at the look of pure revulsion on his face. This is my friend. My best friend since childhood. Does he not believe me? "Sam?"

"You have some fucking nerve," he says, pushing my chest. "You concoct this whole story just to break up with my cousin?"

My mouth falls open. "Sam that's not—I didn't say that!"

"Her dad's an alcoholic, you asshole! You really think she'd follow in his footsteps? Use your brain, Dave. You think I don't see the way you look at other girls?"

"What are you even talking about?"

"No, you know what? You want to fucking break up with Emily? Fine, but don't make up some bullshit like this."

That anger rushes back, and I push Sam hard, nearly throwing him off-balance. "Why the fuck would I ditch the demo taping then, huh? You know there's no way in hell I'd ever miss that. I'm the one who set the whole thing up, remember, asshole?"

"Because you finally figured it out, Noblar," he says, opening his arms up wide with a menacing smile.

"Figured *what* out?"

He laughs sardonically. "We always knew we weren't good enough for the big leagues but you kept pushing until we believed it too," Sam spits, stalking toward me. "But when it finally came down to the moment, you finally saw the truth, didn't you? That we're just a bunch of hacks who can't play worth a damn and if your name ever appeared on something that bad, you could kiss your stupid dreams goodbye."

"Sam . . ." I say, dumbfounded. "That's ridiculous. I don't think any of that!"

"And Emily," he continues, his voice quiet. "She'll never be enough for you. Because your dreams are too big for ants like us. I see you always writing and rewriting that fucking list of yours like it's sacred. Like you'll actually be some bigshot rockstar one day. But you'll see," he says with venom in his voice. "You're just as big a loser as the rest of us, and you'll never get out of here."

He pushes me hard and I stumble back, losing my footing and falling to my ass on the garage's concrete floor. Sam stands over me with an expression I've never seen before on his face.

"You're a fucking *disease*, Noblar. Now get the hell out of here."

He turns and stomps toward the house, the door slamming shut behind him so hard dust falls from the garage rafters. Every happy memory I have has occurred in this garage, but it's suddenly cold and unfamiliar, and I don't know how it all changed so fast without me even noticing.

I drive for who knows how long until finally deciding to sleep in my car. I can't possibly face my father, but there's nowhere else to go. I can't believe Emily. I can't believe Sam. And I can't believe that even after all of that, I still love them. How much hurt can one person endure before that love snaps? Breaks? Destroys? After all, that's what love really is. It's giving someone the power to destroy you, and then standing there with a smile as the world burns to the ground.

CHAPTER 30

You Shook Me All Night Long

DAVE

When I walk through the door, Joel and Key are furiously talking over each other, as though they're both trying to win the same race, and James is sitting about ten feet from them, drinking coffee.

"What's . . . going on?" I ask as I set the few bags I have down on the counter next to James.

"Oh, good, Dave is here. He can help," Joel says, waving me over.

I give James a look, and he just rolls his eyes and walks to the fridge. I amble toward the dining table where there appears to be hundreds of wristbands spilling out of a cardboard box. Picking one up, I examine it. It's a little thicker than a hair elastic but less stretchy. "What's all this?"

"Groupie passes," Key says without even looking up.

I nearly choke. "What?"

Key and Joel both finally stop and look at me. "A code . . . for girls."

My eyebrows may have shot off my head in amazement. "I —" I am speechless.

"We told Jamesey there he could have some, but he had to go and get married."

Hearing a laugh behind me, I turn to see James watching the three of us with an amused expression. "Yeah, because what you're doing looks like *so* much fun."

"Don't be a wet blanket," says Key.

"Whatever," James says, heading down the hall. "Just remember to wrap your dicks."

"We're not morons," Joel yells, but James's door slams, and he lets out a long sigh. "Why do I feel like he's going to judge me every time I hook up with someone. He's the one who went and got married."

"He isn't," I say quietly. "But he doesn't want to be judged for getting married either."

Joel's mouth twists. "Yeah, I guess you're right."

"Plus, I'm pretty sure he's still mad at me. About Izzy."

Joel and Key raise their eyes to me. "Izzy?"

I cough. "Isabella, I mean. She's going to be coming with us on the bus for the last three weeks. Al called me this morning to let me know."

"I guess that means you won't be needing these," Key says, pulling the wristbands out of my hands.

Reaching for them, I grab a handful. "What are you talking about?"

Joel and Key look at me as if I've just grown a second head.

"Well, we just—" Joel starts. "If she's going to be on the bus . . ."

"So?"

Key buries his face in his hands. "My God, Dave. Are you really that dumb?"

I wait for him to continue.

"Are you seriously telling me your plan is to hook up with groupies on the tour bus right in front of the girl you just fucked?"

My mouth opens and closes like a door hinge for a moment. "I mean—"

"Sure, that'll go great for the magazine feature," Joel says.

I shake my head. "It was just one night. We agreed we'd still be friends. That it wouldn't interfere with her job or mine."

"That doesn't mean she wants to watch you hooking up with girls right in front of her."

I slump back in my chair. "No. You're right. I—I promised her I wouldn't flaunt it."

"Do you even want to?"

"Want to what?"

"Hook up with other girls?"

If I'm being honest with myself, I haven't given it any thought. My head has been filled with nothing but visions of Isabella in my bed since Christmas. Before Christmas, even. It wasn't until I walked in on Key and Joel right now that I thought about the potential of anyone else at all.

"Yeah. I mean—of course. Of course I do."

"It would be fine if you didn't," Key adds gently. "We wouldn't even make fun of you for it."

I roll my eyes. "Okay, fuck off. Look, we'll just make a rule for all of us, no sex on the tour bus."

"Wait," Joel says, holding up his hands. "Why are *we* getting punished?"

"You want to screw a bunch of chicks to the soundtrack of Isabella's typewriter?"

"Wouldn't bother me."

I roll my eyes. "How about I just don't want to see your naked asses and she won't either."

There's a long pause.

"Fine," Key finally says. "No one hooks up on the tour bus. Okay?"

"Good."

"Here's your wristbands," Joel says with a scowl. "You're fucking welcome."

I CAN'T SLEEP.

I like to think it's nerves about heading out on tour tomorrow —and it is that—but it's also what Joel and Key said about hooking up with girls while away. *Do you even want to?* Do I? The idea of being in bed with anyone but Izzy doesn't excite me the way it used to. In fact, it hasn't for months. What is wrong with me? I haven't wanted just one woman in years. I'm not like James.

It's okay to like a woman for more than one night.

How is it that the youngest member of the group is the wisest? I'll admit, I thought he was an idiot, falling in love with a girl when his music career was just about to take off. Sure that he would regret it and miss out on so much. But, miss out on what exactly? He found the girl of his dreams on the first try. If sex is the only encouraging factor, then he's already got that taken care of. It's not like the wall between their bedroom and mine is soundproof, and from what I've heard, they can't seem to get enough of each other.

Okay, so it's not crazy to only want one woman as long as she ticks off all the boxes for what a man wants. Does Isabella tick off all of my boxes? First of all, she's gorgeous. Not only does she have a smokin' body but her face is so goddamn beautiful with those chocolate brown eyes and long lashes . . . those naturally dark lips. Fine . . . check.

Then there's the sex. I can't lie. The sex we had on Christmas was, without a doubt, the best I've ever had. Her body, her breath in my ear, the way she felt wrapped around me in every way. Check, check, check.

But then there's also who she is. Her personality. Becks and James are exact opposites but somehow, they make each other better. Would Izzy and I be the same? We don't exactly like a lot of the same things, but I can talk to her. Something about the way she asks questions or . . . listens . . . it makes me open up in a way I haven't since—

I shake my head. It always comes back to her. To Emily. Sometimes it baffles me how one person can do so much damage, how awful things ended up. And I know deep down that Isabella is not Emily. In fact, two women couldn't be more different, but I never thought Emily could do the things she did, and loving her blinded me to so much. Caused me to make so many mistakes. Caused me to feel ashamed of the things I want most in the world and almost caused me to lose out on it all. Emily was sweet once, too.

So getting close to Isabella? Not a good idea.

What if she changes like Emily did? What if something happens and all of this is jeopardized because my heart got in the way?

I need to break out of this obsession I have. For all of Joel and Key's idiocy, the wristbands are kind of a genius move. If a girl ends up backstage, at least she knows why she's there and I'll know what she expects. Maybe that's all I need to do. Just rip the Band-Aid off and sleep with the first girl wearing a wristband. I just need to get back into my regular routine. Of course, it won't be easy. I can't do it in front of Isabella, but I have just over two months on tour before she joins us. Plenty of time to shake her out of my system. Especially since she so easily shook me from hers.

After Christmas she seemed more at ease with our deal than I was. In fact, it was shocking. What if she meets someone else? What if *she* hooks up with another musician on this tour? My stomach twists hard and my fists clench. The thought of Isabella with another man is . . . abhorrent. Nauseating. Rage-inducing.

But what can I say? Nothing, that's what. This is what we agreed on. Besides, there is so much I need to do to prove to myself that I've made it. I pull the little keychain from my pocket. The sun and cloud are starting to show signs of wear. Probably because I'm constantly rubbing it between my fingers.

Dreams are forged out of darkness. Ain't that the truth. My dream to be a drummer came out of the depression after my mom left. Then it was fueled even more after the darkness that consumed me after Emily. Thinking of my list—the one I carelessly left on a table in Vegas—there are so many things I want to do in this life. And while Isabella would be an indulgent temptation, she's not the one who's going to make my dreams come true.

I am.

Dress You Up

ISABELLA

Taking a deep breath, I open the door of the bus terminal, bracing myself against the frigid mid-February winds. With my suitcase in tow, I head for the huge red and silver bus parked at the curb in front of me.

"It's fine. This will be fine," I mutter as I walk toward the towering bus with the Carnal Sins logo along the side. I can't decide why I'm so nervous at this moment. Whether it's that the bus is intimidating, or maybe it's because I don't know what to expect once I'm on board but I wonder if the guys will treat me differently? Will Dave? It's been over two months since I've seen or spoken to any of them.

The door opens and the guys spill out onto the sidewalk with the biggest smiles on their faces. James, Joel, and Key each pick me up in a giant hug, then Dave is there. For a brief moment, I wonder if he won't hug me, but his face relaxes and he scoops me up in his arms and spins me around. The warmth of his chest, the smell of him, it all hits me like a dopamine rush and I feel the tension ease off of my shoulders. When he sets me back on my feet, I smile.

"Hey," Dave says, stepping back.

Those eyes. Two storms brewing over the ocean. "Hi."

He grins wide, showing all of his brilliant teeth at once.

"Come on," James says, grabbing me by the elbow and turning me toward the stairs. "I'll give you the tour."

"Wait, my bag—"

"I got it," Dave says from behind me, and I glimpse him carrying my bag like it weighs nothing, even though I nearly dislocated my shoulder getting it down the terminal stairs. James pulls me up into the bus, and I'm greeted by an older man.

"This is Barney," he says, pointing to a portly driver sitting behind the wheel.

Barney tips his head as I pass, and I offer him a smile. We then pass through a heavy velvet curtain, and my eyes all but bug out. Red velvet upholstery and wood paneling as far as the eye can see. There's a small table with bench seats on either side as well as a tiny kitchen.

"This is the main living area," James says, gesturing around. "It's not huge, but we're not really in here all that much anyway."

I nod and follow along behind him, sensing Dave's silent presence behind me as I go.

"Bathroom is through here," he says, gesturing to a narrow door to my right. "If I were you, I'd try to schedule showers for when we're staying in motels. The shower in there gives you maybe thirty seconds worth of hot water before you're freezing to death."

"Right." I glance into the surprisingly clean bathroom. In fact, the whole place is clean. "It hardly looks like you've been living in here for a few days, let alone nine weeks."

James glances past my shoulder for a moment, then turns and continues down the hall. "Then here we have the bunks. There are only four. One for each of us, but the dining table folds down into a double. Are you cool with that?"

I take inventory of the narrow bunks on either side of the bus, then back at the dining table. "Yeah, that's fine with me. I knew it wasn't going to be glamorous."

James smiles. "Again, we only sleep here when Barney's driving, so it's not all the time. We all long for the nights we get to sleep in a motel."

"I'll bet."

"There's a small cupboard here where you can put your clothes and stuff," James says, pointing toward my suitcase.

"They told me to pack light."

Dave sets down my bag. "This is light?"

Frowning, I shrug. "I had to pack the typewriter and paper."

"Oh, right."

"We're heading out in five, so you might want to double-check you have everything, miss," Barney says, poking his head through the curtain.

"Okay, thank you."

James rubs his hands together and backs up toward the front, pushing Dave along with him. "We're just going to grab some air and let you get accustomed to the space. We'll be back in a few minutes." They disappear through the curtain, and I'm left standing in the narrow hallway of a real tour bus. Never in my wildest dreams would I have imagined I could be here. This is nicer than I expected. I was sure I'd be walking into a party bus, but the place is spotless.

I take a deep breath and pull my suitcase up onto the table. Taking the typewriter and paper, I place them on the counter then grab some of my clothes and head for the back where the cubbies are. There are eight square cupboards, four of which have labels with the guys' names on them. My fingers trail down the wood grain, my thumb passing over Dave's name. He's written his "D" the same way as he did on my shoulder that night so many months ago, and my skin tingles at the memory.

With a sigh, I grab the handle of one of the other doors and pull. I shriek as what appears to be dozens of rubber bands fall toward me and ricochet onto the floor.

"Shit!" I cry, dropping my armful of clothes to try to collect them.

"Miss?"

Wide-eyed, I catch Barney peering through the curtain.

"I—" I fumble trying to grab them and stuff them back into the open door of the cubby, but I stand up too fast and slam the top of my head into the open cabinet door. "Ow!"

Stumbling back, I sink against one of the bunk beds, rubbing the top of my head, which is tender and throbbing. A moment later, Barney is in front of me, helping to scoop up the blue bands from the floor.

"Are you all right?" he asks, jutting his chin at my head.

Scrunching my face, I close my eyes and nod. "Yeah, shit, I thought that was empty. What the hell are these things anyway?" I ask, picking up a blue band from the floor.

"They give those out to the girls," Barney says absently as he finishes picking up the last of the fallen items.

My head tilts to the side. "Oh," I say, pulling the rubber band over my wrist where it joins my other bracelets. "They're bracelets. That's nice."

Barney glances at the band on my wrist. "Should probably put that back," he says seriously.

I grin and wave my hand. "Why? We're all friends. They won't mind if I take one, will they?"

He looks toward the front of the bus then back at me. "Them bracelets aren't for friends, nor are they for nice girls like you."

Okay, he's lost me. "What do you mean?"

Barney hesitates, then reaches forward to take my wrist, pulling the blue band off of me. "They ain't friendship bracelets. They give them to the girls who want to come backstage."

I raise my eyebrows. "Backstage?"

"You don't exactly seem like the type of girl who'd want one of these."

Realization dawns on me and my mouth hangs open. My eyes flick back and forth between Barney, who turns and heads back toward the front, and the cupboard full of . . . sex passes? Is that really what he's implying? The guys hand out these bracelets to girls so they can come backstage and— Does Dave do this? Ugh . . . men are disgusting.

I'm such an idiot. Here I was, wondering if Dave stopped sleeping around after our night together. Thinking that he might have cut down on hooking up with random girls because he had me on his mind. But here *he* is with a closet full of groupie bracelets. Just how many girls does he plan to sleep with?

"Ready to hit the road?"

I look over at Dave, that beautiful, easy smile on his face. But after what I just discovered, something sours in my stomach. My lips seal shut and I clench my jaw. Standing, I walk toward the table, pushing past him with an aggressive bump of my shoulder.

"Yeah, let's go."

He turns slowly. "Whoa, what's wrong?"

I sit down and pull the typewriter toward me, fiddling with the knobs. "Nothing's wrong. Everything's great. Fine. *Peachy*."

Feeling him tense from here, I try to take a deep breath. I can't be mad at him. He promised me nothing and was always up front about what we were to each other. It's my problem. It just stings to know I'm not good enough for him when he's all I ever think about.

"You don't exactly seem fine. Barney said you hit your head. Are you okay?" he asks, his fingers gently grazing the top of my hair.

As if on instinct, I bat his hand away. "I said I'm fine, Noblar."

It comes out harsher than I intended. Fuck, this is going to be a long trip. I continue to fiddle with the knob, aware of his eyes watching me but refusing to look up at him. He's probably trying to decipher what the hell my problem is. After what feels like forever, he turns and walks toward the back of the bus, where I watch as he climbs into the bottom bunk on the left and lies down staring at the ceiling.

An uncomfortable shiver races across my skin. I should apologize. I should tell him I was wrong to snap at him, that I didn't mean to push him away. I have a job to do, and that's what I need to focus on. But I can't lie to myself any longer. I like Dave. I care about him. And I want him to want me the way I want him.

The bus shifts from side to side, and there's a commotion as James, Joel, and Key come through the curtain. I feel rather than hear the bus engine rumble to life then we begin moving.

"Seattle, here we come!" Key shouts, waving a pair of devil horns with each of his hands into the air and banging his head so his dark hair flies everywhere.

Joel jumps into the seat next to me and nudges my shoulder. "Excited?" he asks.

The three of them inch closer, their wide, smiling faces bobbing above me, and I can't help but mirror their energy back at them. "Let's get this party started!" I shout.

OUT ON THE ROAD, I do my best to insert myself into their enthusiasm. To ask questions about what it's been like living out of a bus in such confined quarters day in and day out. What it's like traveling around the country and performing for thousands of people. Before I know it, I've hit my journalistic stride, filling my new leather-bound journal full of their tour stories.

"In Georgia, we played in an open-air theater and it poured rain from the moment we started until the end of the last song."

"At the show in Kentucky, this girl snuck onto the bus while we were playing and stole all of Key's clothes!"

"The fucking seagulls in Maine are terrifying. I swear one was trying to peck my eye out."

For hours, I listen to them talk, while periodically they bust out a guitar and play me something they've been working on. Their joy is contagious, and they've given me so much already.

All but Dave.

At some point, he pulled the curtain across his bunk, and he hasn't emerged since. It's not until James stays behind to help me lower the dining table into a bed that anyone mentions him at all.

"He's glad you're here, you know," James says quietly as he passes me a pillow.

I look up. "Who?"

James gives me a look, and I feel heat rush into my cheeks. Of course. Who else would he be talking about?

"I know he can be a moody bastard, but even if it doesn't seem that way tonight . . . he's happy you're with us."

I look past James toward the bunks. "Oh. Sure, I know that." I shrug. "He's probably just tired and wanted to get to sleep early."

James smiles. "Yeah, we're all a little beat after spending the entire day cleaning."

I raise my eyebrows. "You guys were cleaning?"

He gestures to the spotless bus. "Should've seen this place eighteen hours ago. It was a fucking disaster zone. Dave made sure we cleaned it up before we came to get you."

My stomach flips. "He—oh, that was . . . you guys didn't have to—"

"That's what Joel said, then Dave almost punched him in the face so . . ."

I grin. "Well, I really appreciate it. And thanks for making me feel at home already. I know I'm kind of crashing your party."

He shrugs. "It's not as glamorous as people think." Pushing his long curly hair away from his face, he offers me a gentle smile. "Good night, Isabella."

"Good night."

As I settle into the gentle swaying movement of the bus in my dark bed, the sound of snores begin to reach me from the bunks and I grin remembering the guys' argument in Vegas. Snoring was never something that bothered me. Miguel had snored the few times we had been able to spend the night together.

My chest aches at the memory of his skin against mine. His kisses, so tender and innocently hesitant. In the dark with only the light of the passing street lights I can almost see his smiling, happy face before me. But he wasn't happy with me, or at least thought there was something better out there for him. Somehow, I never seem to be enough for anyone.

Part of me is desperate to believe that he'd be happy for me. He knew this was always what I wanted. To be a real journalist. That he was young and stupid and selfish, thinking his dreams were superior. I suppose all young people think that way. That their dream is the only thing worth pursuing and to hell with everyone else. But then I think, why is *my* dream more important than any he ever had? The spiral continues and pulls me down until the sound of the road grows louder and louder and louder.

I clamp my hands down over my ears and turn on my side trying to muffle the noise, the thoughts, the heartbreak, all of it.

But that soft and gentle snoring breaks through. Amongst all the noise where my guilt, my fear, my shattered heart lives, it pulls me back like an anchor surfacing from the depths of some endless ocean so I can finally sleep.

I CAN'T BE sure whether it's the lack of that gentle swaying movement or the early morning sunlight filtering in through the bus windows that wakes me. Either way, it takes a few moments to get my bearings and I nearly topple out of the bed and onto the floor.

I glance behind me where the boys' bunks are. Everything is quiet and they're likely all still asleep, so I take advantage and quickly get dressed, pulling on a pair of high waist jeans and a T-shirt with the band's logo that Key gave me last night as a welcome aboard present.

Looking around, I don't see a coffee machine, and after the night I had, I am in desperate need of caffeine. I grab my bag then peek through the front curtain to find Barney's gone. Maybe he went to get some coffee too. I step down the bus stairs and out into the frigid damp air and immediately realize I didn't bring a jacket with me. Spending an entire lifetime living in California and Arizona has not prepared me for dealing with northern winter temperatures.

"Shit," I say, wrapping my arms around myself. Looking around, I try to see if there's anywhere in my immediate vicinity that could pass for a decent breakfast, when I spot the doors of a gigantic old-fashioned theater. Above me are hundreds of lightbulbs lining a carved wooden sign that reads "The Alabaster." It's beautiful. Old and ornate like something out of the silent film era. Below the elaborate sign is a marquee which is . . . blank? How sad.

"Isabella?"

I turn to find Dave standing a few yards away with two coffees and a brown paper bag. All powers of speech leave me as he walks forward wrapped in a leather jacket, his blond hair still a bit messed up from sleep the way it was on Christmas morning after we . . .

"Why are you out here without a coat on?"

Blinking, I suddenly remember just how cold it is. "I . . . I might have forgotten to pack one."

"You—" he starts, then swallows and gestures with one of the coffee cups back to the bus. "Get back inside, then."

"Wait." I hold up my hand. "Where did you get that coffee? I'm dying for one."

It's quite possible that Dave blushes, but that could be the cold. "Oh, no, I—This is for you."

"What?"

"I mean I got it *for* you. I felt bad after how I behaved, and I know how much you need your coffee to survive. I can only imagine that need has multiplied after having to sleep on a fold down kitchen table, through snoring and my shit attitude last night."

He gives me the coffee with a sheepish grin. My hands close around the warm paper cup, a shiver racing up my arm as my fingertips brush his. Smiling, I pull it toward me. "Thank you, and you weren't— Last night I was out of line."

For a long moment we stare at each other until a gust of wind blows and my body contracts from the sheer violence of the cold. Next thing I know, Dave is shoving his coffee into my hand, whipping off his jacket, and draping it over my shoulders.

"You don't have to—"

"Shut up and let's find you a coat," Dave says with a smile. He takes his coffee back and turns to walk down the street, giving no indication that he's cold even though he's wearing a T-shirt with no sleeves.

He must sense I can't get my legs to move because he looks back over his shoulder. "Come on, Disco Girl."

Jogging behind him with my coffee cup in tow, we walk down

the empty street until we find a small boutique. A little bell jingles above us as we enter, the saleswoman's smile brightening when she spots Dave behind me. I mean, it's not like I can blame her. He's hot.

Okay, focus. I'm supposed to be looking for a winter jacket. Jacket . . . jacket. There are a few mannequins standing in the center of the store, and one in particular catching my eye. There's a gorgeous white leather cropped number with fringe detailing that catches my breath. It's gorgeous. Completely impractical for the purpose I need it for, but I would wear it all the time. If only I was made of money.

"See anything you like?" Dave asks, crossing his arms over his chest.

I twist my lips. "Yes, but . . . not the kind of coat I should be getting."

His eyes follow my gaze, and he points out the white jacket. "This one?"

When I nod, he glances over his shoulder and waves at the girl behind the counter. "Excuse me, could she try this on?"

My mouth drops open. "Dave, no! I can't."

"Why not?"

"It's not exactly a winter coat."

"So?"

I roll my eyes. "I don't have the money to be buying stuff I don't need."

He stares at me for a moment, then says, "Just try it on. You know, for fun."

"Fun?"

He grins. "Yeah."

The girl sidles up next to us. "Did you want to try on the jacket?" she asks, her eyes flicking between Dave and me.

"Uh—"

"Yes, she does," he insists.

"Sure thing," she says, then pulls the jacket off and takes it over to a three-way mirror at the back of the store.

Casting wildly around me, I spot a navy puffer jacket on a rack nearby and hold one out. "This one too. For practical reasons."

"Anything else?" she asks.

"No, I think that's it—"

"You should try this on too."

I spin around to find Dave holding up some off-the-shoulder dress that I can definitely not afford. "What?" I whisper.

But before I can stop him, he's passing it to the saleswoman and has turned to continue looking through the racks of clothes. My face boils and my stomach is in knots. What is he doing? When he holds up a metallic-silver halter top, I hold up my hand. "Dave, what are you—"

But he leans close to me, his breath tickling my ear. "Just indulge me, okay?"

Now my stomach is flip-flopping like the International House of Pancakes. "You want me to try on clothes for you?"

After he hands the saleswoman a few more things, he smiles slyly at me then sits in the big poofy chair in front of the mirror. "Absolutely."

Again, I hesitate, my heel tapping against the tile floor.

"Come on, Disco Girl," he encourages. "Fun, remember?"

I take a deep breath. Right. Clothes. I love trying on clothes. In fact, it's one of my favorite things and the reason I took the class that led me to meeting Becks. Besides, it's not like I have to buy everything. I'm just trying things on. I've done this hundreds of times before. Just never with an audience.

"Okay," I whisper before heading into the change room and pulling the curtain across with a clink. Shit, there's no mirror in here. Well, obviously, because there's a massive mirror *out there*. Why would you need one in here? I shake out my hands and grab the black dress that Dave picked out, stroking the lace in wonder. How did he know what size to choose? Stepping into it, I'm surprised when it fits perfectly—like a second skin.

"Wow," I whisper to myself, then look at the price tag and nearly choke. Well, I guess this is just supposed to be fun, right? Otherwise I might need to wear this dress while working the street corner outside to pay for it.

Pulling the curtain back, Dave's head snaps up and his lips part. His eyes sweep over me from head to toe, then he leans back and lets out a low whistle.

"What do you think?" I ask, pulling the hem of the dress down a little.

He blinks a few times. "Wow," he says, letting out a breath.

I smile. "That's what I said." I walk forward and turn to look at myself in the mirror. Wow is right. I don't think anything has ever looked so good on me in my entire life. Why do expensive clothes have to be so . . . expensive?

"You look incredible." He says it almost too quietly for me to hear.

I spin around and watch as his eyes look up to meet mine. "You think so?"

"Definitely."

I smile, and so does he. Wait, what's happening here? Is this what friends do? Do men usually pick out clothes for their female friends to try on? If it isn't, it should be. Dave has great taste.

"I think I'll try on that halter top next."

The halter top is another great pick. Who knew a metalhead who wears nothing but ripped shirts and faded jeans knew so much about what looks good on a woman? Actually, never mind. Maybe I don't want to know.

"What do you think about this one?" I ask, showing off the backless halter. The shirt is barely a shirt. It's more like a loin cloth for my chest. A singular scrap of silver fabric that barely covers my breasts, but maybe that's why he picked it. It dawns on me then that he's drinking me in and it causes a flush to spread over my entire body. Is he thinking about what I look like with nothing on? He can picture me anytime he wants now.

He needs to stop looking at me like that.

"I think I'll just try on the jacket now," I mumble. I rush out of the halter top, put on my T-shirt from earlier, and pull on the navy puffer jacket. The whole reason I came in here in the first place. Stepping out from behind the curtain, I do a quick turn in the mirror to make sure it fits right. "Okay, this works. Let's go."

"Whoa, Izzy," Dave says, standing to grab my arm. "What's wrong? You didn't even try on the other jacket."

I blink. "Sorry, I uh . . . I just feel bad that I'm taking up the change room when I don't plan on buying anything but this."

His forehead wrinkles and he looks around. "It's eight thirty in the morning. No one else is here."

"Fine, I just—everything is so expensive and I don't want to damage the clothes then have to pay for them."

"I'll pay for them."

What I planned to say next dies in my throat. "Wh—what?"

He looks at the items I tried on. "I'll get them for you. You know, as a 'welcome on tour' present."

"You . . . you can't," I say, unable to verbalize anything else. *What is happening?*

"Yes, I can. I've made really good money so far on tour and from the album, and while I'm no millionaire, I can afford to buy my friend a few things to wear to parties."

My eyes search his face. "I can't possibly accept," I whisper.

He huffs. "Why not? If you hadn't written those articles, I might not even be on tour and I definitely wouldn't have money to burn. Let me spend it on you." His face softens. "Let me spoil you."

Oh god, this man knows how to pull on my heartstrings. "Okay, fine."

He grins, and an involuntary chuckle escapes my mouth at how happy he seems. He gestures to the lady and points to the pile of clothes I left in the changeroom. "We'll take them all, thanks."

"Wait," I say, "I didn't mean everything! I haven't even tried on the white jacket yet."

"It'll fit," he says matter-of-factly.

"You're awfully confident about that."

He shrugs but grabs all of the items, including the beautiful white leather jacket, and heads to the cash register.

Wrapped up in my new navy coat, I let Dave lead us back toward the theater and tour bus, fresh coffee in hand.

"So," I start hesitantly. "How's the tour been going? Are you enjoying it?"

He shoves his hands in his back pockets as he walks. "Yeah, I mean . . . this was always the dream. It's totally surreal, but we've been able to meet so many other bands and people in the business. Did James tell you about the night it rained for our whole set? I have to admit, as much as I thought touring would be the best time of my life, I find myself wanting to be home more often than not."

Something swells in my chest. "I can imagine it's hard. Sleeping in bunks and always on the go."

His brow furrows but he doesn't say anymore.

"Anyway," I push on. "It won't last forever. We'll take lots of pictures and create amazing memories and you can keep them in that box with all the things you've collected to remind yourself you really made it."

He laughs. "Yeah?"

I smile. "Yeah. You're lucky you have a friend who's a fairly decent photographer," I say with a wink.

He smiles back, but it wavers for a moment. I turn away, swinging my bag of clothes—his smile is too glorious to look at dead-on. Ahead of us, the old theater's marquee comes into view.

"Thanks again," I say. "For everything. The clothes and the coffee. You're right, I can't survive without it."

He nods. "Just don't tell the guys. They'll think I'm playing favorites," he says with a smirk.

I mime zipping my lips closed and tossing away the key. Dave trudges into the bus, but I hesitate on the first step. Looking back up at the marquee, an idea comes to me. Scouring through my purse, I pull out the worn paper with Dave's list.

SEE THE BAND'S NAME ON A MARQUEE.

The sound of a door opening startles me, and I spot someone coming out of the theater door. He must be an employee if he's here this early in the morning.

"Umm . . . excuse me?" I say.

He looks up at me and frowns. "Here already? The show isn't for over twelve hours and it's freezing. Go home and I'll put in a good word for you with security so you can meet the band."

My mouth drops open. "I—excuse me?"

"That's what you want right? A way to get backstage?"

Holy shit, this guy thinks I'm a groupie.

"Oh!" I say, stepping forward, my stomach spinning like a dryer. "No. I'm with the band actually. I'm touring with them, writing an article for *Earworm Magazine*." I pull out my press badge from my purse and show him.

His cheeks turn pink. "Sorry, miss. My mistake. What can I do for you?"

I glance up at the marquee again. "I was wondering if you could do me a favor."

CHAPTER 32

Heartbreaker

DAVE

When I hop up on the stage for sound check a few hours later, I find three wild-haired musicians staring back at me and freeze.

"Hey," I say casually. "What's, uh . . . . What's going on?"

Key leans on the microphone. "Well, you seem to have come to your senses and stopped being such an asshole."

"I—"

"Also . . ." Joel says, dramatically looking over at James. "Was that *your* jacket I saw Isabella walking away in this morning?"

I press my lips together then shrug. "Yeah? So? She forgot to bring one and it's cold as shit."

"Dude, you wouldn't even lend me a pair of socks last week," Key says with an exasperated laugh.

"So what?" I head for the drum kit. "If you wore my socks, I would've had to burn them after."

"Just making observations . . . you know," Joel continues. "For the speech I'm going to give as the best man at your wedding."

"Who says you get to be the best man?" James chimes in.

"Will you all just fuck off?" I say loudly. "I can't even be chivalrous now?"

Key narrows his eyes. "When have you ever been chivalrous?"

I grin. "I always make sure the woman comes first." The less-than-impressed looks on all of their faces makes my smile disappear. "What? She's my friend. She was cold. I got her a coffee—"

"You got her a coffee?" Joel asks aghast. "I've known you for three years and you've never once gotten anything for any girl unless she asked for it."

"She's living on our bus!" I say, pissed off by how long this interrogation is lasting.

"Can you just admit you like her?" Key pleads. "It's so fucking obvious to everyone but you and her."

I toss my drumsticks to the floor and step backward. "I thought this was a fucking sound check. Not *Love Connection.*"

Turning my back to the group, I stomp off the stage and head outside for a smoke, ignoring the sound of them calling after me. I'm so annoyed that it takes me a solid minute in the freezing wind to finally get my cigarette to light. But as the smoke fills my lungs, I'm already calming down. And really, I'm not mad at them. I'm mad at myself.

Because I do like Isabella. A lot. Way more than I thought possible.

I glance back at the theater doors, but shake my head and walk away. God, if they only knew how much I like her. How I barely slept last night thinking about her sleeping mere feet away. How I wanted to be next to her. Not even to have sex . . . just to hold her and feel her against me. How when I woke up, I watched her beautiful face sleeping for longer than I care to admit before deciding to bury the hatchet with the help of a peace offering.

Then next thing I know I'm buying her clothes and loving every second of it. I could watch her try on dresses all day but . . . what the hell am I doing? She knew something was off. Friends don't do that. To be honest, I don't know if we'll ever be able to just be friends.

The bus is gone now, probably parked around back, and I'm thoroughly looking forward to sleeping in an actual bed tonight— the bonus of back-to-back shows in a single city. I'll be able to fully stretch out, have a shower, walk around naked if I want to and jerk off without the bunk squeaking.

And Isabella will be there. In her own room. Alone. I wonder if she touches herself and thinks of me. The image of her naked on a bed, fingers disappearing inside that dripping pink pussy has me hard and straining against the tight confines of my jeans in the middle of the street. I let out a long breath and try to think of literally anything to deflate my raging boner.

"Dave?"

Looking up, I see Isabella standing in front of the theater with her camera slung around her neck, all wrapped up in her new navy coat. Perfect, now how am I going to get that image of her out of my head? Hopefully she won't notice the bulge in my jeans from this angle. "Hey."

She frowns. "I thought you guys had rehearsal. What are you doing out here?"

Walking toward her, I rub the back of my neck. "Had a disagreement with the guys and needed to walk it off."

"Oh."

"How's the coat?" I ask. Anything to change the subject.

She looks down at it. "It does the job. Warm. This one doesn't smell as good though."

As though she hadn't meant to say that out loud, the smile drops off her face and her eyes widen. "I mean . . . I—shit." She sighs and closes her eyes.

I can't help the smile that stretches my lips. "You think I smell good?"

She places her hands on her hips and vibrates her lips together. "Yeah." She pauses. "Yeah, of course I do."

"You smell good too."

"Me?" she asks in a low voice.

Her chocolate eyes look up at me from underneath long dark lashes. Maybe I can do this. Maybe it won't all fall apart if I give this thing with her a real shot. But an iron grip suddenly tightens around my heart. My breath halts in my chest and the memories of my mom leaving, of Emily's abuse, Sam's betrayal . . . It comes rushing back in an overwhelming wave. All of that heartbreak and guilt and darkness flooding me at once.

I step back and clear my throat. "I just mean, all chicks smell good, you know?"

My heart aches at the way her face crumples. "Oh?"

"Way better than four guys living on a bus, that's for sure."

Her eyes search mine for a moment that feels like it'll go on forever. Like I'll be stuck feeling like the biggest piece of shit on earth for eternity. Then she does something I never would've expected. She smiles wide and lifts her chin.

"Right. I can only imagine how bad it gets. Not exactly looking forward to that part."

"Isabella—"

"Anyway," she moves on, looking away. "I was looking for you because I wanted you to see something.

She steps beside me and turns, pointing up toward the massive marquee, where the words "Carnal Sins" are lit up by a hundred lights. My heart pounds in my ears and some strange giddiness washes over me. My band's name. It's really up there. Shining like a beacon at a real theater. I can't believe it. I dig my hand into my pocket, rubbing my thumb across my lucky charm.

"I've been dreaming of seeing that my whole life," I murmur.

But when I look back, Isabella is gone, the front door of the theater swinging shut behind her.

The glimmering euphoria at seeing the band's name up in lights comes crashing down. What I said before is true: I really don't have anyone to spoil, and other than the guys, there's no one I'd rather share this moment with than the girl who I just made walk away from me. I need to figure out if I can continue to play this dangerous game. How many sacrifices does music need me to make? Or will my luck crash and burn, taking everything with it, when it's already too late?

CHAPTER 33

Five Years Ago

To say I was surprised when Charlie said he'd let me stay at his place until I figured out where to go would probably be the understatement of the year. He'd been receptive to me telling him about what happened, but I could also tell that Sam had planted the seed in his mind that what he'd accused me of was true. That I thought the guys weren't talented enough to make it and thought I was better than them.

"You have to know that thought never once crossed my mind," I say, my voice broken.

"Oh, come on, Dave," Charlie says. "You were always lightyears ahead of all of us. Maybe you were just too blind to see it."

I scoff. "Guess I've been blind to a lot of things in my life."

"Listen," he says, leaning forward over his knees. "I'm sorry about Emily. That whole thing sucks. At least the cops believed you. Guys who look like us—" He pauses and our eyes meet. "Generally speaking, usually no one cares about our side of the story."

I nod. "Yeah, I know."

"If I were you," he continues, "I'd get out of here. There's nothing keeping you here anymore. Pack up your stuff, get a job, and hey, if you're lucky you can find another garage band to jam with on weekends."

That awful word again. *Lucky*. "But that's—" My eyes sting as I try to rein in my emotions. "That's not what I want."

"Dave."

I look up at my friend—or who I thought was one of my best friends.

"Most people don't get what they want. Dreams aren't always meant to come true."

Ring ring.

Charlie sighs and stands to walk into the kitchen where the phone is while I sit back and contemplate his words. Maybe he's right. Maybe it's not meant to happen for me.

"Uh, hey, Dave?" he calls. "It's for you."

I look over my shoulder, perplexed. Only a handful of people even know I'm here. Who the hell would be calling me?

Charlie holds out the phone and I walk over, tentatively taking the receiver in my hand. "Hello?"

"Baby, where are you?"

My blood turns to ice. "Emily?"

There's loud music in the background. "Why aren't you here? I miss you," she says, her words slurring and her voice pitching in a sing-songy kind of way. I can imagine her now. Eyes hooded and covered in sparkly eye shadow, her mascara smudged, leaning against the wall of someone's kitchen at a party to call me. It's such a familiar sight I can almost see it directly before me. But rather than it filling my heart with warmth, all I feel now is rage and despair.

"Em, what the fuck are you doing?" I say through gritted teeth.

"I wanted to hear your voice. I feel like I haven't seen you in so long."

My eyes clamp together. "Because we're not together anymore. Or do you not remember telling a bunch of cops I was hitting you?"

Charlie looks up from his place on the couch, and I turn away, the spiral phone cord wrapping around my body with the movement.

She laughs on the other side of the phone. "Baby, what are you talking about? I would never do that."

"You— Yes, you did!"

Heavy breaths crackle across the speaker. "I'm sorry if I made you mad. But we can work through it. Come pick me up and I'll make it up to you."

My stomach turns. "Emily, what are you not understanding?"

"How can you be so mean to me, Davey? I thought you loved me."

I pinch the top of my nose. "Yeah, well, not anymore."

"So that's it?" she says, her voice breaking. "Baby, come on. Just come and get me and we can talk this out."

"It's not fucking happening, Em," I say raising my voice.

"You can't break up with me," she shouts back. "I won't let you."

"I can, and I am. Don't ever call me again. You need help? Call Sam."

A sob breaks through the receiver, and a black feeling resembling a thundercloud spreads over my very soul.

"You can't leave me, or I'll—I'll . . . I'll kill myself."

I nearly punch the wall. "You can't say that shit to me. You ruined my fucking life!"

"If you don't come here right now, I'm going to do it. I'm going to slit my wrists and it will all be your fault."

My heart is pounding, I'm sweating and nauseous. What if she actually tries it? Maybe I should just go . . . one last time.

There's sobbing on the other end. "Baby, please come. I don't want to die."

I open my mouth, ready to say that I'll be there—that I'll come wherever she is. But if I do, she'll do this again and again and again. I can't let that happen. What we had is finished, over.

"You need help . . . but it won't be from me."

I can hear the way her tone shifts, even through the phone. "God, you're such a fucking disappointment. I always knew you never really loved me."

It's as if a burning knife has been stabbed through my heart. Hot tears spill from the corners of my eyes. "I loved you with *everything* I had," I whisper. "But you— You broke me, Emily."

Silence.

"I never want to see or hear from you again," I manage.

"Baby—"

"Goodbye."

She shouts into the receiver, but I hang up. I'm exhausted and shaking as I rest my forehead against the wall, the urge to break down and cry overwhelming. Did I do the right thing? Maybe I should've gone to see her. One last time, for closure. But she's wasted, so what kind of conversation would that be?

The one person who I should have a conversation with is Sam.

Lifting my head, I dial the familiar number, pacing back and forth as it rings. It goes to the answering machine. "Sam, it's Dave. Emily . . . she might be in trouble. She's at some party. Can you go check on her? Sam?"

When he still doesn't pick up, I try calling again and again. On the fourth time, he finally answers.

"What the hell do you want, Noblar?" he says.

"I . . . Emily called me. I think you should go and check on her. She seems . . ." I sigh. "She might try to hurt herself."

"What the hell are you—"

"Sam, enough!" I shout. "You can hate me all you want but I

would never want something bad to happen to either of you. Can you just *listen to me*?"

There's a stretch of silence.

"Where is she?" he asks.

"She didn't say, but it sounded like she was at a house party. Know of any happening tonight?"

"Yeah, there's one on the other side of the bridge," he says slowly. "I'll, uh, I'll go check it out."

Relief loosens the tightness in my chest. "Thank you."

The line goes dead and I turn to slump against the wall, sinking to the floor so I can bury my face into my knees. Maybe Charlie's right. Maybe I need to get away from here. Away from Emily and Sam. Away from my dad. Just . . . away. It's not like anyone wants me here anyway.

"Everything okay?" Charlie asks, standing in front of me.

I look up at him, trying to blink away the moisture in my eyes. I push myself off the floor and wipe my nose. "Listen, I'm going to get out of here."

He frowns. "Where are you going to go?"

I shrug. "I don't know. But I can't stay here. I'm going to load my kit into the car and I'll be back in for my clothes, then I'll be out of your hair."

"Dave, it's almost midnight. Just sleep here and you can head out in the morning."

"No, man . . . I can't—I'm just going to drive until morning and figure it out from there."

I PACK all of the heavy drum equipment into my station wagon. It normally doesn't take me this long, but between my frantic, racing thoughts and shaking hands, it's slow going. When it's done, I head back into the house for my meager bag of clothes and toiletries.

"Are you sure you want to go right now?" Charlie asks.

I nod. "Yeah. Thanks for letting me crash for the week. Take care of yourself." I hold out my hand. For a second I think he won't shake it, but I'm surprised when he throws his arms around me for a hug.

"Drive safe, okay?"

He lets go and I offer him a small smile. I turn toward the door and I'm nearly there when the phone rings again. My stomach drops and I stop in my tracks. It's almost one in the morning. No one would be calling this late, unless . . .

Charlie picks up the phone. "Hello?"

My heart is racing, sprinting like the roadrunner, completely at odds with the rest of me that can barely move.

"Sam, hold on. What do you mean?" Charlie asks.

I turn slowly, and find his face has turned as white as a sheet.

I don't even know how the words come out of my mouth, but I manage to ask, "What happened?"

The receiver drops away from Charlie's face. "There's been an accident."

CHAPTER 34

Strike of the Beast

ISABELLA

By the time the tour makes it to Montana, I've settled into a nice routine. I wake up and wherever we happen to be, I pack away my makeshift bed of a kitchen table, get dressed, then go for a walk to find coffee and stretch my body out. It also gives me ample time to get out and clear my head before I say something stupid again. God, what was I thinking? His jacket smells good? I'm such an idiot. One thing that's been made perfectly clear by that interaction is Dave and I can't be friends.

It sucks, but at least it's given me an understanding of how to be with him. Indifferent and casual. There is an upside, though. I thought that we would be stuck shoulder to shoulder on this bus for days and weeks at a time. But I've seen less and less of him. When we're not driving, the guys are rehearsing or writing new music, and I've been either writing at local coffee shops or at the back of the theater, or sometimes, when there aren't many nice places to go, in a motel room. And when we are all crammed on the bus together? Dave usually goes to sleep, pulling the curtain across his bunk.

At least the rest of the guys are fun to hang out with. Joel and Key are hilarious and James, for being the youngest, seems wise beyond his years. Periodically, I spy Joel and Key opening the cupboard—the one with the wristbands. I haven't seen Dave reach for any, but maybe he's trying to be respectful and not flaunt it in my face. I've seen the girls though—the ones who hang off of him.

The ones wearing wristbands, who end up backstage with hair a mile high and barely any clothes on. But he's been true to his word and when I'm around, he doesn't do much more than talk to them. At least he's not making out with or groping anyone when I'm in the room. I wouldn't be surprised if he took them back to his motel room. I generally don't stick around too much backstage after the show. Thankfully no one has been hooking up on the bus that I know of, but what they get up to after I head to bed, who knows? Maybe Dave hooks up with the girls backstage, like Key and Joel do.

Maybe I just need to accept it and move on.

Everything else aside, I've been writing a lot, and I mean *a lot*. And not just about the guys, but about myself too and how it feels to travel around with them. It'll never make the final version of the feature, but it's something I want to remember—immortalize. The journal Dave gave me is more than half full by now, and I just wish I had some more input from him about the tour and the seemingly ever-growing success of their little band.

Of course, I never told him it was me who ensured the band's name was on the marquee in Seattle. There was no way I could. If I did, he might figure out that I have his list. And instead of returning it to him like a normal person I've kept it with me like some stalker. While I didn't stick around to see his reaction, he mentioned to the guys several times how it was something he had always dreamed of seeing. It felt good to see him happy.

"We're here," Barney says, calling through the curtain as I feel the bus slow down and finally stop.

I look over at the clock on the microwave. It's a little after seven in the evening. I haven't eaten yet, as I've gotten too engrossed in editing my work from the last two weeks, but now that we're here, I think I might try to find a diner.

"Anyone want to get the hell out of here and find something to eat?" Dave asks, peeking out of his bunk.

"Actually, I'm going to try to find a payphone so I can call Becks," James says, grabbing his coat and wallet and heading for the door. "I said I'd call when we got here."

"Yeah, we could eat," Key says. "Miss Rodriguez? Care to join us for some dinner?"

I smile, my eyes briefly flicking to Dave. If he had asked it to be just the two of us, I would've politely declined and eaten a pile of saltines with jelly for dinner. But the fact that it'll be a group of us? That seems safe.

"Sure, sounds good."

We check ourselves into a really rad motel that has an indoor heated pool. All of the rooms back onto it and I find myself wishing I brought a bathing suit. But first we set out on foot to find a place to eat. The Montana air is crisp and clean and while it's cold, it's not unpleasant. After a few minutes of walking, we spot a neon sign in the distance.

"The V Lounge?" I say, squinting to make sure I read it right.

"Oh, brilliant!" Joel says.

"Joel," Dave says exasperatedly. "We can't take Isabella there."

Joel looks to me as though he's forgotten something. "Oh, shit . . . right. Uhh—"

"Why?" I ask.

Dave's lips twitch, then he leans forward, his mouth so close to my ear my whole body breaks out into goosebumps. "It's a strip club."

Heat floods my cheeks. "Oh. Right. Yeah, I'm really hungry. But you guys can go. I'll just head to that place there," I say, pointing to a vibrant blue neon sign next to it with the word "diner."

Joel does a double take. "They probably have food at the club, lots of those places have buffets."

My mouth drops open.

Key laughs, but Dave frowns. "Joel, you're a moron. Only you would think a stripper buffet is acceptable."

He thinks about it for a moment, then looks at me. "I'm sorry. You shouldn't be subjected to that."

"It's fine if you want to go," I say. "I'm a big girl. I can get my own food that hasn't had nipple tassles near it."

Dave laughs, and my chest swells at the thought he laughed because of me.

"You sure?" Key asks.

"Go have fun," I say with a smile.

"Okay, see you in the morning then," he says.

I'm almost at the diner when I hear boots crunching in the snow behind me. I turn around and find Dave on my heels.

"What are you doing?" I ask, bewildered.

"Going to get some food."

"I thought—"

He levels me with a look of skepticism. "You thought my idea of getting something to eat was going to a nasty buffet at the strip club? Come on now."

I glance between Dave's bright blue eyes and the retreating backs of Joel and Key. Maybe this wasn't a good idea. Now we're alone.

"You don't have to come with me," I say quietly as we fall into step beside each other. "We're both adults. If you want to go —"

"Well, I want food that doesn't have sweaty glitter all over it," Dave says.

I catch his grin out of the corner of my eye, and I can't help but laugh.

"I've missed that sound."

It's so quiet, yet I wonder if I heard him correctly. When I turn to look at him, he's watching his feet as we walk. I think a dangerous butterfly springs to life in my belly, and soon we're walking through the door and finding a booth to sit in.

We both look over the menu when I spot something that makes me smile. I take a peek at Dave over top of the laminated paper, watching as his eyes scan over what he might like to eat. When a waitress shows up, I can't help but notice the way she licks her lips at the sight of Dave, then how her smile turns to a frown as she spots me sitting with him. She must think we're together.

"What can I get you?" she asks.

"What are you known for?"

She turns to me and raises her eyebrows. "What?"

Try each city's signature dish. It was on his list.

"We're just visiting, and neither of us has been to Montana before." I shrug. "What food are you known for? What does everyone come here to eat?"

I can feel Dave watching me, but I keep my eyes on the curly-haired waitress. Finally, she says, "Probably the elk burger."

"Elk burger?"

"Yeah, game meat is pretty big here."

I hand over my menu. "I'll have that, please. With fries."

"Me too," Dave says quickly, not taking his eyes off of me as he hands the girl the menu. She walks away, glancing back at Dave just once before she disappears into the kitchen. "You know," Dave says, playing with the sugar packets in the container on the table, "I've always wanted to try different foods from all over the country—all over the world."

I smile softly. "Yeah? That's pretty cool."

He continues with the sugar, correcting the placement of different packets until they're in order. "I always forget though."

"What do you mean?"

He looks up at me. "Whenever I go somewhere new, I forget to ask or check what local food I should eat and usually end up with what I've always had before. So, thank you for reminding me."

"Don't thank me yet. It could be terrible."

He grins wide, and that little butterfly that's been fluttering all alone in my belly now seems to have made friends.

"How's your article coming along?" he asks.

"It's good. It's missing something though," I admit.

He furrows his brows. "What?"

"You."

It hangs in the air for a moment, neither of us moving, neither of us breathing. Finally he sighs and leans back against the booth. "I know. I'm sorry, I've been—well, you know."

I avert my eyes. "It's okay."

"No, it's not."

"It's fine, Dave. When this is over, I'll keep my distance and —" I swallow hard. "We can just be people who hooked up one time."

He frowns. "That's not what I want."

"I don't think you know what you want."

There's a pause. "It's just being on tour and everything that's happened in the last year. I had a plan. But now . . . ."

"You don't think you're achieving your goals?" I ask, concerned.

He drums his thumbs on the table. "That's just it. I am. Quicker than I ever imagined."

"That's great though."

He presses his lips together and doesn't say anything more.

The waitress appears with our drinks and after nearly chugging half of my water, I sit up a little straighter.

"I have a few questions, if you don't mind," I say, pulling out a pencil and the notebook he gave me. "For the article, I mean."

"Yeah, of course."

I nod and open up to a fresh page. "Umm . . . let's see. Oh, right." I look back up. "Why do you think you're able to so accurately sense the emotions of your fellow band members?"

He blinks. "Wow, that was . . . I wasn't expecting that kind of question."

I try to stop the smile that pulls at the corners of my mouth. "Have you always been like that? As a kid?"

Shaking his head, he takes a drink. "No. In fact, most of my life, I lived blissfully ignorant to the feelings of others."

His sad tone surprises me. "But that changed?"

He nods.

"Care to elaborate?"

"There were just a lot of things I should've seen but didn't, and eventually they all blew up in my face. So now? I've learned to pay attention."

"Does it have something to do with your first band?"

I see the way his muscles tense before he clears his throat. "Who said I was in another band?"

Shifting in my seat, I take a sip of my water. "It might have been briefly mentioned by one of the others."

His mouth twists.

"You don't have to talk to me about it if you don't—"

"I *was* in a band," he interrupts. "And I wanted so badly to make it that I looked past the fact that . . ." He sighs. "The fact that maybe they weren't as invested as I was. Maybe I wanted it too much—pushed them too far. But I had dreams and I thought the only way I was going to make it was with them. I needed to prove something . . . at the expense of *everyone* else."

His face darkens and my chest feels tight. "You were too focused on your own dreams to see that theirs didn't match yours."

"Yes."

His thumb taps against the table again. A chaotic sort of rhythm, like he can't make up his mind about which one he wants to play so he plays them all. Then I see it. The way it plays out across his face. Something happened to him. Something that causes him pain. Is that where his anger and darkness come from?

"That's not all though, is it?" I ask softly.

Narrowing his eyes, he clasps his hands together.

"Something else happened. Something you feel guilty about."

He scrunches his face up and leans away from me. "What do I have to feel guilty about?"

"It's where the anger comes from, isn't it? The thing that haunts you."

"I—" His ears turn pink and I can see a hint of moisture in his eyes. Maybe that was too close to home.

My heart starts to race in my chest. "I'm sorry, I didn't mean to push. You're always free to not answer anything I ask."

He swallows, his Adam's apple bobbing up and down. "I'm just terrified that it'll happen again," he whispers.

I don't hesitate. I reach across the table and grasp his hands, his calloused fingers gripping mine instantaneously. "You shouldn't live your life consumed with the fear that things outside of your control will happen."

The waitress comes at that moment to deliver our elk burgers, and he avoids my eyes as they're placed in front of us. She must sense the tension between us, her eyes bouncing from the looks on our faces to the way we grip each other's hands so tightly his knuckles are white. The waitress shifts uncomfortably, slowly asks, "Y'all need anything else?"

He lets go, then sniffs and smiles at her. "This looks great, thanks."

I retract my hands, my heart dancing the samba in my chest as the waitress leaves us alone again.

"So," Dave says with a small smile. "Elk burger?"

I smile back and grab the burger off my plate. "You don't think it'll moo at me, do you?"

"I don't think elks moo." He laughs.

"Grunt? Bleat?" I ask.

"I guess we're about to find out." He takes a bite and so do I. Surprisingly, it's delicious.

I watch as he chews and swallows. "Verdict?"

"It's . . . sweet. But really fucking good. Sadly, no bleating."

"Hold on, let me get a picture," I say, pulling my camera out of my bag.

"A picture?"

"To put in your box," I say.

His eyes skip across my face before he lifts the burger and chomps down.

I laugh and raise the camera, capturing his face buried in the food. "Perfect." Grinning, I take another bite and relish in the rich, sweet flavor of the meat.

"Why do they call it a hamburger if it's not made from ham?"

I blink. "Huh?"

He picks up the burger and points to it. "Elk burger, bison burger, chicken burger . . . why hamburger? It's made from beef."

A smile pulls at my lips. "I'm not sure, but that's a good point."

Dave takes another bite, chews, then swallows. "What did the hamburger name their baby?"

I tilt my head. "What?"

"Patty."

A laugh bursts out of me and Dave smiles. "Where do hamburgers go to hook up?"

I roll my eyes but can't hide my grin.

"A meatball."

"Oh my god . . ."

"I could do this all day you know," he threatens.

"Thank you."

He holds my gaze with a knowing smile for a moment. "Hey, did you hear about the hamburger who couldn't stop telling jokes?"

"Okay, I'm leaving."

"He was on a roll!"

WALKING ACROSS THE COLD, snowy parking lot toward the motel, I feel lighter than I have in weeks. Maybe Dave and I really can make this work. It's not exactly what I want, but it's enough. For now. There's also something that makes me think he acts the way he does because he's still not over something. Maybe if I can figure out what that is, things could change.

"So, Key mentioned you guys are performing a new song tomorrow?" I say, cutting through the silence of the night.

Dave nods. "Yeah. I mean, if the crowd requests an encore, that is."

"What do you mean?"

He shrugs. "Al, doesn't want us to deviate too much from our set, so we compromised."

"Oh."

"Besides, we haven't had a crowd request an encore yet, so I think he's feeling confident about keeping that new song a secret."

I stop. "You haven't played an encore?"

He stops too. "It's fine. We're still small-time. It'll happen eventually, I'm sure."

But my mind is already churning with ways I can make this happen for him. How happy it would make him. "I guess you never know, right?"

"Right."

We arrive at the motel and I walk toward my room. I pause when I get there, only to look up and see Dave standing closer than normal. I'm reminded of the way he looked when he asked me to dance on Christmas. Despite the cold outside, I'm warm and the thought of his body against mine burns brightly in my mind. A clenching sensation in my core causes my hips to push forward as though searching for his.

"Thanks for reminding me to try new things," he finally says with a bashful smile.

"You're welcome."

His breath rises in the cold air between us like little clouds. Then his fingers brush against mine, just for a moment. An accident. Or maybe it wasn't.

"I, uh—" I mumble, pushing my hair behind my ears. "Well, good night."

He blinks then takes a deep breath, stepping back. "Good night, Izzy."

My heart skips three beats, then tries to catch up by stuttering in my chest. He called me Izzy. But he's already moving away to the next door and disappearing inside, while I stand here in the cold with my mouth open.

"What the hell . . ." I mutter. Finally, I push inside my room and fall against the wall with shallow panting breaths.

He called me Izzy. But what does that mean? It could mean absolutely nothing. Or it could mean everything.

I flick on the light and look around the room, taking in

the plaid bedspread, the paneled walls, the brown everything. Even the phone is brown. The phone. Right. I should call my mom. The phone rings twice and a familiar voice answers.

"*Mamá*?"

There's a deep inhale. "Isa! *Mija,* how are you? Where are you?"

"I'm good. I'm in Montana, can you believe it? There's real snow here and everything."

"Snow?"

"Yes, snow. It's everywhere and it's so beautiful and cold and —"

"Isa, listen . . ."

The smile drops from my face. "What?"

"Someone called for you the other day. They said it was urgent that you call him back."

My mouth goes dry. "Him? Who was it?"

"Uhh . . . someone named . . . hold on, where's the—ah, here it is. Simon Cranmer?"

That cruel bastard won't ever leave me alone, will he? What the hell does he want now? How did he even find my parents' number?

"Did he . . ." I swallow against the anxious lump in my throat. "Did he say what he wanted or . . . ?"

"He just left a phone number."

"Can I have it, please?"

She recites the number for me and I write it down on a pad next to the phone. "What's going on?" she asks.

"Don't worry. It's nothing," I lie. "*Mamá*, I have to go," I say quickly.

"Wait! Don't—"

I hang up the phone and attempt to take a deep breath. Before I can stop myself, I'm dialing this dreaded number. It rings and rings and rings. Ugh, where the hell is he? Just before I go to hang up, the line connects.

"Hello?"

"Simon," I spit.

"Ah, little Bella," he says jovially. "You finally got my message, did you?"

I pull my legs under me. "You called my mother?" I shout.

"Should I have called someone else?" he asks.

"You shouldn't have called anyone!" I scream.

"Now, now. I had to get a hold of you, and you are a difficult woman to get in touch with."

I try to take a deep breath, but it nearly makes me choke. "What the hell do you want?"

"No small talk? I appreciate a woman who gets right down to business."

I can picture his smug smile through the phone. There's music playing in the background and people talking. Is he at a party?

"Right, well, I'll cut to the chase then," he continues. "I want your article for *Earworm*."

Did I just have a stroke? The wheels in my head stutter and stop, malfunctioning like my ability to hear sounds and speak words.

"Bella?"

"You—you what?" I whisper.

"I want the feature you're writing for *Earworm Magazine*."

"What?" I shout incredulously. "Why the hell would I give you more of my work?"

There's a pause. "The *Chronicle* isn't accepting any of my ideas. They want more shit about that stupid band—"

"Carnal Sins," I say through gritted teeth.

"Whatever. Anyway, I need you to give me what you wrote about their tour."

"Fuck you!"

"If you're offering, I'm always happy to oblige a casual hate fuck."

My grip tightens on the phone until I'm hunched over, my knuckles white. "I would rather die than give you more of my work to pawn off as your own."

He sighs. "Well, then I guess a whole lot more people are going to get to see that sweet ass of yours."

I blink. "What are you saying?"

"I'll make it crystal clear for you. You fax me your draft for *Earworm* by the weekend or that salacious picture will be seen by more than me."

My face burns red hot and my jaw is sore from trying to control the trembling. "I'll kill you."

"You have until Saturday to decide. It would be a shame to have to humiliate you like this. I've been enjoying having this small part of you to myself."

I slam the phone down and scream. Rage like I've never felt before races through my veins like acid. I want to hurt him, torture him, kill him. Grabbing the ceramic ashtray from the motel nightstand, I hurl it across the room. The ashtray shatters, the sound seemingly knocking some sense into me as I rush over to stare at the wreckage.

There are pieces everywhere. On the desk, on the carpet. I freeze and try to take in a deep breath, but my body shakes so hard I can't even do that properly. This can't be real. How can someone get away with this? I bend down to pick up one of the larger pieces of shattered ceramic when there's a knock at the door. Jumping, the broken piece falls from my hand back to the floor, slicing my palm in the process.

"Shit!" I mutter as I press my lips together to keep from crying out. Blood begins to pool in my hand and trickle down onto the carpet.

"Izzy?"

Looking at the door, I suck in a breath. "Dave?"

He knocks again. "Izzy, are you okay? I heard shouting."

Fuck, fuck, fuck. "Just a second," I say, running to the bathroom and grabbing a towel to wrap around my hand. The rough terry cloth stings, but I head back for the door, opening the lock and pulling it open to find a wet-haired and wide-eyed Dave.

CHAPTER 35

Do You Wanna Touch Me?

DAVE

I don't even wait for her to invite me in as I step past her into the motel room. I'd been getting out of the shower when I heard it. Muffled shouting followed by a loud bang against our adjoining walls. Something primal took over my brain then, spiraling into all sorts of horrible scenarios of Izzy, *my* Izzy, in danger.

"Dave, I—"

"What's going on?" I ask, interrupting her. "Is someone else here?"

"No, there's no one."

It's only then that I notice her red face. Then I spot the blood. The once white towel wrapped around her hand that is now mostly soaked through with crimson. My heart is beating a million times per minute. What's happened here? "Izzy, you're hurt."

We both glance at her injured hand, and she instinctively pulls it in closer to herself. "It's nothing."

You can't leave me, or I'll—I'll . . . I'll kill myself. I'm going to slit my wrists and it will all be your fault!

Panic settles in my heart. No, no. No. *No.* "You're bleeding all over the carpet, Izzy, this isn't nothing," I shout.

She flinches. "I—" Her concerned eyes bounce all over my face. "Dave? Are you—" She steps closer, and I can hardly breathe. The air won't enter my lungs and my vision blurs, the focus darting in and out around me. Her uninjured hand reaches out to touch me, and I realize just how fast my chest is heaving. Am I having a heart attack?

"Dave," she whispers. "I'm okay. It was just an accident."

"An a-accident—" I get out. My eyes finally find the shattered remnants of what appears to be an ashtray.

"It just broke and when I tried to pick it up it cut me," she says calmly.

"So you weren't—you weren't trying—"

Her eyebrows lift. "Trying to what?" she asks.

Relief settles over my skin, sinking down to calm my heart and force air into my tight chest. "Nothing," I say, swallowing around the lump in my throat. "Here, let me see."

"It's fine, I can—" But she flinches.

"Come back to my room. I have bandages and antiseptic."

Her head tilts. "You do?"

I hold up my own hands. "Occupational hazard. Sometimes the calluses split or I get a bad blister that bursts."

"Oh. Eww."

"Come on," I say, ushering her out into the freezing air then into my room. The TV is still on and it's cold in here after stupidly leaving the door open when I ran out. I nudge her toward my bathroom and flip the toilet seat down. "Here. Sit."

She does as she's told while I grab the small kit out of my bag. When I come back, I take out the roll of bandages and the hydrogen peroxide. "Give me your hand."

Sniffling, she holds out her hand wrapped in the bloody towel. I gently unwrap it to find a gash in her palm. "Ouch," I say, bringing her hand over the sink so the blood doesn't drip on the floor. "The bleeding seems to have started to clot, so I don't think you'll need stitches."

"Stitches?" she says a bit hysterically.

I offer a soft smile. "Never had stitches before?"

She shakes her head and shivers. "Ugh, no."

I shrug. "They're not so bad. This is going to sting though," I say and then pour the hydrogen peroxide over her cut.

She hisses and tries to pull her hand away, but I grip her wrist tightly. Our eyes meet. "How did it happen? The ashtray, I mean."

"Oh." She looks away. "It slipped out of my hand."

She's lying. I know I heard that thing hit the wall. "And the shouting?" I ask, peering up at her.

With a sigh, she tilts her head back. "Just a rough conversation with my mom, and I guess I'm just a bit stressed with a problem I need to solve for the article with *Earworm* . . . Anyway, it's fine. I'll figure it out."

"If you need any help, you know you can always ask me, right?" I say. "You don't need to take it out on poor innocent ashtrays."

She turns pink all the way to her ears and she looks so goddamn pretty—even if she is covered in blood. I wrap her hand with a clean bandage and tie it off. "There. A few days and you'll be as good as new."

She sighs deeply. "Thanks for fixing me up, doc," she jokes before standing.

"Do you want to stay here?" I blurt out before I can reel the thought back in.

Her lips part and she blinks at me.

"I just—I mean," I stammer. "I was just going to get some snacks and watch TV. To be honest, I'm kind of bored here all by myself."

"Oh," she says, glancing past me at the small motel room and making me aware for the first time that there's no couch. Just the one bed to sit on.

"Well." She glances down at herself. "I should probably change first. There's blood on my clothes."

"I'll get your bag,"

"Dave, no. I can do it—"

"Seriously? What kind of person would I be if I let you back in there to step on some broken piece of ashtray hiding in the carpet?"

Before she can argue, I'm back out the door and ducking into the next motel room. I pick up as much of the broken ashtray as I can find and put it in the trash. She doesn't seem to have unpacked, so I grab her bag and the keys and turn off the lights.

She lets go of a breathy laugh when I reenter, and I smile. "Come on, why don't you get changed and I'll grab some snacks from the vending machine."

"Are you sure I'm not intruding?"

I nod. "Yeah. You're doing me a favor. Come on, we'll watch TV."

Hesitantly, she smiles. "Okay."

"Here," I say, squatting down and placing her bag at her feet.

When I look up, we're at eye level and she's looking at me with those sparkling eyes. Tentatively, she reaches out and places her hand on my cheek. My breath catches at her soft touch. "Thank you."

I simply nod, then grab my wallet before heading out the door to grab some munchies. The cold air hits me and I can suddenly think a little clearer. What the fuck am I thinking? The two of us hanging out on a bed together? This is a bad idea.

Feeding some one-dollar bills through the vending machine, I choose an assortment of snacks and I momentarily panic, wondering if she won't like what I've picked. I'm starting to lose my mind. Why do I care if she likes my snack choice?

Because I want her to like my choices. I want her to like . . . me. And she does. I know she does. I can see it on her face whenever we're together. The way she smiles slyly when she wants to laugh at something I've told the guys. How her eyes seem to want to memorize every detail of my face when we're alone together. How I want to do the same to her. Would that really be so bad?

You shouldn't live your life consumed with the fear that things outside of your control will happen.

But it is terrifying. Loving anyone is a terrifying ordeal. And I

—

I love her.

A warmth spreads through my veins at the thought. Glancing back at the room, it hits me like a bolt of lightning. Is this why I've had no interest in anyone else? The amount of beautiful girls who've donned our wristbands backstage has been overwhelming. But I didn't want any of them. I just wanted her. God, how could I be so stupid for so long? And I've hurt her. Ignored her and pushed her away. I'm a fucking idiot.

But what if this turns out just like before? My experience with love hasn't been the best. Besides, Izzy is right. She doesn't know what she's right about, but I *am* haunted. Would she understand that pain? Can I bare my soul and have her accept me anyway?

Puffing air into my cheeks, I collect the bags of chips, the licorice and Charleston Chew bars, and head back to the room. When I open the door, she's sitting on the bed in an oversized T-shirt and shorts. Her hoop earrings are gone and her hair is a tumble of thick curls that fall over her shoulder. She looks incredible, even with her hand all bandaged up. It felt nice to take care of her.

"Hey," she says quietly.

Closing my mouth, I walk toward the bed and dump the bags down. "I wasn't sure what you'd like so I got a few things."

She reaches for a bag of BBQ chips and smiles. "This is great," she says. "And . . . thank you again for . . ." She raises her hand.

I grab the licorice and kick off my shoes, then I stretch out on the bed with my back up against the headboard. "It's no problem. Besides, I'm always happy to come to your rescue."

Her lips twitch as she pulls her knees up and sinks back against the pillows. I grab the remote and turn the TV on. "Any preferences?"

She shrugs. "I think *The Tonight Show* will be coming on."

"Okay."

Sure enough, when I flip through the handful of channels, Johnny Carson appears doing his opening monologue. For a while we just contentedly watch TV together, even if I can't help but think about how bad I want her head to rest on my chest.

"Just think," she says, breaking the silence. "One day maybe you guys will be on there."

I fight the urge to scoff. "I doubt it."

She frowns. "Why not?"

"There'd likely be a riot if thrash metal made it on prime time TV."

"I don't know about that."

"We're not exactly Journey."

"Well," she says, turning to lie on her side and propping her head up on her hand to speak to me. "You managed to turn me into a fan. And all I listened to was disco."

I sidle down next to her on the bed. "Well, when your taste in music is that bad, you really can only go up from there."

Her eyes widen, but with my smirk, her lips pull into a toothy smile. Shoving my shoulder playfully, she sighs then nuzzles down into the pillow. "Why metal music?"

"Hmm?"

"What turned you into a metal fan?"

I scooch a little closer and tuck a pillow under my head. "I never really felt like I fit in. I wasn't athletic in the way other kids my age were. I wasn't a brainiac. I wasn't handy with a hammer. I guess I felt like metal music understood me because it was made for outcasts."

"And you found your little family from that?"

"My first band . . ." My throat goes dry. "Sam was like a brother to me. Charlie and John too. I would've done anything for them. Then they—"

I pause and wet my lips, Izzy's eyes holding mine as she listens to my story. Moving a little closer again, I lower my voice as I push through the nervousness that I'm about to tell a journalist my darkest secret. Will she leave when this is over? Will she think differently of me?

"I tried so hard for our little band to make it big. Put all of my money into getting studio time, playing gigs anywhere that would have us, working just enough so we could spend all our spare time playing and writing music."

"So what happened?"

"The day came when we were finally going to record our demo. I had never been more excited or nervous than that day. But just before we left—"

I pause, my heart racing in my chest. Is this the moment? I haven't even told the boys about Emily. But Izzy's watching me with such compassion in her eyes that it makes me want to spill all of my secrets into her hands for her to hold and keep safe.

She reaches out and places her injured hand on my chest. I'm sure she can feel the way my heart pounds, and the subtle pressure is soothing. I take one last long deep breath, then continue on.

"I was dating Sam's cousin, Emily, at the time. At first, everything was perfect. She was great and fit into my life without it changing too much. I thought I was so lucky. I'd hit the jackpot.

Then she changed. She started saying I should give up on what I wanted. That I'd never make it. That I should just get a job like everyone else because my dreams were nothing but that . . . dreams."

Izzy's fingers clench on my chest.

"She was an alcoholic," I admit. "At first I thought she just liked to party and that she was super cool. Then she started drinking more and more. Then stealing money. Then was fired from her job. Maybe it really is my fault. I should've done more to help her, but I was eighteen. I was a kid with no real concept of how fucked up she was. The day we were supposed to record the demo, I got a call from the diner where she used to work. She was at her old job causing a scene and they asked if I could come get her. I told Sam and the others I'd meet them at the studio, but I never made it. She . . ."

My face burns with the memory of that day.

"She was wasted and told some cops I was abusing her. That she was scared I would hit her. Izzy, I've never laid a hand on a woman in any violent way, ever."

"I know." Her eyes are shining with unshed tears. "I believe you."

I rest my hand over hers and swallow. "Thankfully they let me go since there was no evidence of domestic abuse. That's when the band broke up. Sam thought I'd had a change of heart and ditched the recording session, refusing to believe his cousin was an alcoholic. I should've left then."

I let out a deep breath.

"But you didn't?" she asks.

Shaking my head, I continue. "No. I foolishly thought there was still something to keep me there. Then a few weeks later I got a call from Emily. She was drunk, of course. She wanted me to come and get her from some party, and I had to remind her that we weren't together anymore, because how could I be with her after that? That's when she threatened to—" I sniff. "She threatened to kill herself if I didn't come."

"Oh my god," Izzy whispers. Her eyes instinctively glance at her bandaged hand. Does she understand why I was so panicked over her injury? That for one fleeting moment I thought maybe she had tried to hurt herself. That I had ruined another life just by being near her?

"I told her I never wanted to see her again. That she ruined my life."

"Dave—"

"I thought I did enough. I even called Sam to warn him she might try something. But it didn't matter."

"So she—?"

I shake my head and look into her shining eyes. "She stole someone's car then wrapped it around a telephone pole."

The tears leak from her eyes.

"She died instantly," I whisper.

"I'm so sorry."

"It was my fault, Izzy. If I had just gone to get her—"

"No. She made her own choice. That's not on you."

"But it is. I was supposed to protect her, but I cared more about my own ambitions and dreams. If I had paid more attention, maybe I could've gotten her help."

"You can't keep blaming yourself for that. Sometimes," she starts with a sniffle. "Sometimes the people we love are bad for us."

"You sound like you're speaking from experience."

She shrugs. "My ex. I thought he loved me but really, he just wanted someone to take care of him. He didn't care about my dreams, and when he figured out I wasn't going to give up on mine for his, he moved on by sleeping with my best friend Ana."

"Shit," I mutter, my fist clenching on instinct. How could anyone do that to her?

"I hated him for a long time, but now I just . . . I guess I pity him." Neither of us says anything for a long moment until I can't stop the words from falling out of my mouth.

"I hated her too."

She blinks and looks at me hard.

"I loved her so much, but I also hated her. She made me feel worthless and stupid. She manipulated me and I—I'm terrified to think that maybe I was the one who changed her."

"What do you mean?"

"She was fun, beautiful, smart, wanting to get away from her alcoholic father before she met me. But what if I'm the thing that poisoned her? Maybe I'm cursed."

"You're not cursed," Izzy says, placing both her palms on either side of my face.

"But what if it's all because of me? That I'm the reason everything gets destroyed."

"Do you want to know what I've learned while writing this article?" she asks, her lips licking the tears that have fallen down her cheeks. At my silence she presses on. "You're the person who builds everyone up. You are part of all of it. The key moment in everyone's story."

"No, I just—"

"Who gave James the chance he needed? Then a place to stay when everything was falling apart for him? The way Joel and Key talk about you. How they all talk about you. It's like you saved them. So how can you possibly be cursed when you did all of that?"

My mouth twists.

"Despite everything and everyone in your life telling you it wouldn't happen, you wouldn't make it, you were doomed to fail . . . you did it anyway! And sometimes love isn't enough to save a person."

A strand of hair falls across her face, and I push it back, the tips of my fingers brushing against her warm skin to tuck it behind her ear. Her eyes darken and that mask she wears—the one of indifference—falls away. I don't want her to slip away too. Not now. Not ever. So I do the only thing that I can think of. I tilt her chin, then lean forward and kiss her.

CHAPTER 36

Where Do Broken Hearts Go

ISABELLA

Dave is kissing me. He's kissing me without the influence of alcohol, without jealousy, without an unbearable sexual tension ready to burst out of us. He's kissing me because he wants to, and the way his lips devour mine makes me truly believe he's kissing me because he *needs* me.

We melt into one another, like two pieces of butter in a hot pan. His leg wraps over top of mine, pulling me closer. My hands travel down his jaw, over his shoulder, while his hand cups my face. My nerves are alight, singing—but is he just feeling vulnerable after telling me his darkest secret? Do I even care? If anything, it helps me understand him that much more.

He moves over top of me, his lips blazing hot trails down my throat, and my core turns to molten lava. I barely notice the throb in my hand anymore. This feels too good. He feels too good. He's all-consuming, and like a powder licked by flame, he ignites me more than anyone has before or maybe ever will again. I'm so crazy about him that if this ends badly, I may never fall in love with anyone ever again.

Knee pressing against my throbbing center, he pulls down my loose shirt to kiss between my breasts. Oh god, do I love him?

"Can I touch you?" he rasps, his fingers pulling on the strings of my shorts.

My heart is swelling as a whispered "Yes" floats past my tingling lips. My fingers clench in the bed sheets as his rough hand slips below my underwear to find that pulsing, soaking prize.

I gasp out loud when he touches me, and he groans against my shoulder. The noise of *The Tonight Show* in the background fades to a dull drum as he lights the fuses to all of my nerves.

"I can't believe you're real," he whispers. "It's like I dreamed you to life."

His fingers work their magical rhythm, and soon I can't stop myself from grabbing his wrist and riding his hand like a mechanical bull.

"I'm so close," I cry.

Clamping my eyes shut, his lips are back on mine and it's enough for all of my nerves to fire at once as I explode. The orgasm rips through me, and I moan his name against his mouth as he languidly draws out my climax.

His breaths are as ragged as mine, and he rests his forehead against my collarbone. Focusing, I can feel his massive, hard length against my hip. Our eyes lock before I kiss him again. I push him over, bringing myself to straddle his body. His erection fits snugly in the gap between us, and my legs twitch as the pressure glides against my sensitive clit.

He sighs against my mouth, and I slowly trail kisses up his jaw to his ear, tugging on his earlobe with my teeth.

"Tell me what you want," I whisper.

"I—" He gasps again. "I don't know," he says.

"Well," I say, kissing lower, "let's find out."

"Izzy—Izzy, no. Wait."

The sudden grip of his hands on my arms jolts me back to reality. I look up at his face, at his wide and serious eyes zigzagging over me.

"I—" I stammer. "I thought . . ."

"This is just . . . I don't know what I'm doing here."

And just like that, my hot-air-balloon-filled heart bursts and collapses in a fiery crash. I sit up, still straddling his hips, and blink furiously to try to ebb the flow of tears. A knife to the heart would hurt less than this as I move myself off him to wrap my arms around my small body.

"You still don't want me?" I whisper.

Pushing onto his knees, he grabs my ankles. "No, that's not— god, I'm fucking this all up. I'm not saying that. I care for you so much, but I'm . . . I've sacrificed so much so I could get here, and no matter what I feel for you, I can't risk losing it."

"How could being with me put all of this at risk?" I ask through trembling lips.

"You don't know how long I've been working for this. Years. Hell, my whole goddamn life! And no one was going to do it for me. I had to do everything. I made it happen when everyone else thought I would fail, and I can't let my feelings for you get in the way of all that."

"But I'm part of it," I say. "You told me yourself. You showed me with that box of things you keep to prove to yourself you've made it. I'm entwined in all of it."

He doesn't say anything.

"Unless you didn't actually mean any of that."

"No, Izzy—"

But I push him off me and jump out of bed, the throbbing in my hand making a swift comeback. "You unimaginable asshole. I'm going to get in your way?" I shout. "If you really think that, you're a fucking idiot."

His face crumples, but I'm so hurt by his words that I'm about to confess everything. He shakes his head and moves towards me but I back away. "Izzy, that's not what I mean. I know you've done things to help with your articles, but there are other things. Things that I need to do. Things I wrote down on a—"

"On a list?" I interrupt.

Sitting back on his heels he narrows his eyes. "What—"

"Your list of things you wanted to do?" I grab my purse and dig around until I find the crumpled up piece of paper. I throw it down on the bed in front of him. "You left it on the table in Vegas."

I'm shaking and sweating, the rage seemingly needing to work its way out as I watch him gingerly pick up the paper.

"You've had this the whole time?" he asks.

"Yes! And how many of those things have happened for you since then, huh?"

He looks down at the paper list, his eyes traveling down then snapping up to mine.

"That's right!" I shout, tears pouring down my face now. "Your first autograph? Me. Your band's name on the marquee? I arranged that."

"Trying new foods . . . You—"

"*Me!*"

The next thing I know, he's standing in front of me, the paper crumpled in his hand. "Why the hell didn't you tell me?"

"Because I wanted you to have everything you've ever dreamed of."

"So you did this . . . why?" he asks. "As an angle for your article?"

"Oh, fuck you, Dave!" I spit. "How can you say that to me?"

"If not for the article, then why?" he shouts.

"Because I'm in love with you!"

There's silence as we both stand staring at each other, panting

—the gravity of what I just said hitting me like falling down a flight of endless stairs. Covering my mouth with my hands, I try to take it back. Maybe if I can swallow the words, he won't have heard them. But his wide eyes prove to me that no matter what I do now, I can't take it back.

"I'm sorry," I whisper, collecting my things and quickly slipping my shoes on. I need to get the hell out of here.

My fingers are on the handle when his warm hand wraps around my wrist. "Izzy," he pleads, but I can't look at him.

"Just let me go, Dave. Please."

He doesn't let go right away. In fact, he seems to grip me tighter for a moment before finally releasing me. I open the door and, spying a light on in the bus in the parking lot, I head for it, hoping Barney won't mind if I sleep inside for the night.

I knew this would end in tragedy. He warned me. I warned myself. My lonely heart just wouldn't listen. But the pain ignites a fire in me so hot I'm burning even as the snow swirls in the air around me. No one helped him? Bullshit. The truth is that no one helped me! What does Dave know about what it's been like for me?

A small part of me knows that's unfair. I didn't even tell him about the phone call with Simon. Probably because that same small part wants to give in. To hand over what I have because I'm so tired of fighting. But then what will I have? Nothing. I won't have an internship, I won't have Dave. I won't have a future.

Well, screw that. I've earned my future, and Simon can publish that goddamn picture of me in the school paper for all I care. I'm graduating in a few weeks and I never have to set foot back on campus again, so let him do his worst. Besides, Randall would never allow him to publish it anyway, so he's probably bluffing.

Hours later, as my hands cramp from the typing and the words spill out of me, I decide to do exactly what every other man in my life has taught me to do: look out only for myself and make my dreams come true. And they can all think me heartless or weak for choosing myself, but if I was a man, no one would bat an eye.

CHAPTER 37

Little Lies

DAVE

Three pairs of horrified eyes look back at me.

"You did *what*?" James grits out.

I bury my head in my hands. "I know . . . I know. I'm an idiot of gargantuan proportions."

"You might possibly be the stupidest person on the goddamn planet," Key chimes in, leaning on a microphone stand.

"So, she told you she loves you and you accuse her of doing all those amazing things for you as journalism tactics?"

I groan. "No, I accused her of that before she said . . ." I can't even finish the sentence. "The worst part is that I didn't even run after her. I should have. I wanted to but I—I don't know."

"What are you so afraid of?" James asks.

"The last time I loved someone—it almost ruined my life. I guess I'm just . . ."

James frowns. "You really think Isabella would ruin your life?"

"What if something happens? What if what we have disappears, or I choose her over it all?"

"Dave, man, why would you ever need to choose?" Joel says. "From what I know about Isabella, she would never do that to you. No offense, but you really are a moron if you can't see that Isabella is the best thing that's ever happened to you—to us."

"God, I know. I fucking know that. What's wrong with me?"

"Do you love her?" James asks.

I look up at all of them. "Yeah, I do."

"Do you want her to be yours?"

"Yes."

"Then go tell her," Key says. "Apologize for being a giant dick last night and tell her how you feel before you lose her forever."

"What if . . ." I pause, chewing on my lip. "What if she won't forgive me?"

"Then you're no worse off than you are now."

I nod.

There's a sound of doors opening, and a booming laugh echoes from the empty auditorium as Al enters with his curly hair and portly belly. "Big night tonight!"

We all lock eyes. "Big night? Why? It's just a regular show."

But Al is grinning like a lunatic as he approaches the stage. "Not anymore it's not. Because Carnal Sins has now officially hit gold!"

My jaw drops to the floor and next thing I know, I'm being hauled up and dogpiled on. Maybe this is all a dream. Maybe I'll wake up and Izzy will be happily snuggled up next to me in bed. I can't believe it! Our very first album—an EP album—went gold? Five-hundred-thousand copies sold? I can't believe it. This might be the greatest moment of my life, but as I extricate myself from the jumping mosh pit of excited bandmates, I realize that the one person I want to tell the most isn't here.

She's the first one who pops into my head to tell good news. She's the one I want to have wrapped up in my arms when I'm feeling down. I want to wake up to her wild hair in my face every morning and watch her long eyelashes fluttering while she sleeps every night.

Jumping down off the stage, I head for the exit. I can make a fair guess where Isabella might be.

"Hey, Noblar!"

I spin around outside the theater doors, and my stomach flips. "Sam?"

Never before have I thought I might be so high that I hallucinated something, but as I stand on the street, face-to-face with the man who was my best friend, I wonder if this is real. His hair is shorter and his face is thinner. A cascade of memories flit through my mind as I remember all of the time we spent growing up together. Until it all ended.

He smiles at me and steps forward. "Long time no see, man," he says, shoving his hands in his pockets.

"I—uh, yeah. Long time," I say cautiously. "What, uh . . . what are you doing here?"

"Came to see your show," he says, gesturing to the marquee above his head. I wonder briefly if Izzy is responsible for this one too.

"Really?"

"I thought maybe if I showed up early enough, I might catch you, and, well . . . I guess I was right."

I cross my arms over my chest as though preparing to defend myself. "Right."

There's an awkward pause and Sam coughs into his hand before pulling out a cigarette. "Want one?"

I let out a sigh. "Fuck, all right."

His smile grows and somehow the tension eases slightly as we both light up and take long drags.

"Listen, part of the reason I'm here . . . I wanted to talk to you," Sam finally says.

"Oh?"

"Actually, I guess what I meant to say is—I want to apologize."

I choke on the smoke and cough. "What?"

Sam closes his eyes and shakes his head. "The things I said to you, accused you of—I was a first-class fucking douchebag. No one deserves that. It's no excuse, I know, but I was stressed out. I never told you this but my dad had declared bankruptcy that summer. We were going to lose the house and you kept pushing to spend all this money on recording a demo, and when I knew we were facing eviction, I guess it just all seemed like too much."

My cigarette nearly falls from my mouth. "Dude, what? Why didn't you tell me that at the time?"

He shrugs. "Ashamed, I suppose."

"I would've helped you."

"I know." He takes another drag. "And Emily . . ." His voice cracks. "I was distracted, I didn't see what you and clearly everyone else did. She was sick and messed up and I'm sorry that I blamed you for what happened to her."

I blink several times, not believing what I'm hearing. "Sam . . . no, you were right. I should've been there for her. I should've done more—"

"We were eighteen," Sam interrupts. "Not that much younger than now, but comparatively to what I know now in life? We were babies. We weren't equipped to handle or fix her problems. Besides, she's the one who got in that car."

"If I had just gone to get her—"

"Then she would've done something else," Sam says, reaching forward to place his hand on my shoulder. "When I think about what she told those cops about you . . ."

It's getting harder to keep the moisture out of my eyes. "Yeah."

"Anyone who knows you would know you're the last person who would ever hit a woman." He takes a long deep breath.

"Anyway, I just want you to know—what I said . . . you're not a disease, Dave. And it was clear you were the one thing keeping all of our heads above water. Everything turned to shit after you left. I tried for so long to blame you for how it all turned out, but the guys and I . . . we know now you were the star. *We* were the ones holding *you* back."

"I never thought you guys were," I say.

"Yeah." He nods. "You always were too nice for your own good. I'm happy good things are happening for you."

I take a drag on my cigarette to hide the tear that slips down my cheek. "I—" I break off then cough to keep my voice from betraying me. "Thanks, man. You don't know how much it means to hear that."

He grins wide again, that same boyish smile I grew up with. "So, Carnal Sins, huh?"

I release a breathy laugh. "Yeah."

"You really made it."

Shrugging, I look back at the theater, then at the bus. "I got lucky." But as the words tumble past my lips, I don't believe them anymore. Standing here with Sam and thinking of the girl I may have lost forever, it finally hits me that maybe it was never about luck. Maybe it really was my own work and the help of friends. That this time, it can't be taken away from me. That the only thing standing between me and the future I've been terrified of losing . . . is me.

"You living that rockstar life?" he asks, jolting me from my thoughts. "I bet being backstage is wild."

"You wanna come backstage tonight?"

"Seriously?"

I grin widely. "Of course. Here." Digging around in my pocket I find a stray wristband and hold it out for him. "This will get you backstage."

"Yeah?"

"They're usually for girls, but just tell them you're an old friend."

He pockets the bracelet. "A groupie pass?"

"It wasn't my idea."

"It's brilliant."

I laugh. "Yeah, maybe. If I was using them."

"What do you mean? I figured you'd be drowning in pussy."

"No."

Sam twists his face disbelievingly. "You mean to tell me you haven't been screwing around?"

"It's not like that—"

"Oh." He smirks. "You've got a bang buddy?"

"Nah, dude. I love her."

His eyebrows lift. "Damn, seriously?"

"Yeah, but I may have fucked everything up last night." I see Isabella walking toward the theater from a distance, her signature cup of coffee in hand. "Listen, I have to go, but I'll see you tonight." Without thinking about it, I wrap my arms around him in a brotherly hug. "I've missed you, man."

He squeezes me tight. "Yeah, me too."

Backing up, he smiles then turns and walks away as Isabella approaches, her dark hair bouncing with each step. She's watching her feet and as she gets closer my heart beats faster, my palms sweating. When she looks up at me, the indifference painted on her face morphs. Her eyes narrow. I think even her lip curls.

"Izzy," I say, ready to fight for her to listen to me.

But she says nothing, merely brushing past me and running up the steps into the bus. I follow her up and past the curtain.

"Can we talk?" I ask.

"No, I'm pretty sure you did enough talking for the both of us last night."

She grabs some clothes out of the cupboard and stuffs them

into her suitcase. Wait, is she . . . packing? "Where are you going?"

She doesn't even look at me. "I'm leaving."

My stomach sinks through the floor. "Leaving?"

"I just faxed the draft of my article to *Earworm*. I'll stay tonight to cover the album going gold, but tomorrow morning I'm taking a bus home."

She's leaving. She's leaving because of me. "No! Wait—" I put myself between her and her clothes, forcing her to stop. "Izzy, please. I'm sorry."

"Yeah, I'm sorry too," she spits. "I'm sorry I was stupid enough to think you cared about me. I'm sorry I thought coming on this tour would be fine. But most of all"—she lowers her voice—"I'm sorry I fell for you."

I shake my head. "I do care about you. You coming on tour made everything so much better. And I—"

"Stop," she says, eyes widening. "Don't say it. I won't hear those words because you think it's something you have to say to make this all better."

"It's not."

"I'm not even mad at you, Dave," she says, turning and breathing out a laugh. "I'm mad at myself. You were upfront with me. You didn't want commitment and I foolishly thought that might change. I really thought we could make each other happy, but lately all I am is heartbroken."

"You do make me happy."

"Dave," she says and stops her pacing. "Let's just call this what it is. We had a mutually beneficial friendship. You benefitted from my writing and I got the opportunity to write about an amazingly talented band and get all the backstage privileges a writer would kill for. And well, I guess the sex was a bonus."

"A . . . bonus?"

"Yeah."

My chest aches as I discover I have a new worst fear, and it's being realized right now. "Izzy," I say, stepping forward and grabbing her hand. For a moment I think she might push me away, but she doesn't, so I grab her other hand. The bandage is gone, just a Band-Aid in its place. "Please don't go," I whisper. "I'm sorry, I'll make it up to you, please."

Her fingers squeeze mine, and I take the cue to pull her against me, wrapping my arms around her body and burying my face in her soft hair. She grips me tightly and for the briefest of moments, I think everything will be okay. That she'll stay, hear me out. That we can work through it all. "I can't lose you." I whisper.

Her grip on me loosens and my heart cracks as she pulls away.

"You can't lose me, Dave, because you never had me in the first place."

CHAPTER 38

Let Me Put My Love Into You

ISABELLA

"Hey, heart?" I ask aloud, looking down at where my hand is pressed against my chest. "Why him, huh?"

Grabbing my coffee to go, I head back to the theater from the station. The ticket from Billings to San Francisco was so expensive it nearly made me want to reconsider, but I can't stay any longer. Not after everything that's happened. Thankfully, there's a five a.m. bus heading out tomorrow morning. I'll do some last-minute coverage writing of Carnal Sins's album going gold if *Earworm* wants it, and that'll be it.

My heart is in tatters. Not just because of Dave, but because of everything else I'm losing. And Simon? He can kiss my ass. Like hell I'm going to hand over all of my hard work—my internship—to him. Even if he does publish that picture.

I thought I had found a new family with the band. With Becks. Part of me wishes I could stay in contact with them all, but we've tried that, and it's probably best that I just disappear from their lives. Becks is only a freshman, she's sure to find more friends, and Dave—well, he has a cupboard full of wristbands, so he won't be lonely for long.

I hide away from the guys for the remainder of the day in this tiny coffee shop, pounding back cup after cup until I'm jittery. It's not until they tell me they're closing that I head back to the theater, dragging my feet down the cold, damp streets. There's a massive crowd outside now, and I take a moment from a few dozen feet away to take a photo of the spectacular sight. The marquee with *Carnal Sins* above the throbbing crowd of heavy metal enthusiasts chanting to be let in.

What a wonderful image. Hopefully I can include it in the photos for the article. Maybe I'll send Dave his own copy—as a farewell. I march down the alley toward the back of the theater, where security eye me up and down for a moment, then smile when they see my backstage pass.

The halls behind the stage are a flurry of activity. Guys running here and there with arms full of wires and microphone stands. I pass the entrance door to the stage, where lights dance around on the glittering metal of the instruments, but it's still empty. Everyone must still be in the green room.

I take a deep breath. I can do this. One more night. Be happy for them.

When I walk through the door, I'm immediately caught by the blue eyes I've grown to love so much. They widen and his lips part as he goes to stand, but I subtly shake my head. I watch several emotions play out across his face. Hope, despair, anger, and finally acceptance, but he doesn't stay. Without a word, he stands and heads through another door toward the stage. As hard as it is to watch him go, it's easier this way.

James is next to me a heartbeat later. "Hey," he says somberly. "I, uh . . . I heard you're leaving in the morning."

I bite the inside of my cheek. "Yeah. I think—I mean, I'm done with the piece for *Earworm,* so it's probably best for everyone if I go."

James places his hands on his hips and looks down at his feet. "I really think you should stay."

Everything feels worse when you disappoint someone. And disappointing James is the worst of all. "I can't," I whisper.

"Listen, I try not to get involved in my friends' love lives but . . . don't give up on him."

I scoff. "What's the point? He's made his position very clear and while I may be a touch masochistic, I'm not willing to put myself through this constant torture anymore."

He sighs and shoots an angry glare at the door where Dave disappeared.

"I'm really sorry, James. I thought Dave and I could be friends. I so desperately wanted to keep all of you in my life— Becks too—but I don't think I can."

"He cares about you, I know he does."

"Not in the way I need him to," I say, shaking my head. "Besides, he'll forget all about me once I'm gone and no longer raining on his parade."

James's frown deepens. "What do you mean?"

I roll my eyes. "Oh, come on. I know about the wristbands, okay?"

His eyes widen. "You do?"

"Don't worry, I know you don't partake."

"But how—?"

"The first night on the bus, I was trying to find a place for my clothes and it was the first cupboard I opened. Then Barney kind of explained it," I finish, glancing up.

For a moment he says nothing, then laughs. "Fuck, I knew those wristbands were going to get everyone in trouble. Look," he says, leaning forward. "I know what it looks like but . . . there've been no other girls."

"James, you don't have to protect him. I'm not blind—I've

seen them backstage. Gorgeous women wearing them and hanging all over him. There's even some here tonight."

"Yeah, they may be wearing them. But the road crew gives those out. He hasn't hooked up with anyone the entire tour."

I freeze. "He . . . what?"

"Not a single one. Actually, he hasn't hooked up with anyone else since the album came out."

"But that was months ago. That was before Christmas." Before we ever slept together.

He nods.

A tingling rush feathers its way across my skin. "What are you saying?"

James smiles. "He's crazy about you. He's just also . . . unfortunately, an idiot."

"Five-minute call everyone." One of the crew members holds open the door, and Key and Joel pry themselves away from their apparent fan club. Spotting me with James, they both give me an awkward smile then head out.

"Got to go," James says. "Promise me you'll at least stay until the end of the show? You might change your mind."

I look between him and the door, nodding ever so slightly. James smiles wide then heads out with the others. I let out a huge breath and wipe my nose with the back of my hand. Is James telling the truth? Has Dave really not been with any other girl since the night he autographed my shoulder? The butterflies in my stomach lurch to life, then all too quickly fall down again.

If he hasn't been hooking up with anyone, then why tell me he didn't want to be exclusive? Why would he tell me he can't be in a relationship? He's clearly had ample opportunity to be with whoever he wants. Looking at the pile of girls on the couch, I spy two blondes who, months ago, I would've said were just his type.

The sound of the crowd screaming roars through the stage door and I head for it before I can stop myself. In the darkness I watch the guys through the curtains taking their places on stage, before the music explodes to life and my skin is overwhelmed by the rush of electric energy in the air.

While I may not have appreciated this type of music six months ago, I have to admit it's grown on me. The complexity and beauty of the notes. The stamina it takes for them to play so fast and hard for so long. They really are amazing. *He's* amazing.

And James is right . . . he is an idiot. A beautiful idiot. But an idiot nonetheless.

But that's not enough. And even if he hasn't been with anyone else, I don't know if that's enough either. Someone brushes up against me and I tear my eyes away from Dave to look up at Al, the band's manager.

"Miss Rodriguez," he yells over the noise, leaning toward my ear.

"Hi," I answer.

"How are you?" he asks.

I shrug. "Fine." I mean, it's not like I'm going to go into details about my situation with Dave.

"How's it going with *Earworm*?"

I wrap my arms around my chest, remembering to be grateful for the opportunity this man gave me. "Great. I just sent them the draft of the article."

"That's great!"

"Mister Simpson," I say, turning to him. "I want to thank you for getting me that internship. It really . . . It's a life-changing opportunity, and I really appreciate your help."

Even in the darkness of the stage I see his cheeks redden. "I just happened to have the phone number. Can't take credit for the whole thing. Noblar is the one you should be thanking."

I may have just gone deaf because the entire world goes quiet. "Wh—what did you just say?"

"Dave. He . . ." He studies my face. "He asked me if I could get in touch with someone in journalism. I told him I had a buddy from college who was the new editor at *Earworm*. But Dave's the one who called them to ask if they could take on any interns. He submitted your articles."

"I . . ." But as if the floor disappears from under me, my legs wobble and I reach out to steady myself on his arm.

"Didn't he tell you?" Al asks.

I shake my head, my hair flying everywhere. "No . . . he didn't."

Speaking evades me, and at some point, during my stunned silence, Al leaves my side. I step forward to get a better view of Dave. His arms are flying and he bounces on his stool as he stomps on the pedals. Sweat glistens on his skin and his thin shirt sticks to his chest. He got me the internship but never took credit. Why would he do such a thing? There's an expression on his face now. His aggression is gone and what is left in its place is pain.

With a final flourish, the song comes to an end, and instead of smiling up at the crowd, Dave simply hangs his head. Like he's tired.

"All right, we've got an unexpected cover for you tonight," Key yells into the microphone. "A song that means a lot to the man on the drums."

My heart skips in my chest.

"Take it away, man."

I watch Dave take a deep breath, then his drumsticks are flying, the other guys coming in gradually to fill in the familiar rhythm. Wait . . . familiar?

Dave finally looks up from his focused attention on his kit and somehow, it's as if he knows I'm right here. Our eyes lock and the smell of a pine tree hits me, the memory of the low twinkling lights, the feel of Dave's hands on my body as he asks me to dance. *He learned the song I showed him*. It's an important song to me, and so it's important to him.

Maybe that means I'm important to him too.

As the music fills my soul, I realize I've been frozen in my anger. Maybe he only pushed me away so much because he was scared and didn't know how to cope. After all, haven't I been scared too? Aren't I still? The tears spill out of the corners of my eyes as I let the pain and fear melt away until I'm like a puddle of ice cream that's been left out in the sun too long.

By the end of the song, I've reached a decision. To give this idiot one last chance. And maybe it won't work out in the end. But maybe seeing if it does will be the greatest thing I've ever known.

CHAPTER 39

Take a Chance on Me

She heard it. I know she did. I saw her clear as day in the wings. Saw her face as she recognized the song. But when it was all over, she was gone, and while the smallest part of me was thrilled to be called to play two encores, I wanted nothing more than to get the fuck off the stage so I could find her.

"Are you sure you didn't see her?" I ask Key one last time as he wraps his arm around a pretty dark-haired girl with a wristband on her arm.

He offers me a sympathetic frown. "I'm sorry."

"Fuck."

I spin around the crowded room, wishing everyone would just shut up and get the fuck out. But I can't do that. Our album just went gold and we played our biggest show yet. Everyone is celebrating. Even Al, who looks like he's half in the bag already. I see James come through the door and head for him.

"Anything?" I ask him.

He twists his mouth and shakes his head. "Sorry, man, she's not on the bus either."

Everything feels tight, suffocating. I hate not being able to solve a problem, and now here's one I can't fix. And she's gone. I sink down into the closest chair.

"I blew it big time," I mutter.

"I was sure she'd at least stay until the end. She promised me she would," James says from his seat on the couch next to me. "Maybe she didn't hear the song?"

"No, she heard it." It just wasn't enough.

"Well, maybe—"

"James," I cut him off. "I appreciate it, but just . . . I can't anymore."

He presses his lips together and nods before standing. "I'm sorry, man. I was really rooting for you." Holding out his hand to me, I grasp it and he gives me a brotherly hug. "Want me to stay with you?"

I wave him away. "And miss the party? Don't be stupid. Go."

He smiles sadly, then disappears into the crowd, avoiding the group of girls watching him like prey. Unfortunately, those same girls lock eyes with me and before I can even get up, they descend like sharks on an injured seal.

"Hey," the first blonde says as she sits her tiny ass on the arm of my chair, making sure her legs are as close to mine as possible without them being in my lap.

I swallow. "Hey."

"You were incredible out there," the other blonde says, kneeling down on the floor in front of me.

"Thanks." I wonder briefly if they even watched the show or if they just sat back here snorting coke.

The first girl fingers a lock of my hair and twirls it around. "Why so glum? It's a big night for you."

I know what they're doing and I know why they're here, but I hardly have the energy now to ignore them. "Yeah, it is." But it means nothing if Izzy's not here.

"Maybe we could make you feel better," the other girl at my

knees says seductively, her hands tracing up my thighs. "Help you celebrate."

I'm trying to come up with a way to get rid of these girls when I see Sam step through the outside door. Perfect.

"Hey, Sam," I say, calling him over.

He walks up and eyes the two annoyed-looking blondes. "Hey, man, what an incredible show."

"Thanks. Hey, help me up." I offer him my hand and he hoists me out of the seat and away from the girls who pout. I lean forward and whisper in his ear. "Listen, I have to get out of here, but play along with me, okay?"

His brow furrows but he offers me a slight nod.

"Ladies," I say, turning back to the two girls with their wristbands. "Have you met Sam Winston? Epic guitarist?"

They perk up at that like I knew they would. "No, I don't think we have."

"Huge new band out of the midwest. And Sam here is the leading man," I say, patting him on the chest.

"Uh," Sam starts, but I pinch his neck and he coughs. "Yeah, that's right. You better watch out, Noblar, because you'll have some more competition soon."

I watch the girls listen to our exchange with rapt attention. If there's one thing I know about these girls, it's that all of this is a competition. To be the first to hook up with someone famous? It's too easy.

"Well, you should have a drink with us then," the girl on the chair says, pulling his arm toward her and practically dragging him into the seat I just vacated.

"I've got to go," I finally say once Sam is set in place. "Take care of my boy here for me, will you, ladies?"

Sam grins wide at me and I laugh for the first time all night before I grab my jacket and head out the back.

IT'S BEEN an hour of wandering the streets of Billings with no luck in finding her. I've checked every twenty-four-hour coffee place I can find but she's nowhere to be found. Then it starts to sink in—she left. She left without even saying goodbye or letting me try to explain myself one last time. It's really over.

Flicking away my cigarette and lighting up another one, I turn around and head back for the motel. It's not like I want to go back to the party. No, I'll just go wallow in my own heartache and self pity and overthink everything I've ever said or done so I know exactly how much I hurt her. But when I get back to my room, I don't want to be here either. The bed still smells like her hair and the side she laid on when we watched TV is still rumpled. For a while, I just wander around the motel, stopping to stare blankly at the vending machines until I wind up by the side of the indoor pool.

I lie down on one of the lounge chairs and watch the flickering lights from the water reflect off the glass ceiling. Snow begins to fall from the black sky above and collects on the square window panes above me. I take another long drag of my cigarette and blow the smoke up into the air, wondering if it'll touch the glass ceiling before it disappears.

The sound of a splash makes me bolt upright in alarm, drops of water hitting my jeans and arms. Someone glides under the surface of the water toward me from the far end of the pool. With my heart galloping in my chest, I lean forward on the edge of the lounge chair. All of the hope in my heart swells when that beautiful face breaks the surface of the water.

"Izzy?"

She grins, that beautiful dazzling smile. "Hi."

The smile that stretches across my face must be comically large right now. "I thought you left."

She shakes her head, the water beading down the sides of her face. "No, but I had to return that bus ticket. It was crazy expensive, and since I no longer needed it . . ."

I bury my face in my hands and laugh. "Jesus Christ."

"When I got back, they told me you left."

I peek through my fingers. "I couldn't be there knowing you were somewhere else." Her forehead wrinkles as she keeps her eyes on me. "I went looking for you. Do you know how many all-night coffee shops there are around here?"

"I do, in fact, know," she says with a cheeky grin. "Do you want me to tell you or are you going to join me?"

I let go of a big breath and lean closer. "I don't have a bathing suit."

She smirks and pulls her hair to one side. For the first time, I realize she's not wearing anything. "Neither do I." Pushing off the side of the pool, she swims toward the center and treads water. "Well?"

I glance around at the motel rooms with doors facing the pool, but all the windows are dark. It's well after one in the morning at this point, and most people staying here are probably still at the after party. It doesn't take long to make my decision. She watches me as I pull off my shirt, unbuckle my belt, and push my boots off. And all the while she watches me, her brown eyes sparkling in the reflection of the water. With as much grace as I can manage, I dive into the pool.

It's warm, a fine mist above the water as it meets the cooler air. Pushing my wet hair back and away from my face, I spin around to the center of the pool looking for her, but she's gone. I hear a gasp of air from the far side of the pool and spy her watching me again. This little game of cat and mouse she's playing has my blood diverting to my groin.

"Stay where you are," I say. "I've been chasing you all night."

"I'll let you catch me this time."

I swim toward her, her smirk falling away the closer I get until I'm right in front of her. "You didn't run."

She wets her lips. "I'm tired of running."

I stretch out my arms on either side of her to hold on to the ledge of the pool. "Izzy, I'm so sorry. I've been the biggest fucking idiot and I—" I sigh. "I'm just so glad you're here."

She gently places her hands on my shoulders, her expression softening. "Why didn't you tell me about *Earworm*?"

My eyes widen. "How— Who told you?"

"Al."

I scoff and shake my head.

"Dave?"

"You were so upset about that Simon creep and worried you'd never get an internship, and I—" I bite my lip. "I just wanted you to be happy. I figured if I had the chance to help you, I would do anything."

"So why not tell me—"

"Because I was falling in love with you."

Her eyes dart across my face as they glisten in the reflective light.

"I didn't tell you because I didn't want you to know how I felt. Because if you knew . . . you'd fight harder, and I was losing every shred of self-control I had around you day by day."

Her hands trace along my shoulders until they cup the sides of my jaw. "But why fight this if it's always been what you wanted?"

My chin dips into the water. "I was terrified of loving you more than I loved my dream. That somehow, I couldn't have both."

She nods. "So what changed?"

"With Emily, I always had to prove her wrong. Prove to her that I was destined for more than what my father expected of me.

But you—" I follow the bead of water that trails down her forehead to the tip of her nose. "I never had to prove anything to you. You've believed in me from day one and never made me think what I wanted wasn't possible. In truth, a lot of those things, you *made* possible."

I move toward her, our chests brushing together under the water. "It wasn't because I was lucky. It was you the whole time. And if I let you leave, I would be cursing myself."

Her lips tremble.

"I love you, Izzy," I whisper, brushing my lips against hers. "I've loved you from the moment I wrote my name on that perfect shoulder. Please forgive me, and I'll never push you away again."

For a moment that feels like an eternity she stares at me. "So, what do you want, then?" she whispers, her fingers playing in the wet hair at the nape of my neck.

"I want you to take a chance on me. I know that's asking a lot after everything I've done. It's asking the world. I don't care how complicated this gets, I want you, and if I don't ask you to be mine, I will regret it for the rest of my life."

My heart pounds when she says nothing amongst the gentle lapping of the water between us, and I think maybe all of this will fall apart again and she'll disappear. That she's just a figment of my imagination. Then she smiles and it's possible my heart skips three whole beats.

"You played my song," she says simply.

I shake my head, rubbing our noses together. "No, Disco Girl, I played *our* song."

CHAPTER 40

Crazy For You

ISABELLA

ur song.

It's miraculous that, after everything, something could be ours. I pull his face toward me, our lips fitting together perfectly, passionately, hungrily. God, how I've missed his kisses—it's as if they breathe new life into my lungs. I wrap my arms around his neck and pull his body even closer. His muscled chest presses against my nipples and his massive length hardens against my belly. I roll my body against his and he groans against my mouth.

"Fuck, Izzy, let me show you how much I want you to be mine," he rasps.

I lean my head back and he sucks on my neck, bruising the sensitive skin. "I believe I brought a pass for that."

He pauses and pulls back to look at me. I can barely keep my smile contained as I lift my hand with the adhesive bandage from the water to show him the wristband hanging there. His eyes widen in horror.

"Wha— I . . . How did you—" he stutters.

I kiss him quickly. "I found them that first night on the bus."

His jaw drops. "Izzy, I never—"

"I know you never."

"You do?"

I nod. "James told me."

"I thought—" he starts. "I tried to move on from you, but I couldn't. I can't. No one ever came close to you. You're all I think about every day, every night. All I want is you."

"Then fucking have me," I say, throwing his line back at him from Christmas. He smirks, then it's as if the green flag has been waved as he attacks my body.

Hands skimming down my ribcage, over my hips, he grasps under my thighs to pull my legs around his waist. I squeeze him tighter to me. A jolt of pleasure races down my spine as his cock touches my clit. I gasp against his ear as he continues his bruising assault on my neck. His hips roll and his cock slides through my skin, rubbing my clit in the most teasing way. My nails dig into his shoulders.

"That feel good?" he whispers, rolling his hips again.

The slow strokes make my eyes roll back. "Yes," I breathe.

With one hand on my hip, his other hand grasps the wet hair at the base of my scalp and pulls, tipping my head back against the concrete edge of the pool. Every thrust of his hips causes the heat in my belly to spread like wildfire. The water starts to lap and swirl around us, but all I can do is stare at the snow-covered glass ceiling above. My core clenches with the need to be filled by him, and the stupid part of my brain wants to be reckless. If I just shifted my body slightly, he could be inside me. But all risky things aside, I don't want kids right now, and I'm smarter than that.

My moans escape upward, and I almost forget we're in a public place. But . . . would that stop me?

"Dave," I whisper. "Take me inside."

He pinches my nipple, and another loud gasp breaks out of me. "Not until you come."

"Someone might see."

"Then they'll know you belong to me."

Belonging to someone. Belonging to *him*. It's enough, and with a few more thrusts my legs shake and I come hard with a shout of his name on my tongue.

"That's my girl," he whispers with a gentle bite to my earlobe. "You're so gorgeous when you come."

He releases my hair and I slump forward, my cheek resting on his shoulder as my body twitches. I've barely registered that we've moved until the cold air hits my skin and Dave's climbing the stairs of the pool with me clinging to him like a sex-crazed koala.

He slides the glass door to the side, and we're back in the familiar motel room. I think of how different I felt twenty-four hours ago. It's amazing how quickly things can change.

Still dripping, he lays me gently on the bed, only . . .

"Wrong way, doofus," I tease, looking up at him and kicking at the pillows with my feet.

But he just smirks then leans down to kiss me hard. "No, it's exactly the right way." His hand gently grasps my neck and tilts my head back, causing it to hang off the end. He must see the confusion on my face because he crouches down to kiss me, his nose pressing against my chin. "If it's too much, just tap my leg. Now," he says, standing over me stroking his huge, hard cock, "open wide."

The glistening head of his cock nudges my lips and I take him in my mouth. I grasp the damp bed sheets for dear life. In this position he has all the control, and when he thrusts forward a little too deeply, my eyes water as I gag.

"Relax your throat," he urges, his fingers gently gliding up my neck.

I take a deep breath through my nose and will my body to take him deeper. He thrusts forward slowly again and again, and each time it's easier, the ache in my jaw delicious.

"That's it," he praises. "Touch yourself."

I moan around his cock and he shudders, but reaches forward to move my hand down my body. Closing my eyes, I reach between my legs to find myself drenched, and not from the pool water. No, my thighs and lips are slick for him. He thrusts forward again and my pussy clenches hard, a fresh wave of tears spilling from my closed eyes.

"Breathe," he reminds me. "You were fucking made for me, Izzy. Look at you. I can see my cock choking you."

I'm so fucking turned on, and when I dip my fingers inside, my whole body contracts with something finally filling me. My pussy tightens around my fingers and I release a moan, my throat constricting.

"Jesus, you feel so fucking good," he grunts.

Stepping away from me, he pulls out of my mouth, grasps the back of my neck, and lifts me up to give me a bruising kiss. My sight blurs from the unshed tears as I open my eyes. He wastes no time and grabs a condom from his small bag on the dresser. Heat pools in my stomach watching him roll it on. He spins me around and grabs my thighs, pulling me toward the end of the bed where his cock is at the perfect height.

I'm breathing hard, chest heaving, but he looks at me for a long moment until I push myself up onto my elbows.

"You want me to fuck you?" he asks.

I nod. "Yes . . . please."

"No more one-time-only," he says, his blue eyes dark and burning.

Shaking my head, I whisper, "No."

"I fuck you now? You're mine. Forever."

His eyes dart over my face, giving me the moment to decide if this is really what I want. I don't hesitate. "I'm yours. Always."

He thrusts forward swiftly, deeper than I ever thought anyone could physically go, and I see stars. My legs twitch uncontrollably as I come instantaneously.

"Goddamn," he grunts, thrusting over and over inside my spasming walls. "I'll never get tired of that face. So fucking perfect." He leans low over me, sucking my nipple into his mouth. I'm barely lucid. I've succumbed to sensation. To feeling him inside of me. And I can't help but wrap my arms and legs around him, holding him to me, even as I feel the sheer size of him rushing me toward another mind-melting orgasm.

"Oh, god, I don't know if—" I gasp, even though I'm already on the brink of it.

"You can give me one more," he whispers, kissing my cheek and rolling his hips. "Fall apart for me, Izzy, and I'll spend the rest of my life putting you back together."

"I'm coming!" I shout at the same time as Dave groans deep and heavy, his strong fingers pinching my skin and adding to the incredible pleasure.

He collapses over me, his cheek resting between my breasts, and for a while we just lie together, my fingers combing through his tangled hair. Nothing runs through my brain except pure happiness and contentment.

"I love you, Izzy," he says. "So much."

A smile pulls at my lips. "I love you too."

He lifts his head and pushes the damp hair back from my forehead. "I finally figured out your rhythm," he whispers, a smile spreading across his face.

I nuzzle into his side. "Oh yeah?"

He nods, then grasps my wrist to place my hand over his heart while he places his other over mine. "It's the same as mine."

CHAPTER 41

Out Ta Get Me

DAVE

I've been awake for an hour. The sunlight creeps slowly across the floor of the motel room, but all I can do is watch her sleep. Her perfect, beautiful face and kinked-up hair. The light-purplish bruises that have slowly appeared on her skin from where I may have grabbed her a bit too hard. I'll have to apologize for that and be more careful in the future.

The future. There will be a future with her. Having her in my arms now only solidifies that I want to wake up with her next to me every day. How could I have been such an idiot for so long when this kind of happiness was in front of me the whole time?

Izzy stirs and I pull her closer, not quite ready to let her go yet. Her pulse beats in sync with mine still, and it's the most amazing feeling I've ever experienced. Leaning forward, I kiss her nose.

"Morning," I whisper, my voice still croaky from disuse.

She smiles and her lashes flutter open. "Morning."

"Did you sleep okay?" I ask, my thumb feathering over her jaw.

She nods and stretches her legs, her nose pinching adorably.

"Yeah. But I can honestly say this is the first time my dreams haven't compared to waking up."

Reaching around my neck, she pushes forward to kiss me. She rolls me onto my back, her legs straddling me as I continue to kiss her. With a tug of her teeth on my lower lip, I groan, and as her hips press against mine, I'm hard in no time.

"Think you could wake me up the right way?" she says against my lips. She sits up, the sheets falling to reveal her naked body. My cock twitches at the stunning sight of the woman on top of me.

"If you want to be fucked awake, Disco Girl," I say as I reach over to grab a condom from the nightstand, "I'm happy to oblige."

She takes the packet from my hand and kisses me again. Then, in a way that's utterly erotic, she rolls the condom on me and slowly lowers herself on my cock.

Her lips part as she seats herself, and my jaw clenches as I try my hardest not to thrust upward and fill her completely. Watching her face while we fuck is quite possibly the best goddamn thing on the planet. My fingertips press into her hips, but then I remember the bruises from last night and pull my hands away.

Eyes opening, she looks down at me as her hips roll torturously over mine. "What's wrong?" she asks.

I groan as her pussy clenches around me. "Just—don't want to hurt you."

She grabs my hands and places them on her hips once more. "You didn't. Don't worry, I'm not fragile." She punctuates her words by sinking down on my cock.

"*Fuck*, Izzy," I moan.

She inches up my dick again. "I love it when you throw me around," she gasps out, grabbing my hands and interlacing her fingers with mine.

My balls tighten and my breathing shallows. "Yeah?"

I go to turn, to toss her onto her back and fuck her into the mattress, but she tightens her grip on my hands. My brow furrows but she just smiles. "But I also love riding you, so I want you to just lie there."

Fuck me.

Hands moving to my chest, she plants her feet on the mattress then she's bouncing on my dick like a fucking goddess. Face contorting with pleasure, I rock my hips slightly to keep up with her, trying to last long enough for her to get off as she uses me. When her legs start to tremble I know she's close, so I press my thumb between us to rub her clit. She sets off screaming and gasping and it pushes me over the edge of the cliff I've been balancing on since the moment she rolled on top of me.

She collapses in a heap of wild hair. "Oh god, that was amazing." She sighs.

Pushing back her hair I find her happy, satisfied face. "You're amazing."

"Okay, I'm awake now. Are you hungry?" she asks. "I'm starving . . . and I need coffee."

I laugh. "Yeah, we can get something to eat—as soon as the feeling returns to my legs."

WALKING hand in hand with Izzy feels as comfortable as breathing. Even knowing the moment the guys see it they'll tease me nonstop, it's actually something I'm looking forward to.

"Are you sad you missed the big party last night?" Izzy asks.

I shake my head. "I was with you. Best party I could've had."

She squeezes my hand. "I never congratulated you on the album going gold. It's amazing, Dave, seriously. You must be so thrilled."

"It's incredible," I say. "What about you? Have you heard back from *Earworm* about what you submitted?"

"No, but I'm sure it'll take a few days. I submitted it early. Besides, it's the weekend. They might not have the time to look at it right away."

I tug her closer and kiss the top of her head as we walk through the motel lobby. "They're going to love whatever you wrote. I know I do."

"I think you're a bit biased."

"Picturing what you look like naked while I read your work is definitely a perk."

She rolls her eyes then she stops. "Dave . . . there's something I should tell you."

"Did you write how utterly charming and handsome I am?"

She blinks. "What? No . . . I mean, yes, you are, but there's something else."

A knot forms in my stomach. What else could there be? Even if she wrote a sonnet about what an asshole I've been, I'd still love her. But before I can open my mouth, I hear a shrill scream. "Isabella!" Then Izzy's face is obscured by familiar blonde hair. Wait, blonde?

"Becks?" Izzy asks. "What—what are you doing here?"

When she finally steps back, I can see Becks's bright green eyes and James is standing a few feet away staring at her adoringly.

"Al flew me in as a surprise last night for the party, but my flight got delayed. I only just got in a few hours ago."

Izzy hugs her again. "It's so good to see you," she says, the words muffled by her sweater. "I've missed you so much."

Becks looks at me and cocks a smooth brow. Her eyes flick between Izzy and me. Offering her a small nod and a smile, she jumps forward to wrap her arms around me. "I knew you two would figure it out eventually," she whispers in my ear. "But listen," she says, stepping back. She averts her gaze over to where Izzy gives James a hug. "Maybe it's really good you guys figured it out because, well . . ."

My heart rate spikes. "Spit it out, Becks."

She bites her lip and stands rigid like a statue. "I have to show something to Isabella, and . . ." She trails off. "I don't think it'll go over well."

Something hard clenches in my stomach. "What do you mean?"

"It's hard to explain."

The look on Izzy's face and the way she behaved a few moments ago makes me think she might already know what this is.

Becks leans forward and grabs her hand. "Isabella, I . . . there's something I think you should see. But before you do, you should know that we're all here for you and we care about you—"

"Becks, what the hell is all this about?" I ask, growing more and more irritated.

Becks looks at James, who subtly nods, then she turns and pulls out a rolled-up newspaper from her bag. She hands it to us and Izzy takes it.

"This is the *East Bay Chronicle*," Izzy says, looking at the header.

"Flip to the entertainment section," Becks says with a grimace.

Sweat trickles down the back of my neck at Becks and James's reaction to whatever the hell this is. Izzy's hands tremble as she thumbs through to the entertainment section. Then with a gasp the paper drops down, splashing across the floor, and my eyes nearly bulge out of their sockets.

There, on the front page of the entertainment section of the paper, is a picture of my Izzy in nothing but a thong. And . . . is that *my* autograph?

CHAPTER 42

Controversy

ISABELLA

"*Journalist or Groupie?*" I shriek.

There's a droning in my ears as I stare at the picture of myself in the paper. One copy of how many possible thousands that could be out there circulating. I thought he was bluffing. I thought at most it would end up in the *Stoneman Press*. I thought there was no way a real newspaper would print something so explicit. And as surprised as I am to find myself featured in a newspaper, I am completely unsurprised by the name of the author under the title. Simon Cranmer.

"What the fuck?" Dave says harshly, grabbing the paper and hiding the image of me from any onlookers. Why does he even bother? All of San Francisco has probably seen this by now.

My hunger pains turn sharply to nausea.

"I'm going to be sick," I whisper, then push harshly on Dave to move out of the way.

My sight blurs as I try to locate the bathroom. I see it in the distance and run for it, bile rising up my throat as I'm within feet of the door. I don't make it to the toilet, but thankfully I do make it to the sink. Not having eaten anything, yellow bile pools against the white porcelain, and I clamp my eyes shut and blindly reach for the faucet to wash it away.

I'm shaking violently when the heaving finally stops. A gentle knock on the bathroom door forces a deep breath to enter my lungs.

"Isabella?" I hear Becks call. "I'm coming in, okay?"

I don't answer, but when she enters and wraps her arms around me, I sink into her embrace. She may have brought horrific news, but I would rather hear it from her than be blindsided later.

"Izzy," she whispers, "I'm so sorry. You don't deserve this."

I shake my head. "The article . . ." I start, then hiccup. "How bad is it?"

"It's—well, it's not great."

I cover my face with my arms. "Oh, god!"

"You shouldn't read it!" Becks says, pulling my arms away. "And the picture . . . Okay, I know you probably never intended for it to be seen, but you *do* look gorgeous in it."

I laugh despite myself. "Thanks."

"And besides, who cares what that jerk wrote about you. You got your internship because of your hard work."

Nausea rolls through my stomach again because that's no longer true. I thought it was. But really, it was Dave who called in a favor. He submitted my work and pulled god knows how many strings. Maybe what Harold Lewis told me is complete bullshit. What if he saw the opportunity, and it didn't matter if I was a good writer or not. They just knew I had access, and he was desperate. Hell, so was I.

"I could lose my internship over this," I say.

"Why?"

"The secretary practically beat me over the head with how they value professionalism and integrity. And my guess is, that article doesn't paint me in a very good light."

"But that's—" She sighs. "That's not fair."

I take a deep breath. "I'm really glad you're here," I say, offering her the best smile I can.

She smiles, and it slowly turns into a knowing smirk. "So . . . all crises aside. You and Dave?"

Heat rushes into my cheeks. "Uh, yeah . . . me and Dave."

"I knew it!" she squeals. "I knew all that stuff about just staying friends wouldn't work. He's been smitten with you for months."

"He said he loves me," I admit. It sounds strange to say it out loud to someone else. More real. Her eyes widen. "You don't think that'll change because of the article, do you?"

"No! Of course not," she says, waving her hand at me. "Don't be crazy. If I know Dave like I think I do, he'll want to pluck the eyes out of anyone who sees that photo of you while simultaneously framing a copy for his room."

I try to smile as the two of us head back out into the lobby. Before I can walk two feet though, Dave is there and pulling me into a hug.

"Izzy, you okay?" he asks, gently cupping my face.

I shake my head. "Not really," I say, swallowing hard. "There are some things I should do, but I'm—"

"We got breakfast to go," Dave says, nodding toward James, who carries a tray of coffees and juice and a huge paper bag. "We'll take it back to the room. Things won't seem so bad once you have your coffee fix, I promise."

This time, I really do smile, a little at least, as my heart digs its way out of the hole it fell into when I saw that article. "That's —thank you."

He smiles tentatively and wraps his arms around me, then he kisses my head and steers us back the way we came.

When the four of us are back in the motel room and I've drunk my coffee, I admit that Dave was right. Nothing seems quite so terrible. I suppose it could be worse. At least the picture of me is hot.

"Did you read it?" I ask Dave as I pace the room at the end of the bed where he, James, and Becks are sitting.

He nods sheepishly. When I groan, he reaches out to grab my hand. "I only read it to protect you. And believe me, if James hadn't physically held me down, I'd be on my way back to San Francisco to kill this motherfucker right now."

"That's true," James says through a mouthful of bagel.

"Also, I—" He pulls me closer. "You didn't tell me about the photo."

I blush furiously, turning away from James and Becks to whisper to Dave, "I don't know why I took it. I felt—sexy and . . . it was your name and—"

"Oh, don't get me wrong, that picture is the hottest thing I've ever seen, and the moment I destroy every other copy in circulation I want one blown up for my room."

I see Becks roll her eyes dramatically.

"But how did this fucker even get it?" he asks.

"I accidentally left the film at the school newspaper office and he . . . made himself a copy. When I found out, he threatened to blackmail me with it if I ever told anyone he stole my work to get his internship position."

Dave grunts. "Okay, now I'm definitely going to kill this fucker."

"Dave," James groans.

"No, no way, Walton. Are you telling me that if some asshole shared a picture of Becks like this to the public, you wouldn't want to smash his face into the concrete?"

James sighs. "Yes, of course I would, but listen, there's literally nothing we can do right now. We're hundreds of miles away from home, we have a show tonight, and the article is already out there. The best we can do right now is damage control."

Damage control.

"He's right," I murmur. "It's not like we can turn back time. I'll just call *Earworm* and explain."

"But I don't get it," Dave says. "What do you have to explain? None of that shit is true."

I shake my head. "You don't understand."

"Then help me understand." He grabs my hands and squeezes. "Please."

Dave and James might never understand what this means, but I can at least try.

"That article suggests I'm not a real journalist," I say slowly. "That I only got this position, this story about you, by sleeping with a band member."

"But why does that matter?" Dave asks.

Shaking my head, I try to remain calm to explain. "They never took me seriously. Remember? The only reason my article about the band even took off was because I submitted it under a boy's name. No one was going to believe me. I was the one who wrote the dating advice and makeup column and was expected to get all the guys their coffees." My jaw clenches at the memory. "No one was going to believe I could write a hard-hitting article about metal music. Simon implied for weeks—to the entire newspaper staff—that I was only getting content for my articles because I was sleeping with you. Then what does he find?" I turn to the bed and grab the newspaper. "Exactly the evidence he needed to prove I'm what he said—just a *groupie*. That you guys only kept me around because I was a piece of ass. The moment he found this picture, all my credibility disappeared."

Dave huffs. "But that's not true. *Earworm* gave you the internship because you're an amazing writer."

My head tilts and I give him a sad smile. "But even that isn't completely true. You made that happen. Everyone else . . . rejected me."

"What?" Dave says, standing. "That's impossible."

I shrug. "Simon contacted each place I applied to and told them that some silly girl had stolen his work and that *his* was the original."

He turns to James. "Is it legal to buy a gun in Montana?"

"Dave!" I chastise. "You got that internship for me. And it was made very clear to me that *Earworm* only accepts journalists with above average integrity. This?" I say, shaking the paper. "It's ruined any chance of me being taken seriously. And not just by *Earworm*, but potentially any other publication too."

He stands and rests his hands on my shoulders. "We don't know that yet. For all we know, *Earworm* hasn't and will never see that article."

Ring ring.

As if on cue, my knees wobble beneath me and I know—I feel it in my soul—who's on the other end of the line before I even pick up.

"H—Hello?"

"Miss Rodriguez, this is Eliza Watters from *Earworm Magazine*. Secretary to Harold Lewis."

I sink down onto the side of the bed, not brave enough to look at the others. "What can I do for you?"

She clicks her tongue. "It's been brought to our attention that there has been some, how do I phrase this? Professional misconduct, on your end, Miss Rodriguez. A certain article in the *East Bay Chronicle* revealed some shocking things about how you conduct yourself and as you know, *Earworm Magazine* is a serious publication."

"Yes. Yes, I know, but—"

"This isn't some rag magazine or school paper. It is very important to us that we uphold our brand."

"I understand, but—"

"For that reason, I'm afraid we've decided to cancel the feature you were working on."

My heart is breaking. My dreams crashing around me like that fucking ashtray I threw at the wall. "Wait, please! If I could just speak to Mister Lewis personally, I think—"

"With all due *respect*, Miss Rodriguez—" I can practically hear her lip curling. "Mister Lewis doesn't want to be associated with women like *you*. You should be ashamed of yourself."

"But I—"

But the line goes dead, and with it, all of my dreams. And while I know I should fight, that I can't give up, that I need to fix this somehow, I just . . . can't. I'm too tired. It's like I've been fighting for years, and I don't think I can go on anymore. So I slump onto the floor, letting the darkness of my thoughts crash over me, wondering if this time they'll finally take me out to sea where I can drown.

"Izzy."

A sob tears out of me. "I can't . . . I can't fight anymore."

Dave's gentle voice somehow breaks through and before I know it, he's in front of me. All of them are. His hand on my cheek is like a lifeline.

"Remember what I told you before?" Dave says, grasping my face. "What's awesome about having friends, Disco Girl?"

More tears spill from my eyes, but he brushes them away with his thumbs as I take a long shaky breath and look up at the people I've grown to love. My friends. My family.

"They help you fight the battles you can't win on your own."

CHAPTER 43

Don't Give Up

DAVE

After tucking Izzy into bed, I pull my jacket on and head for the theater with James on my heels.

"Dave, what the hell is the plan? We can't let this happen."

I push through the doors and out into the frigid air, grateful that it clears my head. "I don't know, man. But I have to do something. This . . ." I stop. My knuckles clench into fists, and I raise one to my temple. "If I ever see that fucker," I grit out, "I'll fucking kill him."

James's head drops back and he sighs, a little frozen cloud escaping into the air. "Listen, I want to kill him too, but . . . and I can't believe I'm saying this—we need to be smart about this."

"It doesn't take brains to bash someone else's in, Walton."

He grabs my arm. "I *mean*, we need to think of a way that will ruin him without causing any further damage to Izzy, and find a way to help her get her feature back."

"Do you think I should call that guy? The editor?" I ask. "Maybe if I explain that Izzy and I are together . . ."

James smirks.

"Oh, don't give me that," I say, rolling my eyes.

"Listen, about that. I'm sorry I ever told you to stay away from her," he says as he kicks his foot in the snow. "If I had known—"

"You were right to try to keep me away," I interrupt.

He grins. "I fucking knew she was just your type."

"Shut up." I shove his shoulder and we both laugh.

"But, yeah," he continues. "I mean, her article's already been canceled. I don't see how calling to ask them to change their minds would make it any worse."

"Right."

"LIKE I TOLD you the previous five times you've called, Mister Noblar, Mister Lewis isn't available right now."

"If he's so unavailable, then how is he able to make final decisions on projects for his magazine without discussing them personally with the intern?"

She sighs into the speaker. "Again, Mister Lewis is a very busy man, and you should remember that before calling here again."

The line goes dead and it takes all of my strength not to punch my fist through the greenroom wall.

"Still nothing?" Key asks.

I shake my head, looking around at my friends helplessly. After we got to the theater, we found Key and Joel passed out half naked on the couch with three girls who were also mostly naked. It took about fifteen minutes for everyone to get themselves decent and the girls to leave, then James filled them in on what happened while I called *Earworm*.

"Maybe *we* should all take a scandalous picture," Joel says.

James throws up his hands. "How the fuck would that help?"

Joel shrugs. "I don't know, man. Distract the masses with my giant dick?"

Key punches him in the arm. "You're such a moron. We all know a naked picture of you would just embarrass the band."

Joel flips him off and rubs his arm. "It was just a suggestion."

"Wait," I say, an idea forming in my head. "Maybe . . . Maybe Joel is on to something."

"See?" Joel says, aggressively punching Key in the side.

"No, not us," I say, a smile pulling on the corners of my lips. "That fucker who published the article."

James frowns. "What are you talking about?"

My palms begin to sweat as the idea takes hold. I clap my hands together and bounce out of my seat. "I have—and, James, you'll be happy about this—a nonviolent plan that will forever make that douchebag regret he even *saw* that photo."

WHEN I OPEN the door to the motel room after rehearsal, I'm confused and surprised when I find Izzy sitting on the end of the bed with her suitcase.

"Hey," I call out, closing the door behind me.

She looks up, her eyes still swollen despite her dry cheeks. "Hi," she whispers.

"How are—actually maybe it's a stupid question to ask, I know you're not okay," I say, walking over and sitting down next to her.

"It's not stupid," she says. "But you're right. I'm not."

I nod. For a moment, I consider telling her that I phoned *Earworm Magazine* a dozen times and nearly screamed at them half as many more, but it seems pointless. My eyes linger on the suitcase and my stomach tumbles.

"What's with the bag?" I ask.

She takes a quick breath and looks away. "I'm going home."

"Izzy, don't leave. We're all heading back on the bus after the Detroit shows this week anyway, just stay—"

"No, Dave, I mean . . . I'm going home. To Arizona. To my family."

I lean back to look into her face. "What?"

"I just," she starts, voice catching. "Maybe this isn't what I'm meant to do."

"Yes! It is. Izzy, we're not giving up. You can't let that asshole win."

She shrugs. "He already did."

"No," I plead, sinking off the bed to kneel in front of her. "No, listen. You stay with me. Finish out the last week of the tour. We'll all go home together, just like we meant to, and we'll figure it out from there."

She presses her lips together. "And then what?"

"And then . . ." But I *don't* know what comes next.

"I might not even get my degree now. I won't be able to get the job I need to pay off my student loan—"

"You can live with me," I say in a rush. "I'll take care of you. You don't even have to work, I can provide for us both. Just stay."

A sad smile flashes across her face before her eyebrows scrunch together. "But that's not what I want." My grip loosens, but she rushes to grab my face. "Sorry, what I meant was that I don't want to *just* be that. To be the girlfriend of a drummer. I want my own career, my own success. My own dreams to come true."

My eyes water, and I sniff to keep the tears away.

"You got yours," she whispers. "And it's wonderful. Now I have to figure out how to get mine."

"I know you think running home is the answer. I promise you

it's not. Don't run away from the people who are trying their best to help you."

She blinks furiously and looks up at the ceiling. "I don't know," she whispers with a shrug.

"Stay with me—with us. Give it a few weeks. If, once we're home, you still want to go, I'll drive you to Arizona myself."

"You will?" she asks with a quirky smile.

"Yeah," I say, running a finger over her cheek. "If I'm going to be your boyfriend, I guess I have to meet your parents."

She smiles a real smile, that sweet little dimple appearing in her cheek. "So you're my boyfriend now?"

I twist my mouth and tilt my head. "I mean, if you'd rather refer to me as your sex slave, I'm cool with that too."

She slaps my shoulder, but I push forward to kiss her. When I pull away, her eyes open slowly. "Okay, *boyfriend.*"

I grin. "You'll stay?"

With a chuckle, she nods. "Yeah, I'll stay. But I'm going to need to be distracted."

My hands run up her thighs and I whisper against her mouth. "Good thing you have a sex slave to use."

Seek & Destroy

DAVE

I don't think I've ever been as dressed up as I am at this moment. Definitely haven't worn a button-down shirt or tie in over a decade. How do guys dress like this everyday and not suffocate? Pulling on the collar, I take one last look in the window outside of the *East Bay Chronicle* before opening the door and walking toward the front desk.

A young brunette woman with cherry-red lipstick looks up at me and does a double take. "Hello, can I help you?" she asks.

A strand of hair falls out of the makeshift ponytail I threw my hair into to make it seem a little more professional. "I have an appointment. Dave Noblar?"

She raises her eyebrows. "Are—are you really?"

"Uh, yes?"

"Oh my god, my boyfriend is a huge fan!" she says, standing so abruptly her chair falls backward. "Do you . . . Sorry, but do you think I could get your autograph for my boyfriend?"

A smile tugs at my lips. "I, yeah . . . sure. What's his name?"

"Marty," she says with a massive grin. "And I'm Flora." I take the marker from her outstretched hand and the notepad from her desk. "What are you doing here?" she asks when I hand it back. "Are you doing an interview for the paper?"

My mouth twists. "Not exactly. I'm here to see Tony Yahamara."

"Right, yes. I see here you have an appointment. I—thank you for the autograph. Mister Yahamara's office is on the tenth floor. Just take that elevator there."

I drum my hands on the desk then head for the elevator. "Thanks."

When the doors open to the tenth floor, there is a sea of small cubicles that span the wide-open space. People are chattering and phones are ringing. I don't see him yet, but it's better this way.

"Mister Yahamara will see you now, Mister Noblar," says a middle-aged woman as she points to a large wood-paneled office to my left. Opening the door, an older man with a salt-and-pepper beard steps forward and shakes my hand.

"Mister Noblar, please come in," he says politely. He gestures toward the leather seats in front of his desk. "Would you care for a drink?" he asks.

I plop down in the chair, quickly taking in my surroundings. "Oh . . . no, thank you."

He nods then sits down across from me. "How can I help you, Mister—"

"Just Dave, please," I say. Mister Noblar just reminds me of my dad, and it's not like I need that reminder right now . . . or ever.

"Dave," he says. "When we spoke on the phone it was unclear what kind of feature you wanted us to do about the band."

"Actually, I'm afraid I wasn't entirely honest about my intentions, so for that I apologize."

He sits back. "I see."

"The reason I'm here is because you currently employ an intern who . . . well, I'll just come out and say it, stole the work of someone else and passed it off as his own in order to get where he is."

Yahamara narrows his eyes at me. "That's a very serious accusation. But I can assure you that we vet our interns very carefully."

"So I guess someone else isn't doing their job very well either. You see, your intern, Simon Cranmer, stole work published by Isabella Rodriguez from the *Stoneman Press*."

"That's preposterous. We take plagiarism very seriously."

My mouth twists. "Doesn't really seem like you do, or I wouldn't have hauled my ass in a suit all the way downtown on a Wednesday morning."

"I—"

"Not only that, but he continued to blackmail this talented writer with a photo of her in a . . . compromising state. When she refused to cower to his demands, he published that photo in your paper."

His mouth falls open. "But he—he told us quite the opposite —"

"So you *are* aware of such an issue."

His reddening face turns splotchy. "He told us that someone from his school had attempted to steal his work and—"

I pull the original *Stoneman Press* articles out of my jacket pocket and lay them on the desk between us. "These are the original articles," I say pointing to them. "You can check the dates. I believe Cranmer deleted the originals from the school archives to cover his tracks." Who knew holding on to this stuff would be such a stroke of luck?

Yahamara picks up the papers and quickly scans them, his forehead wrinkling further with each new piece of evidence.

"I won't go into too much detail, but the fallout from this has been devastating for Miss Rodriguez's prospects as a journalist. Considering the plagiarism you printed and profited from, and the use of an image without the consent of the lawful owner, I would say you have a fairly substantial lawsuit coming your way."

"This is hardly enough evidence to win a court case—"

"And I assure you that I'll fight this in every way possible."

He clears his throat and smiles uncertainly. "Sir, I . . . Is that really necessary?" Yahamara blunders, putting the articles back down before him.

I shrug and pull on the collar of my shirt again. "I suppose that depends."

"On?" he asks.

"I would expect this intern to be fired immediately, for starters."

He scoffs. "I can't just fire someone based on this—"

"I'll also expect for your publication to pay out a fair image rights wage to Miss Rodriguez since she is the legal owner of the photo you printed."

His eyes narrow.

"Unless, of course, you have another solution. I will mention, though, that we as a band have an upcoming multi-page feature being published in another magazine, and it would be a shame if we had to call out what happened here."

There's a tense silence that settles between us, but I don't look away or back down. Finally, Yahamara huffs. "Right." He leans over and presses the red button on an intercom. "Maria, will you come in here, please?"

A moment later, the woman who led me in here enters the room. "Sir?"

Yahamara finally takes his eyes off me and turns to her. "Do you know Simon Cranmer?"

"Oh, yes, the intern?"

"Tell him he's fired."

She blinks then looks between us a few times. "I'm sorry?"

"Please tell Mister Cranmer that he's fired, effective immediately, and to clear out his desk before the end of the day."

"But sir, I—"

"I'll also need a photo rights check drawn up and made out to a . . . ?"

I lean forward. "A miss Isabella Rodriguez."

"Yes, Rodriguez."

"And that check will reflect your top-tier rate?" I ask.

He closes his eyes and takes a deep breath before opening them again. "Of course. See to that please, Maria."

I grin.

"Yes, sir," she says, then backs out of the office.

Yahamara sighs. "Well, if that's all, Mister Noblar?" He stands and gestures to the door.

"Oh, one last thing," I say, standing up and brushing off the sleeve of my jacket. "The band would be happy to provide a real interview rather than that garbage you printed two weeks ago, with the condition that you make a donation to the San Francisco AIDS charity." I remove a card from my pocket and toss it onto the desk. "This is our manager's contact info. He'll be waiting to hear from you."

With one last look, I turn and head out of the office where I'm delighted to hear some shouting from way down the hall.

"Here you are," Maria says as she hands me a check for Isabella.

"Thank you," I say. "Appreciate your help."

Simon's screaming stops abruptly as he looks at me. I smirk then head for the elevator. The smile that stretches across my face is obscene, but I don't care. No one will treat Isabella like that ever again.

The elevator doors open to the lobby, and the little brunette from the front desk waves at me again with a smile before I reach the door.

"You fucking asshole!"

I turn to find Simon storming over, his face contorted with rage. He raises his fist but I easily duck his swing, my own right hook whipping around to clock him right in the face. The girl at the desk gasps, but I don't even bother glancing over. I stand over this sniveling piece of shit, nudging him onto his back with my boot as he grasps at his bloody nose.

"You're done," I say, squatting down to look into his teary, bloodshot eyes. "You're finished. And if you ever come near Izzy again, I will fucking kill you. Do you understand?"

He stares up at me, his rage making him shake. "I'll have you arrested!" he spits. I stand up and look at the little receptionist who's been watching with wide eyes. "Flora, did you see what happened here?" I ask her.

Her eyes bounce between me and Simon before she finally drops her hands. "He tripped," she says finally. "Nasty fall, but a total accident."

I smirk and look back down at Simon. "You really should be more careful."

With a rough shove of my boot to his side, I grab the door handle. "See you later, Flora." I call back. "Tell your boyfriend there'll be two tickets to this Friday's Carnal Sins show at the box office under your name."

She lights up. "Thank you so much!"

Then I'm gone, pulling the tie from my throat as I walk down the street and tossing it into a nearby trash can. I wish I could string him up by that tie, but he's not off the hook yet, and I smile to myself as I race to my car to put the rest of my plan into motion.

CHAPTER 45

These Dreams

ISABELLA

I t's early enough in the morning that parking right in front of the *Earworm* building is easy. Dave opens the door for me, but I'm quivering and can't stop wringing my hands together.

"What's wrong?" Dave asks.

"Are you sure he wanted to see me?"

"Of course I'm sure. I spoke to him myself. Didn't realize calling after hours was the right way to get ahold of newspaper editors."

"Yeah, they can be a bit of a weird bunch," I say, shifting back and forth. "I just—I don't know . . . it all seems too easy. His secretary was adamant they were through with me."

He grabs my hands. "Maybe she confused you with someone else?"

"No, she mentioned the article . . . the picture. She knew it was me."

He glances over my shoulder at the building, then back. "Listen, I don't know for sure what's going to happen. But he wanted to see you and I promise, if anyone says anything bad against you, it'll be the last thing they ever do."

"But—"

"Izzy, what do you have to lose at this point?" he asks.

I take a long shaky breath, then straighten the white leather jacket Dave got me. With a sharp nod, he clasps my hand and we walk toward the door. As the elevator lights take us higher and higher, my nerves seem to settle. If I'm here, I'm committing to it, and I'm not leaving without saying my piece.

With a ding, the doors open and with only a slight hesitation, we exit out into a quietly busy office space. There are a number of cubicles where a few sleepy-eyed journalists and reporters are sitting, sipping coffee and answering telephones. But I head right toward a mahogany desk at the far end of the room, behind which a sleek wooden door and paneled wall stands like an obelisk.

There appears to be no one around, but when we approach the secretary's desk, there is a steaming cup of tea on the desk and a half-eaten blueberry danish. Wherever she is, she's around somewhere.

"Should we wait?" Dave asks.

I shake my head. "No. I'm not waiting anymore."

Grabbing the brass handle, I open the door and walk inside to find Mister Lewis sitting at his grand desk. When he looks up, his eyes go wide and his mouth drops open.

"Miss Rodriguez," he says, standing and quickly pulling on his suit jacket. "I'm so very glad to see you."

I press my lips together and stand as tall as I can. "Hello, sir."

"Please, come in." He walks around us and closes his office door. "You must be Dave Noblar," he says, reaching out to shake Dave's hand.

"Yeah," Dave says. "I believe we spoke on the phone."

"Indeed," says Lewis, gesturing for us all to sit. "First of all, Miss Rodriguez, I need to express to you how very sorry I am about such a disastrous misunderstanding."

I raise my eyebrows. "Misunderstanding?"

He nods. "Yes."

"I'm sorry, but I did not misunderstand."

He leans forward. "What do you mean?"

"I mean to say," I start, with a look at Dave. "It was made very clear to me that *Earworm* no longer wanted to work together on the feature for Carnal Sins, even though I had sent in my draft earlier the day before."

His head tilts, and if I wasn't so nervous, it might seem comical. "What would make you so sure that we wanted our working relationship to end in such a way?"

"I would say that the phone call I received telling me I was fired was concise enough."

He blinks. "Phone call? From whom?"

My eyes flick to the door, past where the secretary's desk sits. He follows the trail of my eyes. "A phone call, you said?"

Nodding, I take a deep breath. "Sir, I understand the reputation of your magazine and its journalists are of the utmost importance, but she wouldn't even let me explain."

He leans back and holds up his hands. "Whoa, whoa, whoa. Explain what? What exactly happened?"

"You—you don't know about the article from the *East Bay Chronicle*?" I ask.

He scoffs. "The *Chronicle*? That trash? I haven't looked at a copy of the *Chronicle* in ten years, ever since Yahamara turned it into what is essentially a scandal paper."

My mouth hangs open. "So you never—"

"Miss Rodriguez," he says calmly and with a small smile. "I think you better tell me what happened, from the beginning."

As I explain the history I have with Simon, the subsequent article and photo he published, followed by the distressing phone call from his secretary, Harold's face gets grimmer by the minute. I finish the story with Dave convincing me to return and confront the situation head-on versus hiding out in the Arizona desert.

"I'm so sorry if I disappointed you, sir," I say quietly, somehow managing to keep my emotions in check. Perhaps it's because Dave is next to me, his strength bolstering my own.

Harold leans back. "Let me just make sure I've understood you correctly," he starts. "My secretary called you and explicitly stated we were no longer interested in working with you. Even though we had already sunk several hundred dollars into your exclusive feature."

"I know that the picture in that paper makes it seem like maybe I wasn't the most professional, but I swear—"

"We weren't even together when that photo was taken," Dave chimes in.

Harold's eyebrows rise. "But you're together now?" His gaze dips to our entwined hands.

I nod. "We are. But I promise, my journalistic integrity never faltered."

He sighs. "Miss Rodriguez, let me be the first person at *Earworm* to apologize. I don't know what could have possibly been going through Miss Watters's head to make that decision without consulting anyone—then to lie and say you quit—but I promise there will be consequences."

I give him a half-hearted smile.

"I have to ask . . . why did you so easily believe this would be true?"

I shrug. "I've had to deal with this kind of discrimination for years. From high school, through college—I had to work five times harder than the men to be taken seriously. I didn't even have anything substantial to include in a portfolio for internships. It wasn't until I wrote that first Carnal Sins article and even then I had to submit it under a man's name before anyone even looked twice at me except for whether I could fetch them a coffee."

Dave squeezes my hand, and Harold's forehead is wrinkled deeply over his eyes.

"When you offered me the internship, I was certain it was because I knew the band and you were desperate. That, once again, I was just a woman in a convenient situation. So when the call came, I guess it just made all the fears I was already carrying with me seem valid."

"Isabella—I'm sorry that has been your experience in journalism. Please know that an article about you in something like the *East Bay Chronicle* is not something I would have taken seriously. If anything, I would've asked you whether you had approved such a thing, if it was taking a toll on your ability to do your job, and to let me know what you might need. I'm sorry that didn't happen and that you were forced to believe that you are not worthy of this position. Because you are. I wouldn't have hired you if you weren't."

"But even you only hired me because Dave sent you my articles," I counter.

He leans forward and steeples his hands under his chin. "He might have sent them to me, but I still read them and they're still some of the most insightful music journalism to come out of San Francisco in years. I was honored to read them and offer you your spot here."

There's a buzzing noise from the speaker on his desk, and he rolls his eyes before pushing the talk button. "Yes?"

"Mister Lewis, I have those reports for you, shall I bring them in?"

The hairs on the back of my neck rise at the familiar snarky tone from the speaker.

He looks at me and nods. "Yes, bring them in please."

The door opens a moment later, and in walks the secretary from months ago with a stack of papers clutched to her chest. For a moment she doesn't seem bothered by us. "So sorry, sir, I didn't realize you were in a meeting—"

But then her eyes lock on mine, and her face drains of its

color. Her mouth hangs open and a wave of quiet rage settles into my skin.

"Eliza, there appears to have been a very unfortunate misunderstanding," Harold says.

She blinks a few times, then turns toward her boss with wide eyes. "Sir?"

Lewis leans back in his seat, folding his hands over his chest absently. "Did you, or did you not tell me that Miss Rodriguez called you to say that due to an unfortunate turn of events, she would not be able to continue her placement with us?"

"I—I—" she stutters, beads of sweat breaking out over her forehead. I wonder briefly if she'll try to deny it. Blame it on me. That I really did call and drop the project. That I'm only here now because I changed my mind and am trying to pass the blame. But nothing prepares me for the cold determination that takes over her face. "Sir, I did what I thought was best for the magazine."

His brows lift, obviously also expecting her to deny her involvement. "Best for the magazine?" he asks.

She steps forward. "*Earworm* has been a pillar of the music entertainment industry for over three decades," she says in a shrill tone. "When I saw that—that . . . filthy photo of her in the *Chronicle*, I knew that if we kept her on it would ruin us! The reputation of the magazine would be tarnished forever!"

"The magazine would fail because a gossip column with outdated morals published an article about a young woman? While illegally using a photo *she* owns?"

"They'll think we're a joke, sir," she whispers harshly. "When I was made aware of this woman's complete lack of respect for the noble art of journalism, I had no choice."

"How exactly did I disrespect journalism?" I ask, cutting off Harold before he can reply.

She stands up straight, lifting her nose in the air to speak down to me. "I hardly think you can call yourself a professional while sleeping with a devil-worshiping rock band."

My knuckles crack as I grip the chair.

"Then to take a photograph like that—it's abhorrent."

"Look, lady," Dave cuts in. "Not that I care about your opinion, but what year are you living in? Journalists aren't celebrities. Who would even make the connection between that garbage article in the *Chronicle* and the masterpiece that Isabella would provide *Earworm* with?"

"I would know!" she shrieks.

"Eliza," Harold pleads. "I'm sorry, but—you didn't even discuss this with me and—"

"None of my other decisions have ever caused a problem," she says with a smug smile.

The three of us look at each other.

"You—you've made decisions for the magazine before?" he probes.

She blinks, then tries to backtrack. "I mean . . . nothing like this—I . . . uh . . ."

Harold sighs deeply. "Eliza, I'm sorry, but this discriminatory behavior is not acceptable. The fact that you would do this without discussing it with myself or another superior . . . I'm afraid we're going to have to let you go. Please have your things removed by the end of the day."

"You—you can't do this!" she screams. "I am trying to save this magazine!"

"Actually," Harold interrupts, "I now have an inkling as to why we can't seem to get any new blood to stay on. I expect you to turn in the draft that Miss Rodriguez faxed over before your telephone conversation—"

"I shredded it," Eliza interrupts.

My heart sinks. All I have are the rough notes I took.

Harold rubs his eyes, then in the coldest voice I've heard yet, says, "That'll be all, Eliza. You have until the end of the day."

With a mighty huff, she storms out of the office, the door banging shut behind her. Harold leans forward in his seat, looking exhausted.

"Miss Rodriguez, I'm so very sorry. You don't—I don't suppose you have a copy . . ."

I solemnly shake my head. "Not really, no."

"But she's practically written a book," Dave says sitting forward.

"Dave!" I cry embarrassed.

"What? You have."

Harold's eyes turn into saucers. "A book?"

I push Dave back and shake my head. "It's hardly a book. It's just, I don't know," I say, pulling the brown leather journal out of my bag and flipping through it. "It's just, after I thought the feature was down the drain, I simply couldn't stop writing."

"Writing about what?"

I shrug. "Everything, really. Meeting the band, the friendships I made, going on tour—all of it. Aside from a few bumps along the way," I say, pausing to glance at a smiling Dave. "It was an incredible experience."

Harold rises from his chair, rubbing at his chin. "Listen, I know we agreed on an article . . . an unpaid internship. But like I told you back in December . . . the magazine is failing. Partly, I think, due to Eliza shutting things down behind my back. I took over this position hoping to revive *Earworm*. That means taking risks, trying new things. I wanted to make it comparable to *Rolling Stone*, and maybe this is how I do that."

My lips part. "I'm sorry, but I don't—"

"What if," he continues on, "instead of a single article, we did a serial feature over the next few months."

My heart is pounding. "What?"

He holds his hands up. "Think about it. We could market it as a memoir and publish it in parts. If we can hook them with a kickass cover and the promise of a behind-the-scenes look into life on the road as rockstars, sales could fly off the charts. Then those people will want more of the story and subscribe to the magazine to get it."

"But the readers you have won't—"

"With all due respect, the type of readers we have now are living in the past. The same people who thought Elvis was controversial. Wait until they get a load of you guys."

I press my lips together. This could be huge. It also seems too good to be true.

"You don't seem convinced," Harold says.

Smiling nervously, I look at Dave and then back again. "Sorry, I just . . . I'm scared to get excited. I've been burned too many times."

"I completely understand. This time we'll draw up a contract. We'll pay you our standard junior writer rate for the hours you put in to get this finished, and you can keep the rights."

My hand flies to my mouth. "Keep the rights?"

He nods. "Yes. That way, after all of the features have been published in *Earworm*, you can compose it into a novel and pitch it to a publishing house. Any agent worth their salt would pick that up. I should know; my brother happens to work in publishing."

My gaze bounces around his face, trying to decipher his stare or find any cracks in his generous offer. But I don't find any.

"Isabella," he says, "help me save the magazine. And help yourself become the writer you were always meant to be."

I turn and look at Dave. His smile is so warm, so open. He gives my hand a gentle squeeze and a soft smile. When I turn back to Harold, he's nervously tapping his fingers on his thighs, a thin bead of sweat running along his hairline. Maybe he really does need this as much as me.

"Okay," I say finally.

"Okay?" he asks as though trying to confirm my answer.

I smile. "Let's do it."

"Yes." He jumps up off his desk and grabs my free hand, shaking it vigorously. "You won't regret it. Okay, I'll get the lawyers on the line this afternoon to draw up a contract. You outline a writing schedule, and I'll send a courier to come and pick up issue number one on Friday. I don't trust anything to be faxed to me until Eliza's out of the building." He paces back and forth until finally collapsing into his chair. "Now, all I need is to come up with a magazine cover photo that'll get everyone's attention."

Dave raises his hand with a smirk. "On that, I think I might have the perfect idea."

Lucky Ones

DAVE

With fresh coffee and a new outlook on life, Izzy and I drive over the Golden Gate bridge. Her feet are warm in my lap and my fingers play absently on her bare ankles. A smile is permanently ingrained on my face, and I don't think I could wipe it off even if I wanted to. I just want her home. Home with me, where she belongs.

"I don't know if I ever realized how beautiful it is here," she says, her voice hoarse. "I'm glad you convinced me not to leave. I can't imagine never seeing it again."

I grasp her hand and kiss her knuckles. "It's only beautiful because you're back."

She looks over at me with a smile. "You know, I don't think metal drummers are supposed to speak so sweetly."

"Would you prefer I speak about all the ways I'm going to fuck you once we get back home?"

Her eyes widen, her cheeks flushing a gorgeous dark pink, and her muscles tighten in an unmistakable way. "You really do have the filthiest mouth. But I'm curious," she says, sidling up next to me and placing her arms around my neck. "What went through your head the first time you saw me?"

"I thought you were sexy," I admit. "Then when you said you were there because of Becks, I—" I swallow hard. "I didn't want to screw up her only friendship by making you hate me."

She doesn't ask me to go into detail, and I'm grateful not to have to say them out loud.

"Why didn't you tell me about the photo?" I ask.

She slumps down next to me. "I don't know . . . I was embarrassed? Embarrassed that I took it. Embarrassed I left it so carelessly for that asshole to find and extort me with. And at the time, you *did* tell me you couldn't fall in love with me."

"I guess I figured you told me everything else . . . but not this."

She nods. "I wish there was a way to make him pay. Losing his internship is literally the bare minimum that should've happened. Thank you for that, by the way."

I can't stop the smile from pulling up my cheeks.

"What?" she asks. "What's that smile?"

"I may have exacted a little petty revenge of my own."

She sits back. "You didn't—"

"I did."

"So what did you . . ."

But I don't need to explain. Pulling over on the side of the road past the bridge, I point up at a massive billboard ahead of us. Izzy leans forward to look through the windshield, and I laugh as her jaw drops. "That's—but that's . . ."

And there, ahead of us, lit to perfection and twenty feet tall, is a photo of Simon Cranmer with a bold slogan next to his face.

"Struggling with erectile dysfunction? Me too. Talk to your doctor about your options today," she reads, her voice betraying a hint of confusion. "But, Simon—" Then it seems to clunk into place and she gasps, her hand covering her mouth. "No!" she shouts, but when she pulls her hand away, she's grinning like it's Christmas morning. "You did not!"

"I don't think he'll have such an easy time getting a date for the foreseeable future," I say with a smirk.

"But how did you—"

"James and Becks," I admit. "Becks asked him to model an outfit she designed for one of her classes. Told him he had the body for men's fashion. He was quite agreeable to having his photo taken after hearing that. Not sure how she got through the ordeal without throwing up."

"He really is the worst kind of narcissist." She squeezes my hand. "Thank you."

"I would do anything to make you laugh like that," I confess.

The beautiful dimple appears in her cheek and my heart has never felt so whole. I open my door and get out.

"Dave," she calls, "where are you going?"

"Come take a walk with me," I say, coming around to open her door.

She nods, and we entwine our fingers as we head down the boardwalk. When we reach the edge of the pier overlooking the bay, we stare out into the distance and watch the glittering water as the sun rises higher into the clear blue sky above us.

"So . . ." I say, leaning on the rail. "A book?"

She doesn't turn to me, but her cheeks pinch with the smile that grows on her face. "That would be something, wouldn't it?"

"Yeah, it would."

"And Carnal Sins, naked, on the front cover of *Earworm Magazine*?" she says, arching her brow and glancing at me out of the corner of her eyes.

"Mostly naked," I correct. "You have to admit, it would be scandalously brilliant."

She laughs. "You don't need to lie anymore, you can tell me it was your idea."

"It was not!" I argue. "I swear . . . Joel—"

"Oh please." She rolls her eyes. "You just want to show off that body of yours."

I slide a little closer to her. "Are you jealous that other people will see me?" I speak into her ear.

Goosebumps rise on her skin, and I trace a finger down her spine. "Hmm . . ." She pauses to think. "If you had asked me that four months ago, I would've said yes. But, now?" Turning toward me, she steps closer and pushes the hair away from my face. "Now I know your heart belongs to me, so they can eat their hearts out."

I laugh, my belly contracting, and I pull her into a tight hug to bury my face in her sweet-smelling hair.

"Does this moment make your list?" she asks.

Pulling back, I stare down into those questioning chocolate eyes. "It would be at the very top if I ever thought it was possible before a few days ago."

"You really never thought this could work?" she asks with a frown.

Gazing out at the sea, I take a long, deep breath. "I've always had such bad luck in life. From my mom, to school, Emily and my first band. It was a way to keep track of all the good things I thought I *could* make happen."

"I don't think it was ever really about luck, Dave," she says. "You worked hard to get where you are."

I nod. "Yeah, I know. It's stupid, but I have to admit it's hard to let that go."

She lays her palm against my cheek. "Whatever happens, we can face it together."

I smile gently. "Then maybe you should hold on to this," I say. Reaching into my pocket, I pull out the keychain. The one I found months ago when everything started to turn. My good-luck charm. I pick up her hand and drop it onto her palm.

Her eyes lock on the little plastic sun peeking out from behind the cloud, and she freezes. I can feel it in the way her breath falters before she looks up at me with tears in her eyes.

For a moment, I'm horrified. What could I have done to upset her? "What's wrong?"

She grips the keychain tightly. "This . . . this is mine."

It's possible my heart completes a quadruple flip. "What?"

"I lost it," she admits, the smallest of smiles pulling at her lips. "I lost it . . . the night we met."

"You—wait, what?"

"Yeah," she says, smiling. "I figured it just fell off my keys somewhere at the bar, so I knew there was no way I would ever find it. I can't believe . . . You're the one who picked it up?"

I blink several times then shake my head. "I just—everything was kind of in limbo. We had been picked up by Al in Iowa but we were having a hard time finding gigs and making a name for ourselves. The night I met you, our equipment was failing and I couldn't find a replacement cable. I was sure we were going to have to cancel the show, then I found this and all of a sudden there was a perfectly good cable right there. Then your article came out and things started to take off. Everything just started going right."

Then it hits me like a bolt of lightning.

"It's been you this whole time," I whisper.

She raises her eyebrows. "What?"

"It was never the keychain," I say, my voice growing louder. "It was you. Everything good started happening *because of you.*"

"Dave—"

"No, don't you see?" I say, backing up a bit to take a better look at her. "The publicity, the recording studio, the tour, seeing our names lit up, the album going gold . . ."

Her bright eyes dart over my face.

"Everything is— It was always you. Maybe it was never really luck. Maybe it was . . . love."

"That's the corniest thing you've ever said."

"Corny or not. You loved me. You helped make my dreams come true. You made that list a reality, and I would be the luckiest man on earth if you let me prove to you every day that I love you more than anything in this world."

She looks at the keychain for a long moment, then tucks it into the front pocket of her jeans. "That's the dream, then?"

I grin. "That's the ultimate dream."

"It's a good one."

Winding my arms around her waist, I pull her against me again. Her gorgeous smile lights up her face as the sun peeks out from behind the clouds, just like her keychain. "You were my dream forged out of darkness," I whisper against her lips.

"And you were mine."

Our lips meet and my heart floats. "Too corny?" I ask.

"Exactly corny enough," she whispers before kissing me again. A fluttery feeling swells in my chest and belly at having this amazing woman by my side. My thirst for her will never be satisfied. When we finally pull away, there's a peace that's settled in my heart.

"Take me home," she says. "I miss my family."

"You got it, Disco Girl," I say as our entwined hands swing between us. "Any thoughts on a title for the book?"

She stops and looks up at me with a bold smirk. "I know exactly what to call it."

With the smell of the sea in the air and the warmth of the sun on our faces, we head back to my car. I can't help but think that after so much darkness, she's been the brightest light. She fell in love with my dreams, and I fell in love with hers.

EIGHTEEN MONTHS LATER

DAVE

How the fuck do you tie a tie? I've been staring at myself in the mirror for twenty minutes trying to get this damned thing to loop the right way, and everytime it looks like a strange little noose at the end. I huff with frustration and, after pulling the tie from my throat, toss it to the floor at my feet in front of the mirror.

"Problem?"

I turn to find Key standing in the doorway with an amused smirk on his lips.

"No, I'm just fucking dandy," I mutter.

As I stoop to pick up my tie again, I see Key roll his eyes in the mirror's reflection. "Can you stop being so dramatic? All you need to do is ask for help."

I bite my cheek and hang my head. "Fine. Key, can you help me?"

He raises his eyebrows and I want to punch him in his smug face.

"Please?"

With a grin, he walks toward me. "Of course. Can't let you go to the award ceremony looking like a slob. Izzy would never forgive me."

I shove him playfully in the shoulder. "Thanks, man."

"No problem. Turn around."

Facing the mirror, Key confidently slides the black silk tie around my neck and starts doing some complicated thing with the fabric.

"Nervous?"

I look up and Key is watching my reflection. "Is it that obvious?"

He shrugs. "Totally understandable to be nervous. We all are. You're the only one who can't seem to get your hands working right though."

I laugh. "Yeah, well usually I have drumsticks that help balance things out." Key finishes a beautiful windsor knot at my throat and flips my collar down for me. "Thanks. How'd you get so good at that?"

"Nearly two decades of Church on Sunday's," he says with a sigh.

Right. "Thanks."

He slaps my shoulders. "I couldn't watch you fail anymore. Besides, if we don't leave right now, we'll be late."

I glance at the clock on the nightstand. "Shit." As I pull my suit jacket on, I turn and face Key with my eyebrows raised high. "Do I look all right?"

He tilts his head and waves his hand. "You'll do."

I roll my eyes. "Thanks."

Laughing, he follows me out of my room and into the main living area of the hotel suite. It's probably one of the fancier hotels I've ever stayed in, and with all six of us here for the award ceremony, this seemed like way more fun. Joel and Key are always staying at the fanciest hotels and partying all night long. James and I are happier in quieter—more sober—

accommodations. So, it's been a while since we've all stayed together.

We walk out to find Becks standing in an emerald green dress that's sheer through the bodice. She's recently cut her hair a bit shorter, and the effect makes her look incredibly grown up.

"You look amazing, Becks," I say walking toward her. I pick her up and spin her around in a hug.

Her cheeks are flushed when I let her go, but she's beaming. "You think so? I made the dress at school. Hopefully it's not too much."

"Too much?" James asks, appearing behind her and wrapping his arms around her tightly. He kisses her cheek and she giggles. "It's so much, Cindy Crawford's going to have to watch her back."

She slaps his arm playfully. "Come on, we better get going. The limo's downstairs waiting for us."

"Where the hell did Joel end up?" Key asks.

But he appears the next moment, stuffing the last of a Hot Pocket in his mouth.

"Joel, come on, we're leaving," I call.

He runs toward us while chewing. "Yeah, I'm ready."

"Why the fuck are you eating?" Key asks.

He shrugs. "Don't know what the food situation will be like when we get there. You know I get moody when I'm hungry."

"I swear to god," Key pinches the bridge of his nose, "sometimes it feels like we've been married for fifty years."

As the five of us head for the door, he shrugs. "Don't know how we would've lasted that long. You never ask me how my day has been or give me snuggles."

"I swear to—"

"Boys," Becks cuts in. "This is a big night for everyone, so can we just, I don't know, *pretend* like we're grown ups?"

I watch James smirk as his wife puts my two friends in their place, and with half-hearted nods, they mutter an agreement as we all pile into the gilded elevator.

FOR ALL I dreaded dressing up, I'm actually having a hell of a good time. There was beer and champagne in the limo and while I still don't drink, it put everyone else's anxieties at ease. Bright spot lights weave through the sky as we near the theater and my knee begins to bounce. Why am I so all over the place?

James leans over. "You okay?"

"Yeah, yeah. I'm fine."

"Sure," he says. "You look fine."

I close my eyes and tip my head back to rest on the seat. "Okay, you got me. I'm crazy nervous."

"Did you talk to Izzy about the next album cover?"

Album cover? Oh, right. "Ah, yeah. She's excited to do it on one condition."

James frowns. "What condition?"

I grin. "That we send the first copy to that old hag who tried to fire her from *Earworm Magazine*."

He laughs and so do I. "We could definitely arrange that."

"Then she's in."

"And you're sure you're okay with her being on the cover?" James asks me.

I rub my chin. When the guys first suggested we recreate Izzy's leaked photo but with the band's name on her instead of just mine, I wasn't sure what to think. But when Izzy heard the idea, she was more excited than I've seen her in a long time. Part of the reason I'm sure is that she wants to stick it to everyone who has ever judged her. "Yes. I mean, I know I was jealous when that picture got out in the paper, but she wasn't mine back then. Now she is, and I just want to show her off to the world."

"As long as you're both sure."

I nod and realize my heart rate has slowed and my knee doesn't bounce anymore. With a smile, I turn to James. "Thanks for the distraction."

"No problem."

The limo begins to slow down and join a queue of other limos that approach a monstrous white stone building. A giant black box from which the circling floodlights sits at the bottom of a grand outdoor staircase covered in a bright red carpet. When we pull up, I'm the first to get out. There are easily two dozen men in tuxedos with slicked back hair lining the sides of the stairs and helping ladies in long gowns traverse the steps.

"Wow, this is some fancy shit, huh?" Joel says, as he steps past me out of the limo.

"Way to class it up, mouth breather," Key says, shoving him in the back.

I look at both of them, and they hold up their hands. "Swear to God," Joel says, "we'll be on our best behavior."

With a roll of my eyes, I look back and watch as James helps Becks out of the limo in her long green dress. The limo pulls away and as the five of us approach the stairs, a man in an all white tuxedo approaches us.

"Can I help you?" he says.

Key narrows his eyes and opens his mouth, but I step in front of him. "Yeah, we're here for the award ceremony." I hand him the passes that were couriered to us and he looks them over before raising an eyebrow.

"Hmm." He hands them back to me with a touch of disdain on his elderly face, like he doesn't agree with the fact that the coordinators invited us at all.

"Not a fan of metal music?" I ask him with a small smirk.

"I beg your pardon?"

"Didn't think so. Well, I assume we're heading up the stairs?" I ask, pointing behind him.

He hesitates, taking another look at our group. Clearly he doesn't approve of how we're dressed, even though we all tried as hard as we could to look presentable tonight. All this asshole sees is the long hair and tattoos and how awkward we stand here in our suits. Maybe we should've just dressed normally. It wouldn't have made a difference in how we're treated but at least then we'd be comfortable.

"Dave, come on," Becks calls as James leads her up the stairs.

I try to ignore the stares. It's not like I'm not used to it anyway. How many years have we all been judged on our appearance? Our attire? Our taste in music? I guess I just thought tonight would be different, but it isn't.

Ultimately, I don't care. I'm a successful musician with a certified gold album and another coming out in a few months that, if projections are correct, is also expected to hit gold. I have everything I could want and a woman who loves me. Why do I need the acceptance of these stuffy nobodies?

I shake the thoughts away, and as I come to the top of the red carpeted stairs, there's a flurry of popping lights of photographers and journalists. I wonder wildly for a moment if Izzy is among them, if that's the real reason she wanted to meet us here. One thing's for sure, she works hard and sacrifices a lot to get a good story. Harold Lewis had no idea how much he struck gold with her.

As we hang around the bar I hear someone calling my name and look over the crowd to find a short dark haired woman waving at me.

"Dave!" she calls as she makes her way through the crowd.

"Señora Rodriguez," I say, turning fully before she slaps her hands on either of my cheeks and plants two kisses on me.

"How many times do I have to tell you to just call me *Má*?"

Heat floods my face as I spy Key and Joel hiding their smiles. "Sorry, *Má*," I say, awkwardly. "I won't forget again."

Two strong hands clap my back and I turn to find myself face to face with Izzy's dad, Hector, complete with his never missing white stetson hat.

"Long time no see," he says, clapping my back again roughly and making my knees buckle a little.

"Hector, how are you, sir?"

He scoffs. "No need to call me sir, Dave. We are practically family now."

I smile. "Yes, I suppose we are."

"Open bar?" He says looking past me. "*Ay dios mío*, that could spell trouble."

Laughing as he passes me I turn back to Izzy's mom, Carmen. "You look lovely tonight." I say.

Her cheeks darken and her hand flits over the top of her sky high hair. "Such a charmer. My Isa had no chance of resisting you, did she?"

"No, m'am."

She pats my cheek. "Speaking of, where is my—"

"I'm here! I'm here!"

And she sure is. Izzy steps toward us in a pale pink sequined gown with the most devastating neckline that reveals skin almost to her belly button. Somehow she still manages to make me feel like I'm seeing her for the first time—she's beyond stunning. She's the sun.

"Isa! Where is your sweater?" Carmen asks, pulling her own shawl off her shoulders and trying to wrap it around her daughter.

"*Má, tranquila*. I'm all grown up now," she says.

"Yeah, you are," I say under my breath.

Izzy turns a bright shade of pink while her mom huffs and rearranges her shawl back around her shoulders.

"Hi," she says to me. "I'm sorry I couldn't ride in the limo with you all."

I shake my head. "You look unbelievable."

She smiles and brushes her large dark curls over her shoulder. "And you," she says, standing back and looking me up and down. "You look damn fine in a suit, Noblar."

Raising my eyebrows, I reach out and my fingertips grip her waist. "You think so?"

Her eyelashes flutter and she hums in appreciation. Someone clears their throat and I look over at the noise to find Hector with two drinks, one in each hand and looking very seriously at me from under his stetson. I retract my hand and tuck it into my pocket.

"*Pá*!" Izzy says, moving past me. "I'm so glad you both could make it."

"Of course, Isa. It's a big night."

"Hi, Señor and Señora Rodriguez," Becks says, stepping forward. "Wow, Izzy, you look amazing!"

"So do you."

"Looks like everyone is heading to their seats, which means we should too," she says. "But we seem to have lost Key. He went to get a drink and never came back."

I lift my chin and look over the crowd for a solid minute before finally spotting Key over by the employee entrance. "What the hell is he doing over there? Key!"

His head snaps up and I raise my hand to indicate we're about to head into the theater. With a nod, he walks back over, draining the drink in his hand in one gulp. When he reaches us, I can't help but notice a suspicious shine to his eyes. "Sorry," he says, with a short sniff. "Had to use the john. Let's go."

Izzy looks back at me with a nervous grin. "Ready?"

I grasp her fingers, my thumb brushing over the top of her warm hand. "Lead the way."

Epilogue

ISABELLA

My stomach is in knots. I don't think I've ever been so excited and nervous all at once, but as we make our way into the theater and sit down at our designated table I take a moment to breathe. There are photographers and journalists scattered among the periphery of the room and I find it odd that I'm not among them, but there are other priorities here tonight. I'm shocked my parents were able to make it. My dad hates California, so when we invited them to the award ceremony I was sure he wouldn't be able to make it. But, he's here.

Everyone I love is here and it fills my heart with so much joy.

We all take our seats and as the lights dim and the master of ceremonies walks across the stage to noisy applause, I close my eyes.

"Have I told you just how fucking stunning you look tonight?"

Before I even open my eyes, a smile pulls at my lips. When I do look, Dave's gaze is resting on my face. "You did."

He leans a little closer and lowers his voice as the MC tells a joke to the crowd that laughs politely. "How am I supposed to concentrate on being here when you look like that?" I feel his rough hand land softly on my thigh where the dress splits apart under the table.

"Would it make it better or worse if I told you I wasn't wearing any panties?"

The soft smile drops from his face and his eyes become sharp, focused, as his fingers grip my thigh so tight I gasp.

My parents look over at me and I quickly cover the gasp with a cough, grateful that the long white table cloth covers where Dave's hand is moving right now.

"Are you trying to kill me?" Dave asks. "First a suit and tie, now this?"

"Just think of all the ways you're going to celebrate with me later."

The back of his fingers just barely brush against my pussy and I bite down on my lip hard to keep from squirming out of my seat.

"I hope you're well rested, because you're in for a long, long, *long* night."

His hand is gone and he sits up in his chair, straightening his back as though he's not as turned on as I am. My core throbs, and my nipples ache, and for one wild moment I think about abandoning the ceremony and taking Dave to the nearest bathroom so he can fulfill his promise early. He looks so damn good in that suit, but nothing compares to the glory of him in nothing at all.

"For our next award," the MC continues.

Next? How long have I not been paying attention?

"I'd like to call to the stage, musical artist, Dana Aldenberg."

My heart does a triple beat in my chest. "Dana Aldenberg?" I whisper, sitting forward.

"You know her?" Dave asks.

"Know her?" I repeat, my cheeks pinching at the smile on my face. "I'm obsessed with her."

"Isa!" my mother says a little too loudly. "Is that really Dana Raina?"

"Who?" Joel asks from across the table.

I turn to face my friends. "Just the biggest Disco star of the seventies. I can't believe she's here."

My head whips back to watch as the Disco goddess herself walks across the stage in nothing less than exactly what I expect her to wear. A gigantic feathered headdress and an outfit that seems to scandalize most of the older folks in the audience. But damn, she looks flawless.

Stepping forward elegantly to the microphone she smiles. "Good evening, ladies and gentlemen."

Something like a squeal escapes my mouth and I catch sight of Becks across the table who smiles brightly, her eyes twinkling at my excitement.

"I am honored to present the nominees for the next award of the evening—the award for best Memoir."

The smile fades from my face. Oh god, it's happening. Dana "Raina" Aldenberg is giving out the award for best memoir—my category—the whole reason we're here tonight. I think I might throw up.

"Nineteen eighty-seven was an interesting year for memoirs," Dana continues, "with books ranging from Olympic sports triumphs to touring with a rock band."

Yup. Definitely might throw up.

"These five incredible memoirs are not only stories of an individual's life, but are stories that teach us a lesson about life. A theme to ponder. Something we can take and use to shape our own futures. All of these authors have done that in their own unique and beautiful ways. Here are the nominees for best memoir."

There's silence throughout the room as Dana reads off the envelope in her hand. My whole body is shaking and blood is pounding in my head, my ears, my heart. My stomach is churning and the edges of my vision begin to darken as I glance around at the nervous faces of my friends and family. But then my gaze lands on Dave and he's simply watching me with a soft smile on his lips and a sparkle in his eyes.

All of a sudden this becomes real. The fact that I might win an award from the Literary Association of America tonight. At first, being nominated was simply a fun thrill. I thought it would be a nice way to spend an evening with my friends and my parents who I haven't seen in four months. To show them that all the bullshit I put them through moving away for college was worth it. But now that it's here I *want* to win. I want it so badly that I can't even remember the names of the other nominees as they're said out loud.

"And the winner is," Dana announces with a coy smile. "*I'm with the Band*, by Isabella Rodriguez."

The noise explodes around me and the next thing I know I'm being scooped up in two muscled arms. "You did it, Izzy," he says in my ear. "You won!"

I think I'm floating. It's as if my feet don't even touch the floor but I also can't stop the voice in my head from screaming *whatever you do, don't trip in front of Dana Raina.* Next thing I know, I'm walking across the stage and enveloped into a hug by my musical idol.

"Congratulations, sweetheart," she says, squeezing me tightly. "I was rooting for you."

This is a dream. I'm surely dreaming. "You—You were?"

She smiles, gently cups my cheek with her palm then retrieves a beautiful glass statuette from the person behind her. Placing it in my hands, it nearly slips as I realize just how sweaty they are. With a gesture to the microphone, I turn and shakily take in the audience before me.

"Wow."

I'm shaking so hard that it's difficult to take a breath, but as I look out over the crowd I see Dave and the people I love most, and the rhythm of my heart steadies.

"This—Wow, this is such an incredible honor. I would've been happy enough just to have been in the same room as Dana Raina herself, so this is the cherry on top."

There's some scattered laughter and I swallow the nervousness in my throat.

"Thank you so much to the Literary Association of America for bestowing upon me what might be the biggest thrill of my life. When the opportunity to cover Carnal Sins's first tour was offered to me, I had never been lower in my life. I had been blackmailed and betrayed, thinking I would never even get the chance to copy edit at a real newspaper let alone write a feature for a magazine— then later a book.

"I have to thank Harold Lewis. A man whose vision and work ethic for modern journalism is what has turned *Earworm Magazine* into one of the top entertainment magazines in the country in only eighteen months. He took a chance on me, a gamble that anyone would have told him was foolish, and I will be forever grateful for that. He's been the best mentor and I'm very lucky to consider him a friend."

I shift the weight of the award in my hands and take a long breath.

"Thank you to my parents," I say, the first prickles of emotion flowing into my cheeks. "I know I put you both through hell. Not only as an untamable child, a moody teenager, then an adult who left you behind to pursue my dreams. You've both always believed in me. *Espero que estén orgullosos de mi.*"

At the sight of my mother's tears, the first of my own fall.

"To my amazing friends and members of Carnal Sins," Key whoops from the audience, "meeting you all changed the trajectory of my life. You are the family I got to choose for myself and I love you all so much. Without you, there would be no award in my hands."

"Finally, to Dave."

Blinking furiously, I take a long deep breath.

"Thank you for giving me the courage to chase after what I want. For being my biggest supporter and showing me all the beautiful facets of life that were hidden from me for so long. Thank you for loving me unconditionally and always having coffee in hand when I get a bit unruly."

His eyes sparkle like the sun rising over the ocean.

"Thank you for letting me dream my crazy, impulsive dreams and being my strength to fight against all odds. You are the love of my life. Thank you."

My eyes never leave his as I walk down the stairs. All I see is him as he stands and claps. His face glowing with a teary smile. Holding the heavy award in one hand, I wrap my other arm around his neck and kiss him deeply—right in front of everyone.

Fire and light burst inside of me. My body, my heart and my very soul yearns for him and the world around us fades away even after the kiss breaks.

"That was some speech," he says, resting his forehead against mine.

"I love you," I whisper breathlessly.

"I love you, too." His arms wrap themselves around my waist, squeezing me tighter. "How did I get so lucky to have you?" he asks.

"It wasn't luck. My heart always beat in time with yours. Our heads just needed to catch up."

THE END

Want More?

Thank you for reading *A Duet of Darkness and Dreams*. If you enjoyed the book a review would be very much appreciated as it helps other readers discover the story. For updates on future new releases or other works by L.H. Blake, please sign up for my newsletter via my website www.lhblake.com.

Acknowledgments

When I set out to write *A Song of Sin and Salvation* I had no intention of making it a series. It was just going to be a little (or rather, big) deviation from my fantasy romance world and it was simply on a whim that I added the potential for more in the epilogue. Perhaps it's because I just couldn't let the world I had created go. It demanded more of me. Demanded I stay with it longer because it had more to tell, and therefore Izzy and Dave's relationship sprouted. It was the best impulsive decision I've ever made.

Thank you to my family who put up with the messy kitchen and the lack of clean laundry. I'm so grateful that you all allow me to do this beautiful thing that I love. Part of Izzy's acceptance speech are wedding vows I said to my husband nearly ten years ago and they are as true today as they were then.

A huge shout out to the movie *Almost Famous*. If you haven't seen it, it's incredible, and inspired parts of the story. Metallica was also an inspiration, particularly stories from their early touring days.

Thank you to Cindy Ras for her incredible cover design. It's absolutely perfect and I couldn't be more obsessed.

To my editor, Britt, you were a lifesaver on this one. I cannot thank you enough for polishing this rough stone until it was smooth. You're the best.

My beta readers, your feedback was so important to me and I appreciate the time you took out of your busy lives to help me. Becky, Morgan, both Katie's, Michaela, Elodie, and Heather, thank you so much for everything. Every comment, reaction and every missing comma.

Allie Garza, thank you for sensitivity reading and helping me with the spanish. You're the sweetest.

To my IG wives. You sustain me when the going gets tough. You're always there to help or lend an ear or talk through an idea and, thanks to massive differences in home country's, there's always someone awake.

Lety. No one could ask for a better friend. I seriously don't know what I did in my life to deserve you. I love your spirit, your talent, your brain and your laugh. You are truly my platonic soulmate.

Finally, to the readers. Thank you so much for reading my book. I know there are thousands of options for you out there and you chose to support a little indie author. I hope with my whole heart that you enjoyed this book. And for those of you with dreams that people have tried to dissuade you from pursuing, prove them all wrong by chasing them anyway. Even if you fail, you'll regret for the rest of your life not trying.

About the Author

L.H. Blake is a full time high school teacher living in rural Ontario, Canada. An avid reader and creative writer since childhood, Blake has always loved fantasy and romance stories. This is her third full length published novel and plans to release two more this year. Outside of books, Blake has been involved in the arts her whole life with passions for dance, musical theater, crafting, embroidery and backyard astronomy. She currently lives with her three little boys, husband, kitten and two dogs in total chaos 24/7.

instagram.com/lhblake.author
tiktok.com/@lhblake.author